"Howdy,

"Hello." Her blue eyes were cool yet curious.

Longarm's lean jaw tightened. "Nice horse. It's got something in common with my black, there: the brand."

The girl sat ramrod-straight, frowning, her glance flicking from Longarm to the Morgan and back again. Suddenly she snapped out at him, "You blind fool, look behind you!"

"That's too old a trick to catch a man," Longarm replied.

She suddenly leaned forward in the saddle, neck-reined her mount a quarter turn, and raked her spurs. The Chickasaw horse lunged tight-angled at Longarm an instant before the blasting report of a handgun.

Longarm, hastily wheeling to avoid the horse, saw that he had indeed been a blind fool ... The Chickasaw had taken the bullet marked for him.

TABOR EVANS

LONGARM

AND THE LONE STAR SHOWDOWN

A JOVE BOOK

LONGARM AND THE LONE STAR SHOWDOWN

A Jove Book/published by arrangement with
the author

PRINTING HISTORY
Jove edition/August 1986

ISBN: 0-515-08644-4

PRINTED IN THE UNITED STATES OF AMERICA

LONGARM

AND THE
LONE STAR SHOWDOWN

Chapter 1

The badge of a lawman was just a piece of metal, but it was a wicked taskmaster. It made you do things that hurt you, that distressed you, or that quite plain scared you—and there were plenty of those times in the frontier West. You didn't want to, yet you did them anyway, sometimes with your badge so akin to your death warrant if openly worn that you were a damn fool if you didn't keep it out of sight, though not out of mind.

Such a time was now, Longarm thought, as he reined in on the slope overlooking Beulah, Idaho. He had been warned about this town, and he had his silver star pinned inside his wallet in his inner coat pocket, preferring to size up the situation before announcing his identity as Deputy U. S. Marshal Custis Long.

Crooking a leg over the pommel of his McClellan saddle, Longarm rather abstractedly drew one of his long, thin cheroots from a shirt pocket. He hunched, cupping his hands, having trouble thumb-striking a match afire against the crisp Indian summer wind which was breezing down off the Sublett Mountains. The mid-afternoon sun slanted under his flat-crowned Stetson, giving his unshaven jaw a bold, aggressive appearance, although the broad brim shaded his blue-gray eyes while he scanned the area with a gaze of mingled wariness and curiosity.

1

The town below was composed of a couple dozen or so tents, cabin-sized houses, and false-fronted buildings strung out in a ragged line, either flanking the wagon road or facing the nearby southern bank of the Snake River. Much of Beulah was in shadow, its motley hodgepodge tucked among the bouldered outcroppings and timbered groves which paralleled the cataract-strewn gorge of the noisy whitewater river. Eastward behind Longarm, as well as to the south, forested mountains loomed tall and green. Westward and to the north, across the river, began the lengthy sagebrushed plains of the Snake River plateau. It was ahead there, not very far downriver, where Longarm spotted two carrion hawks circling above a stretch of rapids. Occasionally other hawks soared from adjacent crags or tree-crowns, wheeling and diving, darkly suggestive of death.

He turned his attention from the scavenger birds back to the town. At a distance, Beulah looked fairly typical of the land and the breed which infested it: apt to be crude and rowdy without being intentionally vicious or dangerous, and able to supply Longarm's immediate needs of a bath, a bed, and some booze. His horse also needed a rest. From that point of view, it seemed to be satisfactory, but so did bait in a trap. And up the trail he had heard rumors of unsuspecting men who had ridden into Beulah and never ridden out— men such as the missing owner of the Double-O spread, Deaver Osborne.

Longarm continued to idle, thinking and smoking, until his cigar ash measured an inch. Then, hooking boots into stirrups, he jogged on down the hill and entered Beulah. There was an arresting intensity to his features as he surveyed the passing scene. He swung his horse toward the livery yard, reined in, and dismounted by the stable doors.

A lean-faced old man came out, wiping his gnarled hands on a leather apron. "'Low to put up?" he asked around a tobacco chaw.

Longarm nodded. "For the night, maybe longer." He paused while the hostler regarded his sweat-stained clothes, his gear, then the Double-O brand on the dusty shoulder of his black Morgan gelding. He'd chosen the horse for its brand, to give the impression that the Double-O, not the law, was hunting Deaver Osborne. Longarm hoped a private search might prompt folks to answer questions more freely and, if Osborne had been waylaid, as was feared, to stir the culprits into acting rather than to send them into hiding.

The hostler showed no response, however, so Longarm added, "Also, I'm looking for a gent who came this way six-odd weeks ago, riding a Chickasaw with white leggings."

The hostler shook his head. "Don't rec'lect."

"Name of Osborne, Deaver Osborne."

"Names mean nuthin' to me." The hostler squinted at the brand again, then went on tonelessly while he loosened the latigo strap, "Seventy-five for tonight, mister, sixty cents each day after."

"Mite high."

"Depends on how you look at it. Includes feed and rub-down."

"Damn well should. Strip the saddle blanket off to dry and walk him some first, so he won't cool down too fast."

"I know to treat hosses right!" the hostler bristled, spitting a stream of tobacco juice into the dirt. "Cash in hand, though, 'less you got one of 'em infernal put-it-on-the-books tickets from Wolfer."

"I ain't beholding to Wolfer. I don't carry his rope around my neck," Longarm retorted as he paid. Warming to his role, he snapped, "Hell, I don't like him or any of his mob, and I think only a polecat would've mammy'd that skunk. I'll tell Wolfer Goswick that."

"You do, and there'll be another one of them quick funerals here. You'll attend it, mister, but you won't be coming back."

Longarm left then, knowing his horse was in good hands, and knowing the hostler had been lying. Everything so far pointed to Osborne having headed to Beulah, and he must have stabled his mount at the livery stable there. Even assuming names meant nothing, the hostler would not likely have forgotten either the big, well-bred Chickasaw with white leggings or the tall, gray-haired rancher who rode it.

With his saddlebags and bedroll hefted across his shoulders, Longarm walked through the short central business core of the town. At one end was the livery; at the other was the largest of the buildings, the two-story log-and-stone Glory Hole Saloon, of which Goswick was the proprietor. In between were several small taverns, card halls, and crib parlors, as well as the expected smattering of shops and stores. Longarm paused in each place. He was not surprised to hear the same thing everywhere: No, sorry, never heard of Mr. Osborne, never saw hide nor hair of any such stranger.

He got the same flat denial in the only restaurant, a one-room place where a man-and-wife team dished up supper for him. After he ate, though, the woman said anxiously, "Your steak, taters, and coffee'll be a dollar fifty. Sorry. I'm sure it's not worth more'n fifty cents elsewhere, but Wolfer Goswick has a tax on all sales here."

"Of two hundred percent? And you pay it?"

"Now, don't get mad," the husband pleaded. "We pay it, yeah; we don't want our café smashed up. Wolfer don't stand for stallin', and them who've tried buckin' him have been beaten to a pulp and drug outa town. No, sirree! Why, anybody'll tell you likewise."

"If anybody had a voice," Longarm replied scornfully.

Outside again, he moved on, checking every shop and saloon. Dusk was still some time away, yet already early night-bloomers were cropping up among the plain folk doing business, sure sign that, come evening, a lot of merry hurrawing would begin in the rotgut mills. But Longarm sensed a menace which belied the livening street. It was a feeling that grew stronger the nearer he approached the Glory Hole Saloon. Along its front he saw a number of cold-eyed, hard-faced men lounging with studied ease and tied-down guns. And with the menace rose another sensation in him: the gut-wrenching intuition that the Glory Hole was as close to Osborne as he was ever going to get.

He was almost there. It was a bit too soon, though; whatever he might have started cooking here had to have a chance to boil over first.

So Longarm continued his fruitless quest until he reached a barbershop, which happened to be across the street from the saloon. The shop had a faded sign above its door, of a striped pole and the proclamation BEULAH TONSORIAL PAR-

4

LOR * CUTS * SHAVES * BATHS IN SEASON. When Longarm entered, a bald man with a comb behind his right ear rose from the barber chair and asked hopefully, "You want a shave, pal?"

"Haircut, too." Longarm dumped his gear, doffed his hat, and took the chair, which faced a large mirror. His reflection was of a dusty and rumpled man topping six feet and sporting a tousled thatch of brown hair. Amused by his disheveled image, his firm mouth was in a quirked grin, relieving the tanned ruggedness of his features with the blue-gray eyes, rather prominent nose, and high cheekbones. "But don't snip at my mustache," Longarm warned the barber, who was steaming towels. The tall deputy tweaked the ends of his now somewhat droopy handlebars. "I think I'll have a bath, too. Water fresh?"

"This noon. Say, ain't you the one asking 'bout a friend?"

Longarm looked impressed. "Word moves right fast in Beulah, doesn't it?" Before the barber could reply, he whispered conspiratorially, "I reckon the fellow threw in with Wolfer, that's what."

The barber reacted like the other townsfolk, either twitchy from dread or irritable from dislike for Wolfer Goswick, or both. In any case, he used a little more relish than was absolutely necessary as he slapped on the scalding towels, then set to work. When shortly he had finished shaving and shearing, he ushered Longarm into the curtained tub room in back and regarded him critically. "I did a good job on you, pilgrim. Your face is red as a beet."

"It's broiled as a lamb chop!" Longarm growled, undressing.

The warm water felt good. It was the first warm water Longarm had bathed in since he'd left Ogden two weeks before, and he enjoyed this luxury, slouching lazily and flicking cigar ash over the rim of the tub. Close by on a chair were clean longjohns, socks, a gray flannel shirt, and tan covert-cloth trousers, which he had taken from his bags. Under the chair were his low-heeled brown boots, while across its back were hung his coat and vest, his holstered .44-40 Colt within easy reach of his hand.

He heard the front door of the barbershop open and heavy

5

steps walk across the floor. More than one man. Then came voices, and he sat up, wiping soapsuds from his ears and listening intently. But the thick drape pulled across the tub rooms' doorway muffled the conversation to indistinct murmurs, reminding him of his boss's muttered grumblings. Indeed, as Longarm strained to discern their words, for an instant he seemed to hear Chief U. S. Marshal Billy Vail instead, the way Vail had spoken when he had assigned Longarm to this case.

". . . Should've been a quartermaster," Vail had greeted, when Longarm entered his office. His tone had been caustic as ever, yet his normally loud voice had been low and well-modulated. "The 'master at Fort Hall, Idaho decided to buy only black Morgans for mounts. Well, last month he spent ten thousand dollars for a hundred of 'em, all prime and straight color."

"Ten—! Where'd he get such funds?"

"That's the army's problem. Ours is Deaver Osborne, a highly respected rancher and breeder who sold the horses, and who, believe it or not, choused them all the way from his Double-O spread in North Platte, Nebraska. Must've been worse'n an ol' Texas cow drive, but it was worth it." Vail had scowled at a map of the northwestern Territories that was spread across his littered desk. "Osborne was paid half in cash and half in a federal bankdraft. He paid off his crew and, evidently, headed for home two days before they did, leaving Fort Hall alone on his own horse. He hasn't been seen since."

"So I'm to locate Osborne, is that it?"

"The bank chit puts him under our jurisdiction, yes. Though there may be more. Y'see all my red ink dots?" Vail had poked his finger repeatedly about the map. "Every red dot represents apparently isolated or routine reports that've come in over the past half-year—a robbery here, a shooting there, perhaps a complaint of rustling or of thieving. I don't fathom this, but . . ." Vail had hesitated, seeming to grope for words or for his temper, Longarm hadn't been sure which.

6

"Chief," Longarm had said gently, and it seemed irrelevantly, "the word is you haven't lost your temper in days. You sick?"

"Hell, no! Who had the fat lip to . . . Ahem." Frowning, Vail had caught himself just in time, cleared his throat, and said in a controlled voice, "I ain't felt better in years, though right now maybe I'm trying to digest a bomb. Between you'n me—I wouldn't want this to go no further—I foolishly saw a doctor recently, and he told me I'd live to a hundred and twenty if I grabbed a handle on my temper and didn't let it get the better of me. That's all."

"Great news." Longarm had smiled, feeling relieved.

"But, damn it all, this crime spree in southeastern Idaho and the bordering Territories makes me bile inside," Vail had continued irascibly. "Of all places! No logical reason for it, though it does have a pattern of sorts. It's like a gathering of tribes, if these were Indians, like a massing for an uprising. But these're outlaws, filtering into the region singly or in bands from all over for mighty slim pickings. And, if that weren't enough, there's Wolfer Goswick."

"Wolfer's in Idaho?" Longarm had exclaimed. "Last I recall, he was operating blind pigs in rail's-end towns. He must've moved."

"He did—fast. Had a close scrape in Utah when a Morman vigilante committee chased him for selling bootleg hootch to Digger Indians, and he was lucky to've gotten himself and his family out in rags and patches. Took root like a weed seed in some tiny Snake River settlement called Beulah, on the Pocatello–Boise stage route."

"Wolfer's a tricky devil. What's he up to now?"

Vail had shrugged. "To no good. Violent and treacherous, he is, and I suspect as rabid as those coyotes he liked to keep for pets." His voice had risen then. "Now, I don't know if Wolfer's connected to any of this, or if there's any connections at all to any of this!" He'd stabbed a finger at the map, his brows ferocious, then suddenly clenched a fist and whammed it down so hard that the inkwell fell off the desk and the touch-bell rang itself. "All I know is I'm seeing red!"

Henry, the office clerk, had peeked in. "You rang?"

7

"No, cuss you!" Vail had bellowed. The clerk had vanished and Vail had sagged in his chair, grinning. "Hah, I feel better. Couldn't hold it in any longer. Okay. Trace Osborne, which for starters means going to Fort Hall. If, while there, you can make sense of this Idaho mess, or can nail Wolfer or any others, wonderful, but your priority is to account for Osborne and the federal bank draft. Anything to go on? Not a blessed thing. You are strictly on your own."

Never was Vail so temperamental as when he was fumbling in the dark, scenting trouble but uncertain of its nature. Yet Longarm knew his boss was too shrewd to waste his time on mere whims, and during the three-day train trip to his jumping-off point at Ogden, Utah, he conscientiously reviewed what meager information he had.

Deaver Osborne was highly respected, all right, by some highly placed politicians. His wife's missing person enquiry had carried enough clout to hit the top and cause lots of huffing and puffing down through channels. Longarm's copy of her enquiry told him little, though other than that Osborne was fifty-eight, five feet eleven, weighed 210 pounds, gray-eyed, gray-haired, clean-shaven, slightly scarred, and healthy. A subsidiary report from Fort Hall gave a few names and dates, the route Osborne had taken to get there and, presumably, to get back.

The Idaho mess puzzled Longarm, as it had Vail. Owl-hoots marauding off the land while heading for a mass gather—it defied explanation. Assuming such a pattern, and that Vail hadn't read too much into coincidence, where they would converge was still too vague to pinpoint precisely: someplace in the Snake River region between Idaho Falls and Twin Falls. That encompassed innumerable spots—including, for that matter, Wolfer Goswick's current lair, Beulah.

Longarm had never met Wolfer, but he knew of him in the way most experienced lawmen kept aware of notorious mavericks. Years before, Wolfer had come with the railroads across the midwestern prairie, a hulking figure in a dilapidated Conestoga, accompanied by a frowsy wife who seemed a fitting mate for such as he, and a young yellow-curled daughter who was a little spit-kitten in tattered calico.

His history was of pitching end-of-track camps that dispensed poisonous swill, crooked gambling, and verminous whores. Dim in the trail-dust of his past, however, were murdered men and women, burned-out nester homes, and rustled beef which was later sold to the construction crews. Yet this renegade had never been arrested on more than minor charges, there never having been a survivor during those earlier times of killing and plundering. Wolfer had seen to that. Now, apparently, he'd parked his wagon and was settling down as though, Longarm thought wryly, Wolfer was mellowing with age.

From Ogden, Longarm rode a series of livery rentals to Fort Hall, a venerable fur trade post that had been reopened to serve the Indian reservation there. Military bureaucracy, he quickly learned, was in full reign there. The quartermaster was on reprimand for splurging unwisely, albeit honestly, and Osborne's prize horses were under a hold order, preventing them from being rebranded as cavalry stock. Beyond that, facts were scanty. Everybody Longarm spoke with wanted to cooperate, but though they talked plenty, they hadn't much to say.

The 'master and the remount duty noncom, however, added some color to Deaver Osborne. Rawhide-tough and iron-willed, the rancher had forged overland through the Wind River and Snake River ranges, across the pass at Alpine, then south by Idaho Falls and Blackfoot to the fort. He had forded swollen streams when others would have waited, had scaled elevations that would have made a mountain goat quail, punishing his herd and punishing his crew and mostly punishing himself, as if to prove he was still the grittiest drover of them all. Obstinate and impulsive, Osborne had then left two days ahead of his exhausted men, cursing them for laziness while ordering them to stay behind, as he geared up his Chickasaw and pulled out at a rip.

When subsequently Osborne was reported missing, a search was made here and northward, his direction of travel, while some of his departed crew backtracked from their Nebraska end. Not a sign nor a whisper of him was detected. Every known or suspected rogue who could be grabbed was shaken down, but none proved to be suddenly flush with ill-earned loot. Osborne and his money seemed to have simply vanished.

An army investigation reminded Longarm of a buffalo stampede—blindered and unimaginative, but sure chewing up the ground it covered. So he figured it would be futile to retrace what had already been done, at least until he'd tried a few different angles. After some hard finagling, he managed to requisition one of Osborne's detained Morgans, which carried him swiftly to Sontag's Emporium up at Blackfoot.

Blackfoot was a crossroads, the main reservation town and the landing for a Snake River ferry to boot. A hellstorming junction, it was, and the taproom in Sontag's Emporium was the eye of the wind, a clearing house for news of the upper Territories, the Northwest, and the mountain states. Often as not, the Emporium was posted off-limits to soldiers, which suited just fine the punchers, miners, freighters, and drifters who passed through with their wild yarns and wilder boasts of doings in faraway trail towns and trading posts.

Out of the hot breath of it all, Longarm heard stories from up- and down-river, including gossip of Beulah. Teamsters and boatmen spoke of the Snake in oaths, saying it was a torrent of death with its rapids and flash floods. Of Beulah there was dark conjecture. It had always been a roughneck town, but now that Wolfer Goswick was its boss, they growled, Beulah was more a roost for the devil's own, having nothing to commend it except its whiskey and Easter Goswick.

Easter must be Wolfer's daughter, Longarm realized. To believe the talk, that little girl had grown into a stunning woman. Those who had seen her bawdily marveled how so much sass and beauty could have resulted from the union of pug-ugly Wolfer and his drab-boned wife. Yet it had, they ribaldly agreed, Easter was a tasty young morsel, finefeatured and full-figured, as spirited as an unbroken filly and as unpredictable as Idaho weather—one minute all sunny and the next a raging tempest, as the mood was on her.

Listening to this and much other bunkum, Longarm patiently sat in Sontag's the rest of that day and through the next, buying drinks and nursing his own while carefully pumping for information. At noon of the third day, he encountered a dry-goods peddler just in on his monthly sales tour. On his last trip, the peddler recalled, he had glimpsed a man of Osborne's description conversing with a stage driver. He wasn't positive, understand; he had noticed only because the man looked to have the means to buy something, and because he'd frequently ridden with the driver, whose regular run was between Burley and Twin Falls, way southwest of here. Well, the man left before the peddler could show any wares, and the driver turned out to have been fired and was going to Canada. That, the peddler said, was that.

That, Longarm judged, was enough. Obeying a small inner voice, he went to the fort, packed, and headed south on the Snake River road.

In Alameda, he met a blacksmith who claimed to have replaced the cracked right foreshoe of a Chickasaw several weeks ago. The rider had been southwest-bound, and the Chickasaw had white leggings and the Double-O brand on its shoulder. "The same like the brand on your hoss," the smithy declared, giving Longarm a tight scrutiny.

Now, having come to Beulah in the natural course of his search, Longarm tensed in the bathtub and concentrated on hearing the muffled discussion out in the barbershop. He had been hoping to attract some attention, and bet those low-growling strangers out there meant he'd succeeded. After all, in a small pond like Beulah, even a single pebble could throw big ripples. He suspected, however, that the interest in him was due more to his interest in Deaver Osborne. His mind was still probing for the reason that would have drawn the rancher in this direction and away from his route back home.

The curtain across the tub room doorway was shucked aside by the barrel of a sawed-off brushgun. While the curtain was held open, a squarely built man with sandy hair and immense hands came in, his right hand hovering near the pearl handle of his revolver. Then the owner of the brushgun entered, a shorter, thin-faced man with a hooked beak of a nose and eyes like dark, wet marbles.

"Don't try a dumb move for your iron, amigo," the sandy-haired man cautioned. He spoke in a raspy purr, as

11

though he had an injury to his vocal cords, his pale blue eyes darting meaningfully from Longarm to the weapon looped on the chair and back again.

Longarm stayed put, gauging the man, disliking the thin smirk playing around the corners of his mouth. Come to consider, he plain and instantly did not like either of these men, not at all.

Chapter 2

Thoughtfully, Longarm picked up his burning cheroot, which was resting on the rolled rim of the tub. "You'd be more polite," he said as he sat there, puffing on the cigar, "to wait till a man finished here."

The sandy-haired man pulled up in front of the tub, hands hooked in his waistband, rocking a little on his heels. He rummaged cursorily through the clean clothes stacked on the chair seat and glanced at the boots. Lifting the Colt, he studied it as though by the type and condition of a firearm he could read the measure of the man who carried it.

Longarm's lean, tanned face showed no concern. He continued to puff on his cigar and he reached for the bar of soap in the water. "You're a damned fool to meddle with someone else's weapon, old son."

The man, grinning, reholstered the Colt and dropped it to the floor. Tossing Longarm's vest to his partner, he rifled the coat, and was checking the wallet when his partner tapped him on the shoulder. The man did a stupid thing. Having found nothing much of value so far, he didn't bother to inspect further, and he overlooked the badge concealed in the fold. Instead, he dumped the wallet and coat on the chair and turned to his partner. "Whatcha want, Ira?"

The hook-nosed man named Ira showed him Longarm's watch chain. One end of the chain dangled down and was attached to an Ingersoll watch; the other end, held in his hand, was clipped to a .44 derringer. "Ain't this a li'l pip, Mace?" the hook-nosed man said.

Mace, the sandy-haired man, stared at the derringer and then at Longarm again, the grin broadening on his face. Softly he said, "You fork a Double-O cayuse, but you don't outfit and you sure don't tote arms like no ranch wrangler. Name it, amigo. Who are you?"

"Who's asking?" Longarm replied pleasantly. He watched Ira put his chain and vest down atop his coat and step back, rubbing the blue barrel of the brushgun fondly with his fingertips.

Mace sat down on the edge of the tub, pushing his hat back on his head. He was still grinning, but his eyes were narrowed now. Longarm shifted the cigar from one side of his mouth to the other. Then Mace's right hand stabbed out, his fingers snapping the cigar from Longarm's mouth, knocking it into the bath water.

"You ain't tough. Not in this town, amigo."

"Not when there's a scatter-piece dead on me."

"Not any time." Mace chuckled. "Remember that. We don't give a shit what your name is, really; we got a boot hill special for unknowns. If you ain't a genuine Double-O hand, get the hell outa Beulah in ten minutes. If you are, we'll give you fifteen minutes."

Longarm nodded. "Pretty unfriendly place, here."

"You'll find it out." Mace stood, still grinning.

As they were leaving, Mace picked up Longarm's Colt and looped it on the back of the chair again. The gesture was significant, Longarm knew. If he wanted to make an issue out of this, the way was open. It was a clear invitation.

Without haste he finished washing, stepped out of the tub, and dried himself. Dressing, he took time to swat some of the dust from his vest and coat before putting them on, then strung his watch chain with the Ingersoll in his left vest pocket and the derringer in his right pocket. Buckling on his belt, he adjusted his holster until his revolver rode, butt forward, just above his left hip in a cross-draw position. He lit another cheroot and was reaching for his hat when the barber came in, sheepishly wringing his hands.

"Sorry, pal, sorry about that. Did they muss you up?"

Longarm smiled thinly. "Not much. Who were they?"

"Mace McCoy and Ira Berenson, but—"

"Did you see where they went?"

The barber fluttered a hand over his bald head. "If they told you to take a fast hike, pal, I reckon you better do it."

Longarm went to the doorway and glanced into the front room. It was empty and dark, the shades on the window and street door having been lowered. He looked back at the barber. "You closed?"

"Had to. I've too much trembles to cut or shave anyone."

Crossing the room to the window, Longarm peered through a corner of the shade. It looked almost like dusk outside, though he figured the time to be about sunset, for the sky was overcast with slate-gray clouds, and the breeze he had felt earlier was now whipping along, swirling bits of trash and street grit in eddies before it. He saw that his black Morgan was now conveniently hitched to the barber shop hitch rail, complete with the saddle and gear he had left inside. Directly across the way, the Glory Hole Saloon was going full blast, horses lining its rails and men jostling on its boardwalk, and raucous noise erupting out between its batwing doors.

"They over there?" Longarm asked when he heard the barber's step behind him. He noticed the alleys on either side of the Glory Hole and a side entrance in one alley, spilling a square patch of dim lantern light outside when someone opened the door to enter.

"Berenson's likely watching from a front window. He gen'rally does," the barber said. "He'll be waiting for you to ride out."

"He'll have his wait. Say, have you got any mustache wax?"

The barber eyed Longarm as though he might be a lunatic, but he fetched a tin of brown goop from a cabinet. Longarm stroked it on and twisted the ends of his handlebars, then paid the barber and clapped on his hat, only to discover that it wobbled loosely on his head.

"You bought a haircut, pilgrim," the barber reminded him. "I just gave you your money's worth. All you need to make your hat fit is a few lamp wicks under the sweatband. About three, I judge. In a couple weeks, pull out one; couple more weeks, pull out another. Soon as the wicks is all out, it'll be time for another haircut."

"Thanks a lot. Now, where's your back door?"

The barber showed him out and hastily bolted the door. Longarm swung left along the darkened rear of the shop, the cheroot tilted up at a jaunty angle. His face was clean of stubble; his warm bath had been a tonic; his hat seemed to be settling better; and his mustache was now sleeked to the cant and spread of the horns on a Texas steer. He felt ready to start playing his smash performance.

He walked past one more building and turned into a pathway which led back to the main street. He went through there with his revolver in hand, and he didn't slip it back into the holster until he was crossing the street. Using another side alley, he made a circuit and came up behind the Glory Hole, then moved swiftly along to the near corner and dipped up the alley that led to the side entrance. Two hardcases were standing in the doorway arguing drunkenly. Longarm pushed his way past them and inside.

Longarm had seen meaner saloons, but rarely. Smoke hazed the air beneath dingy hanging lamps. The place was roiling with the reek of sweat, spilled liquor, and stale tobacco. Bartenders in dirty aprons served the long bar, built of raw lumber rubbed oily smooth from the countless bodies bellying up to it. At small tables, aging, bare-shouldered whores smiled professional smiles while they cadged drinks. Cards slapped felt, roulette balls clicked, dice rattled in boxes. Above it all rose the bellowing, the laughter, and the profanities of the unshaven men.

At the center of the bar Longarm spotted Mace McCoy, his back to the side door, chunky shoulders bulging as he leaned on the counter. Ira Berenson sat at a table next to a dirty front window, just like the barber had said, glancing out every so often while drinking beer, the brushgun propped upright between his legs.

Stepping up behind McCoy, Longarm touched his shoulder lightly, the way Berenson had tapped him earlier.

16

When the sandy-haired man turned around there was a fat cigar in his mouth. Longarm was grinning as he slashed at that cigar, knocking it from McCoy's mouth. At the same time, his left hand darted forward, ripped McCoy's revolver from its holster, and tossed it spinning back behind the bar.

"Why— Damn you!" McCoy choked in amazement. He lashed with his right hand at Longarm's face, the thick knuckles grazing the lawman's chin.

Swaying with the punch, Longarm slugged his own right into McCoy's stomach, catching him just at the break of the ribs. He heard wind burst from the squat man's lungs, and then he pistoned lefts and rights to the face, driving the man against the bar.

Somewhere a girl squealed "Fight!" in relished delight.

Mace McCoy tried to counter, but that first punch to the wind had weakened him considerably. He hit Longarm in the gut with a right, but Longarm disregarded the blow. He set himself and rammed more one-two combinations into McCoy's battered face, forcing the man backwards along the bar. Drinkers hastily scurried out of range as McCoy lurched toward them, blood streaming from his cut mouth and nose, eyes wild but swollen half-shut. He swung a wild punch at Longarm's head, missed, and then collapsed very suddenly when Longarm hit him in the stomach again, in the exact same spot.

A crowd had gathered around the fighters, and through this group Ira Berenson was trying to wedge his way forward. "I'll blast your head clean off!" he was yelling.

Longarm had been watching for this out of the corner of his eye. When Berenson broke through, Longarm whirled on him as he came lunging with his brushgun, raging, "Here's lead in your guts—!"

Abruptly Berenson lost his voice.

Pivoting, Longarm closed and grabbed the brushgun barrel in his left hand. Instantly he yanked it toward him, pulling Berenson with it, then immediately shoved it back and unbalanced Berenson further. What shut Berenson up, however, was Longarm's right fist. When Longarm jerked the brushgun toward him, Berenson was tugged vulnerably near

17

and unguarded, so in the split second before he pushed on the brushgun, Longarm plowed a short, brutal straight jab to the solar plexus. His fist seemed to sink itself halfway to the elbow.

Berenson staggered backwards, sucking raggedly for air. Before he could resist, Longarm wrenched the brushgun free from his grip. Still holding it one-handed by the barrel, Longarm clubbed the brushgun down hard against the edge of the bar. The sharp crunch of its hammered breech could be heard all over the saloon.

Berenson was hunching now, knees bent, clasping his belly with both hands. Longarm, flinging the brushgun behind the bar, pursued with a left uppercut to the jaw that straightened Berenson bolt upright. Another jolting right smashed him flat on the nose and mouth. With blood flying, he went down, buckling forward and landing face first in the filthy sawdust of the saloon floor.

"C'mon, boys!" McCoy was yelling to the surrounding toughs as he made a wild dive for Longarm's legs and feet. "Help us!"

"You're telegraphin' ahead, friend." Longarm sidestepped, booted him in the ribs, and leaped a few paces away, scanning the others and giving them a growl. "Wade in. The water ain't deep."

"T'hell with Mace's brawl," one ruffian scoffed, and another bystander jeered, "Yeah, it's two agin' one as it is." There was a ripple of callous laughter and a third man hooted, "Up an' at 'em!"

It was then that Mace McCoy surprised them all and lost what little respect they may have had for him as a fighting man. He got to his hands and knees and began a cowardly dash for the front batwings, leaving Ira Berenson crawling on the floor, hugging his stomach, his face twisted and blood-splattered. Longarm followed McCoy. His next kick caught him squarely astern, splitting the seat of his pants and pitching him headfirst out onto the boardwalk. A moment later he was scrambling off the boards, grasping his torn pants as he headed down the street.

Longarm turned from the batwings, doubting he'd seen the last of Mace McCoy. *But for now,* he mused, *the score is about even between us*. Then Longarm saw Ira Berenson. Approaching, he said curtly, "Sure you can trust it now, Ira? Sure you want to try me?"

Berenson was standing now, and he was cradling his brushgun again. A bartender was overly red and fidgety, which explained to Longarm how Berenson got it back. There was hatred in his moist pebble eyes as his finger caressed the trigger. Yet, as much as he obviously hungered to shoot, Berenson made no serious move to aim his weapon.

"You've dug yourself a damn deep hole, stranger," Berenson snarled. "I'll bury you in it, I will, and I'll do it with this."

"Tell me when you get it fixed so I'll know when to worry."

A gravelly bass voice called from the rear of the saloon, "Better hang it up for the day, Ira."

Berenson swiveled to the voice. Longarm glanced that way, too. A large, heavy-set man had come out of what Longarm assumed was a back office or private quarters, and was approaching them from around the far end of the bar. The man wore the long black coat, a snowy frilled shirt, and the kind of black string tie favored by the gambling fraternity, but his clothes did not match his features. He was bullet-headed and bulbous-nosed. He had shaggy salt-and-pepper hair and beard, spatulate-fingered hands, and a ponderous sea-captain's sway to his motions. His thick-lipped mouth was smiling, displaying rot-stumped teeth, but his deep-set lemon eyes were as expressionless as a rattler's.

Longarm knew beyond doubt that he must be Wolfer Goswick. With Wolfer here, the fighting was over, and so was the first act.

"You're a mess, Ira. Go wash off and cool off." Wolfer glanced about and crooked his finger at a lanky, carrot-haired bruiser wearing a hangdog expression and a hickory-butt Colt Navy. "Red, help Ira." Obediently Red came over, though he was mumbling under his breath as Wolfer continued, "In fact, you two catch Mace and get him fixed up. He'll be pleased. Get all of you all fixed up."

Red's jaws quit ruminating and Berenson's eyes grew narrow, as if something extra had passed between them and

Wolfer. "Sure, boss. I reckon Mace'll be at Delores's. She's a great comforter."

"Well, find him. Tell him just to get set pretty and everybody'll come out fine real soon. Same goes for you boys, savvy?"

Berenson and Red nodded and walked to the batwings, with Berenson glancing back to glare at Longarm before going outside.

Wolfer turned affably to Longarm. "You pulled the fastest knockdowns ever seen in my Glory Hole. That's a call for drinks, eh?"

That was a cue to begin the second act, Longarm thought. Wolfer took him by the arm and steered him toward the bar.

Longarm had a simple play: Since folks outside Wolfer's pack didn't know or were too scared to talk about Osborne, he would try to get inside the pack. The only way open for him to do so was to knock hard, preferably on skulls, until Wolfer noticed him and decided whether to let him in or not. The odds were poor; Wolfer was crafty by half and suspicious of strangers, and even if he fell for the act, he might not have need of him. And if Wolfer did not . . .

Longarm glanced at Wolfer. Age and barbarous living had taken a toll, he saw, puffing the man's belly, slumping his shoulders, bagging his clothes. But in Wolfer's casual touch on his arm, Longarm sensed surprising strength in those thick fingers. And when Wolfer shifted his cold eyes upon him, Longarm felt a creeping along his spine, remembering the tales back at Sontag's about strange things happening in Beulah, things no man dared question, for those who crossed Wolfer Goswick died a violent death.

Wolfer poured two whiskeys. "Stranger herebouts?"

"That's right."

"Me, I'm Wolfson Goswick, owner o' the Glory Hole."

"I'll believe that."

Wolfer chuckled. "You're damned close-mouthed."

"I was given on good authority that nobody here cares about names. Other'n that, I figured by now you'd know all about me."

"Some truth to that. In a small town like Beulah, every traveler is scrutinized from many a doorway and window."

Wolfer's lips parted in one of these soiled, mechanical grins. "I 'fess, I did hear you're looking for a certain Chickasaw with white leggings."

"Uh-huh, and its rider, a certain Deaver Osborne."

Wolfer sipped, grimaced, and shook his head. "Don't recollect them, sorry. Mind telling me why you are? He kinfolk of yours?"

"Not at all," Longarm replied, smiling. "There's a reward for Osborne, y'see, five thousand for information of his whereabouts."

Throaty noises rumbled from Wolfer's beard. "He's wanted?"

"By his family, not the law." Longarm iced his smile. "If you think me a bounty hunter, you'll be in trouble drinking with me."

"Perish the notion." Wolfer topped their glasses. "Nope, I hazard you're a Double-O crewman on orders to go out searching. How else could you've gotten a horse of theirs and ridden it so far?"

Longarm picked up his glass, grinned, and downed the drink.

"And you do look like a wrangler. You got the build 'n' all," Wolfer added. "We're pretty good to riders in these parts, if they're the right sort of riders and stay that way once they're here."

"Are you hinting at the kind of men you like in this country?" Longarm asked quietly. "And maybe if I'm that right kind or not?"

"I'm not suggestin' nothin'. Draw your own conclusions."

"Well, you got me pegged," Longarm allowed amiably. "I'm a wrangler, but I've done my stints as cowpuncher, drover, bronc-peeler, you name it. Anything that goes with stock handling."

"Anything?"

"Yeah." A steel-like note came into Longarm's tone.

"Well, well." Wolfer stroked his beard. "Staying in town?"

"Perhaps. You know of any rental rooms with door locks?"

21

"There's a whole upstairs of 'em here." Wolfer polished off his drink. "Well, I got papers to burn. If you decide to sleep over, go stable your horse and come see me. Nice to've met you, friend."

Wolfer left Longarm rubbing his liquor glass thoughtfully. His first reaction was that his act had failed, that Wolfer hadn't believed it. That was all right, because he didn't believe in Wolfer's false camaraderie. He sensed a sharp stink brewing, a stink of details not fitting and three skunks set loose outside. He contemplated the smells a while longer, then went over to the bartender he suspected of having given Berenson his brushgun.

"To spare more misunderstandings, I'll take Mace's gun."

The bartender flushed. Afraid to catch Longarm's ire, he got the S&W .44 revolver from where it had been put on a shelf. Longarm checked it over, found it to be in good condition and fully loaded, and stuck it behind his belt. He walked out onto the boardwalk, on guard, and eyed the curiously deserted street one way, then the other, before stepping off and heading for his horse.

Across in the barbershop, he glimpsed its drawn window shade quiver a little, and he smiled to himself. The barber had been keeping a furtive watch on the saloon all this while, he surmised, probably convinced Longarm would never leave the Glory Hole in one piece. Because of the horses, however, much of the boardwalk over there was blocked from view. Longarm was nearing the middle of the street before he spotted Mace McCoy standing back in the shadows. It was a patch of white he noticed first, McCoy's nose taped up with bandages. McCoy, seeing him, began to walk toward him.

Slowing, Longarm turned his head. Behind, to his right, Ira Berenson was easing out of the side alley of the saloon, armed with a short carbine in place of the brushgun. To his left, Red was coming from the other side alley, where he, like Berenson, had obviously been hiding until Longarm showed. They had rigged this trap before, Longarm thought grimly, as he recalled Wolfer's orders. They'd known how they were meant to "get fixed up" while Wolfer delayed him with whiskey and talk, to "get set pretty" for "everybody"—

his body—to come out. And now the three gunmen had him bracketed in a crossfire ambush.

Longarm took another pace and stopped. Casually, as though hitching up his pants belt, he palmed Mace's revolver in his left hand and shifted it so it wouldn't interfere with his regular draw. Then he rolled a spur rowel through the dust and pivoted on his boot heel, estimating each man's progress and probable position.

He faced McCoy again. "How's the nose?" he asked.

McCoy, now in the street, snarled, "I owe you, amigo."

"Everyone makes mistakes," Longarm said sympathetically.

Red laughed out loud. It was a signal for the three to make their move, and there followed a crash of gun thunder action that sent horses snorting and lunging at their ties.

Out in the middle of the street, Longarm drew both revolvers in what looked an almost careless gesture as he twisted in a cork screw crouch. Their muzzles lanced fire behind and before, McCoy's .44 in his left hand kicking with recoil, the Colt in his right seeming to buck under his left armpit and discharge of its own accord.

Mace McCoy was the first to be hit, a slug from his own pistol punching through the top of his skull and killing him instantly. He did not so much as twitch when he fell. His right arm remained extended, his fingers wrapped around his new revolver.

Red was struck while in a loping stride. He cried out and threw up his arms, face contorting, and then he was shot again, the bullet ripping upward through his pectorals and emerging from the nape of his neck. He dropped sideways with both hands pressed tight around his throat until his life had run out.

Ira Berenson stood his ground, firing and levering, adding much to that initial fusillade which seared about Longarm, nipping his clothes, spraying dirt, whining by his face and body. Then lead from Longarm's Colt shattered the bone in his thigh, and Berenson went down, still firing as he started dragging himself back toward the saloon. Another shot caught him, its impact tugging a moan from him and slamming his face into the dirt. He started raising himself slowly, triggering desperately, the slug from his wavering carbine coming amazingly close by chance, burning a groove in the knee of Longarm's pants. An answering bullet drilled him in his heart, and Berenson collapsed without another sound.

Longarm rose, scanning the street and galleries. Some of the braver townsfolk had come out to stand gaping, but they made no move to interfere. This was clearly Wolfer Goswick's business, and he liked no meddling in his affairs. The only ones who concerned Longarm were a few on the saloon boardwalk—bleach-eyed jiggers, tight of mouth and tense of body, their hands too near their sidearms.

"Any of you paw for a gun, I'll kill you in your tracks," Longarm warned, watching them as he backed a step toward his horse. Then one of those coincidences occurred which make life interesting.

A young woman rode up the street at a sassy romp. She began slowly to pull in by the Glory Hole but, glimpsing Longarm's revolvers aiming that way too, she quick-wittedly reined to a halt behind him. She remained on the saddle, as if gauging the situation, wearing a mannish plaid shirt and fringed buckskin vest and skirt that did little to hide her lithe figure. Her face was a haughty cameo, slashed by scarlet lips and tanned as deeply as any cowpoke's. Hair blonde as cornsilk flowed around her shoulders in a golden cascade. She alone would have made the moment interesting for him.

What really intrigued Longarm, though, was her horse. It was a spirited Chickasaw with white leggings. He gave the men at the saloon a last threatening look, then politely stuck his revolvers away as he turned and went to look at the horse's brand: Double-O.

His hand touched his hatbrim. "Howdy, ma'am."

"Hello." Her blue eyes were cool yet curious.

Longarm's lids pinched down; his lean jaw tightened. "Nice horse. It's got something in common with my black, there: the brand."

The girl sat ramrod-straight, frowning, her glance flicking from Longarm to the Morgan and back again. Suddenly she snapped out at him, "You blind fool, look behind you!"

"That's too old a trick to catch a man," Longarm replied.

24

Her eyes blazed at him. As suddenly as she'd spoken, she now leaned forward in the saddle, neck-reined her mount a quarter turn, and raked her spurs. The Chickasaw lunged tight-angled at Longarm an instant before the blasting report of a handgun.

Longarm, hastily wheeling to avoid the horse, saw that he had indeed been a blind fool. Wolfer Goswick was on the boardwalk, having managed despite his bulk to slip outside with the stealth of a panther. In his fist was a big old Dragoon Colt, still smoking, still held leveled at where Longarm had stood with his back to him.

The Chickasaw had taken the bullet marked for him. Twisting in mid-stride, toppling in an ungainly roll, the screaming horse thrashed frenziedly and one hoof kicked Longarm hard. He was knocked half unconscious to the dirt, while the girl was hurled clear of the tangle.

Stunned asprawl, Longarm was dimly aware of the gunmen rushing to cover him with drawn pistols, and of Wolfer cursing at the girl. "Damn your twitchy li'l butt, Easter!" he heard, and realized the girl was Wolfer's daughter. "What addled you to pull such a stunt?"

"You can't cow me with your vile mouth," she retorted hotly, picking herself up. "I won't sit by and watch any man be backshot!"

"Now, don't fling another o' your tantrums," Wolfer growled. Longarm perceived foggily that he was approaching. "This gent came a-spyin' and was rarin' to leave, and I feared if he ran free he'd fetch gawd-all agin' us. D'you know the brand he's riding under?"

"Same's my horse, he said." Easter was breathing hard.

"Y'see? Your Chickasaw caught his eye and tipped him off. There's naught we can do but be rid of him, chil'." Wolfer was leering over him, Longarm saw woozily, standing spraddle-legged, the Dragoon targeted with a fat thumb on its hammer. "Harper, Peleg, you'n Franks take'n rope him up tight, and don't bungle. Some of you others get a barrow and plant the boys here who did," Wolfer ordered, seeming to forget his daughter. "When it gets a shade darker, we'll go throw this cussed spy into the river."

Chapter 3

On the same day Longarm was plunging into the hellfire of Beulah, Jessica Starbuck and her companion Ki were riding aboard a squall-tossed clipper ship off the southern coast of Oregon.

The storm had hit the previous night, as the ship was passing California's Point St. George. The crew fought the rainy gusts and lashing seas, while Jessie's six Jersey bulls bawled in their pen from the string of spuming cold water, the swirling sou'easterner driving the luff-sailed clipper northward at a tempestuous speed. Finally, around dawn, the brunt of the flurry moved on. By the time they reached jutting Cape Sebastian, the rain had softened, the ocean had quieted, and the whitecaps were dying down.

Now Jessie, Ki, and the captain stood at the rail and gazed across the green, pitching water. To the east, the Oregon shore lay squat and dark, a fine line rimmed by banks of meadow and forest. Yonder rose the timbered slopes of the Coast Range. Beyond them loomed the snow-crested peaks of the Siskiyou Mountains, though they were distant and could barely be seen through the showery haze.

"Almost to Gold Beach, Captain?" Jessie asked.

The captain was a stocky, weather-beaten Swede who had sailed this coast for more years than he could remember. "Yah, just about."

"How close can you get to shore?"

The captain puffed on his pipe. At last he replied, "Miz Starbuck, must you insist on pushing these bulls into the sea?"

Jessie sighed. She had gone over this too many times already. Tall and lissome, in her twenties, she was wearing an oilskin slicker whose yellowish color nearly matched her long coppery-blond hair, which she had tucked up under the crown of her brown Stetson. And though the slicker was buttoned at the neck and completely covered her silk blouse, jeans, and denim jacket, it failed to hide the firm thrust of her breasts or the sensual curves of her thighs and buttocks. Nor did the nippy weather chill the sultry warmth of her suntanned face with its high cheekbones, audacious green eyes, and the provocative if sometimes humorous lilt of her lips.

At the moment, however, her features couldn't help mirroring the exhaustive effects of her long journey. It seemed forever since she had left her Circle Star Ranch in Texas on a business trip through lower California. Then this situation cropped up, and instead of returning home as planned, she bought the bulls from a cattle breeder in San Bernardino, trailed them to Los Angeles, and loaded them on the ship, the *Santa Teresa*, for a week's voyage up the coast. She felt drained by it all and slightly seasick from the storm, though she refused to admit such, insisting it was the food that made her queasy.

Unlike Jessie, Ki had not lost his sea legs or his appetite. He was tired of the boring confinement of shipboard life, however, being a man whose lean, sinewy body was graced with energy and stamina. He too was swathed in a slicker, his hatbrim tugged low and visoring features that appealed to women who like their lovers tempered by experience. Born in Japan to an American sea captain and his Japanese wife, Ki had inherited his father's respectable height and agile strength; from his mother he'd been blessed with his lustrous black hair and almond-shaped eyes; while from both had come the handsome bronze complexion of mixed parentage.

Orphaned young and growing up scorned as a half-breed, Ki had apprenticed himself to one of Japan's last great samurai, the aged Hirata. After years of studying the philosphies and practices of the martial arts, his master had passed away. Ki migrated to San Francisco, where he was hired by Alex Starbuck, a wealthy international magnate. When, ultimately, Alex Starbuck was murdered, Ki became the confidant and protector of Starbuck's only child, Jessica, whom by then Ki had known for so long that they were as close as blood brother and sister.

And, like any smart brother who'd learned not to interrupt his headstrong sister, Ki kept still and let Jessie handle the captain.

She did so, succinctly. "I do. Cows can swim and I can too."

"Very well. Your cattle," the captain growled, his briar belching smoke, "and your lungs, so go get 'em filled with water."

The first mate, a thin man, ambled up and reported, "Nigh lays the mouth o' the Rogue River, Cap'n, hard off'n starboard bow."

Staring in the direction the mate was pointing, Jessie noted a wide, scalloped break in the coastal bankline, and a broad, silt-edged delta where a freshwater flow surged out to meet the surf.

"The lady wishes to beach her cattle there," the captain said.

"Used to ply that stretch, I did, and know it respectably well. If'n we put a hand on the sounding bar and take our ease going in, Cap'n, I'd wager we could sidle within two hundred yards of shore." The mate dug into his snuff can. "Gold Beach is acrook the river, and a snug fishin' harbor it is, too, with friendly lasses and stout malt beer. Makes me yearn to dive overboard with them bulls, uh-huh."

The captain swore in Swedish. "You young lubbers are all the same, always chasin' after mermaids with your pennants at half-mast."

"'Least we're not so old we've forgot how to unfurl 'em," the mate replied with a cherry wink, and rolled his snuff. "Aye, the tide's favorable, and the beach's more'r less level. They can make it. I'll put a man on sounding right now." He hurried away.

The rigging creaked and the deck swayed as the clipper began bearing coastward. The closer it nosed to the shore, the gentler the wind blew, and the shower declined to a sullen drizzle.

Jessie could hear the calls of the man taking depth soundings. Gradually the ocean drew shallower, the landscape clearer, until she could clearly see the surf-pounded rocks, driftwood-laced beach, and funneling mouth of the Rogue River. Above the eroded banks grew low-swept trees, matted brush, and grassy patches, and Jessie thought she also could glimpse a smattering of Gold Beach dwellings. No sign of people yet, but some should be waiting. She had notified the North Moon Ranch of her pending arrival, and of her need for hands to help with the bulls' expected, if surprising, arrival by sea.

Sailing in and making the stock swim ashore, however, was the only sensible way. No train ran up the coast, much less to Gold Beach. To drive from San Bernardino would have taken too long, and wasted the bulls to cowhided skeletons. This way they lost a little weight, but not much, having fed well aboard the ship. The *Santa Teresa* was small and light for a clipper, yet it was no picayune packet boat, either. It would be sorely squeezed to dock at the nearest port, Coos Bay, some eighty or ninety miles north. That would have forced a drive aflank the Coast Range, steep and rugged and hard to work cattle along. South, the port of Eureka lay at a farther and harsher distance, for in between, the Siskiyous joined the coastal spine and bulked out sheer-cliffed to the sea. No; this way she might lose a bull or two by drowning, but by herding them overland, she risked losing them in the crags and crevices of the mountainous terrain.

The man taking depth relayed a short number. The first mate bellowed, "Drop anchor!" and the clipper slowly stopped. It rode the swells rhythmically while Jessie swallowed gamely.

The mate walked over, grinning. "This's as close as we can get, Cap'n."

"Yah, well, then start the sinking."

Jessie, Ki, and the mate went to the two horses penned on

29

deck. The mate hollered for some of the crew to begin chousing the bulls. The horses were trained cow ponies, bought fully geared in San Bernardino for the drive to Los Angeles, then shipped along just in case. Jessie and Ki were staunch believers in planning for uncertainties.

They led the horses to the lowered gangplank. Jessie's roan gelding walked the plank after a slight nudge, and fell into the water with scarcely a murmur. Ki's buckskin mare splay-leggedly balked, but a hard swat on the rump sent it skidding on down to land with a splash that soaked the sailors who were manning a rowboat by the plankbase. Both horses surfaced, swimming strongly as they headed for the beach.

Next came the bulls, led by a husky, very stubborn three-year-old who braced resisting at the gangplank lip. The bulls behind were jamming up and kept prodding, and finally shoved him beyond the brink. One by one they slid down the rain-slicked chute to the ocean. The green water choked their bawlings short. Each came up snorting, then began pawing landward through the swells washing over them.

"Not a loss," the captain allowed, "so far."

The rowboat hove to, and baggage, saddles, and gear were carted down and stowed in its stern. Jessie and Ki shook hands with the captain and mate, then descended to take seats. Oars lifted and dug as the craft headed to shore, pitching and rolling on the crests and troughs of the inclement sea. The clipper had been rough, but this rowboat was worse, Jessie thought, feeling greener than the water.

A sailor yelled, "Looks like your horses made it okay."

The cow ponies were still many yards from shore, but the surf was so shallow that they were wading the rest of the way. Ki said, "That's good. With the water that low, the bulls should do fine."

"I am not interested in any horses or bulls," Jessie said tightly. "I am only interested in reaching ground as soon as possible."

The sailor was sympathetic. "Seasickness is terrible."

"I'm not seasick! I'm suffering from your ghastly sea fare!"

"Yes'm. I understand. We'll grate bottom pronto."

30

The rain ceased about then, and shortly the boat rubbed sand and ditched. While a sailor stayed to anchor the boat, the others helped Jessie and Ki transport their belongings to a strip of dry beach.

After the sailors waded back out, Jessie removed each boot in turn to pour out the water, and watched them start rowing away to the clipper. "What a relief. I'm feeling recovered already."

Their horses, dripping water, were scrounging around some green chickweed, hoping to grub the first growing feed they had for days. They had been habitually skittish and unruly to catch, so Jessie and Ki took their saddle ropes, intending to rope them, but found they were easily approached and snagged by their hackamores.

"Sick," Ki judged. "Must've ate what you had."

Jessie, saddling her roan, shot Ki a testy look. They then chased after the bulls, locating them wandering not too far away. Weary and befuddled, the bulls kicked up only minor scraps as they were gathered and hazed up through a drainage cut in the bank, where they were corraled on a grassy, grove-encircled clearing.

Jessie felt increasingly concerned as the North Moon ranch hands failed to appear. "By now someone should've shown up," she said, when the roundup was done. "I wonder if anything's wrong."

Ki nodded. "Stay put. I'll go check in Gold Beach." He added with a grin, "Maybe they're just enjoying the lasses and the beer."

"Let's hope," she sighed, and watched him ride off.

The bulls grouped docilely, grazing and bedding down. Jerseys were a breed which gave superior milk. These bulls didn't, of course, but she wanted them to give what they had to to as many North Moon cows as they could. The ranch herd was mostly the larger Holstein, raised for beef as well as milk, and not necessarily great at either. Her notion was that the bulls would sire a cross-variety whose cows would produce like Jerseys yet be built like Holsteins, thereby improving quality and profits.

The breeding was a shot in the dark, so to speak. If it didn't work, at least it had provided a reason for her coming here, for though she might have been able to travel covertly, her presence could scarcely remain secret for long. And the owner of the North Moon, Abbott Wyndam, had begged her to use utmost discretion, hinting that threats had been leveled against bringing in the law or any other outsider.

The rancher's plea was contained in a brief letter that had been received at the Circle Star and thence telegraphed to Jessie in California. Wyndam's request for help had been sufficient for Jessie to make plans for this trip immediately. Aware of his ranch, she had dreamed up the excuse of personally delivering breed bulls.

Six years before, Abbott Wyndam had saved Jessie's father's life, taking a great risk to hide him from pursuing killers who were henchmen of a worldwide crime cartel as powerful as it was ruthless. Alex Starbuck had first run afoul of the cartel in the Orient at the beginning of his career, and his discovery of this criminal ring had led to the murder of his wife—Jessie's mother—and thence to a protracted battle between him and the cartel. The deeper Starbuck delved into the machinations of his enemy, the more disquieting was the information he uncovered, for it became increasingly clear that the cartel was bent on subverting and controlling emerging America.

Naturally, Wyndam hadn't been aware of all this, of why Alex Starbuck had struggled for years, of how he'd received his numerous scars and injuries. Wyndam had accepted him without question, even though Starbuck had warned him of the grave peril he faced by doing so. Later, out of appreciation, Starbuck had given Wyndam the funds to buy North Moon Ranch and stock it, and had reluctantly agreed to a mortgage, solely because of Wyndam's pride, as bond for the money. Wyndam had been conscientiously repaying what he considered to be a loan, refusing to acknowledge protests that the money had been "just compensation for nursing and other services rendered," and for the same reason rarely initiating correspondence with Starbuck.

In the meantime, the cartel finally managed to assassinate Alex Starbuck. But by then his business had evolved into a far-flung empire of huge resources and influence, and his daughter had grown into a daring and determined young woman. Using his secret records and her powerful inheritance, and aided by the devoted Ki, Jessie had been carrying on her father's war to destroy the cartel.

Nothing so far, though, indicated that the cartel was involved in Abbott Wyndam's troubles. It didn't matter. Alex Starbuck never forgot his friends, and neither did Jessie. Wyndam needed help—badly, or else he would never have written—and help he would get.

Shortly Ki returned. "Bad news and good news, Jessie. The bad is that nobody from the North Moon has been seen in town today. The good is that I was given directions to the ranch."

"Well, we don't have much choice about it, do we?" She eyed the placid herd. "Seems a pity, but let's start moving them out."

They removed their slickers and tied them to their cantles, gambling that since it hadn't rained for a while, it wouldn't for a while longer. From a saddlebag Jessie took her shellbelt, strapping it on so her custom Colt revolver was holstered on her right thigh. She then checked her two-shot derringer and, finding it dry, stashed it back in its cunning hideout behind the brass buckle of her belt.

Ki was range-clad in jeans, a loose, collarless shirt, and an old leather vest. He wasn't wearing boots, but rope-soled cloth slippers; and he wasn't toting firearms of any sort. Yet he was far from being unarmed, for secreted in his vest were short daggers and other small throwing weapons, including a supply of *shuriken*—little razor-sharp, star-shaped steel disks.

The bulls were rousted and goaded into a reluctant trot. From the clearing, which lay a bit south of town, they headed southeast toward the rumpled emerald foothills of the Coast Range, and pretty soon they came upon a wagon trail going in the same direction.

"This must be the road we're supposed to meet," Ki said.

Turning onto the rutted, mud-puddled trail, they were able to quicken their pace somewhat as it slashed a route through overgrown woodlands, ascended stony grades, and forded marshy pockets. Before long they passed through a brush-clogged, pine-choked break in the striated rock wall of a tall ridge, and entered a foothill basin.

"Bohemia Valley," Ki declared. "It is, anyway, if we're on the right track. The North Moon's somewhere toward the far end."

They pressed on, the slopes falling back at once into a broad floor miles wide and more miles long. Heavy with timber and thickets, the valley also contained much more open pasture of wildflower-speckled grass, good and deep as the water of the rousing creeks which snaked across its fertile ground. Sunlight was spearing through the thinning clouds now, setting the foliage to steaming, and butterflies and bees to humming in the growing warmth.

Bohemia Valley was fit to make some ranchers drool, Jessie thought, but it had one drawback. For ranchers massing larger herds it was insufficient by itself, too split from other ranges, and too mountain-locked and far from major markets. For those raising small herds, though, it would fatten cattle and pockets just fine. Farmers were also faring well, she realized from her glimpses of vegetable fields or nut and fruit orchards. And probably some mining was being done for chromite and gold, as it was throughout this region.

However, it appeared that a bumper crop of trouble was being produced here, too. The valley was fire-splotched and black-squared in places where homes and acreages had once been. The sight of such wanton destruction put Jessie and Ki on alert, and their hands rarely strayed far from their respective weapons while they followed the winding trail on deeper, keeping the bulls in tight file with constant vigilance and cow-pony teamwork.

They were nearing another of the numerous tree- and bush-flanked sharp bends, when suddenly a crackle of gunfire erupted from somewhere close beyond the blind curve. They reined in swiftly, their horses rearing, the bulls bawling and tossing their heads.

Ki swore as he calmed his horse. "Do we hide or go see?"

"I think we—"

The rest of Jessie's answer was drowned out by a solid and conclusive thump and an exultant whoop. Almost instantly the whoop was followed by a volley of squawking howls and a furious drumming of horses' irons. These, in turn, were followed by the bellows of six panicking bulls, and a trampling of hooves as they bolted for the surrounding woods, stampeding in six different directions to parts unknown.

"What in blazes is going on ahead?"

★

Chapter 4

Around the bend tore three riders.

It was debatable whether the men or their mounts were more frenzied. The horses were galloping disjointedly in a white-eyed lather, while the men were careening and cursing, waving their arms and beating themselves with their hats. From the saddlehorn of the rearmost rider stretched a rope, and at its end bumped and bounded a dome-shaped object. The rider kept trying desperately to loosen the end snubbed to his horn, as all three cleared the curve and straightened on the trail, flying like banshees.

Behind them a stocky old man came running, surging around the bend as if blown by the wind, his gray whiskers fanning out over his shoulders. He was brandishing a double-barreled shotgun. Suddenly halting, his boots kicking the dust, he clamped the butt of the shotgun against his shoulder and took quick aim. The rearmost rider, at that moment, was leaning far forward on his horse's neck, letting go of the untied rope with one hand while slapping at his back and neck with the other.

The shotgun blasted with deafening twin roars and gouts of black powdersmoke. The rearmost rider screeched and reared tall in his stirrups, clapping both hands to the seat of his pants. He craned around, half reaching for his pistol, but as the oldster broke open the breech of his shotgun, the rider twisted forward again and rode for his life. The released object, having momentum of its own, continued to bounce and roll along, as if perversely chasing after him.

Jessie and Ki stared in amazement. The foremost rider shouted a warning: "Hightail, or they'll get you, too!" He thrashed with both arms. "Yeow! Into the brush, if you value your hides!"

Needing no further encouragement, they neck-reined their horses and launched off the trail. For several hundred yards they charged through the underbrush, swerving around trunks, bending under low branches, skating across loose stones and briar patches. Behind them forged the rip-snorting trio of riders, still slapping and flailing and ranting curses. Finally they reined in by a stout thicket and waited for the others to catch up. A moment later, the riders wrenched their horses to blowing halts alongside them.

"Didja ever hear of anythin' so loony?" the foremost, a thin man with a huge nose, appealed to Jessie and Ki. "Daubin' a loop on a beehive! Why, I'm stung blistered and bloated worse'n a toadskin!"

The rearmost rider, who stood stiffly erect in his stirrups, gave an injured yelp. "F'get your toad-bloats! Ol' Eustace York centered both barrels of birdshot on my trouser seat!"

"I wish he'd used buckshot on you!" the other declared vindictively. A beefy man with bristly side whiskers, he turned to Jessie and Ki. "I'm Lou Prescoe, foreman o' the North Moon," he announced, "and the beaked gent is Bertie Harte. The idjit with the shredded tail is Clem Shore, who's always a-hankerin' to pull pranks on the beekeeper back there, whenever passing to or fro town."

"Looks more like Mr. York went to town on you," Jessie quipped. "But if you're Gold Beach-bound to meet some visitors and cattle, don't bother. You missed the boat, your guests are here, and your rumpus scattered the bulls." She introduced herself and Ki.

"Lawdy, I knowed we was runnin' late," Prescoe groaned, he and his men visibly wilting in dismay. "Ma'am, we're plumb sorry—"

"Save the apologies," Jessie interrupted, mirthfully eyeing the chagrined trio, "and let's get to gathering those bulls."

"Whoa up," Bertie Harte cautioned. "Ol' York is liable to be prowlin' about, all itchy to dose us with his blunderbuss. I got stabbed enough, without catchin' lead poisonin' like Clem did."

They glanced apprehensively in the direction of the trail. Then the embarrassed foreman addressed Jessie and Ki. "Ain't right to ask this, considerin', but since you weren't part of our set-to, p'raps you might be able to talk him into letting us ride free."

Before Jessie could respond, Ki volunteered. "Well, it has the makings of a hefty chore, but I'll give it a whirl. No sense us both risking it, Jessie, so you stay here, too, out of sight."

Leaving her and the anxious North Moon riders, Ki rode through the brush and back onto the trail. He loped along at a wary pace, scanning for Eustace York or the maverick bees, spotting neither but hearing an odd, tinny drumbeat from beyond the curve ahead.

Rounding the bend, he saw that the flanking woods fell away on the left-hand side, exposing a small field of clover. At its edge near the trail sat a sturdy log cabin, fronted by a flat, bare yard on which were arrayed some two dozen or more of the dome-shaped hives.

One of the hives looked a bit dented and bedraggled, the apparent victim of Clem Shore's roping trick. Eustace York, having retrieved it, was standing beside the hive, industriously whanging a tin washbasin with a stick, trying to attract the bees to swarm. He was succeeding. Bees swirled and buzzed in a cloud around him, and steadily trickled into a hole at the base of their damaged hive.

As Ki approached, the elderly beekeeper turned quickly and reached for his shotgun leaning against the hive. Then, seeing Ki was not one of the pranksters, he waved his stick in invitation. "C'mon, natural an' easy, an' the critters won't bite. Ain't interested in you. Right now they're just interested in winging in home."

"I'd say you're real clever at herding them, too," Ki remarked, pulling up. "Strikes me they'd be hard to ride a brand on."

38

York warmed to the compliment. "They can be, but they can be money-makers if you know how to handle 'em. Have to move the hives about, though, as they work out the clover an' flowers around 'em."

"Happens I met three sorry souls who moved one—and got moved by it." Ki chuckled. "They're still holed up in the bushes, and are mighty ready to call it quits if you're willing to let them go."

"Dadblamed if I am! Them ninnies can dang well scratch low through the brambles. Serve 'em humble for stampeding my bees."

"Well, problem is, in the doing they also stampeded our cattle. They agreed to go root them out for us, and believe me, that'll be powerful punishment. The one who looped your hive can't seat his saddle, and the other two are puffed and speckled as turkey eggs."

Eustace York, still glowering, permitted himself a creaky chortle. "Yep, I peppered that scapegrace Clem Shore fair'n proper, right where his brains is," he allowed, mellowing. "I'm pretty accurate with Ol' Stonewall here," he added, with a proud glance at his shotgun. "Reckon they won't disturb my hives soon again. They ain't bad hellions, just full of the devil. Aw'right, get to telling 'em we made peace, afore I change my mind."

Returning to the thicket, Ki reported, "It's safe."

"Good. Let's find the bulls and fog home," Shore declared plaintively. "I'm almighty tired of standin'. I crave a cushion."

Splitting up, the five began searching. The hunt was short, for the bulls had gouged blundering, readily traceable paths through the woodlands. And, though spooked and robust, they had the imperturbable disposition of most bovines, stolid and disinclined to stray freely when on their own. One by one they were located grazing contentedly, combed out from their grassy patches and flushed to the trail, where they were bunched by the curve. When all were collected, they were herded onward.

"We won't do it again, Mr. York," Shore called, red-faced, as they passed the beekeeper. "We made a sorrowful mistake, we did."

"I'll grant you did," York retorted, eyeing their swollen

faces and the stiffly upright posture of Shore. "You'll think twice an' better next time." Then, with a cackling guffaw, he resumed the banging of his tub to entice the remaining bees into their hive.

A little later they came to a fork. The main trail continued on generally southeastward, while a side track rambled off on a slightly more southerly course. They turned into the side track, rode for a quarter of a mile through heavy growth, and reached open meadowland.

"Half an hour and we'll sight the ranch," Prescoe said. "It's hunkered close to the hills over ahead to the right of us." These were the Coast foothills, which swept southward diagonally out of the northeast, then west in a lofty curve toward the sea. Beyond, like a buttressing phalanx, speared the desolate Siskiyous.

As they drew nearer the craggy, forested masses, Jessie noted that high along one slope clung a precarious path. Much of it was out of view, either masked by timber and vegetation, or hidden behind rock snags and ledges. Enough of it showed, however, to discern the path's route up the precipitous terrain, a line etched in stone and soil wriggling southward until it vanished into a hillcrest notch.

Ki observed the direction of her interest, then Prescoe did. "That's the old Whisper Path," the foreman explained to them. "A lively one it was, back when Oregon was a Territory. Some folks to the south of us smuggled Chinese opium across it, and many a cow has walked it, too. Word has it more'n one Northwest cattleman got his start running stock off California *ranchos* by way of the Whisper, only to have other galoots later on spirit the offspring of those herds back south. Uh-huh, a popular night trek, then."

"Ain't so dull nowadays," Harte complained. "Lotsa cows have got up and gone in this section of late, and if they don't hike the Whisper, how do they dodge all the lawdogs and surrounding ranchers?"

"Other things've been missing, too," Shore added. "That strongbox with the Antelope Mine payroll didn't just vanish when it was lifted off the Brookings stage. And the Rogue Logging Mill is awful curious about riders of the Whisper since their safe got blowed."

The North Moon men nodded solemnly. Jessie looked thoughtful, as did Ki, but neither said anything.

They reached a fenceline and followed it along, hazing the bulls who kept trying to grab at tufted grass growing trailside. Presently the ranch house came into view, its peaked roof projecting above the wide-topped grove of oaks that semi-circled it. Jessie noticed with approval the commodious bunkhouse, set rather far behind the house, the tight corral, roomy barns, and other neat, well-tended outbuildings. It showed Wyndam knew what to do, and did it.

Dogs started barking, and a hand hurried to open a rail-gate in the fence. The bulls were chased into an enclosed pasture. The five riders moved on to the stable barn, where a hostler took their horses. Then they headed for the house while crewmen hailed how-do's and a pair of springer spaniels jumped about, yapping.

The only one seeming oblivious to their arrival was a trim youth inside a nearby corral. Absorbed in trying to rope a bay pony, the boy kept his back to them. His slim figure still lacked the heft and girth of a capable hand, and twice he missed his throw.

Ki yelled, suggesting, "Open your loop, boy, and toss higher."

The youth wheeled around, and Ki had to grin as he touched his hatbrim. "Sorry, miss. I figured you for otherwise."

The girl nailed him with cold hazel eyes, her pert nose tilted in a snit. Eighteen to twenty, Ki judged, with a face full of freckles which in his opinion, looked cuter than hell on her. She patently didn't think a damn of his druthers or his apology, and far less of his mistake. She turned away, ignoring him, irritably poking stray wisps of auburn hair back up into the bun under her hat.

The hands thought it rousingly funny, though, and Jessie was tickled as well. The heartiest laugh, however, came from the man crossing the wide yard, walking very bow-legged. Bulky and broad-chested, in his late fifties, he had gray hair and muttonchops, smoky gray eyes beneath shaggy gray brows, and a deep cleft in his solid chin. He approached smiling, his hand outstretched.

"Miss Starbuck?" he greeted. "Welcome."

"Call me Jessie, please. And you must be Abbott Wyndam." She introduced Ki, and they all shook hands cordially.

"Make it Abe," Wyndam said. "I've been expecting you all day, and would've been to meet you personally, if a stock buyer hadn't shown up early and I had to stay and dicker with him." He glanced at the girl. "Opal? Take a moment and say hello."

The girl, having roped her pony, led it to the fence. "Uncle Abe's spoken often about you," she said pleasantly. Up close, Ki saw that he had erred indeed, for though her body was slender and wasp-waisted, Opal had the large breasts and rounded thighs of a mature woman. Her wide red mouth softened as she regarded Ki. "I'm glad you could come. Maybe we'll have time to talk later."

Opal walked her pony toward the barn, then, Ki watching. Wyndam explained, "She's my brother's child. He and his wife got killed in a train crash, so I took her in. She chores about and keeps the boys towin' a polite line. But, listen, you got here just in time to eat. Cook'll be putting chuck on the table any minute, and the boys'll be washing up out back. So what say we put off serious talk, get the dust off you, and strap on the feedbag."

Jessie and Ki enjoyed a meat-and-potatoes dinner in the company of Wyndam, his niece, and ten hands. Opal was quiet but scarcely demure, staring at Ki with a precocious scrutiny that was downright embarrassing. The crew was garrulous, asking about the voyage and swimming the bulls ashore, squabbling about the breeding of the herd, and joshing about the bee-roping and its results. A cushion was found for Clem Shore, and Wyndam advised, "Clem, you best pry out the shot and the bee stingers before they fester. Same for you other jokers. And stop ragging ol' Eustace. He's mean when he gets riled."

"Don't worry, boss," Shore moaned, squirming gingerly.

Leaving the mess hall, Wyndam invited Jessie and Ki to the main house. They crossed the yard just as the sun finished setting behind the western hills, and twilight's purple shadows were beginning to sink deep into Bohemia Valley.

Entering the house, Wyndam lit a pebble-glass table lamp while Jessie and Ki glanced about the parlor. It was tastefully outfitted with paintings, stocked bookcases, and comfortable furniture, but lacked doilies and bric-a-brac, and other feminine graces, Wyndam being a confirmed bachelor.

After everyone was settled, Jessie prompted gently, "Your letter wasn't detailed, Abe, but you wrote of having problems."

"Problems. What rancher hasn't got problems?" Wyndam sighed. "I've got *troubles*, Jessie. I sunk my profits into improvements and operated lean, and now . . . Well, I'm near ruined. That's why I had to see the buyer today, to cash off part of my herd. It was that, or deeding North Moon to Starbuck in lieu of foreclosure."

"Why, we'd refuse it! Dad gave, not lent, you your funds."

"I don't do business that way. Never have, never will."

"We'll discuss it later," Jessie hedged, not wishing to be sidetracked. "You've got troubles, you say. What kind? Rustling?"

"Among 'em, yes. Understand, if my troubles were mine alone, I wouldn't have pestered you, but mine are the same's a lot of folks'. Raidings and robbings and killings have broke out like Satan's rash."

"Sounds more like a very busy gang of outlaws," Ki said.

"If it is, it rides winged horses," Wyndam replied, "'cause strikes have occurred at the same time at different places. And no specializin', neither. Store thefts, company heists, stage and wagon holdups count equal. Ranches big enough to run crews are having stock swiped wholesale and hands shot from ambush. I've lost a couple of good men already, luckily just winged, and lost so many cattle I'm drained to the toe of my boot. Worse off are the really small spreads and farmers, who're being wiped out, burned out, and run out."

"It sounds more like a land-grab or range war."

"Well, Jessie, I can tell you it ain't no rancher–farmer fight. We get along fine. And open water's plentiful, so it ain't a case of anyone trying to hog it. Nope, folks are fearing, not feuding."

"Leading to tempers flaring, neighbor suspecting neighbor, to accusing at gunpoint," Ki observed. "Then the feuding begins."

Frowning, Jessie asked, "Where's the law? What's it doing?"

"What it can. A handful of town sheriffs, county deputies, and state marshals—a pitiful few, swamped by a plague busting wild from the Sixes River up by Port Orford, far east at least as the Cascades, and south more 'n' more into California. And they're stumped."

"Isn't there anything to go by? Not even a single clue?"

"One." Wyndam stood up. "Anyway, I suspect it is."

Rising from their seats, Jessie and Ki followed Wyndam into a side room that served as the ranch business office. A littered rolltop desk was by the window, and around were several chairs, a file cabinet, and a ledger case, both piled with papers. In one corner squatted a massive iron safe, its door securely locked.

From his desk, Wyndam took an arrow and handed it to Jessie. "This's Northwest Indian, but I'm unsure from which tribe."

Jessie noted the tanged arrowhead and spiral feathering, then passed it to Ki. "Abe, you mean you've got *Indian* trouble here?"

"God knows we've got the Indians. The native Kusa and Tolowa tribes, plus transplanted Moducks after their 1858 wars, and stray Nez Percés from Chief Joseph's rampage just three years ago. As for trouble, I pulled that one out of my front door, where it pinned a drawing of a skull and crossbones. Plenty like it have bitten plenty of other doors, sticking similar death threats or warnings like 'Get out.'"

"As a rule, I thought, Indians don't send notes," Ki remarked, returning the arrow to Wyndam. "To them, the arrow's the message."

Wyndam shrugged. "Habits change, Ki. Maybe schooling taught them differently, or more likely it's the Spanish influencing them."

"Spanish?" Jessie asked. "What Spanish?"

"You forget, Spain once claimed all up this coast by right of discovery and exploration. Oh, there wasn't the push like

44

in Mexico and California, but what with expeditions, landing forays, and shipwrecks, quite a few Spaniards wound up staying, often with natives. Their mixed-blood descendants have double reason to resent—and they do—what they feel is the American occupation."

Ki rubbed his earlobe thoughtfully. "So are you suggesting Abe, the trouble you've all got is from a Spanish–Indian uprising?"

"Go on, scoff," Wyndam grumped, impatiently tossing the arrow onto his desk. "Widespread crime, no specific culprit, can't stamp it out, and, hang it, a plain feeling of something astir—they're all early earmarks of a revolt. That's according to Major Pennington, and he ought to know; he's an authority on insurrections. But then, the major is an authority on everything. Just ask him, he'll tell you."

"I've heard of a Major Pennington," Jessie said. "He's the author of a highly controversial history of General Sam Houston."

"Same feller. Crank him up, he'll talk your leg off about how Houston, if he'd lived, might've carried out his grand scheme to unite Texas, the Southwest, and Mexico into a separate country."

"Just as well General Sam died first. It was a bad idea."

"Probably so, Jessie, but scads of believers back then didn't think it was, and would've joined Houston smack through perdition."

"Abe, as troubles go, there's a prime source of them," Jessie stated gravely. "A good leader can do bad harm, if he gets his followers pursuing a false cause. There've been others before General Sam, and there'll be others in the future. And always there're opportunists ready to take advantage of their misguided dreams, often for purely selfish motives, and then everybody suffers."

Wyndam bent a shrewd look at Jessie, but before he could comment, the plaintive hooting of an owl sounded from somewhere nearby.

"Listen!" Ki ordered sharply.

From southward, off across the valley, the cry was repeated.

"The owls hooted the night I got the arrow." Wyndam

sighed, slumping into his desk chair. "That's the call the Indians always signaled back and forth with, and now outlaws do the same."

"You think one or the other is signaling now, Abe?"

Wyndam's fingers tightened on the chair arm. "I don't know what to think, Jessie. I truly don't know what to think at all."

Chapter 5

The owl hoots ceased. The night wore on, and the talk kept on, supplying Jessie and Ki with minor details but no more real revelations.

Finally Wyndam mentioned money again. "There's six thousand in my safe from the cow sale, Jessie, that I want to pay against the mortgage, your travel costs, and the price of the bulls. I'll pay in cash, or I can go to the bank tomorrow and pay by certified check."

"Splendid. Pay for new stock, pay off local debts, pay into savings, whatever, but you will not," Jessie insisted, "pay me."

"I refuse to accept charity!"

"It's smart business," Jessie argued, hoping to placate his obstinate pride. "Think of your loan, as you call it, as Starbuck investing in you. We lose if you fail, we gain if you thrive. So helping you helps us." She laid a hand on the prickly rancher's arm. "Think of it as temporary help, Abe, and if you need more, just ask. Think of it not as charity, but as protecting our investment."

"Agin my grain, but ... Okay." His eyes rekindled their resolute flare, and his voice firmed with optimism. "I'm sure things'll upturn now. With Starbuck partnerin' the deal, how can we fail?"

After a celebratory glass of brandy to clinch the night, Jessie and Ki were shown to the second floor where they would sleep.

"Most of the rooms are vacant and closed up. The boys used to spread their rolls in 'em, but when I expanded and hired more hands, I had to build 'em a bunkhouse to herd together," Wyndam remarked while climbing the stairs. He rambled on as he led them into the corridor. "I bed in the first room here, and Opal's way at the end by the rear stairs. Half the time I dunno if she's come or gone, and tother half I'm wrong. Let's see, she was making up..." He opened the door after his. "Yep, this'll be your room, Jessie, and Ki, you take the next." He indicated the lamp on the table. "Good night, Jessie. Hammer on the wall if you want anything during the night."

Jessie closed the door and glanced about. Moonlight streamed in through the window, revealing a comfortable bed, chairs, and other furnishings. After lighting the kerosene banquet lamp on the bureau, she sat on the edge of her bed and, sighing, pulled off her boots. The floor was cold to her feet as she padded over to draw the window drapes, then back to where her bag had been placed at the foot of her bed.

The bag was a leather-bound canvas telescope bag, pliable enough not to gouge the horse carrying it, yet expandable enough to contain her necessities. Unbuckling its straps and spreading it open, she removed her nightwear and wash bag, and a green tweed jacket-and-skirt outfit which she hung in the armoire to lose some of its wrinkles. She then stripped naked, filled the washbasin with water from the matching pitcher, and used a hand towel to scrub herself.

Jessie would have loved a hot bath and a chance to wash her hair, but that would have to wait till morning. Constantly rinsing out the towel, she made do by sluicing off a good portion of the sand, sea, and Bohemia Valley that was clinging like a patina to her skin. Briskly she dried herself with the larger bath towel, her flesh tingling and glowing a healthy pink, then she slipped on her floor-length nightgown. Then, after brushing out her hair and pinning it up, she doused the lamp and climbed into bed.

She lay there, feeling stifled.

She got out of bed and went to the window again, this time to let out the mustiness. Parting the drapes enough to grab onto the window pulls, she glanced outside as she lifted the sash a crack. Then, instead of returning immediately to bed, she slid a chair over and sat down, leaned her arms on the ledge, and gazed out while pondering the strange, alarming disclosures she had heard tonight.

For some time Jessie sat contemplating at the window, resting her chin upon her arms, watching the moonlight cast shifting patterns on the ground as the oak tree branches swayed gently in a faint breeze. Through an opening in the foliage she could view the swelling bulk of the hills, with perhaps twenty yards of the Whisper Path visible, a thin wavery line in the distance, deceptive by moonlight.

She continued thinking, staring at the Whisper Path without consciously being aware of it. Abruptly, however, she leaned forward, her eyes narrowing slightly, her attention focusing intently on the slithering scar up the face of the wooded and rock-gashed slope.

Into her range of vision, then out of it a moment later, had flickered a speeding horseman. After the first one came others, until Jessie had counted nineteen ethereal riders flashing silently past in the moonlight mist. As phantoms they appeared, as phantoms they vanished, materializing from the murk to the south, dissolving into the gloom to the north. No click of shod hoof or jingle of bridle iron caught her ears, no word of casual conversation. Spectres of the deadened night, for a moment they *were,* then they were not.

Jessie studied the empty thread of a trail, wondering if perhaps she had been hallucinating. No, they were no ghost riders of the mind she had witnessed, but flesh-and-blood men on horseback heading northward at a swift pace. Of course, she realized, the incident could have been nothing more unusual than a group of punchers on the way to the wagon trail, thence on to home or to town. But she had a feeling that what she had seen was neither a hungry, fagged-out crew, nor a skylarking bunch out for a romp. There had been a sense of alertness and set purpose about the hard-riding pack that was disquieting.

Well, there was nothing she could do about it at the moment. Reclosing the drapes, she went back and slipped under the bedcovers again. Yet she had an uneasy premonition that she would hear more, and something not pleasant, relative to the eerie troop. On that caution, Jessie fell into a deep slumber.

Ki, too, had decided on a quick cat-bath before retiring. He peeled off his soiled duds and exchanged them for a clean set from his traveling valise, stacking the clean set neatly on the bureau for the next day's wearing. Then out of his valise he took his blue-gray suit, hung it in the armoire, and slid the valise in underneath. He was as unconcerned as Jessie about padding around naked in a strange bedroom. Less so, in fact, for he planned to sleep in the buff; he saw no reason to dress in a nightshirt, since he wasn't expecting to go anywhere except to bed.

Ki washed and shaved and was working with the towel when he heard someone stop out in the hall, and knuckles tapped on his door.

"Hello? Ki? Are you there?"

Ki recognized Opal's whispered voice, but he didn't answer at once. Instinctively, his eyes checked the door and the window across from it. The lock was engaged, and the drapes were completely drawn. If he were wise, he'd keep it this way. In a small room, the only trap deadlier than a crossfire ambush was a compromising situation.

"Ki? I'm alone. Please let me in."

Ki padded to the door. "What do you want?" he whispered.

"Hurry," Opal pleaded. "I can't be seen here like this."

The worst, Ki figured; an equivocal answer, dodging the question. But Opal had him skunked. "Don't come in until I tell you to," he said.

He unlatched the door and went to the bureau, where he took his clean pair of jeans and slipped them on for modesty. Then he called out, and the door widened just enough for Opal to ease through. She quickly shut it behind her and locked it without being told.

"Well, at least now your uncle can't catch you pounding

on my door," Ki allowed, "and blame me for the outrage." He scratched his bare chest. "I wasn't expecting any visitors, especially ladies."

"Heavens, a girl doesn't grow up on a ranch without seeing men in all states of undress," Opal said, smiling reassuringly as she stepped closer. "Fact is, it's you who should be thinking improper of me, coming here alone while everyone else is asleep."

"Such a notion never crossed my mind, Opal."

They gravitated toward the bed and sat down, Opal primly smoothing out the folds of her long, pink-striped nightgown. Her feet were bare, her hair was freshly combed, and she had doused herself with some pleasing, if overpowering, perfume.

"I hope Uncle Abe doesn't get his nose up and find me in here," Opal said. She inched closer, her eyes wondrously wide. "Oh, it'd be worse than me in the hall, Ki. He's always lecturing me about not getting too familiar, for fear something might happen to me."

Ki grinned. "What kind of something?"

"Oh . . . you know. The hands around here all the time, and salesmen and visitors coming and going. Uncle Abe gets powerful mad if I stop and talk much to any of them, strangers in particular."

"And you never do?"

"I am now, ain't I?"

She lifted her brows when she said that, and looked sideways at Ki as she eased still nearer. Ki was pretty fairly convinced by now that her nightgown and perfume were all she had on—except for what she may have on her mind. "And is your uncle right about it?"

"What do you think?"

What a vixen, Ki thought. He needed to get entangled with her in this house like he needed ringworm. But if a woman was offering, a man would somehow rise to the occasion. "Opal, I think I know what you need."

She sat with a light smirk on her face and then, because she evidently wanted him to make the first move, Ki slid his hand over her shoulder and kissed her. She responded with enthusiasm, the pressure of her young body like an eager

51

promise, her lips pressed to his, her tongue darting between his teeth.

He glided his other hand down over her arm and across the front of her nightgown. She wriggled some but didn't object, and in a second he was massaging one of her breasts. All things considered, Opal had big breasts for her size. Ki didn't think she could weigh over a hundred and ten pounds.

Opal didn't say a word when Ki started kneading her breasts, but after a long moment she broke her kiss. "I've never done this with a Chinaman before."

"I'm Japanese," Ki corrected, tweaking one nipple.

She watched his hand caressing her nipple until it was firm and distended, tenting the fabric of her gown. Her breathing was growing heavier, and Ki could feel a sensual quivering to her body as he moved to the other nipple. "Ki . . . Take, take me bare . . ."

Ki eased her gown up. Opal raised her bottom so he could hike it from under her, then lifted her arms as he tugged the garment over her head. Naked, Opal was as lovely as Ki had imagined she would be. She stretched back on the bed, her legs apart.

"Has your uncle ever caught you at this?" Ki asked.

"Almost. Once I had to hide in the hayloft for two hours."

Now also naked, Ki eased alongside Opal. She gasped with pleasure, her body undulating in response to his hands while they massaged her flesh to yearning arousal. Ki positioned himself over her, feeling her thighs widen to cradle him, her ankles locking around his calves as he pressed down on her loins, inserting himself firmly.

Thus entwined, they began a simple yet urgent flexing of buttocks, a hardening and softening of the muscles of the lower abdomen, a gentle rocking of one body impaled by another. Balancing his upper weight on his arms, Ki watched the play of emotions on Opal's expressive face. Her eyelids were fluttering, her brow furrowing and smoothing, her throat muscles and tendons standing out in bold relief, then relaxing.

Opal breathed raggedly, her lips drawn down slightly, the right corner of her mouth twitching in response to the sensations coursing up from between her clasping thighs. She opened her eyes slowly, seeing Ki hovering above her. She felt the pressure of his pistoning hardness, the rhythmic contact of his pubic bone against her mound as she writhed beneath him.

Ki lowered his head and their mouths fused together. Their tongues touched and flicked in play, Ki beginning now to plunge deeper and more swiftly. Opal shuddered and moaned, and he quickened to a violent thrusting. Their bellies slapped together, Opal quivering with each sliding jolt, grinding against him, sensing her climax nearing.

Abruptly Opal cried out in release, her fist stuffed into her mouth while she tried to stifle her high-pitched sounds of wanton ecstasy. Clenching his teeth, Ki felt his orgasm welling up, triggered by the clenching convulsions of her spasms. He flowed deep inside her, flooding her. She splayed her legs wide, arching up with pressing force to hold the last bits of joy there between her legs.

Slowly Ki settled down over her soft warm body. He lay, crushing her breasts and belly with his weight, until his immediate satiation began to wane. Finally he rolled from her and gently stroked her quivering breasts.

Opal smiled at him with lazy, satisfied eyes. "You like?"

"I like."

"There's more, much more."

"I hope so."

There was much more. Opal was a wildly wanton young woman. Her imagination and energy seemed boundless. She rode him on top the second time. The third time she awakened Ki from a drowsy half-sleep with her hot lips. She was wild and aggressive aboard him, now squatting astride his hips while leaning back, now lying full length, gasping, clinging, until the third release left them both weak and tired.

In the silent aftermath, Ki thought he detected the sounds of an odd metallic click, as of a door latch, and faint bootsteps easing away. But they were so elusive, and the night hush resumed so quickly, that he gave them no mind while he snuggled quietly with Opal, languid with contentment.

"You sure do make me hot," Opal purred dreamily.

"Mm," Ki murmured, half-asleep. Then he raised his head, abruptly sensing something was amiss. The room was dark and undisturbed, but Ki, sniffing the air, sat up attentively. "I can smell smoke."

Opal giggled. "I'm not *that* hot down there."

Suddenly she too snapped awake and sat up, as a muffled explosion burst from somewhere downstairs. The blast quickly faded to a low, dull crackling reminiscent of a campfire, while the odor of burning wood grew more pervasive. Bolting out of bed and rushing for the door, Ki glimpsed tendrils of smoke curling in from under its sill. He was nearly to the door when a chorus of startled, confused yelling erupted outside, followed by a brief salvo of gunfire and louder, angrier shouting, and ending in a jabber of cussing.

"What's going on?" Opal cried. "Don't leave me here!"

"I don't know, and I'm not," Ki answered, as he cautiously began to open the door. "Hurry, now, put on your gown."

The corridor was empty save for the smoke that was coming from the main staircase, gushing up out of the flame-riddled pit of the well. Turning, Ki peered toward the rear staircase, perceiving waves of heated air but no signs of smoke or fire yet.

Opal pressed close. Ki said, "There's a fire spreading fast below us." He stepped with her into the hall. "You can still make it out by the back if you're fast. You'll be safe. Only ranch hands outside, by the sound of 'em, and whatever they're shooting at is gone."

"But—"

"Move!" Ki pushed her. "I'll be along in a second."

Reluctant to leave Ki, yet frightened to stay, Opal hiked up the hem of her nightgown and fled down the smoke-filled corridor.

Ki watched till she hit the stairs before he ducked inside and slammed the door. His room was cloying, the air choking him as with desperate haste he dressed, packed, then heaved his satchel through the window. Craning out, he glimpsed it and shards of broken glass falling, and a reddish glow swiftly growing in intensity along the wood siding.

The rousted crew was milling, agitated, he saw, some of them gathering about Opal as she dashed outdoors, others calling and beckoning to him. But the ground was too long a drop, the nearest tree too far a leap, and anyway, Ki had no intention of jumping.

Instead he dove back out the door. He had yet to hear movement in Jessie's adjoining room, though sounds could have been blocked by the thick partition wall. The corridor remained empty, however, and if she or Wyndam had been aroused, they surely would have raised a hullabaloo warning all up and down it before seeking to escape.

The smoke was stifling. It was billowing from both staircases, Ki saw as he sprang for Jessie's room; the rear was now as impassable as the front. Rising with it came the noise of roaring flames, frantic voices, and stomping boots. The whole first floor must be ablaze. Ki twisted the knob and shouldered open the door.

The glow from the fire scaling the main stairwell filtered into the room, dispelling enough of the murky pall to show Jessie lying on the floor. Huddled unconscious, clad in her nightgown, she had no doubt been overcome by smoke before she could reach the door.

Snatching the wash basin, Ki flung its dirty, soapy water full in her face. Jessie came to with a jolt, spluttering and spitting, then struggled to sit, only to wilt back on one elbow.

"The house is going up like a torch," Ki said in a calm yet urgent voice. "While I rig a way out, you might want to get ready."

Jessie nodded. In a moment, with the aid of Ki's arm, she managed to stand upright, wobble-legged, coughing and gagging.

"Easy," Ki cautioned, "but hurry."

Jessie snaked off her drenched nightgown while Ki went to the window, his back turned to her nudity as she slipped on her clothes. He could have been facing her, though, for all she cared; this was not the time, nor was there the time, for modesty. She went about stuffing her bag with her personals, hastening as best she could, dizzy, almost voiceless, and wheezing from the smoke she'd inhaled.

55

Smoke was curling in through the cracked-open window, and when Ki lifted the sash higher, he met a cloud of it pluming up along the wall from below. To leap out would be as suicidal as from out his window, and though that tree near his was nearer to here, it still was not near enough. Moving to the bed, he swept off blankets and sheets. Deftly he knotted them together, twisting and twining, then shoved the heavy bedstead against the wall, half-blocking the window.

By now Jessie was functioning more normally, and she came over as Ki was tightening a hitch around the stout bedpost. "I believe this'll hold you climbing down," he said confidently, slinging the improvised line out the window. "Throw your bag out and grab a ride."

Pitching her bag through the open window, Jessie replied darkly, "If you're wrong—if it rips or unravels on me—I'll never forgive you." She inched out onto the sill until she was in a sitting position, her legs dangling down the wall, her boots crisping in the hot fluming smoke. "I don't think I'd be in any condition to," she moaned, clutching the line with both hands and sliding free of the ledge. She turned to give Ki a woeful, parting glance, only to spot him heading for her door. "Come back here, you coward!"

"I have to get Wyndam, if I can," he called. "Good luck!"

The door shut after him, leaving Jessie muttering to herself. "He knows if I'd known what he'd be up to, I'd not've done this." He had tricked her into being saved. Well, maybe; she wasn't down yet.

Steeling herself, Jessie began her descent, aware that Ki had counted on her good sense not to waste the time and effort to shinny back up onto the window ledge. The bed linen stretched, the bedstead above creaked, as for what seemed like ages she drew lower, hand by hand, her lungs bursting for air, her arms aching with the strain. And still the ground was a bone-crushing way down through the noxious smoke, along blaze-roasting plankboard siding, past tongues of flame licking out from crannies and chinks.

Dimly she heard shouts of encouragement echoing up through the fuming swelter. Her muscles were trembling, an ever-tightening band was squeezing her chest, suffocating her, sapping her strength. Then suddenly hands were gripping her legs. With a gasp of relief she let go her hold, and the rescuing hands broke her fall.

"We nigh reckoned you a goner, ma'am," Lou Prescoe declared, solicitously guiding her away from the burning house. "Take it easy, now. Sit down here and rest. You've had a lean squeak."

Jessie smiled faintly, closing her eyes as a wave of nausea swept over her. It passed quickly, however, and she reopened her eyes. "Ki!" she gasped worriedly. "Ki's up there inside."

"So's Uncle Abe!" Opal cried, shrill and fearful. "Some of the boys glimpsed him early on, at his window, trying to climb out!"

A saddened ranch hand nodded. "Yeah, till the smoke got him an' he fell back. We went in after him, but the downstairs was a furnace, the stairs ate through, an' the ladder we put up outside caught on fire. Hey, there goes your rope burnin' up, jus' like a fuse!"

Jessie glanced up toward her bedroom window. She saw that only two or three feet of Ki's improvised rope remained drooping from the ledge. The flames bursting from the lower windows and siding were climbing the outer wall, but were still below the second story. Yet in back of her open second-story window, a flickering crimson glow was beginning to strengthen.

"Fire gnawing through the floor," Prescoe said, as though reading her thoughts. "Stairs blocked, no tree close enough to climb up and swing from, or vice versa. I'm miserable sorry, ma'am, but if Ki's caught up there with the boss, he'll be burned, too." Prescoe sighed mournfully. "Let's hope they've suffocated first."

The fire was consuming the stairway landing now, stabbing at the corridor ceiling, running along the floor almost to the door of Abbott Wyndam's bedroom. Ki raced through the smoke, evading the flames, and thrust open the door, slamming it as he surged inside.

Wyndam was a vague silhouette across the dark room, a black crouching shape by the window, bent on his knees with his forehead touching the floor in an odd, prayer-like

57

position. Ki lunged forward, his eyes stinging, vision blurring, the smoke-boiling air searing his lungs. For an instant his brain whirled, his senses reeling. Then Ki dropped panting in the clearer air near the floor.

Shifting to his hands and knees, Ki started crawling toward Wyndam. Flames flickered between the floorboards. The floor and the walls were creaking and groaning from the pressure of the fire rushing up from the inferno below. At last Ki reached the limp body. Groping, he felt for the man's pulse and found its thready beat.

"Abe," he murmured, "we might make it yet."

He gripped the window sill then, and drew himself up to look out. He uttered an exasperated oath. Directly below Wyndam's window was another that opened into one of the downstairs rooms, and from this lower window, flame was spewing up the wall in a fiery sheet. He could not repeat his bed trick here, nor could he again from Jessie's window. That line was already memory, as would be any other within seconds of being fed down out of this row of windows.

"Hang on, Abe. We'll go find us another window."

Ki gathered Wyndam into his arms. The old man's bulky form was a heavy burden, though he was inches shorter than Ki. Raising him, Ki staggered to the door, a lash of flame whipping into the room the instant he opened it. He bent his head and, with Wyndam balanced awkwardly, plunged through the fire and down the corridor.

It was pointless to try Jessie's or his own window. Ki shifted to the rooms opposite, whose windows would overlook the other side of the house. The nearest door was locked. He lunged to the next, steadying Wyndam with one hand as he nervously twisted the knob. It did not open. Likewise with the third door, and when he hurled his weight against the panels, the stout oak scarcely budged.

He was fast running out of doors.

The fourth was unlocked, but led to a broom closet. The fifth sturdily resisted his determined assault to break in, and he was a bit frantic when he gripped the knob of the sixth door. The knob turned, the latch snicked, and the door opened hallward.

Glancing in, Ki saw a stairway leading upward. With the

fire raging along behind him in the corridor, he took the steps wildly, two at a time, and found himself in an attic over the second floor. The attic ran the full length of the house, with a window at each end, far up near the roof peak, altogether too small and out of reach.

Almost despairing, Ki peered about. Some yards to his left he glimpsed a roof vent which, in case of inspections or repairs, could be opened by a notched bar that hung downwards. It was built into the roof where the eaves were relatively low, and by standing close to the side wall, he could reach the notched bar.

Placing Wyndam on the floor, which was already hot to the touch, Ki thrust the iron arm upwards. It did not move. He pushed against it harder a number of times, but in vain. The wood frame of the vent had warped with age and disuse, becoming as one with the roof.

The smoky air of the attic was choking, the heat increasing by the second. Ki daubed his sweat-bleary eyes, scanning for something he could use as a battering ram, but found nothing. The attic was bare save for a scattering of old steamer trunks.

Ki leaped to one of the staunch trunks and dragged it beneath the vent. Swinging up on the trunk, he had to stoop as he rose and put both hands against the vent itself, but was able to exert the force of his hunching back, shoulders, and arms when he shoved upward. Gradually the vent loosened enough to allow relatively fresh air to pour in, finally lifting enough for a person to climb through.

Poking his head out the vent opening, Ki breathed in great draughts of the cooler, cleaner air while he gazed around. The roof had a steep pitch, but leveled off at the eaves where a stout copper gutter was spiked to the boards. Directly beneath spread the outer crown of an oak growing near the house. The leaves obscured his view of the ground, from which came a clamor of shouts and curses, while up through the branches glimmered the glare of flames, as the fire continued its rapid envelopment of the house. To his dismay, the roof's gutter line was considerably higher than the treetop, so that no projecting branch was within his reach.

Only one slim hope occurred to Ki, but any chance, no matter how tiny or risky, sure beat the no-chance alternative remaining.

Ducking back into the smoke-clogged attic, he picked up Wyndam and mounted the trunk. Awkwardly, balancing precariously, he wrestled the rancher's inert body through the vent opening, and levered it resting on the slight offset above the gutter. Then he hoisted himself out and crouched on the roof, studying the tree branches below.

His slight hope appeared bleaker than ever. Sighing, Ki unwound his rope belt from his waist. It was actually a *surushin*, a six-foot braided cord with a leather-covered lead ball at each end, an arcane weapon that, when sent spinning, would coil about an enemy, maiming and sometimes killing. Now he used the rope belt to bind Wyndam's wrists together securely. He dragged the sagging form partially erect and managed to get the bound arms around his own neck.

Bending over, teetering on his narrow perch, Ki hunched Wyndam on his back. Then, taking a deep breath, he crouched still lower and vaulted from the roof into the heart of the tangle of branches.

The slender upper limbs snapped under the double weight. For an eternally long moment Ki feared they would plummet straight to the ground, but as they crashed on through, his grabbing hand snagged hold of a heftier limb. It bowed under the strain and split, but it braked the rush of their fall. Ki clutched another, which also broke, then his chest struck squarely across a third limb with such force that the breath was knocked from his lungs.

Though the limb bent, creaking and almost splintering, it was sufficiently stout to withstand the shock. For some moments Ki lay draped across it, crushed by Wyndam's weight on his back, half strangled by the pressure of the rancher's tied hands against his throat. Torrents of heat were boiling upward, the leaves around and below him shriveling in the torrid blasts. But the tree stood between windows and escaped the flames geysering from them.

Finally Ki managed to suck some air back into his tortured lungs. He began painfully to inch along the branch, reaching the tree trunk after agonizing effort, then started clambering down the ladder rungs formed by the chunky lower limbs. As he descended, the heat grew more intense. Each breath scorched his lungs, sweat flowed from every pore, hot flashes stormed before his eyes.

Groggily Ki realized that men were running and calling beneath the tree, their dark forms stretching to meet his landing. He felt the strangling arms plucked from around his neck, and the heavy drag of the rancher's body was removed from his back. Hands lifted him to a sitting position while someone pressed a water bottle to his lips. As his head began to clear, Ki recognized the person to be Jessie.

"Thank God," she said fervently. "How're you feeling?"

"Like I was rode hard and put away wet," Ki croaked. "Only not wet enough." He snatched the bottle and swallowed thirstily.

Lou Prescoe approached and tossed Ki his rope belt. "You an' the ol' man are both livin' on borrowed time," Prescoe declared, grinning. "An' he's got you to thank for not waking up with a coal shovel in his mitts. Hey, is he rousin' out of it?" he shouted to the ranch hands who were ministering to Wyndam.

"Coming 'round," a hand yelled. "He'll perk to any time!"

Regaining his feet, Ki looped and tied his belt around his waist, wincing at the pain when he breathed deeply. After he prodded about his sore chest and checked here and there, he decided some ligaments and tendons might be sprained, but no ribs or bones were cracked or broken.

With Jessie and Prescoe, Ki went over to where Wyndam lay on the ground a safe distance away from the house. Clustering around, their figures outlined by the glare of the house fire, his hands were anxiously watching Opal swab his face with a damp rag. They let out a cheer when, moments later, Wyndam fluttered open his eyes.

After cursing a blue streak, Wyndam groped upright, refusing assistance. "Git your mangy paws off, I'm okay!" He sat, head in his hands, looking very sick indeed. "Last I rec'lect is hoppin' outa bed in a room so thick you could carve it with a knife." Told of how he'd been carted to the roof and down the tree, he beamed at Ki. "Much obliged,

61

and I won't forget. Smart work, Ki."

"I don't know. It was mostly falling through the tree."

"Sure, that's how I figure," Wyndam replied dryly. "'Cept it was mighty accurate fallin', without a busted neck at the end of it." He looked around. "But what's this about? How'd the fire catch?"

"Didn't catch," Prescoe growled. "'Twas set deliberate —set in a batch of places on the main floor, stairs, too. What first tumbled us from our bunks was hearin' a big bang. We scooted outdoors, only to trade lead with a couple or so owlhoots hightailin' it away, and by then the house was burning all over."

Ki, nodding, cast a glance at Opal before he said, "That fits. A blast downstairs woke me up. I ran out, and found the front staircase burning. Luckily, my room and Opal's were far enough away to miss the smoke gusts that got Abe and Jessie, or. . ." Ki shrugged.

"Those damned lobos must've blowed my safe and fired my house," Wyndam said grimly. "Guess they must've figured that by torching the stairs just before they set off the charge, nobody could come down before they cleaned the safe and skedaddled."

"By way of Whisper Path?" Jessie asked.

Wyndam tugged his muttonchops. "Reckon could be."

"Anyone have an idea what the time is?" she asked.

"Oh, likely nigh to three o'clock," Prescoe hazarded.

Jessie thanked him, her eyes thoughtful. Something like six hours had elapsed between the time she had seen the spectral horsemen riding northward and the attack on the ranch house.

Wyndam started coughing hoarsely. "Can't seem to chuck that infernal smoke from my lungs," he complained, as he rose rather unsteadily. He stood swaying, truculently staring at his flame-spouting home. "She's a goner, but there's plenty of sleepin' space in the bunkhouse. Boys, see the mess hall and cookshack don't catch, so we don't go short on feedin' our faces. As it is, it's apt to get tight till we can build a new house. We'll start on that soon's the ashes cool on them foundations."

At his orders the hands went to work, and the two closest

in size to Wyndam and Opal went to scrounge up some spare clothing. Jessie and Ki helped keep a sharp eye on the roofs of the outbuildings and barns on the chance that a stray ember might ignite them also, until finally the house was merely a charred shell and the fire was well on its way to burning itself out.

"Well, I reckon that's all we can do tonight," Wyndam announced at length. "Things 'pear to be quietin' down, so's we might as well grab a mite of shuteye 'fore daylight." He coughed some more, and cleared his throat as he turned to Jessie and Ki. "I'll ride to town come morning and tell Sheriff Lydell what happened. Not that it'll do any good. Would you like to side me, if you don't mind, seein' as you caught more of what went on than anybody else. Maybe you'll learn a few helpful particulars, too, like p'raps how the word of my money spread so fast, considerin' the buyer was here only today. So, what say, you'll ride in with me?"

Jessie and Ki nodded agreement.

Chapter 6

About the time Jessie first spied the ghostly riders, Longarm lay squirming, gradually recovering his senses.

His body, especially his rib cage, throbbed with pain. His head pulsed to a dull ache as his reviving wits labored to review what had happened. There had been an uppity girl on Deaver Osborne's Chickasaw. When he had scorned her warning, she had ridden into him. A revolver shot from behind, then his glimpse of Wolfer Goswick with a smoking Dragoon, the horse lurching, bullet-struck, and going down. Longarm seemed to remember being kicked by a flailing hoof, but he couldn't be sure, and after that was largely a blur.... Slurred voices planning to drown him, and calling the girl Easter... Vague hands toting him, stripping off his boots, his guns and belt, swiping anything of value before tying his wrists and ankles... Shadowy men beat and stomped him to unconsciousness before dumping him bloodied, leaving him to wait.

Longarm waited. He struggled to ease his cramped position, able to hear a low drone of talk from somewhere nearby. He could see nothing in a blackness that reeked with stable odors, and by touch alone attempted to loosen the binding ropes. He worked diligently but futilely as he waited, he felt, to share the fate of Deaver Osborne. He had little doubt that the rancher had been robbed and murdered here in Beulah. A town of mystery and death, they'd called it back at Sontag's Emporium, where Wolfer was the law and none had the courage to stand against him—none, apparently, except his daughter, Easter.

There came footsteps and a sliver of light seeped through a crack. A door opened and a lantern was thrust in Longarm's face. Blinking, he made out two hardcases and a third figure with a beard staring down at him. Of the two men, one was long-bellied, hawk-eyed; the other was chinless, hatchet-faced, a bit shorter and a lot wider than Longarm, yet nevertheless he was wearing Longarm's stolen boots, gunbelt, watch chain, and all. The third, when he stepped forward a pace, proved to be Wolfer, his blubbery lips curved in a sneer.

"So you ride for Osborne with an eye on the take, eh?"

Longarm shrugged. "Like I said before, you should know."

"I know you're tough. The sort that arises only from plenty of fisticuffs, practicin' on a quick draw, usin' cartridges by the box shootin' at targets. You're too salty to be a simple wrangler."

The hatchet-faced man asked, "Then who is this hombre?"

"Why, he's got to be a lawdog, that's who! Come weaselin' in here, hoping to fool us, but he didn't, eh, Peleg?" Wolfer's viperish eyes gleamed, and in them Longarm read the man's cunning. Wolfer wasn't aware that he was in fact a deputy U. S. marshal. Wolfer was accusing him as a crafty ploy to fire his outlaw henchmen for the kill, and to keep them beholden to him for their safety here. Wolfer glanced at the hawk-eyed man. "Harper, go have Thorne fetch us a mount. Some ol' plug, not this hombre's black. I already lost one good horse today."

The gunman named Harper hung the lantern on a peg and went out. Peleg and Wolfer picked up Longarm between them, Peleg grabbing the lantern as they carried him to the rear of the barn. Harper then came back, accompanied by the stable's night hostler, who was leading a swaybacked sorrel mare. The hostler was as grizzled and scrawny as the nag, with rheumy eyes and a strained white mustache.

The hostler gave the reins to Peleg, who told him, "'Fore you set again, Arapaho, dig a hole out back for that dead Chickasaw."

Arapaho Thorne growled a protest.

"Shut up," Wolfer said, as he and Harper flung Longarm across the mare's sagging back. "I hired you on to serve my needs here, and I'll fire you if you don't. So do like you're ordered."

Nodding, his watery eyes clouding a little, Arapaho Thorne walked away. His jaw was working, but if he muttered anything, it was drowned by the louder grumble of thunder in the mountains.

When Arapaho was out of earshot, Harper said, "That cantankerous coot don't do nothin' but gargle shellac and piss vinegar."

"Yeah, I'm about fed up with him begrudgin' everything and everybody 'cept Easter. Damn her!" Wolfer snarled. "Listen, afterwards you keep an eye on her. She's home—I saw her lamp on—but she's in one of her damned moods. Better watch Arapaho, too. Watch out for him, though. He was a hardtack frontiersman in his day, and the ol' rummy can still be mean to mess with." Then with a sudden savage insistence, he added, "Let's get it over 'n' done."

They passed through a wide door and by a corral toward the Snake River. Lightning splashed the sky. There was a gusty rush of wind from the hills, portents of a late summer cloudburst. It was not an autumnal howler, this storm, but a short, swift deluge to cleanse the charged atmosphere. Yet rain pours in the mountains meant that soon flash floods would come roaring down streams and dry washes, torrents of muddy water laden with debris, sweeping all before them.

Showers now began, soaking them as they followed a river path that angled away from town. Longarm rode a-stride, his legs unbound but his wrists remaining lashed, aware that any try at a break would be folly. He was flanked by Wolfer and Harper while Peleg led the sorrel, a gluefoot plodder who dawdled along until they reached the river, where it promptly fell adoze on its feet.

Longarm gazed down and his breath sucked through his teeth. The swirling, foaming current below was bedded in fanged rocks and enclosed by eroded, sheer-sided banks. Yonder he could hear a menacing note. Already the Snake was on the rampage as the runoff of the thunderstorm fed angry water into it from a thousand slopes.

Wolfer gloated. "Not only are we gettin' rid of this troublesome star-toter, but we're acquirin' his black Morgan to replace the Chickasaw. 'Pears to me we're even with the board, boys."

Peleg snickered as he patted his pocket. "A slice better'n even, boss. He had coupla bucks on him, plus a few other goodies."

"All is grist that comes to our mill, eh?" Wolfer drew his Dragoon Colt and mockingly regarded Longarm. "Mayhaps you'll meet with Osborne downriver somewheres—what the buzzards ain't picked." He thumbed the hammer, aiming at Longarm. "So long, asshole."

Twisting sidewards, leaning low, Longarm jammed both thumbs into the sorrel's belly and shouted directly in its ear. At the same instant, Wolfer triggered. Longarm felt the burn of a bullet against the upper, more exposed blade of his sloping shoulders, then a spasm of pain along his left arm when the horse, squealing, leaped startled and plunged blindly over the crumbling bank.

Peleg let go of the hackamore barely in time to avoid being dragged into the river. He swore luridly, but Wolfer's surprised oath gave way to a hard laugh. Longarm and the sorrel were haplessly floundering in the icy tide under the bank. The roar upstream heralded an onrushing torrential cascade, looming to swamp the man and the horse as they fought for purchase on the slippery, sharp rocks, their legs resisting the buffeting of the churning flow. Racing wind and rain swept ahead of the flash flood, driving Wolfer and his gunmen in hasty retreat toward town, drenched yet satisfied.

Longarm, tossed from his horse, splashed headlong and deep, the slam of the stony channel sending agony spiraling through his wound. He battled to the surface, gulping air while he struggled toward the shallows along the pitch-dark bank. Wavering, he sank there to his knees in foot-high water and tried again to free his hands, but the wet rope only bit more cruelly into his wrists.

Suddenly, peripherally, he was aware of the lithe figure wading in alongside. Turning, he saw Easter leaning close with a straight-bladed "Akransas Toothpick" knife poised in her right hand.

"Hold still," she snapped as he reared defensively. Crouching, she slid the thin, pointed blade between his wrists and quickly cut off the ropes, then resheathed the knife in her belt scabbard.

Longarm began rubbing his wrists and flexing his hands to restore numbed circulation. He started to thank her, when above his voice and the noise of the horse paddling somewhere in the darkness sounded the ominous surge of the impending flood. A wet hand seized his and the girl, scrambling upright, cried fiercely, "Run!"

They stumbled over rocks and into holes, the tumultuous fury of the plummeting Snake River deafening in their ears. Brush crackled and stones were set rolling. Fleetingly, Longarm thought he glimpsed the sorrel thrashing frenziedly to the gully of a cutbank.

Then a towering swell burst over him and Easter, its breaking wave submerging them deep underwater, its sucking tow pressuring them down to stay. Furiously they strained against the watery crush, kicking and clawing upwards, and finally they surfaced, heads reeling and stomachs knotting, only to be caught by the fast-scudding tide.

They swam with hard strokes, hampered by their clothes, hardly able to keep from being dashed into a morass of jagged boulders, through which the river was boiling in deadly rapids. Half drowned, they wrestled loose of the tugging current and struck for the bank, frantically trying to evade the flotsam of timber and bush, cast-off relics, snagged possessions, and unwary animals that constantly swarmed in around them while bowling on past.

They were perhaps ten yards from the south bank when a lumber beam the size of a roof support abruptly speared out of the surface. Before Easter could dodge aside, the beam rammed into her, hurtling her back into the irresistible grip of the flow. Longarm made a lunge for her, but the girl was already gone, tumbling with the beam toward the roiling, life-smashing maelstrom of the rapids.

Longarm dove after, swimming now with the current in an effort to intercept Easter. He reached out, missed, stroked, and reached again, his fingers clutching the neckband of her skirt. Then, one-handed, he swam once more for the bank. Willing his left arm to thrust and pull, almost losing her again in his painful striving, he managed to maneuver them into a break in the bank, away from the main torrent.

The backwash in this break created a whirlpooling eddy, which Longarm skirted as much as possible while aiming for the far shallows. When his bone-cold, bootless feet scraped against stone, he dug in his toes for leverage and half climbed, half crawled to the end of the break. Here the ground lifted to a low hump, its back wall notched by a runoff cut that continued on into the bank, quite likely forming a path of sorts to the top. Yet here as well the rain had turned the earth into a grease-slicked ooze, and it was only by snatching grass tufts and twiggy scrub that Longarm was able to haul them both out.

Slumping, panting, Longarm realized after a moment that the girl remained as he'd placed her, on her back, eyes closed, arms wide. He knelt and pressed an ear to her chest. "Well, she's breathing," he said aloud.

"Of course I'm breathing," she whispered hoarsely, still motionless. "Wait a minute. It's all I can handle right now."

They lay breathing raggedly, while the rain pummeled down and the angry river whirled below, until Easter slowly sat up. She coughed, spat a little water, then gingerly felt her back where the beam had struck her spine. "I'm bruised and wrenched, but I don't seem broken," she said, wincing. "So much for me. What's your name, mister?"

"Custis Long. You're Easter, Wolfer's daughter, aren't you?"

"Yes." Hastily changing the subject, she remarked while smoothing her denim trousers, "Lucky I'd the sense to change." Then she added as she plucked at her shirt, "My buckskin togs would've soaked up heavy and sunk me like an anchor, though I do feel unclad without my vest."

She faltered, regarding Longarm, who was regarding her —her wet shirt clinging tight as a second skin, her flaxen

69

hair coiling about her shoulders and her softly pulsing breasts. The girl stood upright, tossing her head, and transfixed him with a regal glower. Longarm's eyes only grew more delighted, and his grin more cheery.

"Men!" She sniffed, piqued, and turned away.

The two sodden, bedraggled figures rested there for some time, content for the moment to be alive, as private thoughts engaged them. The Snake River raged riotously a while, then shortly started to subside. After a few more explosive claps, the thunder and lightning receded, blown onward with their bursting clouds by the pushing headwinds. The rain tapered and quit, leaving a washed freshness to the air.

Longarm broke the silence. "Why were you out here?"

"To wait for you."

"You knew what was up?"

"Naturally."

"Well, naturally, that leads to me thinking I'm not the first to've been hogtied and slung into the river for vulture grub."

"You're the first to've lived to tell it."

"Why'd you jump the Chickasaw at me, back in town?"

"I don't know. Maybe because Wolfer was backshooting you." Abruptly Easter got to her feet, sighing regretfully. "I hated to spur in front of his bullet. That was a beautiful horse." Quickly she walked off across the rise and into the storm-draining notch.

Longarm hastened to follow. He trailed her through the crooked, narrow cut, ignoring the roiling water as they wended their way higher, studying her agile silhouette threading through the rubble and evading the spewing runoff. Though he chafed to pull even with her, the cut was barely wide enough for single file, and he was forced to pace behind her all the way up to the top. When she climbed out and paused, winded, on the bluff of the bank, Longarm was finally able to draw alongside.

"You're sure impulsive," he observed amiably.

"Also rude to blind men. Goodbye. Hear me clear?"

Longarm acted deaf, too. "Regular factory here. Pluck, truss, river dispose. Is that what happened to Deaver Osborne?"

"Who is Deaver Osborne?"

"He owns—*owned* the Double-O, down Nebraska way."

"Osborne . . ." She frowned, seeming lost in thought.

"The Chickasaw was his. You ever hear his name before?"

"I hear lots of names." She turned away, her movement like that of a startled deer. "I don't know where you're going, mister, but I'm going home." Then she stopped and swung around. "The night hostler will be asleep in a little while, probably dead drunk." She gestured toward the dark shape of the livery barn. "You won't have any trouble gearing up your black."

"You mean—"

"I mean get the hell out of Beulah, Custis Long! Goodbye!" Easter strode away, heading briskly for the lamplit Glory Hole Saloon.

Chapter 7

Longarm stared after Easter. Twice now she had risked her life to save his, voicing no thought of peril to herself, neither explaining nor excusing the murderous attacks. He had failed to thank her, yet she acted as reluctant to take gratitude as to give farewells. Twice now she had quit him with no more concern than someone discarding a ruined garment. A curious puzzle, this girl of Wolfer Goswick's, a nagging riddle whose few answers only begged more questions.

Her trim figure was a murky blur in the distant shadows. Still, she now seemed to be angling more towards a bungalow just this side of the saloon. Longarm recalled Wolfer's orders then, and wondered if Peleg and Harper were steadfastly watching a room with nobody in it.

Easter vanished into the moonless darkness, shrouded by a melancholy night sky that droned with a crisp toying breeze. Longarm shivered, and as he turned and began walking toward the livery stable, the girl's words flashed to mind. "Get the hell out of Beulah!" A warning, true, and an indication that she was washing her hands of further responsibility.

Back at Sontag's, men had said the town had nothing to commend it except its whiskey and Easter Goswick. Maybe she was the decoy who wormed money secrets from unsuspecting travelers; whiskey and a beautiful face could wreak havoc with the best of men.

Longarm approached the corral behind the barn, stubbing his feet on hidden rocks, sliding in the slick mud. He bumped against the corral fence with his left arm, then steadied himself, fighting the savage pain. Okay, he had some problems—no guns or boots, aching ribs, a whole list of 'em—but those he might overcome somehow, Longarm thought as he gritted his teeth; but with his left arm and shoulder wounded, he wasn't positively certain he was a match for a town that devoured men, that fed human carcasses to the buzzards.

Longarm leaned against the fence while the agony subsided. The ground hereabouts was spongy, indicating it would still be relatively soft when dry, too sandy and fit only for stubble—and for graves. A short distance away was a two-by-ten pit dug to a depth of perhaps four feet, surrounded by piles of mushy dirt, a rusted shovel stuck in one pile like a tomb marker. Obviously the night hostler had been interrupted in his labors—possibly by the storm, more likely by the bottle—and hadn't got around to returning.

On the move again, Longarm crossed to the pit and took up the shovel. He looked it over carefully, then glanced around. The light from a window at the front of the barn made a faint pattern in the blackness, and Longarm went toward it, rubbing his hands along the shovel's rough wooden handle.

About to pass an open side door of the barn, he glimpsed a feeble lantern glowing way inside, then caught faint noises from back there. He flattened against the wall, waiting. At first all he could make out were the shufflings of horses in the nearer stalls, the rest too far to be distinct. Soon, though, he heard the night hostler approaching, muttering a growl, clanging tin trays and water buckets. What followed sounded like a cleanup of equipment. Then Arapaho Thorne snuffed his lantern and toddled off to the front of the barn.

Longarm slithered along the wall to the front until he detected voices filtering from the lighted window. The window was cracked ajar for air, and was curtained by burlap feed sacks that were drawn aside. Keeping crouched and very silent, Longarm risked a swift glance through the window. He spied the hostler and the gunman Peleg.

Peleg stood alert, suspicious, a bottle of unlabeled whiskey in one hand. "High fuckin' time, Arapaho. I been hearin' things."

The hostler had just entered, buttoning his fly. He went and took the bottle, grinning. "This hootch'll do it to you, sonny."

"Don't smart-talk me! Where've you been, anyhow?"

"Pissin'." Arapaho swigged, belched, and flopped in a rawhide chair. "Afore that, I tended the sorrel mare. She wandered home."

"The sorrel! Anybody with it or skulking around?"

"No-o-pe. She was alone, I was alone."

"You heard or seed anythin' while you was out spading that hole?"

"Ain't been out since the rains. I hit cover pronto, an' been chorin' around the barn e'er since." The hostler guzzled, and batted his liquid eyes at Peleg. "Ne'er seen, ne'er heard nothin'."

"He can't of lived through the flood, save by a miracle," Peleg grumbled to himself. "Yep, plumb sorry Wolfer missed plugging him dead sure." He swung on Arapaho again, some tiny doubt squirming in his mind, its persistence sharpening his eyes. "Easter messed us downin' that bastard once, and's liable as not to go try twice. And you 'n' her are thicker'n flies on shit! I'm smellin' lies, *your* lies! I'm of a mind to blow your lyin' head clean off!"

The hostler's right hand fell from the chair arm and hovered by his boot top. "Rip your iron, an' I'll gut you like a rabbit."

They were all of a few paces apart, too close for gunplay. Arapaho Thorne's blade prowess must have some claim to fame, Longarm perceived as he sneaked another look, for Peleg was paling, as if from the vision of a knife butchering his entrails.

"Time enough to settle your hash later," Peleg blustered, going to the door. "Noises hereabouts, I heard 'em, and I ain't restin' till I learn what's what." He yanked open the door, killer light flaming in his eyes, and stomped jerkily out into the barn.

Immediately Longarm slunk away from the window and

sprinted hushed on bootless feet back to the side door. He wasn't sure what had sparked Peleg's hunch—imaginings, the whiskey, plain animal instincts, or his own blundering into the corral—yet it had fired the gunman to go out and prowl, warily on guard and dangerous as hell, but out nonetheless, and alone. That set real fine by Longarm.

He paused just beside the doorway. Hearing Peleg curse over something up near the front, he stole a glance. Seeing the barn was utterly dark, he slipped inside and pressed against the inner wall. Again he listened, while trying to recall what he'd seen of the barn when being carried to the sorrel. Very little, but one stable was much like another, he hoped. Peleg was tossing a swearing fit, the drift of it to do with a carbon-filthy lantern whose wick wouldn't light. He'd soon get it lit, Longarm figured, and then Peleg would be coming out. And then Peleg would be taken out.

Or Peleg would be taking him out.

Quietly, cautiously, Longarm eased forward into the pungent black interior. He worked his way to the main aisle of stalls in a circuitous route to avoid an open area where feed sacks were kept, feeling impatient and frustrated, yet aware that his only chance lay in escaping detection. Once seen or heard, once cornered or caught out in the open, he'd soon be killed by Peleg, or shortly after by the horde attracted by Peleg's shots or other raised alarms.

He dipped along the first aisle. The flanking stalls were gated and separated by tall, thick-planked walls, and the horses in them were too used to men's comings and goings to bother fussing. The gate of an empty stall had been left wide open, and Longarm almost hinged over it, invisible as it was in the total darkness.

At the end of the aisle he stopped to feel, to sense his blinded bearings. Nearby was a post, he dimly remembered, with a ladder to a ceiling trapdoor for the hayloft. Halfway up it was built a platform ledge. Perched there, he could let Peleg get to him. Well, to a point. Once in range, he would have to get to Peleg very swiftly and silently, before any shot or alarm, and he would have to get very close to get in range. Nobody had yet invented a long-range shovel.

After scouring this section and finding nothing, Longarm

darted into the next aisle, his padded tread further muffled by Peleg's barking chortle. He had got the lamp lit, Longarm surmised, and when moments later he came to the end of another stretch, he spotted the lantern glow swaying and winking over by the saddle racks.

Still he had not found that damned platform.

He drifted on with the acrid smells of animal sweat, urine, and manure heavy about him, until he hit a particular aisle that ended short. It gave way to a large bare strip fronting the tackroom, and across it to his left, close by an aisle's end stall, was the post. He crossed the strip along its concealing fringe to the post.

Overhead jutted the vague outline of the platform. The ladder was fastened to the post, and though much wider, rose at the same perpendicular angle. Longarm climbed it slowly, softly, shuttling the cumbersome shovel from hand to hand, refusing to favor his left.

Inwardly he released a thankful sign as he crested the platform. His relief was short-lived, for piled across the entire ledge were horse collars. He couldn't move them to make room; he daren't even touch one, for fear it might upset the pile's sensitive balance. He sighed within again, a different sigh, and from his vantage scanned down and around. The lantern was gradually, inexorably approaching, Peleg flushing the barn like a puncher rooting strays from the brakes. Longarm clung gazing, thinking, but only for a brief spell longer.

Picking the best of a few bad ideas, he climbed down three rungs and gauged the steps ahead. Groping, he eased to the other side of the post, then retained his hold on the ladder by wrapping his arms and legs around the post. From there he stretched one foot out sideways and planted it on the top of the adjacent stall's wall. The last phase was delicate, and he was glad, if only this once, not to be wearing boots. Carefully he shifted his weight toward the stall until he felt he might risk letting go of the ladder. He promptly began teetering on the wall, the shovel wobbling and almost dropping, but he managed to keep hold of both with some judicious thrusting and rearing and a windmill or two. When all had calmed and he felt sure-footed and steady, he started gliding along the connective back wall of the stalls toward the lantern glow.

There wasn't much to the Beulah livery stable. No farm gear, for this was no farm town, and no freight gear, for shipping from here was more by river than by wagon. A generous assortment of horses, likely some with odd or no papers, others with owners who had taken permanent swims. Also sizeable supply stocks, dirty clutters in the stalls, plus a truly imposing manure dump out by the corral. From glimpses and memory Longarm could envision the barn and such, but he could not see Peleg in it. The gunman was back amid stacks of wall partitions, the stall sections looming slab-high but staggered and leaning against one another. Still, if the confused welter blocked his view of Peleg, then Peleg couldn't spot him, either.

Longarm began dashing across a series of support beams, which were more exposed, more risky, for they spanned the aisles to brace the stalls. While Peleg was blind, Longarm bridged the aisles and approached the stacked partitions at an angle, toward a better position to strike from behind and above whenever Peleg got in range.

He was almost to that spot, midway out over the last aisle with only one or two stalls to go, when Peleg hurried from the stacks. Longarm flattened, just as Peleg trumpeted a horrendous sneeze. Well, that answered why he'd hot-footed it out, Longarm thought, figuring all the unswept hay dust back there was the likely culprit.

Peleg wiped his nose on his sleeve, then craned about while swinging his lantern. Longarm could do nothing except hug the beam and pray that Peleg would not come snooping over his way. Looking down, he judged Peleg would poke around this aisle once he saw it. Unlike most of the others, the aisle was cluttered with storage goods and surplus feed, as were the vacant stalls. Directly below were two stockpiles, the beam on a line between them: on his right, a great, squarish, disorderly pile of bagged feed grain; on his left, a mountainous sprawl of used horseshoes, nails, slag, rusty piping, and broken utensils. All grist that had come to Wolfer's mill.

Peleg finally made up his mind and stalked in a different

direction. Longarm kept low, and was starting to push forward, when he heard the beam creak a little, up ahead by a cluster of knots. Nothing more. Slowly and softly he advanced some more, leery of the beam now, aware how batched knots can weaken lumber. The beam gave a dull crack, and quivered ever so slightly. He hesitated again, frowning, so close to his goal he could taste it, yet closer still to those knots. He eased on, trying to be even gentler. The beam remained solid as he was sliding over the knots, until he was belly-even with them. Then came a rapid staccato of tiny pings and cracks, like strands parting of a sudden, and Longarm thought to himself, *old son, I think this beam is going to break.*

It did, right then, in a convulsion. One splintering crash, and the treacherous beam collapsed in two pieces, hurling Longarm down onto the domed peak of trashed metal. He sprawled tumbling, thrust furiously against the clattering slide, dug in his shovel, and hauled himself up, then instantly sprang for the adjoining pile of feedbags. The whole clanking mess of ironmongery started to move underfoot in a miniature avalanche as he lunged laterally across the slope. Again he stabbed his shovel and, levering the handle like a pole vaulter, catapulted atop the feedbags and plunged down through the middle of the pile into a pocket formed by the bags' poor stacking.

The rattling clank of horseshoes had stopped by now, and in the immediate aftermath of his fall there was an eerie silence. Regaining his legs in a pivoting squat, Longarm, checked his surroundings, hearing boots on the run and heading his way. He saw another cubby in the pile that appeared larger and better situated, and after sizing it up for a moment, he wormed his way between the feedbags.

His new burrow, he found, was deeper, went higher, had more peepholes, and formed a sort of trough at the top to ease going in or out or simply to hide within. Longarm was hiding in the trough, scrunching low like a compressed spring, when Peleg came into view.

On guard and highly alert, Peleg was approaching along the aisle as stealthily as his bulk and Longarm's boots would allow. Holding his lantern high, fisting Longarm's revolver, he worked his way closer while inspecting each stall, each conglomeration in the aisle, often straying from Longarm's limited perspective. When he got to the metal heap, he gave it a cursory glance before looking up. In the sweep of his lantern light, the pieces of the broken beam were quite discernible as they sagged from their respective stalls, yet Peleg gave them a similar token glance. He then passed from view.

Longarm didn't move, smelling Peleg smelling a rat.

Peleg had a short fuse. Of that Longarm was certain after hearing the blow-ups at Arapaho and the lantern. And, as he anticipated, Peleg blew up soon again. The gunman abruptly reappeared, weaving and ducking, running toward the feed-bag pile while trying to peer every which way at once. Longarm gripped the shovel tightly, sensing Peleg was coming here because the pile was the next thing in line, and was coming hard because he knew someone was somewhere, maybe in the pile.

Peleg plowed along the slope of the metal heap, well-coordinated yet having difficulty keeping balanced on the loose-rolling irons as he looked right and left. He looked right when he should have looked left once too often, because Longarm was there, leaping from the feedbags with the shovel gripped lengthwise by its handle.

"Crap!" The hatchet-faced thug stood with his chinless mouth agape, even as he swiftly recovered and aimed at Longarm. "I'm gonna make sure o' you goin' dead this time!"

Peleg was fast, but not fast enough. Already Longarm was diving in through the short space remaining, and closing, he flattened Peleg with a combination of shovel to the face and kick to the groin. He smashed the steel blade of the shovel between Peleg's upper lip and nostrils with a spearing upthrusted ram; and while he was lancing it deep, Longarm seemed to spring and pivot, using the wooden handle like a fulcrum, launching in feet first and driving his hard, calloused heel in a hammering crush of Peleg's scrotum.

Peleg reeled, lurching, nerves burning with shock and agony. But he was unaware, for the bludgeoning stab of the shovel blade had shattered his nose and knifed shards of bone into his brain. Peleg was dead before he hit the floor.

Setting the shovel aside, Longarm went to Peleg and quickly yet thoroughly stripped the body of his own property. He promptly put it all on, pleased that his aim had struck as planned, hitting Peleg in two of the few vulnerable spots that didn't have something of his on or about. He spent a minute to check his wallet, seeing that Peleg had not spent all his money, and that his badge lay undisturbed in its flap. The time was fast coming, as fast as the flash flood had come, for him to pin his badge on the outside and go on his own stormy rampage.

After using Peleg's belt to hitch his ankles and the shovel handle altogether, Longarm wedged the shovel blade so it would stay with Peleg, then dragged them out by the belt strap with one hand while his other carried the lantern. A lucky break, that; Peleg had placed the lantern aside before his last rush, wanting both hands free to kill. Longarm took his haul out around the aisles to the barn's side door, where he extinguished and left the lantern.

Peleg and the shovel he towed outside to the unfinished horse pit. He rolled Peleg into it, spaded enough dirt over and around to conceal the body, then stuck the shovel back where he had found it. Longarm greatly doubted Arapaho would return to dig before morning, and if this little secret didn't last much past sunrise, well . . . plenty could occur in the span of a night.

★

Chapter 8

The door of the little stable office eased open.

As the stream of cool air flowed over the whiskey-mellowed Arapaho Thorne, he lifted the lid of one bleary eye and croaked, "Come in or stay out, but close the damned door." He said no more to the sodden, muddied figure poised on the threshold, until Longarm eased inside warily and snicked the door shut. Then Arapaho batted his other eye and asked, "Where did you come from?"

"From the river, if you want to know." Longarm balanced himself, ready to lunge at the first hostile move. "I needed my stuff back."

"Yuh don't tell." The old hostler seemed not at all surprised.

"That's right. And if you're in with Goswick and Peleg, who stole my gear, and all the others, you and me are going to have it out."

Arapaho leaned forward in his chair a little, assuming a half-crouch, as he whisked his wicked-bladed knife from his boot top. "Don't figger to carve you up, sonny, 'less I have to."

Longarm checked the rash impulse to make a fight of it. The hostler went on drawling, testing the keenness of the knife blade with the ball of his thumb. "Scout, buffalo hunter, Injun figher. Fit at Adobe Walls that time, nineteen o' us hunters agin' a thousand redskins. Battle lasted two weeks, stacked dead men like cordwood an' shot o'er them. Never war nothin' like it."

"Now you're burned out, lodged in the backwash of Beulah as night hostler at Wolfer's livery barn," Longarm said through his teeth. "Where a Chickasaw with white leggings and a Double-O on its shoulder got stabled, then stolen."

Arapaho Thorne's faded eyes stared at Longarm and on past him into the mists of yesterday. "Double-O? Ain't that a Nebraska brand?"

Longarm nodded. "Deaver Osborne's, out of North Platte."

"I rec'lect the Chickasaw showin' up a while ago, but where it come from or went I ne'er asked. None of my affair, no more'n other things that go on in Beulah." He offered his whiskey bottle. "Have a drink. Looks like you need one, way you're bleedin'."

"A graze," Longarm assured him, feeling the blood seep down his arm and trickle off his fingertips as he took the bottle. "A bandage will take care of it." The whiskey hit his stomach like a volcanic eruption, and he shuddered convulsively. "What in hell is this made of?"

"Injun special," Arapaho replied proudly. "Always add red pepper for bite and tobacco for blend. Wall, a bandage'll hafta do you, on account there ain't no doc here in Beulah."

"Or jail," Longarm added pointedly.

Arapaho's lids squinched down. "Double-O!" A gnarled hand caressed his scarred face. "Double 'cause Osborne had a son," he continued, again drifting with nostalgia. "Hated horse wranglin', the kid did, so he up an' drifted. Married a purty li'l dance-hall gal in Dodge and took up nestin' in the Canadian bottoms. The disgrace nigh killed his pa, him weddin' a honky-tonker and turnin' a sodbuster, but they's young fools crazy in love. I was by their shack a few times, out miles from nowhere 'cept hell 'n' raiding Injuns. A baby came along, a girl, must've been four, five years old last time I stopped there. Then got me a job down Mustang Springs way and didn't get back up in the Panhandle for a few years. Folks told how a wagon train found ashes of the cabin an' what was left of o' young Osborne and his wife.

82

The Double-O's still Osborne and Son, even after that."

"Hell of a tragedy," Longarm said. "Indians, eh?"

"Mebbe."

"Anyone ever find out what happened to the child?"

Arapaho didn't answer directly, but asked instead, "Who was riding the Chickasaw?"

"Deaver Osborne." Longarm told of the money the rancher had carried and his failure to return home. "I picked up his trail at Blackfoot and got far's here. You know the rest, or can guess it."

Cunning mixed with the wickedness that gleamed in red-rimmed eyes. "Can't go far way you is, and can't stay here," he said as he returned his knife to his boot. Getting up, he went to a nearby cabinet. After rummaging around, he handed Longarm some strips of cloth and a bottle of horse liniment. "Use my place t'night. I ain't."

Longarm got directions and another slug of redeye, and things grew a bit hazy as he slipped from the office feeling fire in his gut. Arapaho lived on a side street not far from the livery, and Longarm had no trouble located the one-room, one-window shanty. Inside, he barred the door and draped the window before lighting the lantern. There was a bunk across from the window, and a bench near the stove with a bucket and washbasin. Everything was rough but tidy, and the window curtains and some other touches seemed to indicate a woman's hand.

Longarm shucked down and hung his wet clothes over the bench to air-dry, including a blood-encrusted shirt and a vest which, to his surprise, had no bullet hole in it. Naked, he viewed his wound in the reflection of a large chunk of clouded mirror glass propped on the bureau. It was a clean furrow along the ridge of his shoulder blade, causing considerable bleeding, but no real injury. Longarm now realized how the shot must have happened. He'd been hunching forward with his arms extended, forcing his vest to balloon against his neck; Wolfer Goswick's fluke bullet had gone through his jacket, in the vest's armhole, drilled under his shirt and straight across his back, and out the other armhole.

He washed and was drying himself with a threadbare towel when a quick step sounded outside. Someone tried the latch, then banged hard on the door. Longarm padded silently across to blow out the lantern, figuring he would then dive for the corner where a Sharps rifle stood, within reach of a nail-hanging shellbelt whose holster held an ancient Spiller & Burr percussion pistol. He was almost to the lantern when the banging stopped and a voice yelled, "Open up, or I'll throw a rock through the window!"

"Easter!" Longarm breathed the name with a show of dismay. Better let her in, he thought as he wrapped the blanket-sized towel around his waist. He would only be inviting more trouble to keep her out. He unbarred the door. The girl entered like a gust of wind, flounced to a halt, and gaped as he slammed the door with a bare foot, clasping the door's crossbar in one hand and the knots of his towel in the other.

"You fool!" Her eyes, though, contradicted her sharp mouth.

"Good evening. What brings you visiting?"

"I couldn't get in my house. It was being watched, and I needed to dry and lie low a while, so . . ." She paused, tight-lipped, and planted her fists on her hips. "Never mind me. Did Arapaho take you here?"

"Well, he kinda suggested it."

"There's not enough brains between the two of you," she cried, "to make a pimple on a fly! Why didn't you go when you had the chance?"

"I'm not finished in Beulah," Longarm said stubbornly.

"You're so finished the undertaker would bury you as quick as a grave was dug," she retorted furiously. "I mean, you're dead!"

"I feel fine." Longarm gave her a slow grin. "Arapaho's whiskey fixed my innards, and his liniment will do the rest."

Easter glared at the cloth and bottle on the bench, then at his wounded back. "Go get on the bunk. You can't bind yourself. I will."

Longarm went and sat on the bed, tucking the towel modestly while Easter pulled the liniment-bottle cork out with her teeth. She sloshed his wound, and it burned the way Arapaho's whiskey had burned his belly. Easter, laughing as he flinched and sucked in his breath, began wrapping the cloth strips around him. "It's made to kill pests," she told him.

"If you want me dead, why'd you save me at all?"

"I couldn't stand to see a man murdered without a fighting chance. There, that's as good as I can snug it." The wildness had gone out of her for the moment, and as Longarm turned to face her, she looked frail and dismal, and her voice was serious. "Wolfer was a plainsman too long to be easily duped. He'll check the river bank tomorrow and watch the buzzards, just to be sure. When he finds our tracks, he'll know you're alive." She was so close that he could feel her warm breath against his skin. "That's why I told you to leave."

"You're an odd one," Longarm murmured. "Most women I've met are either good or bad. Reckon you must be some of both, or you would've quit Wolfer."

Easter trembled as if hit. She stroked a finger shakily across his bare chest and stomach. "I was never so close to socking a man—and didn't," she pouted. "I think you're a danger, Custis Long."

He eyed her, feeling stirrings, thinking *she* was the danger. "I . . . eh . . . I thought about our tracks in the mud. That's one reason why I didn't pull out when I had the chance."

"What was the other one?"

"The Double-O has an overdue account to settle here."

"You mean for the Chickasaw?"

"Owner, too. Wolfer hasn't paid for taking them."

Her lips moved. "Osborne and Son." That was all. Her hand was massaging his naked body now, teasing him by working lower along the line of his towel. Longarm was smart enough to sense she knew more and was trying to avoid being questioned; he was man enough to respond to her diversionary tactic. Her fingers wormed lower, dipping down below the towel to circle around his hips and thighs. She touched his groin once, lightly, and Longarm sucked in his breath, his blood pounding. Then he opened the towel, and her eyes grew smoky and hungry as she gazed down at him.

He chuckled. "How's this for a third reason?"

Her pink tongue glided across her lips. "I did come here to dry and lie low, so . . ." Tauntingly, she started undressing, slinging her wet clothes off to reveal firm breasts with raspberry nipples springing hard from their tips.

Longarm sucked one of the nipples, laving her breast while he fondled her other breast. She wriggled, moaning, removing the last of her bottom garments as his other hand roamed down her nude body. She squeezed her thighs together on his hand, moving her hips in concert with his fingers sliding up inside her.

Easter laughed, low and liquid, and straddled his pelvis with her knees on the bunk on either side of his hips. Gazing with eyes of passion, she rose and impaled herself on his fleshy spear, contracting her strong thighs so that the muscular action clamped her moistly welcome passage tightly around his member.

Longarm clenched his buttocks, thrusting his hips off the bunk. Easter spread her thighs. Sliding up and down, she soon contained the whole of his shaft. Her head sagged forward, then craned back in arousal, her golden hair swaying and brushing down over her shoulders and across his chest.

Longarm grasped her jiggling breasts, toying with them until she bent to kiss him. Then again she arched up and back as she plunged like the rider of a bucking bronco. He pumped up into her with deeper and faster strokes. Her thighs descended with increasing force, as if each time she were collapsing on the downward surge, only to revive just in time to draw her plundered belly up on his rigid manhood.

Tensing upward, Longarm felt the gripping of her loins tearing at his entrails, and he clasped her slim waist and penetrated her to the hilt. Her tight inner sheath kept squeezing, milking, until he felt himself bursting, while her own face contorted and twisted in fiery orgasm.

Then he collapsed, exhausted and drained. With a deep sigh Easter crouched limp and satisfied over Longarm for a long moment, then languidly eased off his passive body, slid away to blow out the lamp, and moved back to stretch cuddling beside him. They dozed off before they realized it, their bodies gently entwined.

Longarm awoke twice. Once, briefly, he stirred when a bunch of drunks from the Glory Hole stumbled past in loud chorus. When he shifted, startled, Easter rolled to curl like a little girl, murmuring in her sleep. He tossed the bunk's single blanket over them, thinking about her and why she had come here, of all places, to use as a haven when she couldn't sneak into her own home. Some strange bond linked her and Arapaho Thorne, something that enraged Wolfer and irked his gunmen yet discouraged open dissension, in deference to Easter's temper and the old hellion's scalping knife. What had cemented this peculiar friendship Longarm did not know.

Then, as he drifted asleep again, a drowsy insight occurred to him. A vision of a sacked nester's cabin on the Canadian bottoms, the work of Indian raiders, so it was said —except by Arapaho, who hinted, maybe not. Longarm saw, instead of whooping warriors, an old Conestoga slogging along, a hard-faced woman at its reins, a brutish man hazing stolen stock behind, while crying in the wagon bed was the only survivor, a little girl with cornsilk hair and blue eyes.

His mind's eye skimmed the passing of years, the growing of the girl and the dimming of her childish impressions. Of time when the wagon landed in Beulah, and of time when old Arapaho stumbled here by chance. And the stirrings of long-buried connections which they sensed more than consciously remembered, but which again were strongly felt and now linked them anew.

Easter Osborne . . . It answered a lot.

With that, Longarm fell fast asleep.

Chapter 9

Shortly after he fell asleep again, Longarm awoke the second time. He was roused by a slight movement at the foot of the bunk, and even then, coming out of a sound sleep, eyes only half opened, his revolver came to his hand from the chair beside the bed.

"No need for that," Arapaho said quietly.

Longarm sat up, blinking. "Hell of a town," he observed. "No privacy in it at all. A pair of gents walked in on my bath, too." He glanced at the door, which was shut but no longer barred. "Well, thanks for closing it after you, Arapaho, but how'd you get it open?"

Arapaho was pawing under the bunk. "It's my shack," he replied, coming up with a jug. He grinned at Easter. "I might've knowed."

"Why, you ol' goat, you've been trying to get me in your bunk all along," she retorted, yawning. "All right, what's happened?"

"Hell has done bust from its banks," he announced, his watery eyes flowing from the girl to Longarm. "Peleg got to be missing too long. Some of 'em took to searching, and one fell in the horse's grave and found pore Peleg. That an' the bay wanderin' back have 'em spooked maybe a certain gent cheated the buzzards. The hunt is on. It'll center around the stables a while longer, then spread to the town."

"To here." Longarm got up and started dressing. His clothes were now dry. He threw Easter her garments, which she hurriedly put on under the blanket before rising to go to the window and peek out.

Arapaho offered his jug to Longarm. "Care for an eye-opener?"

Longarm shuddered as he buckled his belt. "Too rich for my blood," he replied, pinning his deputy marshal's badge on his lapel.

Eyeing it, Arapaho grunted, "I might've knowed that, too," and downed enough of the jug for both of them.

"Here comes Obie Hewitt," Easter said. "He's like that—" she snapped her fingers—"with a pistol. If we get him now, there'll be one less river to cross." She turned from the window while talking, saw Longarm's badge, and stalked to the door with a sour expression. She was outside before either Longarm or Arapaho guessed what she was up to.

Longarm made to follow, but was bumped aside by Arapaho. "Not so fast, y' idjit!" He stood peering out with Longarm, watching Easter walk toward an approaching man. To the east, the sky showed a faint gray, indicating it would start growing light in another hour.

She was swinging her hips like a sassy filly, Longarm thought, and felt prompted to remark, "Your memories are so preserved in liquor, Arapaho, I bet you can recall when Osborne's son's child was born."

"Seems t'me 'twas very early one April, afore Whitsunday."

"Uh-huh." He grinned at the softly cackling hostler. "Eastertide, eh? Yep, and funny how granddads can be sentimental and forgiving."

As they watched the girl approach Hewitt, they saw her bob her head at him, her eyes brazenly inviting. "Hello, Obie," they heard her say. She stopped close, gave a quick glance around, and added in a low tone, "He's back there, Obie. Why don't you go after him?"

"Y'mean this feller?" Obie let his eyes slide boldly over her face and tempting body. "Y'say he's at Arapaho's shack?"

"Sure. Come on, I'll go with you." Easter took the gunman's arm. "The guy's not so tough, and he's a damned star-toter." She gazed at Hewitt. "You're not afraid, are you?"

"Me? Naw. If I gun the hombre, mebbe you'll be my gal?"

"Maybe." She squeezed his arm.

They stopped in front of the shack. Longarm had had enough of whatever Easter was trying to do, and stepped outside with his right hand poised. Snarling, "Git away, gal, gimme room!" Obie Hewitt streaked for his gun. But Easter's lingering grip on his arm slowed his draw and partly threw him off stride. Longarm's revolver blasted and Hewitt's knees jackknifed.

Longarm dashed to the girl, shaking his head, his voice hard-edged. "Okay, now hit cover!" He thrust her toward the shack, then moved on up the alley toward the shadow of the building beyond.

The twin gunshots brought more of Wolfer's gang to the alley on the run. They converged at the street corner, leerily staring along the dark, narrow lane to where Obie Hewitt sprawled in pooling blood.

"Bushwhacked!" Longarm heard one snarl loudly.

"Haw! Like I reckoned, ol' Arapaho must be hidin' the lobo!"

"Let's shoot the damn shack to kindlin' around their ears, boys. Chubb, why don't yuh hightail o'er and tell the boss what's what."

"Sure thing, Nick." The man called Chubb began angling across the street. Suddenly he yelled, "There he is!" and wheeled to aim at Longarm, who purposely showed himself to draw the gunmen away from the shack. The distance was, perhaps, thirty paces. Longarm fired while ducking in and out of view—a miss. Chubb hurried his shot and failed to hit target, and Longarm's second shot punctured his belly, dropping him across the boardwalk's edge.

Nick had been standing by the alley entrance. He trained his revolver quickly yet carefully as he pulled a half-turn to the right, calculating that he had plenty of time before Longarm could bring his gun to bear. He was blind to the

90

gnarled countenance poking around the door jamb at the shack, the scarred butt of an old .45-110 Sharps hard against his shoulder, its muzzle canvassing the street entry ahead.

When Nick thumbed his gun hammer, Arapaho's rifle roared into action. The corner's gallery post saved Nick from having his head torn off, but the burst of splinters ripped his face and the partly deflected slug tore away half of a high-boned cheek. Nick flopped screaming into the street, while the other gunmen hastily retreated from the exposed alleyways. Arapaho shouted out, "Remember Adobe Walls, lawdog! Nineteen agin a thousand!"

Smiling wryly, Longarm dove on as the gunmen milled, confused. For a moment he had the advantage of surprise, but he knew that to keep his gain, he must figure his next move quickly. The longer he delayed, the greater the advantage shifted to Wolfer, whose regrouped forces would move deliberately and cautiously on the attack. Pausing, he used the brief lull to reload, relieved to find Arapaho and Easter nowhere in sight, odd thoughts again flickering through his mind.

He envisioned Deaver Osborne as stubborn and tempestuous—the type who would despise weaklings, yet go all out for a man in trouble, who'd reject his son as rashly as he'd left his crew to their fling. Longarm could see him at Sontag's, hearing talk and a name that sparked remorseful memories, then launching impulsively to check it in Beulah. He perceived Easter as much like Osborne, displaying with the Chickasaw and out there in the river that same rash yet sharp-witted behavior. Then showing just now by her hand on Obie's arm that same decisiveness, that same instant recognition of need to carry the fight to the enemy.

Longarm's thinking took no more time than he spent reloading, but it determined his next move. He plunged through the shadows toward the Glory Hole, still open and noisy, knowing he must pick up where Easter had left off by hitting quick and hard. Considering he was up against a wolf pack, that meant striking at the king lobo himself. Then he heard boots nearing and dipped, hugging the wall, realizing that to reach his goal, he had a number of rivers to cross.

The footsteps hesitated, scrunching as the man turned to

crane. Other boots approached, which Longarm read as being made by a second gunman coming to join the first in somewhat of a hurry.

"You got any makin's, Slade? I'm cravin' a smoke."

"Shut up a minute. I think I heard somethin'."

Silence fell. Longarm, breathless, weighed the fact he had two of them to down quietly, so as not to attract a swarming batch more.

After a long pause, the second man scoffed, "You're just jumpy. Ain't nothin' about to get scared of, Slade." He laughed and the first man cursed, so close to Longarm that he could hear the rustle of papers as they rolled cigarettes. There was the flare of a match, and he glimpsed them huddling to get lights. He launched forward then, hurtling from cover to crash into them, his full weight colliding with their hunched shoulders. While they staggered and fought for balance, he gun-whipped and punched with brutal swiftness, clubbing the neck of the bigger man. That one crumpled, groaning. Longarm felt arms go around him from behind. He put all his strength into his back and lifted, flinging off the other man sidewise, slamming him into the side of the building, then pivoting to knock him unconscious.

Longarm sprinted panting to the street, then raced diagonally across its dawn-gray width toward the saloon's side alley. Startled yells chased him, and when he slewed into the head of the alley, he saw a shadowy figure running his way. He flattened against the wall, his revolver tight in his grasp. Orange flame stabbed at where he had been an instant before, and Longarm aimed return fire by that telltale flash. The man staggered as he sped before pitching forward on his face.

Another man burst out from the side door of the saloon. Longarm tried to blend in with the dark-shrouded wall as the door slammed closed on the light-spewing interior. The man didn't wait for his eyes to grow accustomed, but surged up the alley past Longarm without noticing him there. Suddenly more gunfire blossomed from the street, and the man let out a howl, shooting his own weapon as he lurched on, stumbling. That caused a fresh flurry of shots. The man literally fell into the bunch who had been entering the alley after

Longarm. The resultant consternation stymied pursuit, allowing Longarm a chance to escape.

In three low-crouching steps, he darted into the side entry, shutting the door and throwing its latchbolt behind him. He cat-footed quickly along the short corridor and into the barroom, lamplight reflecting off the badge on his lapel. The drunken remnants of the carousing night crowd lapsed into bleary silence, the piano player stopped on a discord, and a few relaxing gunhands stiffened but wisely chose not to buck his leveled revolver.

"Keep it peaceful," Longarm warned the head bartender as he moved to the end of the bar. "I've got a matter to see Wolfer about, and if any of your swill-sloppers interfere, you'll be the first to go."

"Steady, gents, give him room. Steady, now!" The bartender's voice was a sharp whisper as he slowly lifted his hands. The amazed patrons leaning against the bar scowled but moved, backing away. It left the way clear around the bar to Wolfer's closed office door.

Longarm kept his revolver trained on the bartender, while scanning the backbar mirror for signs of trouble in the room behind him. Suddenly, the batwings slapped open and more gunmen poured in shouting, and a sandy-haired man seated nearby flipped over his table while bringing his pistol to bear. Longarm swiveled; two reports blended as one. The man had upended the table with the idea of dropping behind it after he shot, but he was still standing now, gripping the table edge with both hands, head nodding on his chest. Longarm was springing for the stout wood door, revolver ready, and surveying the room. The man dropped, but not as he had intended, collapsing lifeless as Longarm barged into the office and kicked the door solidly shut.

The office was unkempt, an encrusted spittoon by one foot of a big desk, a glass jug lamp at the near edge of the table's flat top. The burning lamp jiggled, the desk bumped hard by Wolfer rearing from his chair. His eyes swelled wide and wild when he saw Longarm's pointed revolver, his breath catching in an alarmed hiss. "Shit!"

"Stand still." Longarm's voice was level, but there was a feral little grin on his face. He stepped behind the desk, ran his free hand over Wolfer, then opened the drawers to look for weapons there. Dipping to one knee, he even inspected beneath the desk.

"No," Wolfer managed thinly, "there's no scattergun rigged under there. Christ, will you slack off before that gun goes off?"

"You're slipping." Longarm straightened, pocketing the derringer and belt-tucking the Dragoon he had taken from Wolfer. "You've got a rep for hooking a shotgun handy, to blow apart anyone in front of your desk. Yeah, then feeding the evidence to your pet coyotes."

"I've changed. I don't keep none of that no more." Wolfer slumped down in his chair, his hands clasped in full view on the desk. "Now, ease off your trigger, okay? The past is past. What say you help yourself to a seat, and maybe we can come to terms."

"Guess again." Longarm stepped back to an armless wooden chair set squarely in front, facing Wolfer. "Money won't undo the crimes you've committed, won't bring back to life the folks you've killed." Keeping his revolver steady, he settled warily on the chair. "And you haven't changed, Wolfer. You won't give up without a fight if you can, and I'm almost looking forward to you trying. But right now we're sitting along here, me with some questions and you with the answers, and I'm hoping even more you'll balk at making talk."

"Talk? Sure, sure." Wolfer hunched his chair closer, his feet tapping the floor as if nervous. "I'll talk, but . . . but . . . ."

"But what?"

"You won't be here to listen! You're hell-bound, you fool!"

Longarm heard a click under Wolfer's foot, and then heard something snap beneath his chair. He tried to lunge clear, throwing himself forward and grabbing for the desk, but he was a second too late. The chair was flopping downward, a panel of the floor hinged open, dropping. Still groping furiously as he fell sliding off the waxed hardwood seat, his snatching grasp swept the desk, punching it rocking. The lamp teetered, and by its wobbling glow he saw Wolfer hover maliciously just for an instant before the lamp toppled

94

over to the floor, its chimney and glass jug shattering, oil spraying everywhere.

Then the man, the room, and all were gone as Longarm plunged through black space.

Chapter 10

Longarm flailed desperately for a hold, his left hand sliding, his boots and revolver scraping against the slick stone and timber walls of a narrow shaft. For all his kicking and clawing, it was his coat that saved him. It was billowing in the rush of cold, foul air, and by chance, one flapping end snagged the bent prong of a rusty iron spike protruding from a wooden support.

The coat jerked him to a sudden, ungainly halt. The impact of his momentum, though, was causing the fabric to tear. Frantically he twisted in midair, and just as his coat ripped loose, he caught the spike by two fingers. Trembling, feeling the sharp iron cut into his flesh as it had the cloth, he reached and hooked the trigger guard of his revolver on the spike. He dangled then, gripping the revolver and wondering what the hell to do now.

He was in a hole, a long chute whose pit could only be gauged by the vile odors wafting up. Something was dead or had been dead far below in that dank blackness, and pungent quicklime was trying to kill the putrid stench. Above was similarly dark, the panel having snapped back, closing flush as though sealing a tomb.

Yet as Longarm gazed bleakly upward, he glimpsed a thin light along the line of the floorboards. It was acting peculiar, long and quivering at one moment, short and threatening to extinguish at the next. He could make no more sense of it than he could of all the muffled hollering he heard overhead. He scowled, watching the light shimmer between cracks, and it was then he discerned the light was fire, trickling through and beginning to ooze down a wall.

That meant there was more fire above him, and now the shouting grew louder and distinct. ". . . lamp broke and set my office ablaze! Water, damn it! Don't stand there gawping like scared apes! Get it fast, before the barroom catches, too! Water, everybody! Water!"

Longarm listened to the uproar for a few moments, feeling a certain satisfaction at having accidentally knocked over the desk lamp. Obviously its hot wick had ignited the spilled oil, and now, by all the wild yelling and scrambling, it sounded as if the flames were consuming Wolfer's office and spreading hungrily into the main saloon. Hot oil continued dripping from ragged cracks, and as a slow stream of it burned down along the wall, he could see around him. The sides of his trap were of slimy stonework braced by rotted beams, with a nearby set of hand- and foot-holds hacked in the surface to serve as a crude ladder. Why the shaft had been dug was anyone's guess—a cistern, a communal latrine, a miner's folly—but Longarm surmised that Wolfer had found it abandoned, and made it into his private "glory hole" when he built the saloon.

Stretching and angling, Longarm crossed to perch unsteadily on the weathered ladder. It required every bit of strength he possessed to retain a grasp in the slippery chinks, but slowly he worked his way higher. It was as hot as Hades above him and getting hotter all the time. Holes were taking shape in the floor where the fire was starting to burn through the planks. He could hear water splashing, men cursing and running, Wolfer bawling orders to form a bucket-and-hat brigade.

The closer Longarm climbed to the top, the less pleased he felt about that lamp. An oil fire was a hard one to contain, and he was going to have a devil of a time getting free with a place as big as the Glory Hole burning down over his head. The saloon sat on a solid foundation of thick stone, with only a narrow crack left here and there in the rocks for air to circulate beneath it, none wider than the thickness of his hand. A rabbit penned under here would not be able to slip out sideways! He paused to rest, shivering inwardly as he glanced down the abyss and contemplated that alternative.

He was about to move on when he felt a draught of cooler air. Craning, he saw a hole in one wall about the size of a drain, maybe large enough, likely not, and probably leading nowhere. He took it anyhow, worming inside and creeping along blindly, scraping his skin and his clothes, and at one point getting hung up by his holstered revolver. He wriggled on with dogged persistence, dust covering him, smoke settling beneath the floor now in a suffocating cloud, and eventually he perceived a slight radiance ahead of him. As he crept toward it, he discovered it was filtering between the floorplanks from the fire in the barroom above, the glowing streaks illuminating a vast cellar.

Perspiration was pouring out of Longarm when he reached the rock-walled rim of the cavernous basement. It was packed haphazardly with tools and trunks, cases of liquor and bales of garments, crocks, pans, spooled wire— everything imaginable, like a general store gone to rummage. Or, Longarm decided as he dropped to the floor, like a hidden stash of leftover loot, ill-gained and hoarded by Wolfer.

Grinning wryly, Longarm began to wend through the trove toward a stairway rising to a trapdoor in the floor. The smile on his face widened when dimly, in a corner beyond the stairs, he saw where space had been made for another big desk and lamp, plus cabinets and an old safe with its door cracked ajar. Fitting, Longarm thought, veering that way; Wolfer kept an underground office for his underground work.

Not having much time, he concentrated on the open safe. It was crammed with jewelry and gems, but he ignored the valuables in favor of the papers stacked on one shelf. Documents, notes, records, and letters he stuffed into his pockets and shirt, figuring to sort through them later for evidence and clues to Wolfer's cohorts. He reached for the last scraps, but as his hand touched them, he tensed. Straightening, he scanned the cellar, abruptly aware he was not alone.

Out of the array of shadows a form began taking shape. Large, tawny yellow, it moved with flowing slyness, belly low to the rock floor, ears pricked back, long fangs baring in the meager light.

Longarm stared, aghast. Wolfer had told the truth for once, about no longer keeping pet coyotes. He had changed, all right, to keeping an enormous Rocky Mountain cougar. With a predator like that prowling about on guard, no wonder he hadn't bothered to lock his safe door.

Gliding toward Longarm, the cougar nervously bristled from the hot sparks, blazing bits of wood, and near-scalding water showering down. The fire was being beaten under control, but the tumult above was provoking the beast, aggravating its already vicious nature.

Slowly and carefully Longarm backed in the direction of the stairs, trying to think of how to hold the goaded cougar at bay. Wolfer had a flair for wild animals, and must know ways of handling this one to work down here, but Longarm had no idea what they were. Nor did he want to shoot. The firefighting wasn't so noisy that gunfire wouldn't draw notice, then a check of the cellar, and then he'd be dragged out to smell the smoking end of somebody else's weapon.

He kept a firm grip on his revolver, though, retreating until he brushed one of the jumbled piles and his boot heel clinked against a bottle rack of stolen wine. Some dozen feet away the cougar stopped, crouching lower, gathering for a lightning pounce. It snarled, the sound like a cruel warning call, sufficient to jelly a man's nerves.

Reluctantly taking aim, Longarm used his left hand to scoop up and hurl a wine bottle. It shattered right in front of the cougar's nose, splashing burgundy and glass shards, while Longarm darted into a crevice between the one pile and the next. Snout wine-splattered, eyes fixed on Longarm, the startled cougar leaped back as well, its throaty call twisting into a guttural roar that nigh shook the cellar.

In answer came a growl.

Initially Longarm thought that the growl was only an echo from the cougar facing him, but it rose from deep in the shadows to his left. One quick glance showed him the

99

second cat. It was slightly smaller than the first, and he guessed it was a mate which had been asleep somewhere back there in the darkness. Aroused now, the mate slinked forward and was joined by the first, then together they eased silently to hunch by the crevice, claws working, setting to spring.

Whether he wanted to or not, Longarm saw, he would have to start some fast, accurate shooting if he ever expected to get out alive. Thrusting closer, he trained straight-armed on the bigger cat of the pair.

They both jumped back, lashing their tails and snarling, enraged, yet making no move to attack. Puzzled, his finger taut on the trigger, Longarm jabbed, pointing at the mate. Again the cougars retreated, growling more fiercely, arching stiffly, poised defensively. They were intimidated by his revolver, Longarm realized. Likely the gun more than the smashed bottle had caused the first cat to react. That must be how Wolfer handled them. He probably came down to work firing pistol blanks to drive and cage them, until now they feared any waving gun.

The cougars bayed by his menacing revolver, Longarm angled for the stairs with thoughts of working up to the overhead door. Then he had second thoughts. He'd be bad off as if he shot down here, for as soon as he poked his head out, Wolfer and every gunman in the saloon would be trying to fall on his neck or open fire on him. Glumly he regarded the restive cougars, and a third thought occurred to him.

Above, the fire was about licked with everybody fighting it, the flames doused by enough water to send plumes of steam boiling. The last smouldering dregs were being snuffed when Wolfer Goswick got another shock that left him speechless for a moment. There was no one in the alcove off the side entry, and had not been since the fire spread to the barroom. A burly red-beard gestured to it now with a yell. Wolfer whirled, and saw huge, billowy clouds roiling from there.

It was only the collected smoke and steam from under the floor escaping out the opened trapdoor to the cellar, but Wolfer did not know that as he turned. He took two lurching steps toward it, then stopped. The barrom was suddenly clamorous with terrified shouts and the crash of tables and chairs, men panicking flat against the walls or fighting one another to get behind cover and hide.

Hell was coming! At least it looked like hell. Out of the murky fog gushing from the alcove appeared a great cougar. Snarling mean and savage enough to make eyes pop and hair stand on end, the cougar loped into the saloon and sprang to a halt near the counter. Just then a thump sounded from back by the alcove, as if something heavy had rammed the closed side door, followed by a second, slightly smaller cougar padding out across the floor to pause with its mate, fangs bared, saffron eyes casting wickedly about.

Instinctively Wolfer reached for his Dragoon, forgetting he was unarmed. He shuddered, his expression mirroring his consternation, for however his pets had managed to break loose, they were here and he was without means to control them. And he was all too aware that each of those snarling cougars hated him as only cats could hate.

"Clear—clear the way to the door!" he yelled. "They'll run quicker'n they'll fight if they have the chance!"

Longarm spoke before anyone was aware of his emergence from the cloud. "No such chance for you, Wolfer. You're under arrest."

From start till now spanned a few heartbeats; what came next passed in one wild eye-blink. Though at first Wolfer froze, seemingly stunned by the sight of this smoke-wreathed figure, unnerved at the thought of this man returning from death *twice* to deal retribution.

His gunhands needed no time to think. They knew their own hides were in tall danger, and reacted instinctively by swinging out weapons to plug the lone marshal. Immediately the cougars hunched, rooted, squalling fearsomely. The men were still swinging when Longarm's revolver struck one flat. In a swift staccato came another shot, the breath of its slug past Longarm's ear, his answering fire at the shooter bobbing up behind the bar. Going down, the man took a shelf of glassware along with him.

Longarm paid the crash no heed, his attention focusing on Wolfer. Hoarsely bellowing for his men to protect him,

Wolfer was shifting to scurry away. Longarm triggered while dodging lead, and his snapshot missed Wolfer but drilled one of the men closing in to side the boss. The man stiffened, howling, staggered some, and died, crumpling over. Wolfer reached out and pulled this man against him as a shield, snatching the pistol from lifeless fingers with violent swiftness.

Longarm ducked behind a pillar, holstering his empty revolver and hauling the Dragoon from his belt. The different heft and grip felt strange yet damn good to him, and he moved to return a chunk of the Dragoon to Wolfer, cursing as a bullet chewed wood where Wolfer's head had just been. Wolfer was facing this way, he saw, busily trying to shove the sagging body on his left arm in order to free his gun hand.

The cougars were breaking. Initially they had responded as trained, but while one or two pointing guns cowed them into obedience, a mass of fanning guns drove them confused. Roused by the surrounding ruckus to a feral pitch, they were reverting wild, up and pacing now in a squalling frenzy. The female cougar was looking as though she intended to charge Wolfer, body and all, and damn any pistols.

Glimpsing the cougar, Wolfer hastily pivoted to meet her challenge. Before he completed his turn, the cougar was bounding his way. The gunmen clotting around Wolfer scattered every other way, and as if distracted by their mad flight, the cougar veered past Wolfer toward the front of the saloon, the male right behind her. There was a crash of glass, then another, and as quickly as they had come both great cats were gone, racing for the timbered hills.

For a split second Wolfer was left standing unguarded and exposed to Longarm. Then he wheeled, his face a mask of fright and fury, a powerful arm clutching the corpse against him and his right hand tracking a bead on Longarm. He turned fast, fired fast—too fast, too soon, his bullet straying wide.

Ignoring it, Longarm kept on coming. Remembering the vultures and the shaft and the men they had claimed, he triggered the unfamiliar Dragoon coolly, deliberately before Wolfer shot again.

Wolfer slapped both hands against his shattered face, the body slumping to the floor. Blood streaming from between his fingers, Wolfer stumbled blindly in a half-circle, to lurch hard against the bar counter. He wavered and sunk down in a sitting position, his death-rattling gasps carrying across the saloon's sudden hush.

"Done for, boys! Wolfer's over and done for!"

The gunman who had blurted this was the first of many out the door. It was an old story to Longarm. Now that the chief lobo was out of action, all of his pack that saw their chance were stampeding away, not about to risk a neck-stretching by sticking around a lost cause. He let them run, having little to stop them with, and stepped to Wolfer. Incredibly, he was still alive, his breathing a horrid sound.

"Wolfer? I want you to listen, Wolfer, while you're here," Longarm said softly. "You're hell-bound, you fool."

The mist of death was stealing over Wolfer's eyes, obscuring them. "Damn you!" he muttered, and he said no more.

Longarm reloaded his revolver, then left the saloon. Outside he saw Easter hurrying toward him and managed a grin.

A bit breathless, she said, "I was worried. Scared."

"Not as much as I was, I bet."

"Are you all right? You don't look it. You don't *smell* it."

"Truth tell, I'm in bad shape," he said. "I'm starved. I haven't eaten since sometime yesterday, and I'm dying of hunger."

"Even a condemned man gets one good meal," she replied. "I go down and get breakfast for Arapaho lots of times." She placed her hand on his arm, the way she had Obie Hewitt's, only now her face was a little wistful. "Can I be your girl, Custis Long?"

"Well, for a while, anyway."

"Long enough to take me to the Double-O with you?"

That's what she's after, Longarm thought, and he couldn't blame her. She wanted to go to a clean, decent place, a safe life, somewhere she could forget Beulah and Wolfer and his wife. The Double-O; she belonged at Osborne and Son's. Easter Osborne wanted to go home. "I'll take you as far as I can," he replied earnestly, "and I'll make sure you're properly escorted the rest of the way, okay?"

She gave his arm an affectionate squeeze.

Bacon was sizzling in the skillet, the aroma of coffee filling the shack. Easter set the table for three, her blue eyes glancing now and then at Longarm, at Arapaho, and during the meal she told the rest of her story. Her childish mind had retained the name Easter, and Wolfer and his wife had humored her insistence that she be so called. The name Osborne had not been as deeply embedded, had meant little, yet had somehow clung to the back of her mind over the years. Her friendship for Arapaho had been born, here in Beulah, of his tales and lore of the plains, and of his stories of his visits to her parents' homestead. Easter recalled little of the tragic night other than the flames of a burning house and the journey in a wagon with strangers. They had sought to impress her then and later that her parents had been killed by Indians and that they had found her nearby. And thus she had lived . . . until finally Deaver Osborne rode here, curious, likely asking about the girl as soon as he stabled up, and getting murdered real quick, before any word could reach Easter.

After the meal, Longarm took a bath. He washed in Arapaho's big tin tub and, since he was alone, studied the papers he had grabbed from Wolfer's safe. He wound up with Deaver Osborne's stolen chit, two thick stacks, and a third pile of discards from the other two.

The first stack included originals and copies of telegrams, and an expense sheet for their costs and related expenses. The cables were usually sent via Pocatello, to and from a set of names that read like an outlaws' dishonor roll. What their messages said was innocuous blarney; what they meant was easy to detect, after Longarm found they fell into a pattern: the crooks agreed or refused to bring in their gangs on a joint, unspecified deal; if yes, they got money and directions where to meet locally, with promises of further instructions to come.

The second stack was like the first, except that the messages were mainly letters and they all involved the same name: Valhalla Land Development Company, General Delivery, Reno, Nevada. Again Longarm had to read between the lines. Wolfer was a bad writer and a worse speller, but it was mostly progress reports on the gangs. Valhalla used stilted lingo that would have boggled understanding even if genuine, but Longarm managed to extract the general idea that, within the next month or two, Wolfer was to move his owlhoot horde to Southern Oregon, there to work on some vague scheme called "Quivera" that eventually would take them far into California.

By the end of all this, Longarm had formed some ideas. Wolfer was the ringleader of a mass outlaw gather, which would scatter the instant news got out of his death. So, essentially, that part of Longarm's assignment was through. Wolfer, though, had left a trail to his boss. Valhalla was going to start some horrendous crime operation, and the fact that Wolfer had to keep detailed accounts meant Valhalla ran it like a business. That spelled only one thing: Valhalla was in the cartel.

Longarm knew something about the cartel, which was more than most people did. It led him to suspect that despite these incriminating papers, an official investigation would slam into so many false fronts and crooked bigwigs it would just die out. The only real expert on the cartel, Jessica Starbuck, needed to get involved in this, fast and unofficially. He couldn't snitch the evidence for her; he had to turn it in. But he could memorize it and contact her directly, wherever she was, the first chance he had. And he would, too. He sorely enjoyed getting involved with Jessie whenever possible.

Longarm felt no regrets when at last they got ready to leave Beulah. Easter eased her horse close to his, her blue eyes smiling as they headed out by the mountains that skirted the town. The surrounding terrain was big and clean, and made the weathered buildings of Beulah seem small and mean, with their untidiness and litter. And yet, when Longarm turned in his saddle for a final glance back, he could see past the rooftops to where the buzzards were circling downriver.

A shiver shook Longarm.

★
Chapter 11

Earlier that dawn, around the time Longarm was tipping over the lamp that set the saloon on fire, Jessie and Abbott Wyndam were regarding the ruins of the North Moon blaze. Ki was also up, scouting the ground about the ranch house yard, although there was scarcely enough light to see by in the pre-sunrise grayness.

The house itself was a fuming, charred heap. Amid the ashes and the remaining embers of beams and posts could be seen the massive iron safe, its door wrenched from its hinges. Robbery had undoubtedly been the motive behind the arson which had destroyed the dwelling, the cost of the damage far exceeding the loss from theft.

Ki found where the raiders had left their mounts to approach on foot. "Five of them," he reported, "including one who stayed with their horses. The tracks came and went due west, though I'll have to wait for better light to give them a follow."

"Well, it's your druthers, and maybe you can take a whack at 'em when we get back from town," Wyndam replied dubiously. "But there's a big rock-flat o'er thataway I'll wager they skedaddled for, and I'd be danged surprised if anyone could trace 'em across it."

On that disheartening note, they retired to the mess hall for breakfast. Afterwards, with pale pink smearing the eastern horizon, they saddled and headed for Gold Beach. Sunrise was in full glory by the time they reached the fork and turned onto the wagon road.

"This's the north boundary of our ranch. Ingram Harcourt's Lazy-H picks up t'other side of the road," Wyndam remarked, gesturing. "East valley back beyond us has some smaller spreads an' farms, but most of it's held by Ramon Valasquez." The name was spoken curtly, Wyndam frowning. He didn't explain, however, and was quickly chipper again as they rode along, chuckling reminiscently when they came to Eustace York's beehives. York was nowhere in sight. The bees were busily minding their own business and gave them no trouble in passing.

The morning grew to a promising day, clear and wispy-clouded. Leaving Bohemia Valley, Jessie and Ki were treated to a scan of the coastal expanse that had not been visible yesterday. They continued on, gazing approvingly at the meadowlands, the numerous groves and trickling creeks which stretched from shoreline to mountain range.

"Yep, the whole blamed area's a garden spot," Wyndam proudly replied to their compliments. "What you're admirin' is a smidge of Major Pennington's Ninety-Three, the largest spread in the county."

"Ninety-Three brand?"

"In honor of 1793, Jessie, the year Sam Houston was born."

"I should've guessed."

The sun was well up in the sky when they sighted the sprawling buildings of Gold Beach. As they drew near, they dipped off the trail to get by two ponderous, mule-drawn wagons escorted by four armed men.

The guards, drivers, and Wyndam nodded affably. Returning to the road, Wyndam remarked, "Ain't that nice. Always a boost to the local economy whenever Antelope sends out a gold shipment."

Ki glanced back at the wagons, making a rough estimate of the contents under their tarp covers. "If those're bricks of milled gold, they'd be hauling . . . why, maybe a hundred thousand dollars' worth!"

Wyndam nodded. "More'r less. Oh, not all out of Ante-

107

lope's mine, not by a long shot. But it's got a stamp and reducer, y'see, and lots of the real li'l miners find it handier and safe to take their ore there for handlin'. When enough is collected, Antelope makes a trek to the railroad at Grants Pass, on the other side of the hills."

"Have they been robbed much?" Jessie asked.

"Nary once. Lost a payroll a while ago, but no gold heists." Wyndam chuckled. "They cast the gold in hundred-pound ingots, is why. Robbers with their mounts weighted down by them chunks would be overtaken in a hurry, 'specially as the only route through the hills is the Douglas Trail, and it's a roop-loopin' heller. There ain't no other way to pack it off fast enough so they'd have a chance at a getaway. Soon's the wagons pull outa here onto the Trail, word is send on ahead to Grants Pass, and folks know mighty close just how long it takes for the wagons to make the trip. If they don't show up right on schedule, a big slug of armed men ride out the Trail to find out why. Nope, the Antelope shipment is plumb foolproof."

"Perhaps *too* foolproof," Jessie said thoughtfully. "People who're sure they've plugged all the holes can get careless, and be easy targets when someone smart comes along and figures a new approach."

"P'raps," Wyndam conceded indulgently. "But I reckon this is one where there ain't no holes."

Some distance along the street they reined in before the small sheriff's office and one-cell jail. Entering, they found Sheriff Lydell at his desk glowering at a report. A lanky old-timer with sunken cheeks and a droopy mustache, he acknowledged Wyndam, swept cool gray eyes over Jessie and Ki, and cocked an attentive ear. Because a lady was present, no doubt, he dang'ed instead of damn'ed in weary disgust as Wyndam outlined the happenings of the previous night.

"Same crop of scalawags that's been preyin' on everybody hereabouts," the sheriff declared with conviction. "Didn't see 'em, eh?"

"M'boys got a glimpse, but not close enough to tell much. Miz Starbuck and Ki, though, they've some details maybe worth adding."

Sheriff Lydell listened to them, cupping his ear to hear over the noise of the gold shipment rumbling past outside, then nodded gloomily. "Those tracks leading west sorta tallies with where them night riders were gallopin'. They're using that cussed Whisper Path!"

"Ever try keeping watch on it?" Jessie asked.

"Have I! Twice I figured I'd got the bast—er, *bandits* snared, but each time they ne'er popped up where they was supposed to. They know the holes and cracks 'round here so good, I sometimes think it might be a local mob, 'stead of one from the outside, hit-an'-runnin' as everyone reckons. But I can't figure any crew here pullin' such hijinks."

"Someone local might be directing them," Ki suggested.

"Thought of that also, 'cept I still can't figure nobody. That is, unless . . ." The sheriff did not finish, but Jessie saw him and Wyndam exchange significant glances. He looked capable, yet she had a suspicion he was not the brainiest of lawmen. Lydell would be tough and effective in any physical fight, but he was under-powered in a battle of wits with such a gang as was undoubtedly working here.

"Well, we've done reported," Wyndam said, "and I should get to seein' about building materials. Have to toss some kind of shack together. The boys ain't too shabby with hammer and nails, so I guess we'll manage a roof that'll keep the rain off our noggins."

"Come back when you're through in town, and I'll ride with you to North Moon for a look-see," the sheriff said. "Who knows, maybe I'll luck out and learn something. Least we can hope."

Wyndam sighed as he opened the door. "Blast them hellions! I just hope the day'll come soon when I can line my sights on 'em."

The first stop after the sheriff's was the general merchandise store. It was comprised of four low, shedlike barns linked by ramps and boardwalks, and if the signs across its main entrance could be believed, it catered to NEEDS OF EVERY TRADE, WHIMS OF EVERY NATURE.

Coming out as they were going in was a tall, robust, handsome man in his late thirties, impeccably garbed in the latest gentleman-rancher style. His hair was a rich, burnished red, as were his well-barbered mustache and beard, and his eyes were a black of depth and sheen. His voice, when he returned Wyndam's greeting, was quiet and well-modulated. Introduced, he seemed genuinely pleased to meet Jessie and Ki, especially Jessie, and Jessie found herself intrigued by him as well. He had a potent charm, this Mr. Ingram Harcourt.

"How're things at the Lazy-H, Ingram?" Wyndam asked.

"Fair to middling. And you?"

"Fine, just great," Wyndam responded sarcastically, and launched into a terse account of the raid while Harcourt grimly shook his head.

"Tragic, Abe, tragic. Count on my help," Harcourt declared. He added in parting, "Don't know where this country's heading to."

"T'hell in a handcart," Wyndam growled, saying goodbye. After they entered the store, he remarked, "Ingram's the salt of the earth and a top-notch rancher. Everyone's taken a real fancy to him since he moved here a coupla years ago. The ladies plumb swoon over him."

That, Jessie thought, she could well believe.

When they finished purchasing the hardware and construction supplies, they visited the lumber yard to contract for materials. Then Wyndam led them to the town's sole restaurant, which was decorated with old fish nets and cork floats, and specialized in day-fresh seafood.

"Breakfast was a mite early and scrimpy for my taste," Wyndam explained, as they settled in a booth. "We're early for fetching the sheriff anyway, not that there's much sense in him riding out with us, but I reckon he feels he ought to. Speakin' of such, tomorrow I ought to begin getting cows rounded up for shipping. I've got to raise cash to pay for COD's, come delivery of all the big bulk stuff ordered today."

Jessie shook her head. "Don't sell off, Abe. Starbuck will—"

"Aid when needed to save your investment, as we agreed," Wyndam cut in gruffly. He paused while their lunch of broiled red snapper was served, then continued in a more conciliatory tone. "Step in my boots a spell, Jessie. I'm

110

already beholden for the breathin' space you gave by forgoin' the heisted six thousand. But I've enough fat beeves ready to cover these buildin' costs, and the California market is good right now. Since the stuff won't arrive till next week soonest, there's plenty of time for some of m'boys to clean up the mess, while us others make a small gather and short drive to Crescent City, so I— Uh-oh."

Wyndam was glancing past them, frowning at a man who had just entered. This sparked Jessie and Ki to turn and eye the stranger. He was perhaps a year or two younger than Harcourt, a bit shorter and more ruggedly featured, with crisp blue eyes and darkish blond hair. He was rancher-clad, yet there were certain details of his dress that set him apart from the usual, much less the fashionable. And, unlike Harcourt, he appeared somewhat rumpled, as if he'd been working rather than preening. His manner was assured, almost arrogant, as he strode to one of the tables. But his smile was cordial when he greeted the waitress, and his speech was soft and pleasantly courteous.

"Who's he?" Ki asked Wyndam.

"Ramon Valasquez. A Spanish don, so he says."

"Blond, blue-eyed . . ." Jessie nodded thoughtfully. "He may well be a don, Abe, a descendant of royalty from old Castile or Navarre."

"He's a Spaniard, period, an uppity one who refuses to fit in," Wyndam grumbled stubbornly. "Uh-huh, and there's quite a few wonderin' if he ain't a *segundo* of them Spanish breeds and renegade Injuns I was warnin' you about. Y'know, the trouble-makers trying to stir revolt, who're behind the raidin' and arrow-slingin' going on hereabouts."

Jessie and Ki didn't reply, not wishing to argue, and not particularly surprised by the accusation. The people who conquered the West, of whom Wyndam was a typical example, were strong, determined, the majority of them honest, yet sometimes domineering, subject to strong prejudices and passions. All too often they did not understand foreigners, and from that lack of understanding arose distrust.

A pity, Jessie thought, for her initial impression of Don Ramon Valasquez was favorable. In fact, if forced to choose between him and the elegant Harcourt, she suspected she'd pick Valasquez, wrinkles and all. She sensed he was a man's man and possibly a swooning lady's man, but he was also— and to her, more importantly—a woman's man.

After their meal, they started back to the sheriff's office. They were almost there when a clatter of hooves sounded ahead, and approaching down the street rode a bloody-faced man, wild of eye and babbling hysterically. He jerked his horse to a sliding halt before the office, slumping limply from the saddle. Ki jumped forward, catching him, and carried him inside and laid him on the cell bunk.

"Water," Ki ordered the startled sheriff.

"Whiskey," the man croaked feebly.

The sheriff found a bottle of rye. "Pull on this, son."

The man managed to swallow a mouthful. Coughing and sputtering, he quieted enough to be coherent. "Antelope . . . gold . . . ambushed."

"What's that? You was held up? Where?"

"The river crossin', as we was climbing the far bank of the Rogue. They caught us in that slot of boulders there, opened up from both sides without a word. Mules 'n' all, a slaughter." The man took another nip before going on. "I's driving the second cart, pitched 'tween my team and they rollled on me, hid me. Saw 'em put our gold on a pack train, string of horses . . . Headed north, left me . . . Just me and pore Gilbey's horse, only ones left alive . . . Get here, had to . . ."

"Rest easy, son, you got here," the sheriff comforted, then turned to the others with an exultant look. "And we've got them! They can't have much over an hour's start, and can't've run fast or far under that heavy a load. To gain time is why they must've killed everybody, 'cept they failed to, lucky for us. Abe, go bring the doc. You two, keep an eye on things here while I collect the boys for a posse. I know a shortcut to the Douglas Trail, and by damn, we'll be hard after their arses soon's we ride. And I mean, we'll *ride!*"

★

Chapter 12

Within twenty minutes a doctor was tending the driver's wound and Sheriff Lydell was ordering his posse to mount up. Eight local men were willing and able to join when asked, Harcourt and Valasquez not being among them. Included were Wyndam and Ki, though, plus Jessie, as an unwelcome bonus that threw the sheriff into a snit.

Lydell objected that ladies were too delicate and would hamper their war-pathing, "likely sufferin' spells o' the vapors to boot." Jessie countered that this lady was going, either with the posse or close behind, and she straddled her roan and waited. The sheriff couldn't wait. Muttering about contrary females, he grudgingly allowed she'd be better with them where, leastwise, her innocence could be sheltered.

Under loose rein and busy spur, the posse thundered out of town. Instead of turning on the Douglas Trail, which headed inland along the near bank of the Rogue, they crossed the channel mouth of the river and angled northeast to the coastal hills. From there the sheriff led the climb along his shortcut, a faint track that wound through thick brush and timber, rocky gulches and flinty hogbacks.

As they rode, Wyndam gave Jessie and Ki a brief overview of the region. Sixty-odd miles due east of Gold Beach lay Grants Pass, where the new Oregon & California Railroad down from Portland had ceased construction.

Those miles, however, were blocked by a craggy vastness of solid forests, sheer ravines, and 4600-foot elevations. The Douglas Trail could only follow the Rogue for some twenty miles before having to cut northerly in a long, circuitous loop around the worst of it, a nonetheless difficult route for even the hardiest traveler.

So was the shortcut. But, perservering, they eventually descended the far sag of seemingly endless ridges and struck the Douglas Trail.

"Right like I figured!" the sheriff exulted, pointing to deeply scarred hoof marks in the bare earth surface. "It rained hard yesterday, and the sun don't get to this road much. Chasin' down these owlhoots will be as easy as fallin' off a slick log."

"They're not making any speed," Ki remarked, studying the prints.

Quickening their pace, the posse rode northward along the Trail. Occasionally they spotted branching paths for animals or remote camps, but otherwise they followed a lonesome rut, twisting and slewing uphill and down, right and left, the deviations so frequent and erratic that it took them a time to realized the Trail had begun to wend generally eastward. A while later they curved in along the bank of a whitewater river, its cascading torrent bedded deep between tall, gullied bluffs and flowing westerly toward the ocean.

"That's the Coquille," Sheriff Lydell informed Jessie and Ki. "Snakes worse'n the Trail does, I swear. We hafta cross it about a mile ahead and then again to get back this side, and thank gawd for them fords, 'cause they're nigh-on the only two to be had. Up to its headwaters the river's a mountain maverick. From here to the coast, it rips north into a gorge that makes this part look like a ditch. After, oh, ten miles it spews out and snaggles across an open stretch a while, then dives into another canyon and don't come outa that hole till the hills peter down way over by Myrtle Point. Then it's okay."

The posse galloped on parallel with the Coquille, eyes focused on the scored hoofprints before them. Only Jessie and Ki appeared to take interest in their immediate surroundings, the broken stone ledges, the timbered breaks and the churning, cataract-strewn river. Always, however, their gazes returned to the marks in the trail, which Ki especially continued to study intently.

Abruptly the Coquille swerved, coming in from the south, and the Trail had to bend with it. Soon, though, came a section where the banks softened into round, swaybacked slopes. The river widened slightly at this point, swirling in gentler swells from the base of a long series of rapids to the beginning angle of its swerve. Dipping to the water's edge, the Trail kept to rocks as much as possible to avoid the soft and muddy ground here. Luckily, where it rose on the far side, the bank was mostly composed of slab stone.

The horses pranced, shying. The riders kept firm rein and kneed forward, plunging their reluctant mounts up to their cinch straps.

"Careful," the sheriff cautioned. "The ford's narrow with deep water on either side. Slip off and you'll hafta swim for it."

Urged on, the horses struggled across, hoofs fighting for purchase on the slippery bedrock, legs resisting the buffeting of the icy current. Finally, lurching, a few almost falling, they clambered up the other slope. The stony stretch lasted for perhaps a fifth of a mile, and then the Trail surface once more became soft earth.

Before they had ridden another hundred yards, Ki called out, flagging the others to stop. "Hold it! We've been outsmarted!"

The posse jostled to a halt, volleying questions.

"What ails you, boy?" Sheriff Lydell demanded. "They're the hoofprints leading on in front. Them crooks came thisaway, all right."

"They did. The gold did not."

"What d'ya mean, not? How'd you know?"

"Look at the prints, Sheriff. They're much shallower than they were across the river, meaning they're carrying less weight. And see the distance between the marks. They're running fast, which they'd never be able to do if the ingots were still weighing them down."

Sheriff Lydell craned, checking, then nodded. "You're right, drat it. But what'd they do with the gold? Chuck it in the water?"

"Maybe, but I don't think so." Ki glanced ahead, scan-

115

ning the Trail. "They've got a good start and they can probably keep ahead of us till dark. I'm afraid, Sheriff, they've about given us the slip."

"And foolin' us into goin' on after 'em!" The sheriff swore, glimpsed Jessie, and choked. "I'm stumped, I admit it. Now what?"

"Try and find out what happened to the gold," Ki suggested.

The sheriff agreed with a melancholy sigh, and led his disheartened posse back to ford the river again. Reaching the other side, they dismounted and poked about for anything that seemed odd.

Jessie and Ki began walking downstream, studying the mushy bank below the rocky strip that accommodated the ford. Abruptly Jessie paused and pointed to a deep, wedge-shaped indentation in the soft earth at the water's edge. "There, Ki, like you thought!"

"Sure is." Ki waved for the others, and when they grouped around, he explained, "That's made by the prow of a boat, and look at all the boot tracks about. They must've had the boat tied up here waiting, stopped off and loaded the gold into it, and sent it on."

"Well, that blows all," the sheriff groaned. "We dang well can't ride the river after 'em. The water's ten feet deep and there ain't no banks inside them cussed gorges."

"No, but didn't you say there's an open stretch between them?" Jessie asked. "There's a chance we might get ahead of the boat if it's moving slow, and be ready for them when they come out. Would you know another shortcut to there that wouldn't take much time?"

Mulling, the sheriff brightened. "Yeah, I do rec'lect one. A half-mile back along the Trail is a path that kinda wanders northwestish. After a fair length an ol' game track crosses it, leadin' to where there's food and water smack-dab at the mouth of that first gorge. If we can make it there before the boat does, we'd oughta be all set to turn their trick on them. Let's go!"

Hastily the posse returned along the Trail. They veered onto a skinny defile of sorts that unraveled across the broad rise of hills, seemingly going nowhere for no apparent reason. At Sheriff Lydell's command, they followed him single file off into the woods on what he swore was the game track he remembered. He blazed their way through blanketing timber, fissured escarpments, and clefted, boulder-strewn culverts, insisting he was taking a familiar path, yet one that was utterly bewildering and invisible to everybody else.

Mile after mile they forged in grim silence, while the sun slanted westward and the shadows grew long. Eventually they rounded the beetling bulge of a cliff and saw they had been right in trusting the lawman. Before them was the open stretch, a broad upland valley with canyons at each end and the Coquille River surging through it.

They saw more. Perhaps half a mile distant, bobbing along in the middle of the river, was a flat-bottomed boat of considerable size containing three men, one of whom bent his weight to a long sweep with which he steered the unwieldy craft.

Letting out cheers, the posse goaded their weary horses to renewed speed. Swiftly they bore down upon the slower-moving boat, which was headed for the dark gorge mouth a mile or more yonder. As they drew within easy rifle range, the sheriff gave a bellow.

"Turn that rig ashore and surrender!" he roared.

The three men, who had been glancing at the approaching riders, hunched low. Gunsmoke puffed from the boat, slugs whining close.

"They ain't going to obey," the sheriff said. "Open fire."

Immediately the posse shouldered rifles, triggering and levering and triggering again. One of the boatmen flung erect, wavered, and pitched over the side into the water. The other two continued to shoot. The boat drew ever nearer the dim maw that spelled escape.

Again the posse raked the boat with a fusillade of rifle fire. One cursed as an answering bullet creased his arm. Then they lowered their smoking weapons and stared at the crumpled figures lying silent and motionless across the stacked gold ingots. The boat, its unmanned steering sweep swinging wildly, swept on toward the gorge.

"Confound it!" the sheriff snapped. "They done skunked us after all. There're rapids in that canyon and she'll never ride 'em. With nobody steerin', she'll bust up on the rocks. The gold's a goner!"

The grumbling posse slowed to a halt, all except Ki, who kicked his buckskin mare to greater effort, lashing reins and urging it on. He tore across the valley on his plucky horse, heading toward where, within a few yards of the gorge mouth, a long fang of rocks extended almost to midstream. Before the rest of the posse divined Ki's intentions, his buckskin's irons were clashing on the flat surface of the ledge. Where it narrowed, Ki reined in sharply, sprang from the saddle, and sprinted to the point of the spit. There he poised, leaning forward tensely, his eyes fixed on the approaching boat.

"Ki's goin' to try and jump in her!" Wyndam exclaimed.

The posse stared intently, silently rooting, Jessie holding her breath as they saw him bend his legs and launch his long body through the air. They grinned and cheered as he landed on the pile of gold ingots, reeled, caught his balance, and turned toward them.

"I'll beach her where the river comes out this canyon!" he shouted. "Think up another shortcut, Sheriff, and follow me there!"

"We'll follow, but there ain't none but a long way around!" the sheriff yelled back as the lurching boat vanished into the gloom of the chasm. "Good luck, boy. Hope the rapids don't eat you alive!"

Ki scrambled across the ingots to the stern of the boat, stepping over the bodies of the slain bandits. He seized the handle of the steering sweep, which fortunately was secured in place by an oarlock. Steadying the boat, he glanced about. The gorge was steeply sloped, hopper-shaped, its heights heavily overgrown with pine and scrub, its depths just smooth rock washed by the river and all quite murky, for the sun was now low in the sky.

Soon he became conscious of a low murmuring that swelled to a mutter, a rumble, a deep-toned roar that vibrated between the walls. Rapids, he figured, big ones, with plenty of rocks, and he didn't know the channel—or if there was one. He peered ahead, narrowing his eyes, bending his weight against the sweep. Pretty soon he could see the white froth where the water spouted foam from the black rocks that stabbed above its surface. Jaw clenching, the muscles of his arm and back tightening, he gripped the steering oar in readiness.

The cumbersome barge pitched and bucked when it struck the beginning of the rapids. Bracing for balance, Ki maneuvered the sweep while plunging on into the maze of writhing currents, gouts of spray, and sawtoothed cataracts. He felt the grind of submerged ledges raking the shallow keel beneath him, and shuddered as a fang of stone planed off a long, curling shaving the entire length of one gunwale. Frenziedly he strove to guide the yawing boat clear, only to smash against another jagged outcrop and ricochet off the next, their glancing jolts causing the planks to creak and almost buckle.

With vast relief Ki steered through the final fringe of the rapids. The rearing boat quieted, and for several miles sailed rather smoothly down the rippling swift river. Then again the slick chasm walls echoed with a hollow murmur, the ominous portent of rapids yet to come, more treacherous because of the thickening dusk.

Soon Ki could see ghostly spume spouting from jutting rocks. Soon after he was slamming deep into the rampaging hazard. The boat tossed and tilted in an ungainly fashion, threatening to capsize, scraping over bedrock and crunching against projections. More than once Ki was sure it was holed or staved in, but somehow it jarred glancing past the obstacles and continued its wild progress with only minor leaks.

Dunking between the last stony tiers, he careened into calmer water and floated with the carrying tide. For an exhaustive, seemingly interminable stretch, Ki sped on without encountering further perils. Eventually he noted that the side walls were lowering, indicating that he was nearing the canyon's end. Shortly he spewed out of the gorge mouth and saw the rolling fields opening out before him.

The east bank of the Coquille was still precipitous, but the west was low and heavy with growth. Working the sweep as an oar, Ki angled shoreward and beached the boat on a little gravelly strip between the tree-laced brush and the water's edge. He stepped out, stretching his cramped limbs, and glanced about, then stiffened as a harsh voice spoke from the underbrush behind him.

"Hands up, pal, we gotcha covered!"

Turning his head, Ki glimpsed two rifle barrels trained on him. He carefully raised his hands shoulder-high. From the dark bristle of foliage stepped four men, all of them wearing grubby, nondescript work clothes and boots, and all of them pointing rifles or pistols. All of them looked ready, if not downright eager, to fire them.

"Well, looka what we nabbed!" the shortest of the four exclaimed. "If he don't fit the gink the boss was describin', I'm a blue turd. Say, you, what's your name, and how'd you come to be in that boat?"

"Never mind, Hank," a thin, chinless man ordered. "We're runnin' late, so just tie him up and leave him for the boss to wring dry."

Under gun, Ki stood quietly while he was checked for firearms, a cursory search that missed his concealed weapons. His wrists were tied behind him with a rope that was then lashed to a tree. The men left him tethered there in constant view as they worked.

One, whose face was badly scarred, entered the underbrush. The other three went to the boat, swearing luridly and glaring viciously at Ki when they discovered the two bodies. They rifled the pockets of the dead men and callously dumped them overboard, then began transferring the ingots ashore, still cursing Ki with angry indignation.

Seemingly stung by their insults, Ki slumped helpless and ejected while he discreetly tested the rope binding him. It was tight and well-knotted, but not tight enough or knotted enough. He twisted and flexed his wrists, sensing weak points that, given time and effort, might just loosen enough for him to break free. Meanwhile he must play the prisoner and learn all he can, so as he convertly strained on the rope, he watched the men through downcast eyes.

The scarred man led a string of packhorses from the brush and started loading the gold while more was brought from the boat. Then horses were led out, including three spares that had evidently been intended for the dead boatmen. The rope holding Ki was cut by the tree and, his wrists still secured, he was ordered to mount one of the extra horses. Struggling, he straddled the saddle, then his legs were bound to the stirrup straps.

They set off riding in the waning blush of sunset. Initially heading west, they shortly turned south and skirted the lower slopes for many miles until, dipping to the coastal flats, they forded the Rogue River and crossed the flanking Douglas Trail. Immediately they angled east, climbing back into the concealing timber before winding southward again. In line near the rear, Ki continued pressuring the ropes with his wrists and legs while trying to keep some sense of direction and location as they jogged along. But the paths they followed, when they took any at all, were overgrown threads as poor as the sheriff's game track, and the terrain was unfamiliar yet all too similar, shrouded not only by the dimming sky but by the canopying trees whose bottom branches were usually higher than Ki on horseback.

Full night had long since descended when finally they arrived at a stoutly built cabin, isolated and well hidden by growth. Here the men dismounted. The short one called Hank lit a lamp in the cabin, then helped the others unload the packhorses and carry the ingots inside. Afterwards the animals were hobbled out to graze, and at last Ki was untied from his horse and ordered into the cabin.

He found himself in a fairly commodious room outfitted with wall bunks, a rusty cookstove, a table, and several chairs. There were some utensils and crockery and a supply of food on the shelves, and the place had a lived-in feel; evidently it was used often.

"Dump our pal in the back room," the thin man ordered. "Flagg, stay guard till we show up with the boss tomorrow. Take no chances, y'hear? He's rattler mean if he's who Hank here reckons he is."

Nodding, the scarred man named Flagg shoved Ki ahead of him, causing Ki to stagger slightly. "I can handle this son of a bitch, no fear. I ain't lettin' him out for nothin'." Pushing Ki forward again, Flagg thrust him through a dark, gaping doorway and slammed the door shut, laughing. "I won't give no never-mind how bad he bleats, 'cause he won't be hollerin' long once the boss gets here."

121

Ki heard the chunk of a shot bolt, followed by a rumbling of voices in the outer main room, then the slam of the closing front door. Moments later came the click of horses' irons, fading swiftly into the distance, and the sounds of Flagg preparing some food.

So much for playing prisoner, Ki thought sourly. Now he was locked in his death cell awaiting execution. His only chance was to escape before they returned with their boss sometime tomorrow.

Simple.

All he had to do was figure out how.

Chapter 13

Sheriff Lydell had been right.

The posse was forced to trek a lengthy, bone-wearing detour around the hills to the Coquille's exit from the second gorge. They reached the riverbank shortly after sunset and found the empty boat but no sign of Ki or the gold. Nosing worriedly about, they located numerous tracks of men and many horses, and stared bleakly at where the hoofprints led off into the brush, unsure what to think until one asked aloud just who this Ki was and just what was his game.

Ignoring the voiced suspicion, Jessie concentrated on studying the ground, trying to discern what had happened. Her practiced eye caught the faint scuff-mark of Ki's distinctive rope-soled slippers. Hunting for more, she detected a few, scarcely enough to point her toward the tree where Ki had stood bound. Her pulse quickened.

Somebody blurted, "Yeah, stacks of ingots make heaps of loot." Abruptly all the possemen were looking askance at one another. Then a third cottoned to the opinion that maybe Ki was in cahoots with the owlhoots, or some gang of like sort, and had skunked them out of the gold. Wyndam threatened to whup the socks off any jigger who didn't latigo his jaw, and was preparing to when Jessie called out sharply.

"Clamp your lips and open your eyes," she scathed. "Ki was tied to this tree. He didn't take anything; he was taken prisoner!"

The sheriff, hastening over with the others, viewed the footprints and the cut rope, and nodded, sighing. "Looks it, yep, and not hard to figure. I should've seen it before, 'cept I was so busy getting us through these infernal hills, I pure disremembered to think the bandits must've been waiting somewheres downstream for the boat."

"Perhaps that's how Ki slipped up, too," Jessie said anxiously. "He came ashore assuming it was safe, and got a loop dropped on him."

"Now don't fret, ma'am, we'll find him. Won't we, fellers?"

"Hell, Sheriff, we hafta go after Ki! He's with the gold!"

Remounting, the posse followed the tracks west from the river toward the sunset's dying afterglow. The packhorses had left a trail that was easily traced through the underbrush, but as it entered deep forest, and twilight faded into dusk, it grew increasingly vague. Shadows thickened until the trail blurred, indistinguishable from the surrounding gloom. Finally the glum, tuckered posse gave up.

"We can't go back," Jesse insisted.

"We can't go on," Wyndam replied sympathetically.

"But Ki could be hurt, or . . . dead."

"If he's dead, he's dead, and us thrashing blindly about won't make him come alive. If he's hurt, he's no doubt lying low, hiding away where we couldn't find him, either." Wyndam leaned to pat her arm comfortingly. "I'm sorry, truly. But we must quit until morning."

She sighed, reluctant, then nodded. "Till morning . . ."

In silence the posse jogged down through the murky hills to town. Jessie hunched in her saddle, scanning the darkness and trying to shake off her apprehensions. A concern for Ki was natural, but to fear the worst was futile. As Ki liked to josh, she wasn't bit yet, so she should stop alarming herself. Forging ahead as if he were here, she knew, helped the most. Ki was not here, undeniably, a dismaying fact.

Though the night was still young, the main street was tranquil when the posse arrived in Gold Beach. It disbanded quietly at the sheriff's office, the men plodding off with their mounts, promising to resume the search at dawn. Thanking them, the sheriff apologized to Jessie for considering her unworthy, and tottered into his office.

Jessie turned to Wyndam. "Is there a place to stay in town?"

"Yep, Buckram's. Might as well spend the night there, if we gotta be ridin' at the crack of dawn." He rubbed his sore rump. "I fear me 'n' my nag couldn't make it home now, anyhow."

They walked their horses to the livery, Ki's buckskin following her roan, as it had since Jessie retrieved it at the valley and snugged its reins to her saddle. At the livery, they told the hostler to give the horses the works. The hostler refused to take them in his stable. Their coats matted with muck, burrs, twigs, and needles, the horses were panting as though spavined and lathered as if with shaving soap. The hostler relented after a bribe of double charges and the promise of a tip.

Buckram's was central in town, between a pharmacy and a drowsy saloon, and across from the restaurant. On the way there from the livery, Jessie and Ki almost bumped into Don Ramon Valasquez as he was about to enter the saloon. He pivoted fast, wary, reminding Jessie of a cat when caught unawares. Just as swiftly Valasquez recovered, his motions quick and decisive as he swept off his hat and nodded amiably at Wyndam.

"Excuse me, Abe. I wasn't looking at where I was going."

Nor by then was he looking at Wyndam, but was eyeing Jessie speculatively, as if he had overlooked her in his desire to make amends. *"Perdone,* Señorita Starbuck, *lo siento mucho."* He flashed a softly teasing smile while he humbly murmured how very sorry he was.

"No hay de qué, Don Ramon. De nada," Jessie replied lightly, returning his challenge, then switched to English. "Don't mention it, really, it's nothing. But how did you know who I am, Don Ramon, and why'd you speak to me in Mexican instead of your native Spanish?"

"I saw you in the café, Señorita, and I asked. Your name is on the tip of every wagging tongue in town. As for the other . . . *por qué no?"* He added a shrug, half hesitated as though inclined to converse, then thought better of it. Clap-

125

ping his hat on, Valasquez politely bid them good evening, and went into the saloon.

They moved on.

"The nerve of that man," Wyndam grumped. "Valasquez sized you up like a side o' beef. Like he knows you, or should. Do you know him?"

"No, we've never met before," Jessie said, thinking over the encounter. Don Ramon took his eyeful, all right, darn near to the nubbin. Rarely had she felt stripped so naked in public. Still, his eyes also gave, and watching them watch her, Jessie had glimpsed virile admiration, the usual male gloat and throb of conquest. And pride. A well-earned pride, perhaps, but it fit his use of Mexican Spanish, though precisely why he'd done so escaped her. Maybe it was a sly trick, to squash stupid Miss Starbuck down to lap size, or a test, daring her to keep up with him. Whatever it was, she sensed less of arrogance than of mockery, a pride that at its worst would not be contemptuous but scornful of others. And yet, when she answered in Mexican and then challenged him on it, she perceived new respect and even pleasure. And with that rose a personal awareness of each other, a mutual attraction hinting at sexual arousal. As Wyndam said, more rightly than he realized, Don Ramon did look like he should know her, for he sure felt he should—intimately. Not that she had any such fancies in mind, she hastily thought. After a day in the saddle, her bottom was thoroughly buffeted and needed to rest with her off it.

She glanced at the fuming Wyndam. "I'm not offended, Abe, so don't get cranky. Tell me something nice about Valasquez, can you?"

"Be a chore," Wyndam grumbled. "Well, I'll allow he's a good rancher. Major Pennington likes him, but then, he favors Mexicans. With a zeal. If ever you hear the major start on how they're misunderstood and'd change Mexico if given the chance, flee for your ears, else he'll lecture on the chance Sam Houston offered, and on Cortes, on and on till you're deaf. That reminds me, I . . . Oh, here we are."

Buckram's was a converted home, painted ivory with chocolate trim, and was as clean inside as it was spruce outside. They rented the last two rooms from Mr. Buckram, who was incredibly aged, but passed Wyndam the lewdest wink Jessie had ever seen.

When they were outside again, Jessie declared, "I caught that dirty old man's wink. Valasquez pales in comparison to Buckram."

"Well, he has his funny notions. Also the only beds in town." Wyndam grinned sheepishly. "Jessie, I think I'll visit the major while the hour's still reasonable. He's got a quarry on his place, with cut stones that've just stacked about for years. They'd be great for the foundation blocks I need to replace, if I can buy 'em cheap enough. Stay here if you like, though I wouldn't mind the company."

Jessie brightened. "Let's go rent us a couple of horses."

After a minor hassle with the disgruntled hostler, they trotted away on two dapple bays, past town limits, and cut onto the Pennington private lane. It meandered southeast toward the hills abutting Bohemia Valley, through an estate that was perhaps not giant by Texas standards, but was large enough to be impressive. And wearying on one's tender seat, Jessie reflected uncomfortably. She was beginning to think of the ride in terms of miles, when the drive scaled a rise between two posterns, angled toward a spacious clapboard ranch house through cultivated rows of hardwood, and looped in a circle as it curved by the fantail-stepped front entrance. They hitched the bays at posts by the steps, and went up to the broad porch and front door.

Answering Wyndam's tug on the bell cord was a stout housekeeper, who ushered them into a library den to await the major. The room had a smattering of furniture, most of it grouped near a small fireplace, and a few gilt-framed oil paintings of famous heroes in heroic poses. Otherwise, from floor to ceiling were tiered bookcases, map drawers, and file cabinets, many with world globes perched on them. The room bespoke money, Jessie saw, but not ostentation, for it was also well used.

Moments later, a man wearing a plum-colored velvet smoking jacket strutted in and greeted them with a hospitable bellow. "Mighty glad to see you, Abe. Glad to see your lady friend, too . . . Miss Starbuck? Rings a faint bell, but where? Never mind. I'm glad to meet you now, Miss Starbuck. Well, light off and squat."

He was in his early sixties, Jessie estimated, his muscular body down but not out, though his shoulders were slightly stooped. A jut-jawed square face with keen brown eyes and a high, wrinkled forehead was topped by sparse gray-brown hair neatly plastered to his skull. All in all, he looked his image, the retired warhorse turned gentleman scholar and cattle baron, Major Xerxes Pennington himself.

"Why am I honored, Abe?" Pennington asked when they were settled. "You payin' a social call, or something I can do for you?"

"In case you ain't heard, Major. . ." Wyndam recounted the tale from the fire to his visit, mentioned the quarry stones, and ended back at the fire. "Losin' the money hurt, sure, but roastin' my home 'round my head was nigh a crippler. If it weren't for Miss Starbuck, well . . ."

Wyndam didn't go on, for which Jessie was grateful. Pennington beamed approvingly at her. "A friend indeed, Miss Starbuck. Alas, as a guest to our area, you must be confounded by all this violence."

"It's no stranger to any area," she replied enigmatically. "I've a question, though, that a long-time landowner such as you can maybe answer. After robbing Abe, the outlaws couldn't have run very far, or they wouldn't have gotten set in time to attack the gold shipment. They must've stayed in this vicinity. Where're some logical places?"

"Dozens. And you're assuming that it's the same gang."

Jessie shrugged. "Well, it hardly stands to reason that two quite similar gangs would be operating in the same locale, does it?"

"It can, if the gangs are *dis*-similar in motives. Hardened crooks are greedy, so they go after loot. Revolutionaries strike at political oppression, though lines can get crossed if funds get too low. Mexico is rife with examples of single districts with varied gangs."

"Mexico is a long way off, Major."

"It's here," Wyndam said. "I dunno about two gangs. I hope not; one is more'n plenty. But, Jessie, an uprisin' is growin' here."

"Over what, Abe? For what gain? Nothing's here to grow a revolt."

128

"Come here." Pennington led them to a shelf, selected a large portfolio, and opened it on a nearby table as he spoke. "Revolutions are over injustice, and for the gain of lost rights and status. Doesn't that fit the downtrodden descendants of a once proud nation?" He pointed to the open page, an antique Mercator's map of North America. "Like Quivera, there. For over two hundred years the kingdom was shown on all maps, charts, atlases and globes. It's on Mercator's maps from 1569 to 1750, which is the year of this one. Quivera existed, Miss Starbuck, right here."

"You mean Gold Beach?"

Pennington nodded. "The site of Quivera the city, the capital, discovered by the Spanish explorer Martin d'Agulai. I've an edition of his journals in here someplace." He started off to peruse his shelves, adding, "Excavations have begun near Flores Creek, in fact. It was reported in the *Port Orford Post* that's around here, too."

Jessie gazed at the Mercator's map, still unsure she believed what she was seeing, much less what she was hearing. Quivera's boundaries were ill-defined, but appeared to stretch north to Oregon's Sixes River, as far east as the Dakotas, and south to a point about in line with San Jose. It was a healthy chunk of real estate to revolt over.

Pennington returned with three books. "Found these instead. Top one has a record of Quivera's trade with China. Next tells of Philip III of Spain's father hiding a sworn declaration given by a traveler to Quivera. Understand, Spain ruled the waves at this time, and the kings wished to keep secret the existence of Quivera, which is why so little was written about it." He opened the third book. "This's a fair reference on that fact and about Quivera in general."

Glancing at the book, Jessie's interest was intrigued by the engraved portrait of a tall, classically handsome bearded man. His apparel was rich and embroidered; his right hand rested on the hilt of a sword that hung from his hip; and his eyes seemed to stare into the distance and see splendid visions.

"He's Tatarrax," Pennington said, noting her focus. "The last great king, under whose rule Quivera flourished prosperous and powerful. Tatarrax looks like the leader he was, an inspired leader."

"He looks oddly familiar," Jessie murmured, concentrating on the picture. She'd seen someone somewhere who resembled him somehow, and recently, too. But damned if she could put a tag on it. With a shrug, she dismissed the minor coincidence which was, after all, of no significance, and turned her attention back to Pennington.

". . . a man of vision. If his principals had been adhered to by those who came after Tatarrax, Western America would be a different land. He died too soon. World-shakers always die too soon, like Cortes, and Lincoln, and General Houston. But they live on in others."

"And their mistakes can also live on in others."

Pennington looked hard at Jessie, as if mustering a retort. Then he mellowed and admitted contemplatively. "A novel point, Miss Starbuck, never thought of it from that facet. I do hope, however, you're able to appreciate the good great men try to accomplish."

Jessie smiled gently. "Perhaps."

That seemed to satisfy Pennington and to close the subject. He clapped Wyndam on the shoulder, declaring, "Sure, Abe, you can have the stones. Right price, too. The codger who owned that section had something in mind for 'em—he quarried 'em—but I don't know what, and've been wondering what to do with them for quite a while."

"Thanks. I'll hire the freighter in town to pick 'em up."

"What for? My crew'll deliver 'em. How about tomorrow?"

"Well, we're grouping a herd together in the comin' days for a drive down to Crescent City. Next week would be better for me."

After agreement was reached on price, Wyndam and Jessie enjoyed a glass of cordial with Pennington and then departed, for it was growing late. Once back in Gold Beach, they turned in the rental horses, ate supper, and adjourned to Buckram's, where the wizened proprietor handed them their room keys with a cackled wish for sweet dreams.

Jessie stomped up the stairs before she punched Buckram in the nose. Her simply furnished room was next to Wyndam's, near the head of the second-floor corridor. Locking the door, she removed her boots and holstered shellbelt, loosened her jeans, and retired to bed thinking she would go right out. But sleep proved elusive. Her mind was too distressed by the events, too disturbed by Pennington's claims, to let her relax. She lay pondering in the dark long after she should have dozed off, hearing a subdued murmur of night activity from the main street, though Buckram's itself seemed to rest in a pool of stillness.

So intense was the quiet that what sounded like the slight creak of a stair tread brought Jessie alert. The sound was not repeated, however, and she concluded it was merely from the old house settling, or a mouse under the floorboards. Then a second sound perked her more quickly—a faint, metallic scratching at her door.

She shifted in bed, staring across the room just as the door eased narrowly open, and a shadow glided stealthily inside. Jessie was not given to fright, yet the quick stealth and menace of this form were unnerving enough to make her gasp. Abruptly it straightened, arm whipping.

A throwing knife, metallic gray and invisible in the darkness, aiming directly at the gasp, lancing straight toward Jessie—all within one silent split-instant.

Chapter 14

Jessie never saw the knife coming.

She recognized the figure's throwing motion, however, from her years with Ki. Instantly she dove, rolling sideways out of the bed.

The blade slashed her pillow and thunked into the low wood headboard. Spinning up on one knee, Jessie drew her derringer from her belt and fired both barrels at the blurry intruder. Echoing their sharp discharges came a strangled cry, a dull thud as of a falling body, then a strange tapping, as of boot heels beating a tattoo on the floorboards. From the next room erupted the pound of Wyndam's feet, plus an aroused bellow that burst with him out into the hall.

"Don't come in! Keep clear!" Jessie shouted. She sprang for her shellbelt on the chair. Snagging her pistol from the holster, she pivoted, aiming, preparing to shoot, but found she had no target. The drumming of heels had ceased, and the shape on the floor was unmoving. Her room was deathly still, though the hall was noisy with querulous voices as other startled guests joined Wyndam outside her door.

"Hold it till I strike a light," she called. Setting a match to the bedside lamp, she saw by its glow a man sprawled lifeless on the floor. Stepping by, she opened the door to admit Wyndam. To her surprise, behind him entered Don Ramon

Valasquez, wearing only his trousers and a worried expression. Glimpsing a key in the lock, she hastily took it and shut the door on the handful of other guests.

"Lucifer!" Wyndam blurted, ogling the body. "What happened?"

"He snuck in and . . . well, didn't get as far as he hoped."

"By the looks of that knife stuck to your bed, Señorita, I'd say romance was not the hope he had in mind," Valasquez remarked, eyeing the long blade driven deep in her headboard. *"Muy estúpido, no?"*

His innuendo brought a sharp scowl from Wyndam and a thin smile from Jessie as she crossed to holster her pistol. Examining the key, she held it out and said, "He unlocked my door with this, a pass key, but how'd he get it? Who . . . ? Hey, where's the old man?"

"Buckram? He sleeps downstairs in the back," Wyndam replied, then exclaimed. "He ain't here, is he? C'mon, and bring the lamp!"

Barging out through the small flock at the door, Wyndam led the way downstairs and to the rear of the building, where a closed door indicated the location of the owner's living quarters. He swept open the door, Valasquez and Jessie rushing in, bearing the lamp aloft.

Across the room a bunk had been built against the wall. On it lay Buckram, bound and gagged, writhing and flopping and mumphing unintelligibly. His face was smeared with coagulating blood that had flowed from a gash high on the side of his grizzled head. As quickly as his bonds were removed, he reared up, sputtering, dabbing his injury.

"'Twas a knock, and I no sooner unlatch the door than a hand flang in and bent a gun barrel over my skull," he replied to their questions. "Next I knowed, I's in here, hogtied. What's goin' on?"

Jessie explained in a few terse sentences, adding, "Sheriff Lydell should be fetched, and maybe the doctor to look at that cut."

"I'll go," Valasquez offered, and hurried out.

Wyndam frowned in his direction. "Ain't we ever goin' to be clear of that blasted rascal? Everywhere we go, he has to show up."

Jessie, too, was gazing at Valasquez as he left, admiring his grace of motion, the flex of muscles along his thighs and bare torso. "Abe, he was here before us. We rented the last two rooms, remember?"

"We weren't follerin' him. But trouble always does, Jessie, and it wasn't no surprise to me to find him here when it bust loose upstairs."

Jessie smiled slightly, an amused gleam in her green eyes, but said nothing. As weary as she was, she preferred peace to an argument.

Shortly Valasquez and the sheriff arrived, and they all trooped up to Jessie's room. The sheriff glanced disgustedly at the corpse, then went to look at the knife, tugging hard to work it from the headboard. He studied it curiously, for it was a peculiar-looking weapon, thick and heavy of blade, and extremely short of handle.

"A homemade throwing knife, ground out from a file," he concluded. "Brand-new file, it appears like. Yep, you can still make out the maker's name, up close by the handle."

"Crude but nasty," Wyndam observed, his face grave. "Jessie, if you'd been a second sleepier, you'd have sprouted that sticker 'twixt your ribs. And I gotta fear there're more where it came from."

The doctor came in. He was also coroner and was panting from haste and still buttoning his vest. He gave the dead man a swift inspection, pronounced him deceased, and answered a question from Jessie. "Nope, you won't need to attend the inquest. The sheriff can take your deposition, then he an' I'll open an' shut the formalities sometime later." With that, he bundled Buckram out and back downstairs for treatment.

Jessie had been holding her lamp to the body for the doctor, and continued to now for the sheriff while he searched the pockets. He found nothing of interest, no identification. Frustrated, he asked if anyone could recognized the corpse even remotely, so they all peered close at its swarthy, unshaven features now grimacing in death.

Wyndam shook his head. "Ain't seen this'n before."

"Nor I," Jessie said. "He looks a bit Spanish, doesn't he?"

"If he is, it's blood of a forebearer from the southern provinces, Catalonia perhaps, well diluted by mixed generations," Velasquez responded. "But, yes, Sheriff, I saw him once, today in the saloon. He was drinking around, rude and belligerent, finally leaving after Señor Harcourt entered and they traded words. Surely the señor will recall it, for whatever he muttered sent this hombre packing *rápido*."

"Apparently not fast or far enough," the sheriff said grimly. "Well, we never met, and I'm glad we won't ever again. Would've been nice if he'd lived to talk some, though, and maybe given us a line on why he picked on you, Miss Starbuck, or who might've put him up to it."

"He may've given us a line, anyhow," she replied, but did not elaborate, despite the puzzled glances. Instead she suggested, "If you men will carry the garbage out, perhaps we can all go back to bed."

"Good notion," Wyndam agreed, yawning. He picked up one leg, Valasquez the other, and with Sheriff Lydell at the head they carted the body away—to the doctor's, Jessie presumed, but wherever they took it, Wyndam and Valasquez weren't long in returning. While they were gone, she went and located a mop and bucket, and was cleaning up the pooled blood on her floor when she heard them clump up the stairs, brusquely say good night, and part for their respective rooms.

When she was done swabbing, she brought the mop and bucket downstairs to put them back in the washroom, pausing first by a pantry door to pour the dark ruby water outside. Going through the pantry to the washroom, she saw the door was closed, and though she thought she'd left it open, she then thought either she was wrong or it had swung shut after her. Thinking no further, she unlatched it and walked in.

She stiffened, halting, almost dropping the mop and bucket.

Over by the laundry tubs, the rosy glow of a bracket lantern revealed Valasquez scrubbing his trousers. Naturally they had become blood-spotted from lugging the body, and naturally he had taken them off to wash, so *very* naturally he was stark naked. He wheeled around, startled, then saw Jessie and began chuckling, not in chagrin but in relief. *"Bueno, bueno.* Close the door, Señorita Starbuck."

"Sorry, I . . ." Flustered, Jessie set the mop and bucket down, preparing to retreat hastily. "I never dreamt you'd be . . . Oh, dear."

"Shut the door. Hook it, and better than I did. Pronto!"

For an instant more Jessie stared at Valasquez, who was impatiently motioning at her instead of modestly cupping his hands like a figleaf over his . . . but no figleaf could conceal the size of him, she thought dizzily. Maybe a whole fig *tree* could, if the trunk was positioned just right! And he was so nonchalant and in control that it was almost like a challenge, like another mocking trap or test.

"Well, we need to talk, anyway." Jessie shut and fastened the door, sensing her perverse response as she faced Valasquez again. "I need you to put me straight on something, Don Ramon, if you would."

"If I can. What d'you need put straight between us?"

"An uprising," she replied. "As in revolution."

"Complex and rarely straight. With the right leader, a revolt can hatch most anywhere, at most any time, for most any wild cause."

"Here? Now? To reclaim Quivera?"

"Quivera—the Northwest's Eldorado." Chuckling, Valasquez padded toward her. "Countless explorers hunted in vain for its reported riches, but found only poor native settlements. Still, despite the secrecy and disenchanted seekers, maps kept charting Quivera, and many kept believing it existed. And, though no one can reclaim what never was, revolutionary causes thrive on faith better than on fact."

He was standing close, leaning closer, so close that Jessie could feel his breath against her face, and smell the scent of his masculine body. She refused to budge, even as an intriguing tingle teased her nerves. "So there really is an active rebellion brewing?"

"So the stories go. Men are arming and drilling, I've heard, and other strange rumors of a great leader coming soon, one descended from Quiveran royalty. Even, it's whispered, one reborn—the legendary King Tatarrax, returning to life to restore his empire and people to glory."

"Hah!" she scoffed, while clenching her buttocks to resist the tendrils of desire budding in her loins. "A dead ruler revives, leads people of a mythical heritage in a revolt, and reconquers his mythical kingdom. Of all the crazy schemes!"

"But not so loco to the dirt-poor who live for hope, nor to the ignorant and superstitious who dote on faith. Plenty will believe they've family roots in Quivera, and'll accept Tatarrax or whoever it is. They've nothing to lose and, who knows, it just might work."

"But not to any good end, Don Ramon."

"Speaking of good ends . . ." Valasquez wrapped his arms around her in a wide, loose embrace. Softly he touched her, massaging, kneading, his fingers easing along her back with a gentle pressure that encouraged her to lean against him. She could hear his breath deepening, and could feel her own pulse quickening, her blood flaming through her flesh and goading her to reckless abandon.

With her last ounce of will, Jessie broke away. A slight twinge of self-consciousness stole through her as she looked at him, seeing his eyes once again roam heatedly over her clothed figure. "Let's keep to speaking the naked truth," she teased shakily.

"Just the bare facts," he replied in a husky voice that sent chills down her spine. "And one fact is, you're going to be bare."

"No, Don Ramon, not here."

"But my bed is very noisy, and any sound from yours will alert Abe."

"Well, this washroom has no bed, but Buckram is lia—"

"The doctor doped him with laudanum. Come, I'll help."

"Don Ramon, please, don't—"

Valasquez grasped her forearm in a light grip, yet it sent vibrations through her senses. And as she looked up from her arm and stared into his penetrating blue eyes, she knew he was beyond heeding her pleas . . . and, for that matter, so was she.

"We'll do fine," Valasquez said confidently, as his dexterous fingers loosened her shirt. "We'll come up with something."

Jessie stood transfixed, unable to defy him even if she'd wished to, and watched his hands roll her shirt up over the thrust of her breasts. Her glance moved to his torso, drifted lower. With a flutter of trepidation, she noticed that Don Ramon had already come up with his something, in a big way. Blinking, she extended her arms so that Valasquez could tug her shirt off.

He then knelt to undo her jeans. They were the ordinary, men's-style denims, except that they were custom tailored to fit Jessie, and Valasquez had no trouble with them once Jessie opened her derringer-concealing belt buckle. He snapped her waistband button, his eyes sparkling while he tugged her jeans down. She stepped out of them, leaving them pooled on the floor.

Remaining were her lace-edged silk drawers. But not for long, Valasquez having an intriguing ringside view of the golden delta between her thighs as he untied the drawstring and eased her drawers off her bare legs. "You are truly a *belleza delirante*, Señorita Starbuck," he murmured, drawing her hips toward him. He kissed her right upper thigh, then her left. "Yes, a raving beauty."

Slowly he rose, and there was an impact as their naked bodies slid together. Jessie curled her arms around his neck, her hardening nipples pressing against his chest, her mouth insistent and bruising against his. Valasquez moaned slightly, deep in his throat, his hands gliding down her back to cup and stroke her tensing buttocks, until Jessie found she was moaning quite a little, too.

Breaking their embrace, Valasquez ran his fingers over the mounds of her breasts and down across her smooth belly to the soft, pulsing warmth below. Jessie sighed, trembling, as she stood delighting in his caresses, and urged him to quench the fires in her loins. He kissed her lips, her cheeks, the tender hollow of her neck. Slipping lower, he darted his tongue across her hardened nipples, then moved it wetly along her abdomen, feeling the satiny skin ripple under his taunting. Above him Jessie mewled, tormented, her body quivering.

Kneeling, with Jessie standing astraddle his bent knees, Valasquez flicked his tongue playfully along the entire cleft of her plump, delicately haired mound. Again and again he swept ever deeper between her nether lips, while his mouth suckled and his lips nibbled, and Jessie whimpered in ecstatic pleasure. She twisted and writhed on quaking legs as Valasquez continued his hot liquid delving of her sensitive inner flesh, crooning as her throbbing arousal increased, her fingers entangling in his hair to keep from toppling.

"Stop, Don—Oh! Stop, before I . . . I fall over."

"Don't worry. I've got a cane that'll support you."

"You mean skewer me," she panted, convulsing as Valasquez renewed his probing of her moist, pink furrow. She shuddered, beginning to spasm, gasping and yearning.

Valasquez abruptly drew away and stood up, his hand sliding in between her legs to replace his tongue. "Come with me."

"I was coming swell, with you," she gasped frustratedly as she followed close. "Bastard!"

Valasquez led Jessie the few feet to the tub where he'd washed his trousers. He produced a chair from back alongside the tub. "Buckram probably stands on it." The chair was an armless dining-room type and, swiftly positioning it, Valasquez sat and grinned lewdly. "But I plan to ride on it."

"Rest on it, y'mean. You're already winded," Jessie teased, well aware of what he meant.

Kneeling between his legs as she spoke, she bent closer and used both hands to clasp his erection. Her eyes closed and her mouth opened, and her pink tongue fluted out to lick the crown of his manhood.

Valasquez shivered. "Easy. . ."

Jessie ignored his plaintive warning, fitting her mouth over to swallow him whole. Her teeth scraped along his aching girth as she tightened her lips and began a tentative sucking motion, her hands stroking his thighs, gently squeezing, while she bobbed her mouth up and down. Valasquez gasped and grimaced, his body shuddering as she sucked harder and absorbed more of his shaft into her mouth, his hips beginning to flex in concert, his groin boiling, threatening to volcano. He fought to hold back, muscles stiffening, sensations billowing exquisitely until he could feel it was too late, his climax rushing to the verge.

Jessie released him, standing up and smiling demurely. "Turn about's fair play, Don Ramon."

"Heartless woman!" Then he laughed. "Climb on."

She turned around and pressed back, leaning with legs splayed wide and her bottom squatting over his spearing erection. Then she sat down, feeling his warm thickness throbbing against the crevice of her buttocks. She draped one leg and then the other over each of his legs, so that she balanced astride his pelvis and thighs. She reached under with her right hand and grasped his hard girth, positioning his blunt crown, her wide-stretched loins absorbing the width of his stabbing shaft as she thrust herself slowly yet eagerly upon it.

She hunched forward, wriggling a little to ease his entry, then levered on his massive erection as she leaned back, gasping. She glued her mouth on his and played moaning, electrifying tongue games with him. Her distended nipples and aching breasts throbbed sensuously as Valasquez fondled and massaged them, while she ground, undulating, until she contained all of his rigid, lust-burgeoning rod within her.

Valasquez asked, "Too much? Hurt?"

"Yes . . . no!" Jessie twisted on him and felt his swollen bulk stir and shift in her. She began sliding on him, slowly at first, then with increasing enthusiasm. Her head sagged, then tautened again in arousal, her mouth opening and closing in mute testimony to the savage sensations plundering her loins, her long blond hair swaying and brushing down her back and against his chest.

Valasquez continued toying with her breasts, drawing hoarse moans from her slackened lips. She arched her back against him for a whisper of a kiss, then curved forward to plunge deeper, faster. Bending, she could see their merging loins in the dim lantern light.

Her breathing ragged and openmouthed, the erection pummeling her, she felt the searing pulsations from her gripping inner sheath. She heard Valasquez gasping against her back, their tempo matching as they raced for completion.

"*Venga rápido*—come quickly!" Valasquez urged. "*Venga!*"

140

Her passage kept rhythmically squeezing, squeezing. Finally Valasquez began a low grunting, his body quivering. A warning rumbled inside Jessie, a gathering tremor like the advance of an earthquake. She poised, breathless, tensing . . . felt Valasquez shuddering, and his warm eruption spewing far up inside . . . and that triggered her orgasm.

She wept, her nails raking Valasquez's legs. He wrapped his arms around her and tilted back a little, hugging her tight while her loins milked and her belly spasmed around his erupting shaft. Her legs twitched kicking as she nuzzled hard against Valasquez, her face contorted with her jolting release.

Gradually they relaxed. Valasquez remained buried in her, becoming flaccid, yet still feeling very large to her. She cuddled against him with her head on his shoulder, the calves of her legs hooked across his knees. Valasquez nuzzled her hair, tenderly kissing her earlobes, still pumping slowly with a dwindling erection.

He chuckled, a satisfied sound. "Nice, very nice . . ."

"Very nice indeed . . ."

"There's more."

"Oh-ho! Listen to the man brag," Jessie teased. "But we really should be calling it a night, Don Ramon, before someone calls the night on us. In a few minutes . . . Then we'll get dressed . . ."

They sank back into shared lethargy now that their bodies had shared passion. Gradually Jessie became more aware of the sweet ache in her stretched loins, the fatigue of her whole sore body. She sighed, thinking it was about time to ask him to withdraw, but then she felt his manhood regaining hardness and length.

"God . . ." she murmured, shivering. She was drained, aching, yet as Valasquez continued his gentle thrusting, she found that her loins were responding in kind. She choked it down for a moment until, despite herself, she moaned softly as she sensed those familiar erotic throbs starting to pulse between her thighs.

"Oh, all right, you've good reason to brag," Jessie wheezed. "You're insatiable."

141

"So are you."

Jessie began undulating, feeling passion rekindling inside her. "If we are, I guess we are . . . But again like this?"

"It's your turn for ideas, Señorita Starbuck. Pick one."

She did.

Chapter 15

Ki was after ideas, too—for hot-footing, not hot sex.

He began as soon as he was locked in the back room. While the three outlaws left and the one named Flagg started to cook, Ki was working on the rope around his wrists and looking for means of escape.

The room was dark, though light from the cabin's main room slipped through a half-inch-wide crack between the door and the jamb. The slivered glow revealed the room to be small and trashy, with shelves and a tiny barred window. The walls were of stout logs fitted closely together. The floor was of thick-slabbed planks, as was the door, whose iron strap hinges were secured by heavy screws driven deep into the wood. The door's outer bolt was unreachable, and nothing inside was usable as a crowbar or battering ram. Anyhow, such a breakout would require Flagg to go off a while, and he doubtless had no more intention of taking a hike than he had of opening the door.

While he was considering the room, Ki sat and freed his wrists. Purposefully, methodically, he dislocated the bones of his wrists, then his hands, even his fingers. By carefully twisting and stretching his ligaments and muscles, he slowly wormed his limp, formless flesh through the enlooping rope. Finally the coils dropped to the floor.

Snapping his bones back into joint, Ki began a thorough

search of the gloomy room. That he remained in a predicament was all too evident. He gathered from what the outlaws had said that their mysterious boss knew him, or knew of him, implying an awareness of Jessie and, perhaps, an acquaintance with their mission. At any rate, this boss judged him a menace fit to kill, and would kill, come tomorrow.

Ki could hear Flagg eating, and the tantalizing aromas of coffee, steak, and potatoes only made it worse, reminding him of his own hunger. The outlaw washed the dishes, and went outside twice to either fetch or pass water. Both times he returned within minutes, certainly not long enough a spell for Ki to have bashed through the door, even if he had found something to do it with, which he had not. He continued searching doggedly, reaching the window just as boots dropped, a bunk creaked, and the light dimmed low. Ki leaned against the window sill, listening and watching.

The bars he peered through were crisscrossed iron rods, firmly imbedded in the solid beams that framed the opening. The sky beyond was foggy, obscuring the moon and stars, and Ki could discern little other than a dark mass of foliage growing near the cabin wall.

The night was rather quiet, save for Flagg in the next room. He yawned, belched noisily, presently farted, and gradually settled into a steady rumbling snore. Outside the window came an occasional stamp or snort from one of the horses hobbled nearby. From the black depths of some yonder canyon drifted the lonely plaint of a timber wolf. An owl perched amid the pines responded with a mournful call. A slight breeze soughed in with the fog from the ocean, rustling the branches.

Ki moved from the window and hunted on, checking the shelves, scrounging through the trash, to no avail. He eventually ended back at the door, which he again examined with care. The bolt which held it shut was obviously ponderous and snug-latching. The planks felt rough but ungiving as he ran his hands over them, testing for play. His fingers rubbed along the pitted surfaces of the strap hinges, his nails scraping at the slotted heads of their screws, digging into the rusty grooves.

Abruptly he stiffened, his eyes widening. One screw, it

144

seemed, felt a trifle loose. Swiftly he tried the rest and found them to be as tight as those before this one. Yet a single loose fastening might indicate that the wood of the jamb was softened from dry rot. If so, he might just possibly be able to remove the screws, assuming he had something to serve as a screwdriver. And, come to consider, he had.

From his vest Ki took a precision-balanced throwing knife. Its honed edge fit easily into the head-slot of the supposedly loose screw, and after some persuasion the screw came out, but the knife edge got kinked while he was turning it. Ki sadly regarded his bent dagger, then promptly warped it further by prying on the next screw, which was stubbornly tight. Finally, with much effort and many crimps, he cracked the second screw, applied more leverage, and soon had it set aside with the first.

But there were four screws in each of the straps securing the hinges to the jamb. Before he had unseated them all, Ki was sweat-soaked, his hands were sorely cramped, and three expertly crafted daggers were mangled ruins. When the last screw came free, the door sagged slightly against the jamb. After making sure it would stay put, Ki sagged wearily against the wall until his strength returned. Then he cautiously approached the door again. Flagg continued to snore, fast asleep in one of the bunks. No other sound disturbed the peace.

Carefully insinuating his fingers into the crack between the door and the jamb, Ki gave it a gentle, tentative tug. The door creaked, swaying inward. With meticulous care he drew it toward him little by little, until he could get a firm grip on the boards. Then, summoning his inner energy, Ki hefted the door and wrenched, twisting, ripping it unbolted with a metallic screech. It swung inward and he pitched it behind him. The door slammed thunderously against the floor while Ki bounded through the opening toward the dark-shrouded row of bunks.

Startled awake, Flagg barked cursing from one of the black recesses. Ki veered for the bed-thrashing yell, readying a *shuriken* to fling the instant he could discern his target, glimpsing instead a wavery gleam of metal, and hastily swerving aside. Gunfire blazed in his face, lead snapping past one ear in the erupting billow of smoke and flame. Blinded and deafened, Ki leaped headlong into the powder-clouded bunk and plunged, groping for the pistol. He missed it, but caught hold of Flagg's gun arm before the outlaw could trigger again.

"Leggo, you fuckin'—!" Abruptly Flagg stopped ranting and started howling as Ki squeezed vulnerable nerve points with piercing fingertips. He lashed at Ki with his left hand, squirming and jerking to break free, but Ki increased his grinding pressure while yanking savagely on the arm, pulling Flagg far enough out of the bunk space to grab the pistol without fear of shooting himself. He bent it back, fracturing Flagg's trigger finger with the spasmodic firing of one shot, the bullet drilling up through the thin mattress of the bunk above.

Ignoring the explosive blast and smoke, Ki kept on dragging Flagg from the bunk as he tore the pistol loose and lobbed it away. The outlaw was squawling and struggling, but was still half dazed with sleep, frantic from the paralyzing pain in his right arm, and rattled by it all happening too fast in a single fell swoop. One instant Ki was tugging his outflung arm, the next Ki was dipping to a knee and scooping Flagg into a *seoi-otoshi*, a kneeling shoulder-throw, adding a small variation of the "flying mare" toss to increase momentum.

Flagg arched through the air and landed on his back, screaming as his pelvis cracked. He ceased screaming as Ki kicked in the side of his head, shattering the temple bone, causing instant death.

Giving Flagg a quick, slightly sad smile, Ki turned away.

Free now, he had a desire to make tracks. On the stove, however, were some pan-fried potatoes, a chunk of raw beefsteak, and half a pot of coffee. Resisting his cabin fever, Ki lighted the lamp, stoked the still glowing coals, and cooked a quick, satisfying meal, which he ate while prowling around. Other than the stacked gold ingots, there was not much worth finding—not that is, until he poked into a bulky cupboard wedged in a rear corner.

The cupboard resembled a big, double-doored wardrobe. Opening the doors, Ki stared amazed at an interior whose depth stretched beyond the cabin rear. Not till he stepped in with his lamp did he realize that the cupboard fronted another back room, the twin of his prison in the opposite corner. The contents were also a surprise. The lamp glow reflected off the parallel barrels of four dozen or more carbines propped neatly in racks. A spot inspection showed Ki they were all '73 or '76 Winchesters, mostly .44-40s, either new or in mint condition. Stacked alongside the carbines were cases of ammunition.

Someone was sure collecting quality arms in quantity, Ki mused as he closed the cupboard. So much firepower indicated the gang was considerably larger than was supposed. It would be such a pity if all that weaponry went up in flames. Trouble was, that was exactly what it would do, go up in a spectacular blast that'd draw every owlhoot swarming.

A swift survey of the rest of the cabin revealed nothing more of interest. As he ate the last of his meal, Ki thought of going now. Obviously this cabin was a long way from town, but he had only the vaguest notion of where he was, and none at all of how to reach town. It would take time, and already it was well past midnight.

Grimly Ki eyed the stacks of ingots, and knew all his arguing to leave was just pissing in the wind. Perhaps a cabin fire was too risky. So maybe the gang could keep their carbines another day. But they weren't going to get the gold, at least, decidedly not that.

Ki set to work hauling the gold. The hobbled horses afforded no difficulty, but loading twenty hundred-pound ingots into their packsaddles was an exhausting task. When he was finally done, Ki geared up one of the saddle horses and mounted. Leading the string of burdened horses, he moved out down the canyon.

Fog continued drifting inland from the sea, its whiskery tendrils curling amid the woods and rocks. Ki rode the mists cautiously, alert for gunmen as well as for recognizable landmarks. He sensed he was generally following a west-northwest heading that should bring him eventually to the coast, or the Rogue, or anyway someplace within a reasonable distance of town. But now the terrain was reversed for him and opaqued by fog, and the stars were too obscured for him to take any bearings. Keeping on his mental trail became one lengthy headache.

Half a dozen times, Ki had to rein in the pack train to study the deceiving perspectives. Twice he found he'd strayed off course, and had to backtrack, tempering his impatience. Once he got lost and wound up in a box canyon, turned the string around, then passed the point where he should have resumed his unmarked way, and had to reverse the string back again. He moved on through the early night hours, slowed by the shambling pace of the weary, overladen horses, near exhaustion himself, but grimly hanging on to complete the chore.

Jessie awoke from a restless sleep. Alone in the dark silence of her room, she drowsily lay recovering her wits. Presently she eased, dressed but unbooted, from bed, her body stiff and throbbing with a peculiar satisfying ache. Moving slowly and gently, she lit a lamp, groomed as best she could, then slipped on her boots and gunbelt and quietly left Buckram's.

Outside was soupy gray, a fog-diffused dawn barely rimming the hills. The posse was to muster soon, but Jessie was set to take off now. After all, her search for Ki might lead in a different direction from the posse's hunt for gold. Anyway, like most impromptu groups, the posse would probably get rolling late and trail noisily in a bunch. Scanning the crestline of the otherwise murky slopes only fueled her resolve, and hoping for clearing sky by the time she reached Ki's tracks, Jessie headed toward the livery stable, a slight shuffle to her walk.

At this hour the town was dead, not surprisingly, though a few far voices of fishermen starting their day echoed from up by the river mouth. The street was hushed and deserted, lightless save for a pearly glow in the sheriff's office window. Also unsurprising, Jessie thought as she approached; Lydell was the posse boss, and most of the possemen must have already gathered in his office, judging by the number of horses lining the hitchrails there—

Jessie halted and stared. She rubbed her eyes and stared again.

Half expecting a mirage, she rushed diagonally across the street to the horses. They looked real, and *whew!* smelled for true, and felt solid as she skimmed her touch over the sweaty, sway-footed, slumping mounts and their stretched, seam-bursting, lumpy packs.

Jessie darted around to the sheriff's office, sprang up the steps, and burst through the door. "Ki! Where's Ki?"

Sheriff Lydell was seated with his legs on the desk, on duty with his eyes closed. The boots reared up and the chair sailed over when Jessie dashed in, her sharp, impulsive query drowned by a flustered howl from the sheriff, a brief yet moving cry which choked off abruptly in a jarring, tumbling crash. The impacted chair and floorboards wobbled and splintered but managed not to break, while years of suddenly disturbed dust and grit fountained up from behind the desk and rained sifting down from the ceiling.

"Sheriff Lydell?" Jessie fanned the air. "Sheriff?"

"Nigh scared the shi— Er, what's the idea?" Wreathed in dust, Lydell clambered up and righted the chair, his eyes glowering. "Wall? What et yuh, to cannon in brayin' and pouncin' at an innercent lawman?"

"Sorry, I was excited. Y'know, we learned some about the train from tracking it yesterday, and I was flabbergasted when I saw a train here that fit. When I checked and discovered it's *the* train with *the* gold, why, I'm afraid I got carried away. From now on I'll knock. But never mind me," Jessie said impatiently. "How in heaven's name did the train get here, and from where? And where's Ki? Tell me!"

"Ain't much to tell. Ki rode the string in twenty, no more'n thirty minutes ago. Not bad hurt, just worn to a frazzle and needin' a bed. He turns the train over to me, not that there's much 'sides keeping an eye on it I can do till morning. Soon's the town stirs, I'll send word to Antelope and have the horses tended," Lydell explained, then lapsed into silence as he settled gingerly back in his chair.

"And?" Jessie prodded.

"And nothin'. Ki refused to tell. Said he'd talk in the morning, so he wouldn't waste sleep time now repeating hisself, and did I know o' any beds at this hour. I tol' him to go tumble on the bunk in there." Lydell thumbed toward the door of the dark cell. "Conked right out. He must've been beat to fall asleep in his position."

Jessie went into the cell. It was dim, yet enough light spilled in from the office lantern for Jessie to discern Ki quite clearly. He sat motionless on the bunk, cross-legged, arms crossed, with his hands cupping his ears—a position Jessie had seen him in countless times, and knew he used for more than simple relaxation. To a Westerner such as Sheriff Lydell, Ki's posture looked peculiar and uncomfortable; to an Oriental, one versed in the martial arts, it was a vital position for strengthening his intrinsic energy, that inner force which was fundamental to health, power, agility, and clarity.

Relieved simply to see him here and basically well, Jessie left the cell and let Ki savor his brief respite undisturbed. She told the sheriff, "I doubt Ki even twitched, when your chair dumped over."

"Y'mean he's still fiddled in a granny knot?"

Jessie nodded, her lips quirking. "And I didn't try to change him. People that hard asleep shouldn't be moved or tampered with."

"Has my blessin', if he wishes to sleep that way, 'cause it gives me a handle to grab him fast by. I'll be setting beside him when he wakes up, and all his contortin' better not've harmed his voice box!"

Sheriff Lydell was as good as his word. When Ki awoke around mid-morning, the lawman was sitting beside the bunk. Waiting as well in the office were Abe Wyndam, who greeted Ki enthusiastically, and Jessie, who smiled warmly, though her face looked drawn from lack of rest. It did to Ki, at least, and her usual svelte grace seemed hampered by a rather bowlegged gait, yet he had the decent sense not to mention it.

"Okay, untether your tongue," Lydell demanded. "What happened?"

Ki told them, in detail. There were questions and interruptions, and digressions into last night's attack on Jessie and so forth, but for the most part Ki just talked, explaining completely yet quickly to get it over with, uneasy whenever he was the focus of any such hoopla.

"Well, if this don't skin the hide off the bull," Lydell marveled when Ki was through. "What'd you say you used to loosen them hinges?"

"Oh, a little strip of metal I had on me," Ki hedged, then turned thoughtfully to Jessie. "The fact of the cabin backs up your idea, Jessie, that there's one gang staying close around the area."

She nodded. "You think they headed there after Abe's fire?"

"I didn't find anything pointing to it. Maybe, but I kind of suspect the cabin is an outpost, one of several, and not the main hole."

"Sounds probable," the sheriff agreed. "I'll give it a real thorough goin'-over, though, soon's I go locate it."

Ki grinned. "Good luck. I sure can't tell you where it is or lead you there. In time I might, by working out my back-trail, but I doubt it's worth busting a gut over. Two seconds after the gang finds me gone and Flagg dead, the cabin will be stripped empty and abandoned. Of course, when nothing happens, they may start using it again, so perhaps in a week we might give it a try."

"About when my cow drive'll be done, if I can ever get goin'," Wyndam grouched, eyeing the sheriff. "You got any more need of us?"

"Well, it ain't I can't use help and ain't grateful for all y'all did, but I don't need you here courting trouble." Lydell paused, his face grave. "Miz Starbuck, them hellers made a stab at you last night, and now they'll really be after you and Ki. They ain't goin' to forget losin' the gold. I hate to say it, but I've a notion the best thing you two can do is to ride outa this region pronto."

"Good advice," Jessie allowed. "We're not taking it."

"Didn't reckon you would," Lydell admitted. "So do us all a favor and stick with Abe and his crew for protection. Just a while, till we thin the gang down more. We've already got a good start at whittlin', and at this rate they soon won't have enough to operate with."

"They'll always get enough, so long as the head of the gang is running free," Jessie responded with conviction. "I've got a notion, too, Sheriff, that they counted on the gold, and losing it will put a crimp in their plans. I'm afraid we're soon to hear from them again."

Shortly the three left the sheriff and headed for the livery. On the way, Ingram Harcourt came riding toward them at a very slow lope, sitting erect and soldierly, left hand resting on his hip, his face wearily blank and his eyes gazing off, preoccupied in thought.

Glancing at Harcourt as he drew even, Jessie had an unpleasant, uncertain impression which lasted for a scant instant. For right then the rancher turned, noticed them, and smiled genially.

"Glad you pulled out of that ruckus all right, Ki," he called in cordial greeting. "Lydell told me about it. You did a fine job."

They returned his greeting pleasantly and continued to walk as Harcourt moved on past. After a few yards, Jessie took a quick peek back over her shoulder, curious, and glimpsed Harcourt still on the saddle, gazing moodily into space. Whatever intuitive fancy had sparked in her, though, was cold and gone now. Jessie shrugged it off.

★

Chapter 16

Work on the shipping herd began late that afternoon, and was projected to last for the next several days. Wyndam split his North Moon crew roughly in half, with the foreman Prescoe in charge of those riding herd, and his niece Opal advising those clearing the fire debris. Jessie and Ki pitched in as well, and continued to bunk in the barn with Wyndam and Opal, although Ki warned the girl he would move in with the crew if she didn't let him also *sleep* in the hay once in a while.

As Wyndam predicted, the ranch had enough beeves for a fair drive, but it was no easy task to round them up. The gather was done with deliberation, for the cows were heavy with flesh and fat, the punchers scattering to comb the foothills and gullies carefully for hiding cattle.

Before the North Moon herd was finally ready for the drive, cutbacks and culls would be separated from the beef cut. Wyndam, with an eye to a possible raid by the gang operating in the section, personally selected the holding spot where the cutting would be done, a shallow box canyon with perpendicular walls two hundred feet high, virtually impossible to enter except by way of the mouth. There the herd, growing steadily day by day, was held and bedded, guarded by shifts of armed crewmen around the clock.

Wyndam felt ease of mind the night before the final cutting and preparation for the drive. He and Jessie rode out there that evening, about the time Ki was finishing a tour of work, and he voiced satisfaction to them as he gazed at the canyon-penned cattle.

"The boys done good, considerin' the short notice. Choused in more critters than I expected, and nary a speck o' trouble, either."

Past the cattle, farther back in the stubby canyon, was a brush corral for the horses of those assigned to guard duty. The guards themselves were comfortably camped under the overhang of the cliff, their position only assailable from the front, and nobody seriously feared that the outlaws would attempt such a suicidal attack. Beyond the canyon mouth was open field on the east. But on the west was a long slope densely grown with timber and scrub, and it bothered Ki.

"Before it gets dark, I want to ride a quick sweep in through there," he said, glancing at the sunset blazing behind the western crags. "You start back to the ranch without me, and I'll catch up."

"I 'preciate your concern, Ki, and I won't stop yuh," Wyndam replied, "but everythin' around here's been scoured for unwanted gents."

"I think I know what's nudging Ki," Jessie remarked with a light smile. "We had an experience with one of our neighbors, who was holding a herd in a *vallecito* boxed much like this one. Nobody could get into it without passing the guard at the mouth, and that was fine, but they neglected to know for sure what was back in that pocket. As it happened, some rustlers hid there the day before the herd was assembled for trailing, waited till dark, then tore out, shooting the guard and stampeding the herd. You just can't take anything for granted."

"You're darn right we can't," Wyndam agreed heartily. "Have at it, Ki, and I'll get the boys to again at daybreak. If you're sure you don't want me to side yuh, I'll take yuh up on your offer and head back. I'm hungry an' wrung out, an' hankerin' to get home."

"I'm sure. You go on, too, Jessie. I'm only scratching an itch."

"Well . . . it has been a hard day," she admitted. Leaving

Ki, she settled in the saddle for the long ride back with Wyndam.

Turning, Ki sent his buckskin trotting into the canyon, deciding to check the outer slope after he made a survey down around the walls, where dusk would collect earlier and thicker. It took him longer than he thought, for the base of the cliffs was haphazardly bordered by a jumble of rocks, underbrush, and debris that required time-consuming scrutiny. Meanwhile, the hands guarding the herd were heeding the cook's strident bellow to "Come 'n' get it or I'll toss it!" On the little shelf beneath the overhang they filled their plates and cups, and Ki cast frequent glances their way, his stomach growling as he watched them shovel food away with an appetite rivaling his.

Presently he worked his way around to the horse corral. Dismounting, he hitched his horse by water and fodder, figuring it could use a short break before hitting the slope and the long return trek. He then walked to the shelf, about a hundred or so yards farther, where the men were mopping up seconds and hinting for thirds. Lou Prescoe, who was chewing as contentedly as the cows on their cuds, sauntered over and asked Ki if he wanted to grab a dish and chow in.

"Thanks, but I'll be eating back at the ranch shortly," Ki declined reluctantly. "I'm going up on that slope and maybe some of the canyon rim first, though, so tip off your boys that if they hear something, not to pop trigger-happy until they're sure it's not me."

"I'll pass the word. Smart o' you to let us know, too, 'cause standin' orders are to shoot and then ask," Prescoe said. "Not that I reckon anyone'll be idjit enough to try scalley-hootin' the cows, but we ain't taking no chances. Ol' Abe would nail our balls to the barn door if anything happened to his herd. We . . . *What'n hellzat?*"

From the cliff top two hundred feet above, something dome-shaped spun hurtling through the air, landed in the horse corral with a smash, and flew to a thousand fragments. As the astounded crewmen leaped up from eating, another followed it, then another and another, some striking within the corral, others dropping among the cattle.

"Them's hives!" Clem Shore yelled, clapping both hands

to his rump in painful remembrance. "Someone's chuckin' beehives off the rimrock! Yeow! An' them ain't empty hives, neither! Look out!"

To their horror, the others saw Shore was right. From the broken ruins of the hives swarmed thousands of enraged bees, all spoiling for a fight and ready to take it out on anything to hand. Almost immediately the frantic horses in the corral were speckled with yellow demons. Nor did the cattle lack for attention.

The maddened horses vaulted the corral and fled up the canyon, trying to escape the countless stings that stabbed at their sensitive ears and other exposed parts. Into the milling herd they charged, kicking and biting. At this onslaught the cattle, already fractious with fright and wild with pain, stampeded all at once, all together. In a frenzied mass of rolling eyes, clashing shorthorns, and thundering hooves, the Oregon-bred Holsteins matched Texas Longhorns in blind rampaging, surging from the canyon mouth with the horses slashing their way through the herd and taking the lead.

"After them cayuses!" Prescoe roared.

The crew and Ki sprang from the shelf and headed up canyon, only to meet clouds of vengeful bees. Another second and they were in full flight down the canyon, howling and cursing and slapping and thrashing. Into the brush they dived pell-mell, burrowing deeper in hopes the bees could not get at them. As they scrambled around to peer back at the swirling enemy, Bertie Harte pointed and shouted.

"Hey! Hey, looky out there! We's being robbed!"

His swearing companions saw over a dozen masked men riding out from the wooded slope in the wake of the fleeing cattle. They swiftly overhauled the herd, spread around it, guiding, compacting.

"The rifles!" Prescoe raged. "Get the rifles and line sights with the cussed wideloopers! We can't let 'em get away!"

The men gamely tried to obey orders, but their rifles were on the bench beneath the overhang. Between them and the spot were clouds of bees still hunting for trouble. Although Ki had no firearm there to retrieve, he joined the efforts as three times the punchers strove to reach the bench. Three times they were driven back, many with faces puffed, some with eyes swollen almost shut.

"It ain't no use!" Shore moaned. "We'll hafta hole up here in the brush till it's black-dark and the li'l shits can't see us."

Again Shore proved correct. Not before full night had fallen were they able to sneak from their retreat, collect their gear, and begin limping in their high-heeled boots on the long tramp to the ranch proper. Ki was lucky in that he wore flat slippers and wasn't stung too badly, yet somehow his fortune failed to hearten him one whit.

When, hours later, they straggled in and reported, Abe Wyndam had a fit but didn't lay blame. "Stampedin' a herd with bees. Now there's a wild new wrinkle!" he declared. "That many of 'em, mad as they'd be after bein' brought that distance in plugged-up hives, would've stampeded a herd o' elephants! Aw'right, where'd the cows go?"

"West, that's all we saw. We was busy." Prescoe dabbed his bee-stung nose, wincing. "Some fast way outa the valley, I bet is where."

"Southwest, out by way of the Whisper Path,' Jessie suggested.

"Most likely." Wyndam nodded, his face screwed in a bleak scowl. "Lou, how many of the crew'll be willing to ride after them rustlers?"

"All," Prescoe stated flatly. The others nodded agreement.

"Gettin' everybody would take too long and it'd leave the spread wide empty," Wyndam countered, mulling this over. "Besides, someone's gotta notify the sheriff to foller us with a posse. And ol' Eustace York oughta be checked on. They couldn't have swiped his hives in daylight without downin' him first, I just hope not permanently. So what say to four or a half-dozen remaining here with the women—"

"This woman is going," Jessie corrected.

"Oh, nobody should go," Opal snapped fretfully. "The rustlers will certainly be on the lookout, and if you did catch up with them, chances are you'd only get yourselves trapped. Please don't try!"

Wyndam regarded his niece, his features almost vindic-

157

tive. "Now, don't you worry, we'll be ready and careful—to spill their blood. Don't get no notions either, child. You ain't no investor pullin' rank. You're staying to help here." He sighed then, and looked sternly at Prescoe. "Okay, Lou, give the boys their druthers, but be quick about it. The skylarkers got a long head start on us, but it's a hard pull through the notch, and the cows are heavy and'll slow 'em down. If we get bustlin', we might have a chance."

In a short time, most of the North Moon crew were tracking out of the ranch yard. Even the swollen-faced, half-blind victims of the bees were included, along with Jessie, Ki, and Wyndam, as they swept in massed force toward the Whisper Path, their horses irons ringing across the valley grazeland. At length they cut into the gloom of the southern hills, the timbered flanks rolling upward till their jagged crests stood out pale and silver in the misty moonlight. Soon they were urging their mounts up along the devious Whisper Path. As swiftly as possible they climbed, the outlaw trail shrouded in dark peril, each stony gap and forest thicket a potential menace.

"No question the herd passed here," Wyndam said, noting fresh droppings and puddles of urine. "Still a helluva ways ahead of us, though. C'mon, you lummoxes, lather sweat! We ain't licked yet!"

They snaked higher, peering for ambushes, the night quiet like a hushed yet vibrant warning to their suspicious ears. Up to the summit's craggy notch and into the crooked black pass they thundered, watchful and alert. But they found no trace of the rustlers there, nor on the long decline that curved through a hollow, skirted some wooded banks, and weaved among a series of wind-buffeted ridges and tables.

Whisper Path would be a dream for an outlaw, Jessie perceived. If pursuit became too hot, he'd be able to leave the trail and strike out on either side, where he'd be swallowed by upland forest. She turned to Wyndam. "They might turn off somewhere down there," she cautioned. "We'll have to take double care to watch for tracks."

"Well, they might," Wyndam conceded, "but I'm far more worried they'll drive the entire Path on through to

Crescent City. It's a raw port town, I happen t'know, wide open for smugglers and the like. Once they get there, my beef'll vanish like the earth swallered them."

The trail ribboned on, capping a knoll and lazily rutting southward along meadowed steppes. An offshore breeze, fanning in from the southwest, flitted erratically among the fringing crags and trees and, like air pumped through organ pipes, produced low, mournful notes as if soughing a dirge. It gave Jessie a chill, and when she rose in her stirrups to stare ahead, the funereal sounds almost seemed to be blowing at them from the dark, pursed mouth of a canyon a mile beyond.

"I'm hearing Opal's warning," she murmured cryptically to Ki, and as they neared the canyon, she slid her carbine from its scabbard.

Like a signal, her move prompted the others to follow suit with rifles or sidearms. Ki alone did not draw, though he had accepted the loan of a saddle carbine just in case of need for long-range weaponry.

The trail bored deeper into another stretch of hills. Gradually the canyon grew narrower, the sides closing in until it eventually funneled to a ravine. The high, steep banks were shaggy mats of high grasses and vines, interspersed with clinging clumps of shrubs and stunted trees, all rippling gently in the breeze moaning up the defile.

Hoping to anticipate danger points, Ki tried to scan the slopes further on, but the Path twisted and the foliage screened so that at no time could he see any appreciable distance. The trail sign left by the passing cattle was easier to discern, however, and after studying the marks a while, he said, "We're gaining, and they're slowing."

Wyndam nodded. "The cows would've got almighty tired by now."

"That's a help, but . . ." Jessie sighed, shaking her head. "Abe, if Crescent City is as bad as you say, then the rustlers are liable to have a buyer already lined up waiting. They'll deal fast, outside town, making two gangs for us to brace even if we could find them in time."

"Yep, it'll be touch 'n' go to catch 'em. So let's go."

Wyndam quickened his horse's pace until the hooves beat

a drumroll on the hardpan surface of the trail. The horses of the others were hard put to keep up along the winding bed of the ravine. Jessie let her gaze rove freely, still restless from the lamenting wind in her face, while Ki's eyes continued surveying the brushy slopes ahead.

Suddenly Ki sniffed sharply, catching a familiar odor. Jessie then whiffed the same pungent tang of burning wood, and was beginning to frown quizzically when Wyndam growled, "I must be barmy. Them wideloopers surely wouldn't have stopped to build a campfire and cook!"

Now some of the other riders spoke up, questioning the smell, and eyes began focusing intently on the surrounding skyline. It seemed to Ki that yonder ahead was slightly hazier than before. Even as he gazed, the haze deepened, becoming a darker smear against the soft black of the night sky, and wisping swiftly northward on the wings of the wind. Another moment and it was a cloudy smudge pluming above the rimrock, quickly thickening, increasing in volume and blowing toward them.

"There! See?" Ki called pointing. "They torched the brush!"

Wyndam blurted a curse. "Whoa up, boys! The way's blocked."

The group reined to a jostling halt. Seated on their panting horses, the crewmen gabbed and stared at the boiling cloud ahead.

"This won't do," Jessie snapped testily. "The fire's coming this way fast, and we have to get out of here before we're trapped!"

A wild yell from one of the rearmost riders answered her. "We're trapped already! Lawd o' May, look at the smoke b'ilin' up behind us!"

Jessie turned, craning, as did the others, her face setting in granite lines as she saw a dense gush against the night sky in back of them. The smoke was in line with the canyon, and though too dark to discern, the fire was undoubtedly burning down close to the trail.

For a brief moment the alarmed crew erupted babbling, until Ki's voice, cool and incisive, stilled the tumult. "We'll have to climb the slope," he stated. "It's all we can do.

160

Rustlers've set fires in front, and a few must've hidden back behind to light more after we'd passed by. It'll be hard going, but hurry, up to the left here!"

"The right slope looks easier," Prescoe countered.

"Yes," Ki agreed grimly, "and chances are they'll figure we'll take it because it *is* easier. And we're apt as not to run smack into a few more gunmen holed up on the rimrock, all set to blow us apart."

Wyndam nodded. "You got a point, Ki. Go left, boys, single file so's you can help anyone whose hoss goes down. If shootin' starts, just keep a-goin'. The fire's deadlier'n lead right now."

Into the brush they spurred their nervous mounts. White-eyed and half spooked, the snorting horses gamely tackled the steep ascent. The thick, entangling vegetation retarded their progress. There were spaces of slippery earth and slides of loose shale, and gravel rolled under their irons. From the south, dense clouds of smoke were rolling before the sepulchral wind. Soon there were sparks and whirling brands, and before the riders were halfway up the slope, they could hear the seething crackle of flames consuming grass and brush.

The undergrowth was not tinder-dry, but it didn't need to be, for once a ground-fire started burning solidly, it created its own parching vortex. The heat indeed became oppressive, the air almost unbreathable. Clouds of ashes sifted down, causing riders and horses to cough and gasp. They were relieved when, some two-thirds of the way up, the greenery thinned. The relief was short-lived, for as the lead horses clambered into the open, something whined ricochetting off a rock.

"Je-hosaphat! You reckoned right, Ki, there are bush-whackers up 'cross on the east slope!" Wyndam shouted. "And we're in range!"

Ki nodded, his eyes cold, his lean face hard-set. "Ride!" he called to the rancher, even as he was reining in by a shelf of stone. Snatching his carbine from its saddle sheath, he dismounted and ducked into the shadows of the shelf. Gouts of powdersmoke were blossoming up from the distant rimrock across the ravine. Slugs were whipping all around him, but the rolling smoke made accurate shooting difficult, and Ki ignored the buzz of lead as he shouldered his borrowed carbine, eyes glinting along the sights. He triggered, levered, fired again, and kept on raking the rimrock until the carbine was empty.

The ragged salvos of other firearms burst from here and there, yet Ki paid them little mind as he concentrated on swiftly reloading. While he was thumbing in fresh cartridges, a clump of brush tufting the opposite rim was violently agitated, and peripherally he glimpsed a body pitch from it and tumble down the slope.

"Got one!" he heard Jessie call. Turning, Ki saw her smiling with grim satisfaction from a spot of cover diagonally up behind him. She motioned with her carbine. "C'mon, Ki, the fire's closing in!"

Glancing along the sag, Ki could see the blaze racing out of the south. With an answering wave, he resheathed his carbine, mounted, and heeled his horse, charging toward Jessie. "C'mon, yourself!"

The air was clogged with ash and sparks and glowing embers, and the billowing smoke restricted their vision to a few yards. Jessie and Ki muffled their noses and mouths in their neckerchiefs, leaning low across their horses withers and urging greater speed. The horses screamed as reaching tongues of flame licked their hocks, but continued to bound forward, upward, into the scalloped wall of flame.

Jessie gasped with the unbearable heat. Ki felt the sting of the fire against his face, hearing in his ears a mighty roar. They both buried their faces in their horses' manes and, reeling in their saddles, twined their fingers in the coarse-haired manes and held on with a death grip. The fire raged about them. Flames singed their hair, their eyebrows, the smoke a stifling cloud thick with ash and sprinkled with lung-searing sparks.

Then, abruptly, they were in comparatively clear air once more. Behind them the fire boomed and snapped. Ahead the growth continued thinning until it petered out, leaving several hundred sheer yards of naked stone and earth swelling to the beetling rimrock.

Abe Wyndam, far up the slope, bellowed encouragement

as Jessie and Ki shot into view from the curtain of smoke and flame. The North Moon punchers, already clustered on the rim, rooted lustily while the two oncoming riders sent their mounts scrambling higher, toiling the last few yards till they finally gained the crest. Below, the fire raged furiously as it swept northward, the smoke so thick now that the eastern rim was invisible.

With little to say, the scorched troop rode along the ledge of the ravine in the cloying darkness of the smoke-veiled night. The depths of the ravine were a welter of flame and smoke, but the breeze toying across the rim cleared the upper air. For the next grueling hour they were prevented from returning to the Whisper Path, and were forced to forge their own hazardous course south through jagged rock and raking thorn until they were well past the fire. Then, locating what appeared to be a likely route, they sent their flagging horses toiling back to the trail, tensely alert for more ambushing rustlers.

"The ones left behind to set fires and stall us might've hightailed, or could be cookin' up new trouble somewhere close 'round here," Wyndam declared bitterly. "One fact's plain, though. The rest sure spent the time shoving my cows along. They've got a big lead on us."

The Whisper Path rambled on amid growth and over ledges. The horses were often blowing hard by the time they reached the crests of rises, and it was necessary to call halts for a while to enable them to catch their wind. Frequently the descents were more perilous, with broken necks being risked if ridden at a reckless clip. The moon was low in the night sky now, and everyone became increasingly anxious. The chase was consuming too much time, but to try hurrying it would be suicidal.

Eventually the Path took a downhill bender like a curlicue slide. The banks began to fall away, and finally, when dawn was barely a promise in the east, the coastal plateau ahead became visible. The sharp grades continued to lessen, until they met and blended with the gradual slopes of the wooded plateau. Though no longer as steep, the trail kept sinuously slewing downwards as it skirted the lower flanks of the foothills, then spread off scattering into the timber like the outlaws who traveled it. Seaward, a stretch of the main wagon road could be glimpsed rolling south toward Crescent City, which was merely a misty shimmer of tiny lights and dull blots in the distance.

Of the rustlers and the North Moon herd there was no trace. Not even any telltale dust cloud marking their passage could be spied.

"Well, reckon that ends it," Wyndam said gloomily, sweeping the terrain with an embracing glance. "They made town, and likely a sale."

Jessie, shaking her head, turned her horse's nose down the trail.

"Where're you goin'?"

"After the herd, Abe. If we can just find out where it's being held, maybe we can still hit before it's disposed of. I know I'm grasping at a straw, but it's the only straw, so I'll chance it."

Wyndam looked at her and turned a shade red. "By gadfry, then so am I, and m'boys if they're a-mind to," he replied with renewed determination. "Come to consider, I know a gent or two in Crescent City who might could help us. I'm with you, Jessie. It's worth a try."

There was a chorus of agreement from the crew. "I still want to even up for them cussed bee stings," Prescoe growled, his scorched whiskers bristling on his angry face. "What are we waitin' for?"

"Nothing!" Grinning, Jessie headed down the slope, Ki and Wyndam and then the punchers all charging after her.

★

Chapter 17

Pale streaks of light were slashing through the brightening eastern sky when the group gigged their footsore mounts into town.

Fronting the harbor bay, the docks were lined with fishing boats and skiffs and coastal packets. Fishermen and stevedores were already hard at work, while laborers bustled about the wharfs, lumber stacks, supply depots, and stockpens. On the adjacent streets were stores, honkytonks, pawnshops, and gaming halls, while on lanes and open tracts huddled shanties and canvas tents. Along with those from the docks, buckskin-clad hunters and trappers, bearded timberjacks and dirt-grimy miners, greenhorns and tinhorns were out about their business despite the early hour.

The morning was active but far from rowdy. And, of course, even at its bloody worst, Crescent City was tame in comparison to the lawless depravity of hell-ports such as New Orleans or San Francisco's Barbary Coast. Nevertheless, Jessie and Ki could sense a rip-snortin' spirit to the town as they rode along the ugly main street.

"Pull up here," Wyndam called, when they came abreast of the Del Norte Hotel. "Wait outside, boys, while we go in and check."

The Del Norte was a graceless, two-story hulk with a

musty-smelling lobby and a marble-topped counter, behind which were an array of pigeonholes and a spectacled clerk. As they crossed to the desk, Wyndam remarked to Jessie and Ki, "This's the only fit hotel in town, an' nobody who's anybody stays noplace else. Manganaris, the stock buyer who paid me the day you came, he plumb lives here."

The clerk, asked if Manganaris was in, motioned toward the adjoining dining room. Thanking him, they went through a side archway and, after a quick scan of the breakfast crowd, Wyndam led on into the room to a corner table. There, two men sat across from each other, rangemen by the cut of their garb. A third man, a gaunt, watery-eyed fellow, coatless and shirtsleeved, was seated between them, eating a sausage while conversing about market conditions. The gaunt man stopped, abruptly aware of company, and turned to glance smiling at Wyndam, while his breakfast companions looked up, vaguely expectant.

"Sorry to intrude, Frank," Wyndam said. "Can we talk?"

"Sure, Abe. These're associates of mine, so feel free to."

"Well . . . I've a herd down here rarin' to get sold."

"Show me to 'em, and I'll see what I can offer."

"That's the snag," Wyndam replied, and told of the rustling.

Frank's eyes chilled. "Abe, you're not hinting I'd buy . . ."

"Heaven forbid!" Wyndam protested, genuinely shocked. "We're hoping you may've been approached, or heard talk, or something."

"In my trade, I regret, confidences must be strictly kept."

Jessie, provoked by his pompous stonewalling, snapped irritably, "Maybe customs are different in this area, but everywhere else I've ever been, ranchers take mortal offense at folks protecting rustlers."

After a moment of tense hesitation, the gaunt man said, "'Pon reflection, a cowpoke came by earlier this week, wondering if I'd care to top the bid on some plump, juicy beef due in on a drive."

"Uh-huh. And what ranch was him an' this prime stock from?"

"Didn't ask, Abe. The deal smelled like the funny kind

that it don't pay to get personal about, so I just listened and turned it down."

"Who made the bid you were to beat?" Jessie asked.

Frank shifted uneasily, and when he spoke, his voice was hushed and a bit quavery. "The 'poke claimed T. T. Bunce did. Likely a lie."

"To find out," Wyndam growled, "where do we find him?"

Frank shrugged, but one of his companions suddenly spoke up. "If I were you, I'd sniff around the scurviest dives in town, where thievin' hounds akin to Bunce usually hanker to conduct their affairs."

"We will," Jessie said. "D'you also know where he lives?"

The other associate pointed ceilingward.

"Obliged. And this's to stay private 'tween ourselves," Wyndam said, nodding to each man. "I appreciate it, Frank, I really do."

"I doubt you will for long," the man replied, half annoyed and half apprehensive. "Not 'less you forget about it and go pound leather back to Oregon. Or else y'all might not live to be a day older or wiser." Turning, the stock buyer resumed eating, ignoring them.

They strode from the dining room. On their way into the lobby, Jessie commented, "There's patently no love lost for T. T. Bunce."

"Then why was Manganaris reluctant to tell?" Wyndam countered.

"He was scared," Ki suggested. "He wished to heed his own warning, to forget. I think they as much fear Bunce as dislike him."

Reaching the desk clerk, Wyndam asked, "Mr. Bunce's room?"

"One-eleven. He's occupied, though, with another visitor."

"Okay, we're expected," Wyndam assured. Then, as they headed for the stairs, he muttered. "A damn convenient confab, yuh ask me."

They climbed the steep stairs, Wyndam still grumbling while he twitched his revolver a few times in his holster.

Jessie and Ki were a pace behind him, Jessie brushing her pistol with her hand. T. T. Bunce, after all, was an unknown quantity of questionable repute.

The corridor was feebly lit and reeked of dust, sweat, and soiled linen. Jessie wrinkled her nose. "If this is the best hotel in town—"

A scream cut her off. It was high and piercing, yet it was unmistakably the cry of a man. They plunged along the hall for the room whence it came, while the scream faded to a whimpering gurgle. Not bothering to learn whether it was locked or not, they hit the door to one-eleven in a flying wedge that almost twisted its hinges off.

The room was neat, almost pristine, and was lit by the same type of bracket lamp used in the corridor. The light was low, yet sufficient to illuminate a thick-bodied, bristle-bearded man doubled over in a stoop, moaning piteously, one hand grasping a chair for support, his other pressing against his belly. Also present was a shorter man, trim-suited, whose small blunt face had a spoiled mouth, like a little child's, and close-set eyes, lusterless and yellow-green. He was swiveling from the bigger man toward the splintering door, a skinning knife in hand, blood smearing its slender blade.

They rushed at the man, Jessie gasping, "Quinalt!" and running toward the man with the knife.

"Starbuck!" the man blurted, dodging aside, reversing the knife to toss it, while cross-drawing a Remington .44.

Ki launched into a *tobi-geri,* a flying snap-kick, aiming to strike the man's solar plexus hard enough to incapacitate but not to kill. Simultaneously with his spring, the skinning knife flashed by to bury itself in the doorjamb, and Wyndam impulsively shot the man in the chest. The man lurched askew from the slug's impact, and Ki slammed into him off center, clipping his ribs. The man reeled away, falling in a spiraling crumple as his legs gave beneath him. He landed face-up, the final pumpings of his heart spurting crimson across his chest, while the big man keeled over twitching in agony.

"What kinda fool stunt was that, bouncin' at him unarmed an' all!" Wyndam barked at Ki. "I came near to plug-gin' you instead!"

"Dead men can't talk," Ki replied, exasperated.

At that moment the clerk trotted in, yammering, "The Del Norte cannot condone altercations in— Gracious! Mr. Bunce's been shot!"

"Dead. He and his visitor were fighting," Jessie explained, kneeling beside the big man. "This one's still alive. Get a doctor!"

Nodding, the clerk dashed back out. Ki and Wyndam carried the big man over to the room's iron-frame bed. The man was whining tormentedly, writhing and clutching his belly as he stared at them.

"L-leave me alone . . . No, don't . . . don't . . ."

"Not us," Jessie soothed. "Bunce did. Why?"

"No! Don't let him!"

"We won't. Who're you, and why'd he knife you?"

"I dunno, he . . . 'pose to pay for cows, not . . ." The man hesitated, licking his lips. "Ne'er mind . . . An' ne'er mind who I is, either."

"If you don't help us, we can't help you," Ki said shrewdly.

The man swallowed thickly, his eyes glazed with pain and fright. Perhaps from desire for protection, or hunger for revenge, or simply because his wound had robbed him of resistance, he nodded weakly after a moment and confessed. "Bunce was buyin' beef we run down, only he's payin' gawdawful cheap. Thought we'd try to up our take, but, shit . . . couldn't get anyone willin' to buck Bunce's game, and he must've been tipped. 'Cause I was mum when I came for our payoff, but after I . . . showed him spot the herd's at, he called me a double-dealer . . . stab . . ."

"What spot?" Jessie prompted. "Where's the herd?"

"Hollow . . . N'good at tellin' . . . Map, I druh . . ."

"Drew? Draw? Y'mean you've made a map, or'll make one?"

"Cold . . . Dark 'n' cold . . ." His faltering whimpers trailed off, then he sucked in one last raspy breath which expired with his life.

Wyndam groaned. "Now the devil only knows where my herd's at."

"Well, maybe this rustler left directions," Ki replied, fishing through the pockets. "Nothing," he said disgustedly when he was done.

Jessie, meanwhile, swiftly rifled Bunce's clothes. She dumped out six cigars, a pencil, a cash-fat wallet, and a brothel token from Reno, plus a silver match box and a turnip watch engraved with the initials E. Q., and a folded scrap of paper with scribblings on it.

Ki regarded the watch. "E. Q. Eldred Quinalt, all right."

Jessie nodded while studying the scrawls. "Cow speculator, he called himself. Rustler's go-between, actually, for you-know-who."

"Who?" Wyndam asked, as Jessie handed him the paper.

"Oh, some crooks we chanced across in Wichita last year," she hedged, preferring not to go into details about the cartel. She began rummaging through Quinalt's bureau. "See if you can figure a map out of those doodles, Abe, then go look at the outlaw's gun, will you?"

Inspecting the paper, Wyndam shared his findings with Ki. "Yep, this's the town, that's the coast road, and here's a cutoff to . . . I can't read all the hash marks, but I betcha this X refers to my cows."

"It also means ducks," Ki said, as Wyndam crossed to the outlaw. "Sitting ducks—the rustlers who're waiting for their pal here to return with the payoff, and for Quinalt's, or Bunce's, men to come take the herd. They can't know they're stuck, and won't be expecting us."

"Great. Now let's go git before I'm stuck here on a shootin' charge," Wyndam replied, growing nervous. "Jessie? C'mon, I've looked at his pistol, and other than it bein' better'n mine, so what?"

"So swap pistols—and the blame. Maybe it's not legal to pin him with Quinalt's demise, but it's justice." While Wyndam was trading weapons, Jessie gazed around, muttering, "Only clothes and stuff."

They left then, striding along the corridor and downstairs to the lobby. The clerk was gone, probably still trying to find a doctor or a lawman. They didn't waste time inquiring about him, but hastened across the lobby and on through the entrance to the North Moon crew.

"Mount up, boys!" Wyndam announced. "We got hides to skin!"

Together they headed northeast out of Crescent City. The sky turned from pearl gray to slate blue, and was budding for a warmer color, when they cut off the road onto a wagon track. In due course they took other tracks at branches and crossings, yet all were deeply rutted, bore roughly eastward through rock outcrops and thick groves, and followed Wyndam's interpretation of the crudely sketched map.

Presently their route began twining in and out of steepening culverts and ridge-flanking woods, flexing toward an increasingly tumbled country of staggered slopes, creek-bottom gulches, and dense strands of timber. At one intersection of trails, where a rivulet formed a patch of soggy ground, they noticed a morass of recently churned horse and cattle prints. The marks joined in from the other trail, out of the north, up Whisper Path way, and they continued on ahead to a dry, flinty rise upon which hooves left no sign at all.

The prints gave them a heartening boost.

The sun had just passed mid-morning when they came to a broad knoll. Here the trail abruptly split, one fork wandering away from the knoll, the other advancing straight toward a hill of rock. There were no obvious hoofprints along either fork, so they reined in to scout about, only to find their attention diverted by the rock. A half-mile off amid low spurs and ledges, the rock soared about two hundred feet high by three hundred around, towering like an eroded, fissured monument, giving the impression it could topple any time. Despite its appeal, though, soon Ki detected a fresh white score on a stone slab—the kind of scrape made by the iron of a shod horse.

"To there?" Jessie asked, motioning at the rock.

Wyndam nodded, consulting the map. "Yep, Ki's scratch confirms these directions. My cows may be close as t'other side o' the rock, but even if not, we just keep on that trail fork, we'll come to 'em."

"Abe, let's get off it," Jessie urged. "We keep on, we'll

171

warn the outlaws. They must've posted sentries to watch their backup and trial, and they've only to hear us, and we'll reap a hot welcome."

Prescoe spoke up stoutly. "Let 'em hear us. Not much chance to sneak in when they're on the lookout, but ain't they expectin' fellows to come take the herd? Okay, we act like 'em, and go in bold as brass."

Ki chuckled. "Good idea, Lou, for a real black night. Problem is, they're bound to've spied on the ranch enough to recall who everyone is, and we'd be caught at once. No, the only way to catch them unawares, I'm afraid, is to attack from an unexpected direction."

"And even that's chancy," Wyndam growled, and gestured at the other fork. "Where's it go? Y'think maybe it skirts the rock?"

"Let's find out,' Jessie said, and nosed her roan forward.

They all turned onto this second trail, constantly surveying the terrain ahead, on both sides, and behind. Soon heavy brush flanked the trail, obscuring details, though with the rock hill as a landmark, it was apparent the trail was hooking at an angle around the far end of the hill. As they approached the hill on this curve, boulders and large stone slabs crowded the trail, until finally they came to a little open glade, with the rock looming near on the right.

"Looks 'bout close as we'll get," Wyndam said. "Now t'see if the herd's here, but it's too risky, too noisy, to go on horseback."

Everybody quietly dismounted. Single file, toting their carbines, they led their mounts up a gentle slope toward an aspen-crowned ridge. At the crest, they ground-reined their horses and glided hunching to the other side of the ridge, where they knelt down in the concealing brush and stared down into a hollow below.

The hollow was compact, its sides gentle and profuse with briar, thickets, boulders, and copses—except for the side formed by the rock, a grizzled slab ending in a barren, shale-slide embankment. The hollow's dished bottom was verdant with field grasses and shrubs, especially around a shallow spring near the middle, where Abe Wyndam's herd was grazing. Past the rock by the mouth of the hollow, four

172

men were lounging about the ash circle of a cookfire. Almost directly below Jessie and Ki, two men were standing and drinking from a leather water bucket. Another seventeen or eighteen could be seen elsewhere in and about, armed to the teeth, while they strolled and loafed.

"Well, let's snag 'em while they're nappin'," Wyndam murmured, motioning Prescoe over. "Split up, slip low, and ring 'em from the sides. I'll open the show. If they don't surrender, smoke 'em."

Wyndam's orders were passed along. The punchers, remaining dismounted, took up reins and nudged their horses along the ridge, while Jessie, Ki, and Wyndam began threading down through the boulders, brush, and trees. Cautiously they inched their way, while the punchers were fanning out to surround the rustlers as much as possible. At last they settled into position, hunching still, the minutes crawling by.

Ki studied as many outlaws as he could, trying to take the measure of each as a threat. Wyndam concentrated on the two with the water bucket, as if they personified all his antagonisms. Jessie viewed the outlaws meandering about, ignoring their scattered gear and the loose cavvy of untended horses, yet always carrying their weapons.

"They're cautious and sharp on guard," Jessie remarked to Ki, "but they're also lazy, just fooling around wide open. Strange . . ."

"Smart, Jessie. By spreading out, they can check the area and catch any enemy in a crossfire. And they can use the cows for cover. It won't be easy to get the drop on all of them, all at the same time."

"Then we'll get a few and parley 'em," Wyndam said, rising.

"Wait—"

Wyndam didn't wait. With an impulsiveness born of resentment, frustration, rage, and anticipation, he charged out and down the rest of the grade, risking a tumble in his haste. He was risking his life and others' as well, yet he was impetuously convinced that this was how best to tackle these rustlers—short of shooting them outright, perhaps. But even if it was the worst, he was doing *something*.

Or so Jessie and Ki sensed Wyndam was feeling, as they leaped after him. They were almost as startled as the two rustlers when Wyndam's rash assault actually worked. "Claw sky, yuh varmints!" Wyndam bellowed, leveling his carbine, catching the pair before they could turn, dump the bucket, and bring their weapons to bear.

Astonished, they froze, save for their hands beginning to rise. In the same moment, Jessie and Ki were just moving to disarm them. The North Moon crew was converging on cue down the encircling banks, yelling and cursing, sliding and skittering afoot and ahorse with the same careless abandon as their boss. The horde of rustlers dispersed about the hollow first whirled and staggered, but for this moment, they seemed to hesitate, milling in agitated confusion.

The next moment some tried to rally, clawing for weapons. Shots rang out. Then everyone began shooting at everyone else, and the hollow reverberated with the salvos of gunfire. Lashed by a hail of bullets, everyone desperately sprang for shelter. The two outlaws Wyndam had bagged scuttled into the thick of the herd in a frenzied attempt to escape. The punchers dipped and dodged as bandit lead stormed up around them, while the rustlers, with cow-waddie slugs whining about their ears, were not slow to duck and hunt cover. Off aside in the neglected cavvy, the horses were increasingly skittish, pawing and snorting and wrenching on their ropes. Also growing alarmed by the flashing tumult, the cattle were lumbering, churning around and bellowing, the portents of a stampede.

Wyndam dug in and began returning fire with his carbine. Jessie started triggering and levering as fast as she could, ignoring the heat from the barrel burning her fingers, and the ache in her shoulder from the brutal recoil. Ki shifted aside to reload, and as he glanced over to see how the others were doing, a lead chunk drilled into the earth where he'd just been. From somewhere up on the rock drifted the throaty blast of a .59-90 Express round, and Ki, twisting around, shouldered his carbine and scanned the rock.

The hollow resounded with crackling gunfire, blood-curdling screams, and the squeals of frightened stock. Calmly Ki ignored the melee around him, concentrating on

174

the splintery façade of that rock, and his patience paid off. Spying a man moving stealthily out from one niche and starting toward another, Ki sighted carefully before triggering. The man jerked, then tumbled over the edge and fell to the ground.

As if this were a signal, there was a sudden upsurge of gunfire, a raging fusillade which made the air fairly sizzle. A creased bullet or rock shard of suchlike must have stung an outlaw's horse, for abruptly it bucked, squealing, broke its cavvy hitch, and bolted, ripping pins and loosening ropes. Freed, all the cavvy's horses spooked and ran scattered. A few, then some, then all the cattle panicked as well, creating a heavy confusion of cows blundering, jostling, crushing.

The crescendoing battle was deafening. Ki could not hear the distinctive discharge of the Express ammo, nor could he swear positively from where the shot came which sang angrily by his neck, or the slug which flicked chips off a stone he was bracing his foot on.

But he had his suspicions, and he kept an eye on the rock.

Jessie rose, hunching, to relieve a leg cramp.

"Watch out!" Ki cried, then swore when lead cut her sleeve.

"Thanks," she gasped, promptly sitting down. "The rock?"

"Another one's up there, or more. He can pin us here, keep us from the herd." Ki ducked, a slug ricochetting next to his head. He tossed Jessie his carbine. "It's no fun to climb with. Cover me!"

Ki launched out along the field, gunshots snapping and whining about him. If and when he reached the rock, its crevices and cracks should protect him fairly well. Ahead in between, however, was a bleating, grinding jumble of terrified cows, followed by the rock's exposed slide of loose gravel and shale. And at any instant now one of those rustlers would get his range or get lucky, and plug him.

Plunging among the hysterical cattle in a zigzagging sprint, Ki sensed they were on the verge of stampeding. The way they were bawling and bunching and floundering back for no reason . . . Well, all it would take would be a starter

175

cow, or another minute, or crack explosion. It cut down considerably on being shot at, though he now ran the risk of being squashed to jelly by rampaging beeves.

When Ki popped into the open, Jessie responded with increased barrages. By now Wyndam had realized what Ki was attempting and had joined in to side Jessie. In a one-two punch, Jessie winged a bearded man in the thigh, while Wyndam blew the face off another. Yet another yelled painfully as a bullet burned his ribs; he stumbled, fell, and was trampled underhoof, a fitting end for a rustler. There were others who went down, but there were more others who hadn't yet, and many of these concentrated on Ki. Nor was North Moon left unscathed. Three bodies already lay lifeless; a fourth threw up his hands and collapsed. Another ranch hand was crying out from a wound.

Ki dove up the shale slide, and sank at his first step. Pulling free, he struggled higher, trying not to slide back, clawing, almost swimming, the incline sucking him in and down as treacherously as quicksand. He found a few solid places, but every inch was a fight, a slow battle that left him exposed to the outlaws.

Bullets whipped close or plowed deep in around him. One man rose to take a careful bead; an instant before he triggered, Jessie fired, her slug glancing off the man's belt buckle and tearing up through his belly. His carbine empty, Wyndam drew the revolver he'd traded the rustler, only to stagger, feeling a quick burning cut across his scalp. Blood flowed down from his furrowed wound, but he disregarded it, blasting two shots at a thin scoundrel jumping for a better vantage. The man sprawled grotesquely, holding his shattered leg.

Ki continued his gradual slogging up the loose-packed slide, expecting to be shot with every torturous step he took. Eventually he gained the top and slipped along a series of thin, angular ledges. The ledges petered out and he began the slow, difficult ascent up a steep wall, fingers and toes clawing for the slightest hold. He could hear someone firing from above him, yet as impatient as he was, he forced himself to climb carefully, to converge silently. Stalking his prey, Ki could first only go by the throaty blasts . . . then he could add the stinging odor of gunpowder . . . and finally he could also rely on the gouts of gunflame to guide him toward the sniper's nook.

Finally he could make out the Stetson and torso of a man on a shallow stone ledge, kneeling on one knee while shouldering a Winchester Express repeater. Silently Ki withdrew the slender, curve-bladed knife from his waistband, and began a slow pad, trying to be careful in case the sniper should hear something and shoot at the noise.

A pebble rolled, clicking against another.

The sniper heard the noise. He didn't say a word, but he moved, swiveling about like a scalded ferret and shooting at the noise as rapidly as he could. He was as accurate as he was fast.

Ki was hard pressed to match the man's swiftness. He twisted in a low, rolling circle, the bullet from the man's large-caliber carbine ricochetting off stone between Ki's legs. The man tried to lever and refire, but by then Ki was coming out of his slewing somersault . . . coming up with the swift force of his straightening body to add power as he blocked the carbine barrel with a diagonal upthrust of his left forearm, while thrusting his *tanto* blade high in a belly-slitting skewer.

The sniper coughed, shaking. He dropped his carbine, which clattered down among the rocks, then sagged and sprawled. Ki took little notice, his attention focused on locating the next attacker, should there be one . . . or more.

Cautiously Ki began working his way up and around the rock, always keeping to cover. More than once he tensed, listening intently, but if somebody else was up here after him, the man was like a snake. Few men were that good, and Ki felt there was a greater chance the man was slouching behind a boulder or the like, waiting breathless, motionless. Ki continued his gradual and noiseless progress.

He was pausing in the crook of two outcrops when he heard a soft grunt and heeled around, eyes darting, left hand thumb-hooked in a vest pocket, his right hand sweeping his *tanto* in a parabola. The second attacker was suddenly facing him, but staying out of knife range, snarling, clenching a heavy Colt .45 dead-aimed at Ki.

Both men acted at the same instant. The outlaw's revolver erupted point-blank, and Ki felt a smarting along his left thigh. But the other man was toppling backwards, with Ki's left-handed-flicked *shuriken* sliced deep into his chest. The man rolled, wailing, the Colt blasting into the air, and blood spewing like a geyser.

The *shuriken* had inadvertently severed a main artery. Ki was prepared to hurl another *shuriken* if need be, but the man died exceedingly quickly.

Ki pressed flat against the rock, catching his breath and straining his eyes and ears for sign of other attackers. Satisfied at last, he wiped his *tanto* clean and returned it to its sheath in his waistband, then hastened back down the rock to the hollow.

Crossing the shale slide was easier this time, but going along the field was near-suicidal. The cattle had been finally set off, and they were caroming around the field and pouring out the mouth of the hollow. They were leaving at a rapid clip, not a hell-larrupin' stampede pace, yet they were still heavy, blinded animals charging about, and nothing could halt them.

Eventually making it through, Ki was relieved to find that Jessie and Wyndam had survived the fray. Wyndam had knotted his kerchief around his bullet-furrowed scalp, and was hobbling about searching for a boot heel that had been shot off. Jessie was tending the wounded when she wasn't fighting, for though the battle had lost its initial savage punch, there was still deadly skirmishing going on. The North Moon punchers, who'd been courageous before when attacked by the rustlers, were ferocious now in dishing out retribution.

Of the rustlers, some were dead, some soon would be, and the remaining gang was disintegrating into a mob bent on escape. They scrambled afoot along with the stampede, using it as cover, the bawling of cows blending with the howls of men. The herd flowed on out of sight with drumming hooves and clouds of dust that glinted golden in the sunlight, the rustlers also vanishing into the timber.

Wyndam's eyes were sparklers and his face was gnarled with vexation. Beside him, Lou Prescoe was swearing and shaking his fist toward the unseen rustlers. Then he turned to scowl at the crew.

"Okay, boys, let's go round up our cows again."

Grousing, the North Moon punchers complied, riding out to comb the forestland and regather the herd. There were also, in the hollow, the injured to tend and the dead to bury. At length it was all done and, bone-weary yet elated, they drove the regrouped herd east on the trail and trudged toward Crescent City.

As sunset was blazing scarlet and gold out at sea, and the crags were tipped with saffron flame, they delivered the cows safely to the dock pens near the port and went to locate Frank Manganaris. When the stock buyer offered and Wyndam accepted the price for the herd, the whole North Moon outfit there breathed a sigh of relief.

★

Chapter 18

The return to North Moon Ranch was uneventful.

"We're soon due for trouble, though," Jessie told Ki at breakfast the next morning. "Involving the cartel, I fear, and a very real uprising. No backwoods bandit gang could handle so costly and complicated an operation as a revolution, but the cartel could, and would. And *is*, I'm convinced, after finding Eldred Quinalt mixed in. We must discover quickly who's the big spider in the middle of the web."

"Valasquez," Ki suggested. "He shows his Spanish blood, and admits it, and he certainly has the ability to lead. Or Major Pennington, obsessed as he is with his dreams of empire building."

Jessie sighed, Valasquez's rugged features floating up in her memory. "Ki, if Don Ramon were tied in with the cartel and spotted who we are, he'd hardly let on. His game would be to pass us without a second glance, to keep in the background, but he's been, well . . . ."

"Very open, very straightforward."

"Ah, yes, so to speak. As for Pennington, I admit that like so many of his kind, he seems to figure he's a law unto himself, but with limits. I somehow can't quite picture him resorting to robbing and killing, no matter how crazy his ideas. I'm not ruling him or anyone out, of course. The only thing I'm sure of is that this is a puzzler."

"I've a crazy idea," Ki offered after thinking a moment. "If you like, let's go locate that cabin I was in. I hope it's now empty."

While the crew resumed work on the ranch house, Jessie and Ki saddled horses and rode swiftly along the route out of Bohemia Valley. Outside town, they came at length to the farthest point Ki definitely recalled having passed with the pack train. There they dismounted and studied the ground, piecing together a pattern which fit the size, weight, and general behavior of the string of horses.

Striking overland, they scouted steadily through the roughs of brush, rock, and timber for familiar marks that would lead them to the cabin. Because Ki had been lost, his path wasn't always logical, nor was it as evident as when he had forged it. Three times they followed false sign and had to retrace. The wasted effort frustrated them, as well as irritating Ki. If he was good enough to find his way out at night during a fog, he chastised himself, then he ought to be able to track his own backtrail in clear daylight.

Eventually, deep within the forested hills, Ki gestured ahead at a canyon. "The cabin's in there, I believe. Careful, now."

They proceeded up the canyon with quiet, tense caution, pausing every so often to listen. But the canyon remained utterly silent and apparently deserted. The sun was at its zenith when they reined in by the cabin, which stood blank-windowed, its door left wide open. Approaching warily, they found it was stripped bare and abandoned.

"You got your hope," Jessie remarked, inspecting the vacated interior. "Nobody here but some ghosts, maybe, to shoot at us."

"I wanted it empty for another reason," Ki replied as he went out. "The carbines. They took them, and perhaps we can learn where."

Jessie joined him by the entrance, where he began examining the muddle of horses and boot tracks in the packed earth. "I've an awful suspicion where," she said. "To Major Pennington's. Unless I'm badly turned around, we must be on or very close to his property already."

"What makes you think that?"

"Well, from Abe's to here took us north and then looping back south. My feeling is, we're far enough south to be about in line with where I cut off the town road onto Pennington's private road."

"Interesting . . ." Ki gave her a quick, knowing smile, then returned to work in fanning sweeps out toward the edge of the clearing. After a while, he commented, "Those prints appear to've been made last." He scrutinized them minutely, detecting that among them was a left foreshoe with a notched toe. He straightened, heartened, and pointed to one of the paths leading away. "Went down there, is my hunch."

They started off, the thread-thin track squiggling south with a tendency toward the southeast. For a time it and the new hoofprints vanished, lost among the layers of conifer needles and the hard clay crumblings that shifted, impressionless, under pressure. Ki dismounted again, walking his horse as he bent studying the ground. Shortly he discovered the mark of that telltale shoe, and occasionally after that he discerned other prints or sign. But mostly he followed his intuition, a combination of knowing the line of travel already taken, and of sensing where it would most likely continue. It wasn't instinct, and he wasn't a blood hound; it was solid logic and long experience.

Presently the tracks reappeared in the richer loam of a sloping field. Ki and Jessie traced them higher. The path kept close to the contours of the foothills, rarely up along the ridges, but down through clefts and gullies. Continuing on, they had to rein in twice more to study the terrain, deciphering the route as it wove among the spurs and timbered banks. At last they entered a narrow culvert and, while scanning the rimrock, glimpsed a pale drift of smoke rising from the hill beyond. It was scarcely more than a wisp, yet it was sufficient to confirm that somewhere yonder, someone was using green wood to fuel a campfire.

"If this path doesn't lead there," Jessie said, shading her eyes as she surveyed the smoke, "it leads to a trail leading there."

Ki agreed. As they rode out of the culvert, he said, "No sense risking it. Let's walk from here."

They ground-reined the horses in a grassy patch where

they could graze unseen. Then they began climbing in the direction of the smoke, the ascent relatively easy at first, but growing increasingly steep and treacherous. Nearing the crest, they groped for handholds and tested each move before placing their weight on it.

Finally Ki scaled the broken ridge. Turning, he helped Jessie draw her weary body over the lips. Then they both sat down to catch their breaths before hiking toward the gauzy trickle of smoke. As quietly as they could they burrowed through snarled underbrush and cluttered groves, ultimately emerging where a rotted tree had settled, roots upended, by the very rim of a sheer-dropping second cliff.

Crouching on the ledge and concealed by the tree, they peered over the side into a vast depression. Shaped like a huge bowl, it was entirely enclosed by the chain of high ridges, except where a small brook flowed out a thin passage cut through the western wall.

The brook, which snaked along one side from a splashy waterfall, was bordered by crabgrass and sparse copses. In the weedy growth were clustered bedrolls, flimsy tents, and makeshift lean-tos. The cookfire was smoking, and about a dozen gunhands lounged under the shade, keeping a bored watch on the broad expanse of open center.

This large middle area was a flat, dusty stone-and-gravel arena. Parading back and forth across it were almost two hundred other men, some appearing to be of Spanish, some of Indian blood, but the majority looking to be breeds of every possible mix. Yet all were similarly clad in grubby shirts and pants and needed shaves and trims. Shiny fine, however, were the carbines with which they slovenly drilled, marching and counter-marching, forming lines of squads, of twos, wheeling, reversing, turning to a ragged company line.

Bellowing commands at them was a tall, pout-chested man flashily uniformed like the Zoaves, Napoleon's French Algerian troops, in baggy pantaloons, sashes, spats, and a braided jacket. "Lock step, you pucker-arsed farts!" he bull-roared. "Late tonight King Tatarrax himself comes to review you, so shape up! You're sharp as crap on a candle, and His Majesty must take pride in his legion of liberation!"

But Jessie and Ki observed nothing militarily proud about the shambling recruits, nor about their camp, which lacked pickets or emplacements; the ringing hills evidently were assumed to provide sufficient protection. They were in a natural fort having only one gap, after all, needing only one shot by a lookout to warn them of an attack.

"And they're armed well," Ki noted. "I sorely doubt they were given loaded guns or any ammunition, though, and if they're as stumbling tonight as they are now, this Tatarrax actor will likely wonder why they were armed at all. Just the same, I bet those poor dupes are the makings, Jessie, of the trouble you said we're soon due to face."

"Face," she repeated, pondering. "Tatarrax . . ." Then, abruptly, the elusive detail nagging her thoughts popped to mind. "That's who! It resembles him! Ki, a book about Quivera that Major Pennington has shows a portrait, supposedly, of Tatarrax. It looks extremely like Ingram Harcourt. Change his clothes, add props, and Harcourt would pass as the pictured image, could pose as Tatarrax. Why, sure, it fits!"

"As suspicion, not fact." Ki rubbed an earlobe. "Y'know, he's also suspect in a way you touched upon earlier. Right off somebody spotted who we are—rather, what we are to the cartel. The bandits who caught me at the boat and the man who tried to knife you had our descriptions, meaning their boss must've spread the word by posse-time our first day in town. We met Harcourt that morning. So it's possible he runs the outlaw gang while, as Tatarrax, he leads the rebellion. And that is what we're after, the top head in control of them both."

Jessie nodded contemplatively. "Oh, it's Harcourt. As only he could, he took Pennington in proper through his resemblance and calls for revolt. So Pennington offered him the use of his land and probably agreed to help, which isn't surprising. He sees things as he'd wish them to be, a visionary, yet blind to crimes under his very eyes."

"Well, the major's in for a fall," Ki said. "when he learns of the raidings and killings he's become party to, if only indirectly."

"Others will fall harder and farther," Jessie vowed grimly,

184

Thoughtful, they scanned a bit longer, then slipped into the brush and hiked back to the bluff overlooking the culvert. They went down the spot where they'd climbed up, sliding and plunging, digging in their heels and clutching with their hands to keep from tripping into a headlong dive. Once at the bottom, they hurried to remount and return the way they'd come, still keeping a cautious eye on the surrounding terrain.

They had traveled perhaps half the distance back to the cabin when, on pausing on the crest of a sag, they saw a man riding toward them. The man rode furtively, studying the growth on either side, hesitating from time to time to peer and listen. Quietly they eased their horses into a shouldering fringe of huckleberry and young oak until they were concealed from the path. Senses acute, they waited.

Presently came the click of hooves, and through the foliage they watched the man's approach. After another moment they exchanged soft grins, recognizing the lanky figure of Sheriff Lydell. They remained hidden, though, while the lawman loomed over the sag, paused to glance about, then rode on slowly, apparently satisfied. Not until Lydell was past them did Jessie call to him, a note of amusement in her voice.

"You're on the right track, Sheriff!"

Lydell jerked disjointedly and whirled in his saddle, his hand pawing for his revolver. Then abruptly his hand dropped and so did his jaw, as Jessie and Ki emerged casually from the brush.

"What brings you by?" Ki asked conversationally.

The sheriff twitched. "Well, okay, I follered you here," he admitted. "Lost you a while ago, then staked out that cabin till I learnt it was empty, and tagged you agin. Wouldn't have done it if I'd knowed what else to do, but I've been combin' these hills since you packed in the gold, and've gotten precisely nowhere."

"You may have this time, and you certainly saved us a trip hunting you up," Jessie replied, her smile widening. "C'mon, we'd better move before anybody back behind us fancies some whim to ride this way."

The three proceeded toward the cabin at a gentle lope.

Jessie told the sheriff of their tracing the prints to the culvert and discovering the hole-in-the-wall camp, and briefly sketched the situation and her suspicions, while avoiding all reference to the cartel. Lydell had enough to digest as it was. His jowls reddened with growing ire.

"God knows how long they've been nesting up there!" he sputtered when Jessie concluded. "Swoopin' down like vultures, murderin' an' wideloopin'! Soon's I get to town, I'm gonna organize everyone from everywhere into the biggest damn posse, and then go mow 'em down!"

Jessie shook her head. "Don't risk a posse. It'd take too much time to reach them all and explain and get together, and meanwhile, it could tip off the gang. No, choose a few of your most trusted friends, Sheriff, while we go gather the North Moon crew. They'll be pleased to get in some licks, and I know they can be depended on. Between them and your picked bunch, we'll have all the posse we'll need."

"What, agin a two-hundred-soldier mob?" The sheriff balked. "We'd have as much chance as a rabbit in a hound dog's mouth."

"Those poor devils aren't fighters," Ki assured him. "Most of them looked eager to desert, and besides, they're armed with empty guns."

"Put it that way, we might capture the whole kaboodle."

"The outlaws are a saltier proposition," Jessie cautioned. "Let's meet at the cabin at ten tonight. I'm guessing that'll be a good time, but I'd rather be too late than too early. Don't want to have any tardy arrivals coming in behind us. We'll attack so swiftly and surprisingly that they'll be caught off guard, and won't have a chance to prepare a defense." She mulled this over for a moment, then added with a frown, "Even so, it could readily turn into a fight to the death, no quarter given."

Chapter 19

Along about ten o'clock that night, Jessie, Ki, Abe Wyndam, and the North Moon boys jogged into the clearing by the cabin. Sheriff Lydell and five picked companions were already there awaiting them.

After the lawman swore in the outfit as deputies, they all departed on the southerly path Ki had traced earlier that day. They wove, skirting the foothills, eventually filing through the culvert and past the spot where Jessie and Ki had left their mounts, continuing on cautiously, darkness blurring the rugged harshness around them.

Midnight was nearing, and the quarter-moon and sprinkle of stars were casting meager light, when the path they were on joined a larger trail. A fast-rippling brook slashed across the juncture, switching for no apparent reason from flowing along one side of the trail to flowing along the other side, as it and the trail descended westward.

Turning, the riders headed slowly up the trail, scrutinizing the terrain for signs of life—life that spelled death. Slopes on both sides rose higher and drew closer, fashioning a cleft of sorts wrapped in gloom, falling steeply away from the ridge in black, corrugated smudges of boulders and brush. The brook burbled and stewed, making an S-curve, tall grasses and saplings sprouting in its bend. The trail curved with the brook and, approaching the bend, Ki glimpsed banks of stone around beyond. He held up his hand as a signal to rein in, and the men clustered silently about him.

"That dogleg ahead is the start, I think, of the cut into the camp. It's a great place to post a guard, and not a great place for us to get trapped," Ki whispered. "Sit tight. I'm going for a look."

While the others backed their horses off the trail into undergrowth, Ki began climbing the slope on the eastern flank of the trail. He reached the jagged crest and levered himself onto the rocky top, then stole carefully toward the far rim that overlooked the camp. The wavering glow of many well-stoked bonfires came from the pit, resembling the luminous vapors rising from some gigantic witches' cauldron. It did little to illuminate around the summit where Ki was, and clouds were sifting in front of the moon, hampering its frail light.

And yet, perhaps because it was so dark, Ki caught a spark winking among the rimrocks over by the cut—a spark no brighter or longer than a firefly's wink or the flare of a match. Dipping to his hands and knees, Ki approached, focusing intently. Shortly he perceived three vague outlines, easily mistaken for boulders, if they hadn't shifted restlessly. Closing, Ki now slithered scarcely an inch at a time, gliding around the back of a boulder with his body flat to the ground. Finally, not two feet from him, he was able to differentiate the three men, one of whom he recognized as the short robber named Hank.

". . . Heard noises down thataway," another was saying.

"You always hear noises," the third man scoffed. "Nobody's come by us on the trail, have they? I see your noises, I'll believe 'em."

"Wouldn't hurt to check, just to be sure," Hank said. He rose, pausing while the other two stood up. "The stretch will do us good."

Ki killed them.

He straightened and tossed daggers with efficient dispatch, having no intention of making it a contest. He had to silence the men as well as drop them, and made it a swift execution before they could cry out. Hank was first, because his back was to Ki and he would be harder to hit once he started to turn. The blade sank deep into the base of his neck, passing between the vertebrae, slicing his spinal cord and bringing his misspent life to an end without so much as a whimper. Even before Hank's chin nodded forward against his chest, Ki speared the next man at the lower jawline of his throat, lancing through his larynx and the root of his tongue. The man's startled shout died stillborn. The third man had his mouth open wide to yell, but could not because his windpipe was severed, along with his jugular veins, which fountained blood as he toppled over.

Ki was immediately on the move again, prowling the rest of the crown for more lookouts, and reaching the opposite rim without finding any. He glanced down at the camp, gauging the scene revealed by the blazing fires, then turned and quickly hiked back to the waiting posse. They slid from the concealing brush and again crowded around.

"There shouldn't be any problem," Ki told them. "The soldiers are lined up against the side cliff, more or less in company formation. Tatarrax and his gang are grouped in front of them, facing away from the trail."

"Who's playing Tatarrax? Harcourt?" Jessie asked.

Ki nodded, grinning. "From what I could see, yes. And wait till you see the clothes he's wearing; they're like something out of a museum. Anyway, he's haranguing his legion of liberation. We should be able to catch them setting, if we pile into them right away."

"All right, boys," Sheriff Lydell said, gazing about sternly. "We've got surprise on our side, and maybe we can corral 'em without firing a shot. Let's hope. But if they start slingin' lead, hit 'em hard with all you've got. Understand?"

A low muttering of agreement answered him.

Spurring into a hard gallop, the posse swept around the dogleg curve and streamed on through the narrow chasm. Before the outlaws realized what was going on, the speeding riders were pouring from the gap and surging out around the camp, brandishing weapons, grim and mute. Sheriff Lydell's voice alone rang out: "You're all arrested! Put your guns down and your hands up!"

For a moment it appeared as if the surprise was complete,

189

and capture could be made peacefully. The outlaws, "caught setting," and covered by a score of guns, dared not make a move, for resistance would be suicide. Ingram Harcourt, his face ashen and wild-eyed, stood tensely quivering in his King Tatarrax regalia—a high-collared doublet and breeches of purple velvet festooned with gold thread, garnets, and amethysts; a cape similarly ornamented and bordered in reddish-bronze tissue; thigh-high boots of buff leather with "butterfly" spur-leathers; a fancy sword whose hilt and scabbard were of silver and gilt; and a brassy morion-type helmet with fluted decorations around the crown and the tipped, curving brim. Harcourt cut quite a dashing figure, but he had nowhere to dash.

Then the unexpected happened. One of the so-called soldiers went berserk in terror, flung his carbine down, and bolted screaming for the gap. The next second his compatriots were all following his example, and the second after that, a squirming mass of panicked humanity were wedging between the posse and the grouped outlaws. The outlaws, with the courage of desperation, seized the opportunity handed them and scattered afield, whipping out guns and blasting indiscriminately as they ran.

"Then let's hit 'em!" Lydell shouted, launching his horse forward. Instantly his posse sprang into action along their line confronting the camp, a long crescent of thunderous guns plunging forward in pursuit like an avenging tidal wave.

With yells of shock and pain, the vicious outlaws dove behind boulders or into copses, or dodged in and out among the fear-frantic soldiers, trying to swing past and escape through the gap. The determined posse charged to stop them, their onslaught turning the camp into an inferno of pounding hooves, rearing horses, and roaring guns. Repeatedly the outlaws were repulsed, thrown back or shot down; yet repeatedly they rallied in frenzied efforts to burst out of this ring of death, firing a deadly response to the posse's challenge.

Three North Moon crewmen were wounded almost at once, and one of the sheriff's deputized friends was drilled through his thigh. The flamboyantly uniformed drill master

190

raised his pistol and triggered at Jessie the same instant she shot at him. The man who chanced to be alongside Jessie gave a half-twisting lurch, as if grazed along the hip or over the ribs. Jessie's truer aim snatched the drill master off his feet, her bullet smashing into his stomach. He landed on his rump, his head wobbling as if shaking to deny he was dead.

Gradually gunfire from the outlaws lessened, as their weapons emptied and their numbers dwindled. They fought on like the cornered rats they were, the attack becoming a close-quarter melee of knives and hand-to-hand struggles. One maddened bandit rushed at Ki with a Bowie. Ki shot him so close that the flame of his carbine scorched the man's shirt, then swiftly loosened two *shuriken*, his whirring disks stabbing another oncoming man in the chest and ripping through the throat of the man just behind. A couple more North Moon crewmen received flesh wounds, but continued to pull their triggers.

The surviving outlaws could withstand just so much punishment. The sheriff's continuing call for surrender began to take effect, and a growing number of outlaws dropped their weapons and lifted their hands. Only those off to the sides with any chance to make it sought to escape by scrambling, crawling, battling to the gap. Most were caught in the crush, but a few succeeded in their desperate bid for freedom.

One such was Ingram Harcourt.

Jessie had been keeping her eyes sharp for Harcourt, and had caught flashing glimpses of his ancient outfit during the conflict. Now, for the first time, she saw Harcourt and two gunhands spurring horses out the defile.

"Harcourt's making a break for it!" she shouted at Ki.

She raced to her horse. Perversely, the roan shied mincingly as she vaulted into the saddle, helping Harcourt by causing Jessie to waste precious moments. Regaining control, she wrenched the horse about and, with Ki galloping a pace behind, set off in fast pursuit.

Through the pass and around the dogleg bulge they sped, lashing their mounts faster down the trail, glimpsing Harcourt and his henchmen far ahead. Their quarry vanished over a distant crest. On they chased, though their horses were panting with raspy, harsh breaths.

Another rise, and again Jessie and Ki spotted the fleeing trio and realized they were losing ground to them. Those other mounts were fresher, more rested, while theirs were of stout heart, but winded from a long day of riding. And again the three ahead dipped down the opposite side of the sag and disappeared for quite a long distance, the trail curving through gullied slopes and wooded ledges.

The outlaws next came into view when they crossed an open patch to veer onto the coastal wagon road. Jessie snapped a quick shot at Harcourt. Her bullet struck rock near his head, making him flinch as he swiveled around and fired back. His gunmen fired as well, their shots all flying wild. Jessie and Ki raced after them along the road to Gold Beach, ignoring the bullets zinging past them, firing salvos from their carbines, but their aim was no better than anyone's could be when shooting from the back of a galloping horse. Their horses were slowing under them, still game, but simply too fatigued to keep up the grueling pace. Yet they refused to give in, fearing the consequences should the boss of the outlaw gang and the figurehead of the uprising elude capture. Harcourt must not escape.

The outlaws, hunching so low across their horses' withers that they were almost invisible, tore along the final straight stretch before town. Jessie raised her pistol to fire, but the hammer struck an empty chamber. Their carbines were also out of ammunition. And then it was too late. The outlaws swerved around the last bend and dropped from sight behind a blocking wedge of trees.

Jessie holstered her pistol and, like Ki, gave all her attention to riding. The roan stumbled, recovered, and took the bend at an ungainly run. Ki's buckskin was flagging to a haggard lope.

As the road straightened again and became the town's main street, Jessie yanked on her reins, pulling the horse to a sliding, staggering halt, while hearing Ki behind her wrench his horse to a slithering stop. Directly ahead at no great distance, she saw, Harcourt and his flanking gunmen sat their blowing horses, their revolvers out and ready, their black muzzles lined with her chest. Harcourt was squeezing his trigger.

Why they had headed to town instead of to Harcourt's ranch, and why they had decided to make their stand in the street, smack in the midst of witnesses in front of Buckram's and the restaurant, Jessie could not understand. She hurled herself sideward from the saddle. She got an impression of a window sliding up on the second floor of the hotel, and of two revolvers roaring as one as the slug from Harcourt's gun whined by her. Then she struck ground and was tumbling on her knees, rolling out into a dive as she saw the other gun men aiming.

A revolver cracked from Harcourt's left just as Harcourt reeled in the saddle of his rearing horse, hand clawing at his chest. Lead from Harcourt's sidekick ripped through Jessie's hat, followed by more gunfire. All three men slid crumpling from horseback, the two gunhands also sprouting *shuriken* in the face and upper body. They hit the street and lay motionless in bloody sprawls.

Jessie got to her feet, walked forward, and gazed down at the distorted features of the dead outlaws. When Ki came up alongside, she said, "Thanks for nailing them. They had me pegged."

"I just added dessert," he replied, and gestured at the bodies. "You fed them the main course. Look at those bullet holes! That's some of the best shooting on the wing I've ever seen you do, Jessie."

"Me! You didn't see *me* shoot them, Ki. My pistol's empty."

"Then who . . . ?"

Jessie turned her head and looked up at the hotel window. It was indeed open. Leaning out with his elbows on the sill, his smoking revolver in one hand, was Deputy U. S. Marshal Custis Long.

"Longarm!"

"Evening, Jessie," he hailed genially. "Howdy, Ki. Chanced to spot that jasper in the costume and his buddies leveling at you, and figured I'd better do something. Trust I did right butting in."

"You get your bu—yourself down here, and I'll tell you just how right," Jessie called back, smiling. "What are you doing here?"

193

Longarm didn't answer, having already ducked inside. Jessie hurried to meet him at the hotel entrance, and when he came outside, it seemed only natural that he should take her in his arms. When his lips found hers, that seemed more natural still.

By now a throng was converging on the scene, pouring from nearby establishments and clustering around to gawk at the three corpses.

"Wha' happened?"

"Where's the sheriff?"

"How come Mr. Harcourt's all fooferawed up?"

Hastening from the restaurant, Major Pennington broke through the crowd, glanced appalled at Harcourt, and then faced Jessie. "I suppose you'll be wanting to take me into custody, Miss Starbuck."

"No, I'll leave it up to Sheriff Lydell to charge or arrest you if he sees fit. I doubt it. You've been a cat's paw, well intentioned but misguided," Jessie responded. "Remember what you said about great men dying too soon? Well, what's happened may help you realize that great men can live too long, if their greatness isn't handled carefully."

"True," Pennington agreed, sighing. Still visibly shaken, he mounted a Morgan thoroughbred stallion that was hitched by the hotel, reined it about, and paused to add with a doleful smile, "Anyway, it was a great dream. Tell the sheriff I'll be available."

"Something to have dreamed," Jessie murmured compassionately, turning away as the man jogged off. "Something to have dreamed."

"Who is he?" Longarm asked.

"Major Pennington." Acquainting Longarm with the situation, Jessie concluded, "Deceived by Harcourt, Pennington believed a separate outlaw gang was working around here, never realizing his own 'patriots' were responsible. Now, tell me, why're you in this neck of the woods?"

"My story can wait," Longarm snapped brusquely, again drawing his revolver. "Your Major Pennington won't. We have to stop him."

Startled, Jessie restrained him with her hand. "Why?"

"I read some letters between crooks, naming the top hon-

194

cho to contact in this region. It's not Harcourt, Jessie, it's Pennington."

"He couldn't be!" She gasped, abruptly aware how Pennington could be. Beckoning to Ki, who was standing discreetly nearby, she charged out into the street. Longarm was alongside, braced for action.

They were too late.

They halted in the middle of the street, faces taut. Ahead, all too far ahead, Pennington was into the wooded bend of the road, his long-shanked spurs raking his mount's flanks. Before they could aim, he was gone, and their own horses were too exhausted to give chase.

"I let him go," Jessie said sourly, quivering with frustration and anger and self-recrimination. "I let the bastard get away."

★

Chapter 20

Jessie and Ki spent the night in town, a sensible decision, considering how long the posse took to patch the wounded, bury the dead, and return with the prisoners. Sheriff Lydell was pleased to meet Longarm, though he was openly skeptical when informed about Harcourt and Pennington. "Are you plumb certain the major hooked Harcourt, Marshal, and not the t'other way 'round?"

"Greed hooked Harcourt," Longarm replied. "But it was Pennington who located a Tatarrax lookalike, and persuaded Harcourt to be field leader of his uprising and his desperadoes. Sure, Harcourt was so eager it's hard to tell who wangled whom, and on the surface, it could've been either one. In fact, if I hadn't seen correspondence linking Pennington, I admit I'd have figured it same as you and Miss Starbuck."

Jessie shook her head. "I should've caught on as soon as Harcourt and his gunhands rode here instead of to his ranch. They were after help, the help only a boss could give...a boss having dinner out for an alibi."

Wyndam now spoke up. "Jessie, you've already done more'n you should've. We'll get a line on the major, but if not—"

"We will," the sheriff insisted. "To save their necks, the prisoners will spill his whereabouts, or if they can't, any owlhoot runnin' loose may know. And there're all them revolters scramblin' through the hills, though danged if I'm sure what to do about 'em."

"Forget them," Ki advised. "The legion's broken up, and they've learned a lesson they'll go pass on to others. They're harmless."

"And brainless." Wyndam shrugged philosophically. "My point is, if nobody knows, if all fails, well . . . You win one, you lose one."

"I lost the big one," Jessie reminded him, adding with a mirthless grin, "but I'm going to find Pennington. Starting tomorrow, I'm going to track that man if I have to scour every inch between here and Mexico."

For this night, however, Jessie got as far as the hotel.

Buckram regarded the two sober-countenanced men flanking her, and grew mindful of his manners. "Glad you ain't holding that incident agin my place, ma'am. Y'know, it 'pears you weren't the only target."

"Oh?"

"Yep, m' washroom. Vandalized. You oughta seen the mess."

This time, rooms were plentiful. There was no need to share a bed or inconveniences like that. Nonetheless, Longarm was soon bunking with Jessie.

In the aftermath of their first explosive union, Longarm drowsed beside her, his breathing trembling in her ear. Jessie nestled against him in the cramped bed, blissfully contented.

At last, she stirred. "Custis . . . ?"

"Mm."

"Remember your promise."

"I lied. It won't really rise from the dead on command."

"Not that. I mean, about what brings you here. You've given scraps, promising to explain fully once we were alone, then once we were, to explain afterwards. Well, it's after. I'm listening."

"Of all the times to . . . !" Sighing, Longarm related how he found papers documenting a cartel conspiracy, and how they involved Wolfer and the West Coast. He skated over traveling to Ogden with Easter Osborne and arranging her escort to the Double-O, emphasizing instead how he had learned where Jessie was by contacting her Circle Star

Ranch. He then bulled through an assignment to investigate the Valhalla Land Development Company, and took leave—of his senses, according to Marshal Vail—to detour via Gold Beach. "I pretty much followed the Oregon Trail, then rode from Portland to here," Longarm concluded. "Sooner or later, and sooner if I know what's healthy for me, I must report to Marshal Cheney Nicodemus, in Reno. He's semi-retired, and still damn sharp."

Jessie was thoughtful. "Valhalla's in Reno. . . . Quinalt had a brothel token from there. Can you recall more about the letters?"

"Everything." Sighing again, Longarm began reciting chapter and verse of the papers he'd memorized. He was just settling into a good droning clip when Jessie shot bolt upright.

"What was that name? The one signing the letters?"

"Ah . . . Gustav. Usually it's Henry Gustav."

"Custis, dear Custis, oh, have I got news for you!"

"I don't want any more news."

"Henry Gustav is the personal secretary of Herzog Von Blöde. I've never met him, but from my father's notes and other references, he's apparently a petty bureaucrat, all celluloid collar and spats, devotedly serving Von Blöde."

"He's news? Sounds fairly typical of the breed."

"No, he's best of his breed. Von Blöde wouldn't retain him otherwise, for Von Blöde is one of the top five of the cartel. You see? Gustav himself is unimportant, a glorified clerk, yet where he goes, so goes Von Blöde and, perhaps, the rest of that *sanctum sanctorum*."

"More likely, where Von Blöde goes, so must go lots of bodyguards." Longarm glanced away. When he looked at her again, it was inquiringly. "Okay, Gustav and Von Blöde might go to Reno, but don't bet on it. I never saw any envelopes, so I can't say where Valhalla posts its letters, but its Reno address has to be a mail drop, its mail forwarding on."

"Perhaps. But why forwarding? Reno's convenient, is set up, and cartel men visit it. No, someone probably comes to post and collect at Reno, and doesn't go too far afield. I wouldn't be surprised if Von Blöde is based there, or if Major Pennington's heading there to report."

"I wouldn't faint, either. But even if Gustav and Von Blöde are there, they'll be well bastioned and shielded by muscles and firepower."

"Oh, we always hit the cartel somehow, guarded or not. Till now, we fought on the defensive, countering assaults, blocking schemes, knowing we'll make errors like I did tonight, until some fatal mistake. No longer. Now we'll launch strikes. Assuming, of course, Von Blöde and, I hope, his associates are around Reno or somewhere in the West."

"Taking them on, y'know, is taking on a hell of a gamble."

"Yes, but the odds won't be improving, and the jackpot's big. One or all of those cartel leaders were compelled to come from Europe by either a major crisis or some tricky, delicate intrigue prone to erupt at any moment. I suspect the latter. Big boys like Von Blöde plot big for big stakes, but take big risks, even to being vulnerable at times," Jessie said with a tigerish smile. "Such as now, perhaps. The cartel might be overextended, and a loss could cause a crash. Or possibly Von Blöde or someone high as him would disappear. The time's right to attack, and it's the only game I have to play."

"Fine, if it wins." Leaning up along Jessie, Longarm cupped a hand to caress one of her breasts. Just before he clasped his lips to her distended nipple, he asked, "What if it doesn't?"

"It'll win," Jessie vowed adamantly. "It has to." She stiffened once, then felt weak as she looked down at Longarm sucking her breast, while his hand kneaded her other breast, his thumb and forefinger tweaking her nipple into hardness. Her breath began to quicken, along with her pulse. "I-in the midst of an informative, serious discussion, you . . . I don't know why I let you spoil it."

Longarm eyed her, grinning. "Spoil? Not at all. I'm not merely giving lip service, I'm attentively keeping abreast of our conversation."

"Oh, you are a liar," Jessie protested, her eyes feverbright. "If you dast force your lewd behavior further, sir, I shall scream."

"Go ahead."

"Eek," she whispered.

Longarm laughed and reached for her, drawing her close as she snuggled down alongside. His mouth pressed against hers once more. Her lips melted to his, her arms sliding around his neck, while she could feel down between their rubbing bodies that his erection was now reviving hard and strong. He started nuzzling the nape of her neck then, nipping tenderly at her earlobes while his hands eased in between them to fondle her aching breasts. Jessie responded fiercely, draping one bent leg over him in an effort to thrust closer.

In response to her urgent yearnings, she pressured her naked body against him, writhing back and forth and up and down. She stretched out beside him, snuggling affectionately, her legs crooked and parted to display her privates. "I want you," she whispered huskily in her ear. "I want you in me." His hands touched off new sensations in her, and she trembled.

Watching her all the while, Longarm entered Jessie very slowly. It was diabolical torment, and Jessie feared she was going to cry out before he was fully buried within her. She could savor the feel of how hot his spearing flesh was, how his body quivered when finally he was entirely in, his thick rod throbbing deep in her.

Longarm began thrusting repeatedly into her with long, pummeling jolts. Jessie moaned at the tempo, an ever-growing sensuality pervading her inflamed nerves. There was no reserve to her, no holding back. She surrendered to him in a series of delighted pantings and half-convulsions.

Longarm's passion was made thunderous by her upward thrusting each time he tightened his own muscles to drive into her, and the joy he felt was not mere passion. Jessie was so alive! Her body was vibrant as she pistoned strongly up to match the rhythmic batterings of her flesh, while he hammered into her stormy loins and her bottom squirmed on the squeaky bed beneath her. Ever faster, ever deeper, Longarm heaved his body up and down between her extended legs. Desire flamed up and caused his blood to sing in his ears and made his heart try to jump out of his rib cage, while his excitement mounted higher, until he sensed he was on the brink of release.

"Ahhh . . . yes, Custis, yes, now, my love . . . !"

Jessie moved wantonly in concert with Longarm, totally unable to control her swiftly approaching orgasm. Tears welled in her eyes, and her hands clawed harder into his flesh as, groaning up against him, her passions erupted with the force of a tidal wave. Jessie's peak seemed to be the trigger for Longarm, and he spasmed violently with his second climax in as many hours.

They shared their passionate outpourings, taking nothing from the other, but adding to their entity. They were beyond flesh, and moved in mystic union, Jessie arching her greedy loins and squeezing the last of his surging, plundering eruption.

Slowly calming, they lay coupled, limp and satiated. Even after Longarm withdrew from Jessie, they dozed intertwined, listening to their heartbeats and the plaintive howl of a coyote far off, serenading the stars.

★

Chapter 21

A cloudless sunrise was just beginning to blaze above the Coast Range when Jessie, Ki, and Longarm rode into the North Moon ranch yard. Abe Wyndam was on hand, as well as most of the crew, and though partings were poignant, everyone kept a fairly chipper face on the good-byes. Except for Opal, who would frequently burst into weeping sobs, for no particular reason she cared to divulge.

"I can never thank you two enough," Wyndam told Jessie and Ki, beaming heartily. "And that goes for m' boys too, by jove."

"No need to thank us, Abe. After all, we were acting in our own interest," Jessie replied lightly. "I believe you shouldn't have any more trouble from rustlers and raiders." She gazed about, her eyes warm with approval. "We're glad to have come. You've got a nice area here, with plenty of nice folks living in it."

"In peace," Ki added. "And let's hope it stays peaceful."

Jessie murmured agreement to that, but already she was thinking ahead. There was another fight to be waged, and for all the peace here now, a trail of danger and death lay beckoning.

As soon as was practical after their belongings were packed, they left the ranch to head south along the coastal wagon road. It was the direction in which Major Pennington had fled, and though the fugitive could easily have circled back and run north or along the Douglas Trail, continuing south seemed the most logical way to start.

They hunted slowly, methodically, asking about Pennington in every village, gossiping with every bystander and passerby they met. The scrub telegraph, source of entertainment in an otherwise humdrum existence, was the lifeblood of a tracker. Finally they picked up their first trace of Pennington at Klamath, a wide spot in the road twenty-four miles below Crescent City, where he'd stopped to eat.

In the settlements after Klamath they drew blanks, and weren't surprised. By estimating Pennington's timing, they figured he'd been flogging his horse unmercifully, and could have stayed overnight in the next town, Eureka. He damn well should have, if he'd wanted a live horse to ride the following day. But nobody in Eureka had seen him.

Backtracking twenty miles to a junction, they took a cutoff angling inland. It was a guess—the fork was in a field of markless stone—which was why they had first tried Eureka. But it was an educated guess, based on Pennington's passing by Eureka, and on Jessie's idea that his destination was Reno. And, anyway, Longarm had to go to Reno.

The trail was a soaring squiggle across the Salmon Mountains. Occasionally from higher elevations they could scan far vistas, though not so far they could see Pennington. But they had a basic notion where the man was heading; east, since north and south were hemmed in, rugged and remote. Eventually they began descending toward the Sacramento Valley, and on the morning of their third day, they rode across the rolling country and entered the crossroads town of Redding.

They felt Jessie's hunch was cinched after discovering that Pennington had horse-traded. In a sense, they were lucky. They had no way of knowing that Pennington's Morgan would get bone spavin from overexertion, or that he would dicker with a skinflint codger who boasted of his deal. The geezer was lucky, too, not to have had his head blown off or his horse simply stolen; Pennington was a desperate fugitive who had killed before and would kill again if provoked.

So a stranger resembling Major Pennington had ridden southeast out of Redding on a moleskin grulla. Longarm, finding the telegraph office, wired the particulars and a request for detention to Marshal Nicodemus. Then they doggedly pressed on.

Sun burned their eyes and the heat made sweat trickle down into them and sting. Jessie and Longarm removed their jackets. Ki licked his lips, tasting the salt of his perspiration. They crossed the blistering high-desert valley at a steady lope, but were forced to a picky walk when they traversed the crippling lava beds around volcanic Mount Lassen. Rather than camp, they spent the night in Susanville.

Next morning, clean-clothed and hot-bathed, they left on their last leg to Reno. A good wagon trail went the distance, toiling across broad stretches of jagged rock and massed boulders, through dry washes and stands of bull pine, along grades profuse with buckbrush, vetch, and bright thistle poppy.

They entered Reno in the early afternoon, the dull stretch before the flurry of evening trade. Jogging along, they shared the street with farmers and ranchers and mine laborers moseying on horseback or in wagons. On the boardwalks, a few bonneted women shopped, while bored storekeepers leaned in the open doorways. A dog snoozed under a bootmaker's porch roof. Beside it, a man resting in a rocker occasionally scratched its ears, both seeming oblivious to the few quiet stirrings around them.

The block of Ralston between Third and Fourth consisted of plain, solid residences for plain, solid citizens. Number 342 was made of block stone, with painted wood trim, a picket fence, and flower patches bordering the front porch. It was the home of Marshal Nicodemus.

Longarm swung from his horse and lifted his arms to assist Jessie from her saddle. For a moment his body was molded against hers and his face was very close; then, giving him a fleeting smile, she pulled away to loop the reins around a fence slat.

The marshal met them at the door as they stepped up on the low front porch. Garbed in a somber blue-black town suit, he had shaggy white hair, the bowed legs of a wrangler and the massive shoulders of a miner. First Ki, then Jessie found themselves looking into a pair of dark eyes as sharp and clear as polished agate.

"Bring your friends right on inside, Custis," Nicodemus said quickly. "I'm proud to make your acquaintance, Miss Starbuck, and . . . was that Ki? Yes? Well, just find a chair and make yourselves at home."

Jessie and Ki sensed that true hospitality lay behind the greeting Nicodemus gave them, and smiled in response as they entered. Inside, they glimpsed the comely, intelligent face of the marshal's wife, as she looked out for a moment from the kitchen. After that they could hear her gently moving about with her work.

The furnishings were few, yet substantial and sufficient. A reflection of their owners, Jessie sensed; those who pioneered in the thinly settled West learned to travel light.

Nicodemus shut the door and shed his jacket, chatting with Longarm. "You look better'n ever, Custis. Has it been four, five years, since we were on the Toomey brothers feud? And, hey, how's Billy Vail?"

"Fine. Asked me to remind you that you still owe him six dollars from that poker game up at the XT spread over a dozen years ago."

"Why, that ornery reprobate! That game was crooked as a snake hoop. Why, one hand Billy showed up with had four aces to my four kings, and I'd been extra careful to deal him four queens!"

Jessie studied Nicodemus with interest as he reminisced with Longarm. Coatless, he appeared taller and more erect. Being a U. S. marshal would place heavy responsibilities upon his shoulders and keep him away from home. Like the simple room furnishings, time had battered the marshal, too. His silvering hair failed to conceal an ugly scar that looked like a tomahawk wound, and his white shirt must cover other scars from bullets and knives, Jessie reasoned, for he was an older edition of Longarm. He was what Longarm would become, should Longarm live so long. Yet, like Longarm now, the marshal possessed an inner strength that would serve his purpose well, even as he would always serve the law. Jessie read that in his eyes, too, as his face became grave and thoughtful when responding to a change of subject.

"Oh, yes, your cable about Pennington came yesterday afternoon. I see you still don't believe in allowing much advance notice, do you?"

"Sorry. I wired as soon as I knew, soon as I could."

"So I reckoned. So, it being too late to nab Pennington in Reno, I cut his sign and tracked him toward the Devil's Minarets till dark." Nicodemus waved off Longarm's thanks, demanding, "What's this case about?"

"Mad murderin' and mayhem." Longarm told of Pennington's joint outlaw gang and Quiveran legion, refraining for Jessie's sake from involving the cartel. "Pennington ran his area behind the scenes, and when the scenes folded, he ran here to the biggest boss. He deluded many people about himself and about Quivera, maybe fooling himself, too."

Nicodemus paced, listening, then growled, "I've heard similar Quivera lies here. Friendly Indians have reported riot talk. Quivera's growing from threat to deadly force. Any idea who's the real boss?"

"Herzog Von Blöde."

Nicodemus shrugged blankly. "Stranger to me."

"Von Blöde will cheer hearing that," Jessie remarked. "He's spent fortunes buying discretion. But he's our only suspect who's sufficiently rich, shrewd, and connected to work it. And he's here."

"With Von Blöde is his secretary and stooge, Henry Gustav. Gustav is also involved with Valhalla Land Development Company of Reno, which Von Blöde uses to excuse his travels and to contact his gangs. When he mails instructions or whatever, he writes them equivocally to read like legitimate business letters." Succinctly, then, Longarm connected Valhalla by the letters to Wolfer; Wolfer by his outlaw meet to Pennington; and Pennington by his escape to Reno. "It all seems to connect, and it all seems to gravitate back here, to circle one. That's why Jessie feels it important that Von Blöde is here at the power center. Hell, it's just common sense that Von Blöde is the ringleader."

"Seems sensible," Nicodemus allowed. "But common sense don't stand up in court, Custis. You've got to submit hard evidence."

Longarm turned to Jessie and Ki. "Short of digging up Wolfer for a gravesite confession, I'd say finding Pennington is our best shot."

"Well, showing the letters surely is not. If we won, Gustav but not Von Blöde would be axed," Jessie cautioned. "Locating the major sounds good, but he mightn't want to be found, and if we did, he mightn't speak to us—and perhaps not for years, at least not on our behalf."

"True enough," Ki said with a soft smile. "Let's agree, then, that until Pennington appears live and talking, he cannot be considered as evidence. However, we've very few options, and I'd like to learn where and to whom Pennington was heading up into that peaked country."

Nicodemus grinned, his eyes sharpening with interest. "I've had twinges like that last night when I gave up m' tracking, and during the day today when more pressin' matters interfered. Uh-huh, I'd like to find out where he's been going."

"Sir, you're a family man," Longarm reminded him gently. "You had best turn this li'l mission over to me."

Nicodemus brushed the suggestion aside. "I've always been a family man. I was born married. And I'm also getting old, Custis, but not too old for another jaunt at my trade." He glanced over and looked into Ki's eyes. "And you want to come along, even though it isn't your job? Tell me, Ki, what's your reason?"

"Why, because it'll be fun," Ki replied, straight-faced.

Nicodemus frowned sternly. "Fun? You think this is fun?"

"It's the only reason I can put into words." Ki quirked his lips. "You see, I just do not like outlaws."

Nicodemus nodded thoughtfully. "Yes, well . . . What we oughta do is start tonight, cross the flats under dark, and make the peaks by morn. We must surprise whoever will be there, for being only three—"

"Four," Jessie chimed in.

"Oh, Miss Starbuck, I cannot permit it."

"You cannot stop it," she countered, "unless you jail me."

Nicodemus, startled, glanced at Longarm for male support.

"Jessie's a crack shot and steady under fire," Longarm said. "And she is the expert authority on things such as this

207

Quivera scheme. I can also vouch that if you plan to leave her behind, you'd better chain her to something very solid."

"I suspect she'd break any chain I could get," Nicodemus said, and eyed her again. "Very well, Miss Starbuck. When Custis Long vouches for someone, that someone is all right to take along. I'll take you and Ki. But, remember, this is no pleasure trek. It is grim, dangerous business. We may not all come back."

Preparations were begun. Later, as the shadows fell, Mrs. Nicodemus called them for dinner in the kitchen. As they sat around the table eating, Nicodemus and Longarm calmly continued to make plans and to speak in matter-of-fact tones of their dangerous business. Jessie, attentive, thought this was an example of why she and Longarm weren't married. When on occasion the subject arose, they skated it like thin ice—lightly, briefly, and left unresolved. He was a lawman; he *was* his job, and she would not have him change even if he was willing. Yet what wife could watch the man she loved ride into peril without fear and dread clutching her heart. However, throughout the meal Mrs. Nicodemus was calm and smiling. Jessie felt a strong impulse to talk with her, and after the others left the table, she lingered to help Mrs. Nicodemus clean up.

Soon they were done. Mrs. Nicodemus poured two cups of coffee, put them on the table, and sat down with a sigh. "I envy you, Jessie," she said with a smile. "You're brave and determined. You'll need to be, and more, when you're out there following an outlaw's trail."

"It's you who has real courage," Jessie replied, "the great patience and fortitude to take the constant worrying and waiting."

Mrs. Nicodemus reached across the table and laid her hand on Jessie's hand. "I hate to see you go—all of you. You're all good people. But it takes good people to put bad ones in their place, and that don't seem right, only I guess that's the way it has to be. It's the price we've got to pay. I'm not finding fault with the design of things, mind you, except . . . Except, hold fast and keep a cool head."

It was there. Jessie saw it, that haunting anxiety that had been hidden in her heart. "I'll stick by. You can count on it."

"Dear me, I wasn't suggesting you'd run out. The marshal and Deputy Long are good fighters, but impulsive, and might use a little cinching." Mrs. Nicodemus tightened her fingers on Jessie's hand and continued gently, intuitively, "Before I married, my seadog of a father said Cheney had the chartings of a rowdy, full-reef-gale life. Some men are fated to such lives, as I think you know. And I remember being afraid that for him to settle down with me would cheat us both out of it. Lord, just the opposite. Oh, I'm prattling, I'm sure, but you'd be surprised how many supposed bad matches do make it well and lasting, by taking the rough with the smooth, all in a day's stride."

"I'll remember that, if the time comes." Jessie paused, then added with a soft laugh, "Well, if it has, it's never seemed to be quite the right time, but somehow a mite too early or too late."

"Too late?" Longarm said, materializing beside her. "Why, if you'll get cracking, I'd judge we'll be right on time."

Both women laughed, realizing Longarm had not overheard their conversation and had misconstrued the last comment by Jessie. Soon the horses were saddled and led from the back-yard stable, and Mrs. Nicodemus came to stand beside her husband as he was about to mount. Goodbyes were said, and then, with a whispered farewell, the marshal swung quickly up into his saddle and reined away.

Mrs. Nicodemus stood there in the starlit gloom while they rode from the yard. Jessie turned and glimpsed her, still peering, her eyes straining to follow the vague blur of departing riders. Even after they passed from sight, Jessie knew Mrs. Nicodemus would stay there, watching and listening. For what else was there for a lawman's wife to do but listen and watch and pray?

Chapter 22

From up in the lead, a low, aimless humming by Marshal Nicodemus drifted back to Jessie's ears. Just ahead rode Ki, who had been silent and contemplative, and at the moment was taking a nap in his saddle.

Longarm was bringing up the rear, leading a packhorse that carried supplies and light camping equipment. A water keg topped the load. He seemed less than enthused by the arrangement, yet he had only himself to blame, having pointed out that the last in line was often the first to die. Yet it wasn't Jessie or Ki who demanded they ride buffered between the lawmen. It was Longarm who insisted his badge gave him the right and duty to expose his backside. Jessie was tempted to chuckle softly as she listened to his grumbling voice.

"Why, Custis, are you ailing?" she finally asked, hitching around in her saddle. "Did the three helpings of supper you wolfed down cause you indigestion? Or was that half a cake too much?"

Longarm gave a snort of disgust. "This club-footed jughead keeps dragging back on the lead rope like he's coasting on a sled."

"Well, then try riding on the pack and lead your saddle horse."

Abruptly Longarm reined to a halt. Jessie drew in, wondering if perhaps she had gone too far in her joking. Longarm had moments when he was very cross-grained indeed, and she could vividly recall a time or two when he had exploded like a firecracker lit at both ends.

Instead of exploding, Longarm grasped the packhorse by the nose and half-hitched the hackamore rope on the lower jaw. Then he swiftly remounted and rode ahead. For an instant the stubborn horse pulled back, then reared and lunged forward, following Longarm's saddler with alacrity, keeping plenty of slack in the lead rope. Quickening their clip, Longarm and Jessie soon caught up with the other two, and again eased to the slower pace of the line.

"I bet the crowbait won't hassle me for a while," Longarm said, now high with humor. "If I'd my wits, I'd have fixed him right off."

"I wondered why you didn't try that Indian trick sooner."

"Speaking of Indians, I wouldn't object to having a sharp one along to help read sign. Jessie, you're good, and me 'n' the marshal aren't bad, either, and Ki is the best I've ever worked with. Still, run an unshod horse up through those peaks and canyons, and it'd need a tracker who's part Comanche and part coon hound to trace it. When did Nicodemus get his notion we'd take any outlaws by surprise? He knows better, and if he'd asked me, I'd have reminded him."

"The marshal didn't ask you, Custis," Jessie teased. "He only brought you along to herd the packhorse."

With an injured sigh, Longarm lapsed into silence. He enjoyed their banter, which was based on affection and trust. Joking also helped release the tensions and anxieties that grew screaming inside during risky ventures like this. Longarm would have answered Jessie barb for barb if it wasn't for Nicodemus, who had acute hearing and chronic chivalry. The old marshal was an old knight at heart, saving fair ladies from various dragons—insulting deputies included—without realizing that most fair ladies owned dragon farms.

A night wind whispered across the Sierra foothills west of Reno. The stars became more brilliant and sparkled like cut diamonds in the velvet sky. The hooves of the horses caused only a low padding shuffle in the gravel and loose rock and the dry, flaky soil.

The easy motion of her horse rocked Jessie to sleep in her saddle. Now and then she opened her eyes to view the vague, sinister outline of the mountain peak country, and each time it seemed a little closer. Before dawn they were climbing slopes that were either too steep or too stony or both for blanket forest growth. The few trees which had managed to root and survive had thick, wind-twisted trunks and clumsy branches that waved in the breeze like flagging arms, warning of the pinnacles above. Jessie awakened then, senses alert.

Presently they were entering a canyon where, in ages past, raging torrents had gouged and ground a river bed. Now the canyon's floor was parched, and choked with an accumulation of rubble sluffed off from the eroding heights above, making progress slow and dangerous.

In the growing light of dawn, Marshal Nicodemus checked his mount and stared around. He sighted a secluded spot under a frowning ledge, and rode in under the perpendicular rock wall. Ki followed, scrutinizing the canyon floor, while Jessie and Longarm closed in.

"Marshal, here's a set of horse tracks," Ki called. "They look recent but not fresh. Day-old. Would these be Pennington's?"

The marshal came over and looked. "I think so . . . but it was black by the time I got here, and I couldn't make much of anything. Hell, let's follow 'em. First let's rest our horses and cook some vittles."

With the hundred-foot cliff at their back, a tiny cooking fire was kindled. Packs were removed, cinches loosened, and the horses were staked out, and by then they had prepared a quick breakfast of bacon, bread, and coffee. While they ate, they surveyed the rough slope facing them, where cedars and scrub pine maintained perilous footholds on its steep pitch. Ahead the canyon forked, and beyond lay another peak, higher, more rugged and massive, its broken crest visible through the bottleneck of the canyon between.

This pinnacle was already catching and reflecting the first rays of dawn. As the sun peeked a degree higher, other summits began to glisten with a cold splendor. Yet, the lighter and clearer it became, the more disordered the peaks appeared, while the surrounding terrain emerged into day as a chaos of angles, lines, strata, and cleavages.

"It's magnificent," Jessie remarked, scanning the view. "It's also a spectacular ruin. Custis, do you know the trails in here?"

Longarm smiled and shook his head. "I know a few, and the marshal knows many more, since he was raised hereabouts, but not all."

"I doubt anyone ever has or will," Nicodemus declared. "This all looks distractingly different, while at the same time it all looks confusingly similar. And there're hundreds of canyons like this one. You've no idea how easy you can trek all day and end up at the camp you left that morning. Well, not us. We're traveling by compass."

"It'd be better to follow a cougar," Longarm suggested. "These peaks breed mean cats and meaner men. The cats know their way around."

"They know their way to food, water, and shelter," Ki said. "Man has to work the same. The men we want will be holed up where they've plenty of cover, good water, and graze for their horses."

"Well, the tracks aim toward a promising region, with several spots I rec'lect will fit the bill," Nicodemus said. "Soon's we find one that the tracks tend to head for, we'll go see if anyone's there."

"If not, if we don't find them at all, don't worry. They're sure to find us soon. But I think we'll find them," Longarm said, studying the ledges above. "We'll find them wide awake and waiting for us."

"We'll soon find out about that," Nicodemus stated grimly.

Breakfast was quickly eaten, cinches were tightened, the packhorse was deftly reloaded. Remounting, they rode into the narrowing canyon just ahead, keeping in the same order, Longarm the last in line.

During the brief interval of rest, the packhorse had found time to free its lower jaw from the biting turn of rope that Longarm had placed there. Now the horse began dragging back on the lead rope more obstinately than before.

Longarm turned in his saddle and gave blistering voice to

his annoyance. When he heard Jessie laughing he added, "Jessie, come get behind this slab-sided son o' Satan and prod him along."

"Smile, Custis, and talk soft and pretty to the bronc," Jessie said, grinning over her shoulder. "It'll gentle right down like the ladies always do, and'll eat cake right out of your hand."

Longarm, muttering, reined in and dismounted. "It won't be cake I feed you. I'll make you eat the rope," he remarked coldly to the horse, and untying the lead rope so he could work with it better, approached to throw another hitch on the packhorse's jaw.

Marshal Nicodemus was leading the way with care, his mount traveling at a slow walk. Ki was stringing along close in under the towering cliff upon their right. Jessie was not far behind and was moving at a dawdle while she kept a mischievous eye on Longarm.

Suddenly a rending, muffled detonation shivered the canyon.

Instantly Longarm yelled hard and sharp, "Ride! Ride like hell!"

"Ride for your life!" Jessie shouted to Ki and the marshal. She caught a glimpse of Longarm springing toward his waiting saddle. Then he was gone, buried, and she was about to be. With the blood freezing in her veins, she spurred her horse into desperate headlong flight.

The canyon walls trembled as if shaken by a giant hand. The air was filled with an increasing sullen rumble as of thunder, and the narrow strip of sky overhead darkened. Looking up, Longarm saw great slabs of rocks and boulders spilling downward in a mighty flood. He flashed a look at Jessie as he leaped for his horse, and it was then she glimpsed him, and he caught a split-second portrait of her face blanched in frantic horror.

The next instant everything was blotted out before Longarm's searching eyes. A ferocious gust of wind nearly ripped him from his saddle. Dust blinded him. Cataclysmic sound deafened him. Fragments of splintering stone pelted his body, cutting, numbing.

Yet Longarm's racing, lunging, fear-maddened horse ran

214

from under the outer edge of the cascading avalanche. It carried its reeling, choking rider safely up the canyon in the wake of those who had gone before. Well out of danger, Longarm stopped and looked back. One by one the others slowly returned and checked their mounts beside him, and the four sat in their saddles, deeply shaken. Motionless, they watched the last dribble of rocks trickle over the broken crest of the high cliff above, heaping higher the colossal mound under which the packhorse was buried.

In a voice ragged with emotion, Jessie said, "You asked me to help with that pack, Custis, and I—I only laughed at you. You asked me to ride behind and prod it along, and, oh, if only I had! We would've been free and clear before it even came, and you . . . you wouldn't have been trapped in there, almost. I'll never josh again!"

Longarm had a great desire right then to comfort Jessie in his arms. But there was no practical way he could vault saddles and bear her to the ground, and convince his superior office he was extending a gentlemanly pat. So he spoke kindly. "Don't look at it that way, Jessie. You didn't know the slide was coming. None of us did, none of us could."

"Yes, that's just shock talking," Nicodemus said paternally, turning from Jessie to Longarm. "I'll be putting you in for a commendation. You cottoned to that slide before us and, looking at death, you gave a warning quick as a shot, saving us all. Well, I got to write you up. If you'd stayed asaddle, you'd have ridden clear with no problems or hysterifying young ladies or losing government materiél."

"The packhorse. I'm to blame." The irony tickled Longarm; his lips twitched as he replied. "The lead rope was untied. The packhorse was free, but didn't budge. Okay. I'm riding, the rope's tied, the slide comes . . . and the packhorse drags back, anchoring my horse and me under it all. If it wasn't for losing our food, water, extra ammunition, and so forth with it, I'd celebrate that stupid horse's death."

Now Ki spoke up. He had been listening peripherally, his attention focused on the slide. A massive pile of boulders blocked the canyon to a height of forty feet, and no telling to what depth, perhaps a hundred yards or more. Toward one canyon rim he discerned the black surface of a huge stone block, the telltale smear of a powder flash. Blasting powder had been poured into deep cracks up along the rim, kegs of it, and set off when they came along underneath.

Now, impatient, Ki spoke up. "Let's move. Killers tried to blast us once with the slide. I don't know where they are now, but I don't like where I am, sitting horseback out exposed in the open."

The marshal, nodding, set his horse trotting. "Yep, Custis's hunch was right. Outlaws saw us coming and blocked our trail behind us. There may be more around us, watching above us, up ahead with another ambush." He ran his fingers through his hair and, replacing his hat, eyed Jessie morosely. "I'm sorry, ma'am, to've let you and Ki get in on this. It's beginning to look like we're on a one-way trail."

"No apologies needed or accepted. Ki and I have ridden one-way trails before, Marshal, and the one ways are always the same way," Jessie said resolutely. "The only way. Hunt them down and wipe them out."

The marshal viewed Jessie keenly, but whatever he thought he kept to himself. He slowed instead, and shifted so he could address everyone. "We'll push on up this canyon. Space out a hundred yards apart, same order. No use bunching all our eggs in one basket." He reined his horse around and rode slowly on, carbine out across his lap.

"One hundred yards. No closer. Ki, you're next," Longarm reminded them calmly. "Shoot to kill at the first flicker of a gun."

With his horse at a walk, Ki slowly followed the marshal. Jessie filled her pockets with rifle shells from a saddle pocket and slid one shell through the loading gate, filling her magazine. Then, wrapping the reins around her saddlehorn, she let her horse move at a walk.

Because of the frequent sharp bends in the canyon, a hundred yards apart frequently put them out of sight. She found it reassuring when she would see Ki riding lean and wary, just like she'd glimpsed him last time and the time before, and hoped she would the next and the time after that. Occasionally she could hear Longarm checking his restless mount with a steady rein, the nervously spirited horse having not yet fully recovered from the landslide. There was a lingering effect on Jessie as well. When she would turn and look back at Longarm, she would feel warmth and relief and renewed desire. Then she would see his face looming in her mind's eye, as she had seen it in that last instant before a thousand tons of rock engulfed him, every feature of his expression etched starkly as if with acid. And she would brush her hand across her eyes, but she could not always banish the haunting picture.

The sun rose and the morning brightened. It was still fairly early when Jessie again saw Ki and watched him pull his carbine from its scabbard and lever in a shell. Something had changed. For Ki to draw and cock a firearm, Jessie knew, meant its probable and imminent use. So something had come up, something that could only be worse.

Ki studied the rimrocks and along the canyon walls, then gazed up the trail where the marshal was searching out each possible ambush in advance. The marshal observed fresh sign of the rider, presumably Pennington, and when in due course Ki moved up to that area, he examined the sign. He was now as familiar as the marshal with those prints, and the kind of horse, shoes, and rider that would produce them.

Except for those prints, the marshal hadn't detected any more than Ki, which was nothing. After having watched Nicodemus work this morning, Ki figured if anything had been around, Nicodemus would have found it. Yet he couldn't shake a sense of unease. And though it remained perversely vague, as elusive as tracks on the trial, it nagged him until he unsheathed his carbine and toted it "just in case."

Coming to a fork in the canyon, the marshal paused and examined the area. Accordingly, Ki reined in to wait. From his vantage he could see enough of the north fork to tell that it threaded among a vista of high peaks. The left fork meandered southwesterly and was soon cut from view by other high peaks. Apparently the marshal was having trouble discerning which of the trails had been taken by Pennington. The tracks had all but vanished by now on the hard canyon floor.

Ki wasn't sure he could do any better, but he thought he should offer to help. He was about to disobey orders and ride to the fork when the marshal made his decision from some scant sign, and took his horse onto the left fork. The narrow defile seemed not to change. It continued on and on, twisting and writhing as if tying into knots.

Again everyone stopped when the marshal reached another fork and had to inspect each branch carefully. His horse stood motionless, its ears pointed forward. Ki wondered why, and as a precaution, made sure his mount stayed quiet and still. Strung way behind him, Jessie and Longarm seemed to have hushed their horses too, but that was probably his imagination, for they were hard to hear anyway, and besides, they wouldn't know what was happening here. Neither did he, but he'd been lucky again, and was positioned where he could watch.

The silence tensed . . . stretched . . . strained. . . . The marshal, frowning warily, cupped his left ear to catch any faint noise. It was his horse that made the next sounds, soft ones, turning its head a trifle, then flicking its pointed ears, toward the shoulder of the peak that split the canyon.

At that instant, a camp robber took wing from a bushy, gnarled cedar growing on a jutting ledge. The marshal caught the flash of its wings as the startled bird swerved in erratic flight, then returned to the cedar, where it gave voice to its annoyance and curiosity in noisy, petulant scolding. The bird was like a pointing finger marking out the spot where a vague blur of blue under the cedar showed at variance with the gray wall behind.

The marshal's rifle was shouldered in a smooth, swift movement. The rifle spoke immediately its butt was cushioned, and its sharp report ripped the silence and rolled off between the canyon walls. It was answered by a wild shot, then by a wilder scream. A rifle pitched from the ledge under the cedar. The rolling gunfire acted like a coiled spring upon Ki, launching him forward in a great leaping gallop by his horses. The clattering ring of hard iron chiming across hard stone mingled with the echoes of those two rifle shots tumbling back across the canyon's fork.

Without warning, a rifle shot lanced at the marshal.

Although Ki had anticipated that more than one killer might fire from ambush, he still felt stunned when he saw Nicodemus rock violently in his saddle. The smashing lead impact jarred the rifle dropping from his hands down awkwardly acant his saddle-lap area.

Despite his shock and anguish, Ki responded as the trained fighter he was, jabbing his already rocketing horse to greater speed. He scrutinized the canyon walls and adjacent heights, for the ambusher's bullet had come from a different angle. He swept his carbine into firing position, for another bullet would swiftly follow.

Reeling, the marshal clutched desperately at the saddle-horn to steady himself. His rifle continued its fall, tilting across his saddle-lap, angling, slipping off. For an instant, sunlight winked off the metal as the rifle slid free and dropped.

Closing fast, Ki chanced to catch that wink and, curious why blued steel would reflect, he glanced at the rifle. It was falling; he saw enough before it hit ground. The breech block had a shiny little crater where it had been punched by something very strong. Marshal Nicodemus's rifle struck the rocky ground with a noisy clatter, but Ki paid it no attention, moving on with a glance at the marshal.

Smiles were traded but words were unnecessary. Ki went by on his running horse, aware Nicodemus hadn't been shot. His rifle had been shot in the breech block, and the bullet's force and his rifle's recoil had hit him off guard. He'd been knocked winded and akilter, and would be sorely bruised for a while, but had already recovered enough to spur forward. Ki saw him slide his hand under his coat and bring out his heavy revolver. Then, with a wave, the marshal angled off to check a different stretch of the canyon, to double their chances of finding this second target before it was too late —all this while an ambushing gunman could load a rifle.

Ki surged on, his predatory eyes sweeping the area around the gnarled cedar and jutting ledge upon which the first killer lay. He saw a faint gray trickle of smoke . . . or was it? Ki slewed about at hard rein, approaching from a different angle. Clearer now, the smoke appeared like a thread hanging over the same ledge, but much farther to his right. It was dissipating fast, as though it were the residue of gunpowder, rather than coming from a cooking fire or the like.

Moving to a better line of attack, Ki charged at a gallop

with his carbine pointing the way. He triggered, levered, triggered again in rapid salvos. Hearing hoofbeats behind, he glanced back and saw the marshal tearing toward him, Jessie and Longarm just arriving and coming determinedly. Grinning, Ki turned frontward and pumped four shots straight across the rim of the ledge. There came a scream and a man raised up his head and shoulders.

Nicodemus emptied his revolver with a steady hand.

The man settled back slowly with a dying curse.

Nicodemus reined in by Ki. While they were busily reloading, Jessie and Longarm pulled to sliding halts, concerned and quizzical expressions on their faces as they stared at the men.

"There were two," the marshal said before they could ask, a fierce glitter in his eyes. "We ironed 'em out. End of report. And it wouldn't do no good to bunch here hashing it over. The shooting is liable to draw others in pronto. If you're ready, let's move out."

★

Chapter 23

The marshal took the lead, choosing the left fork and continuing what had become a general drift toward the south and west. They fell in behind in the same open formation as before, scanning the terrain with their probing eyes, keyed to a high tension now, traveling on a hair-trigger. The sun arched higher overhead, measuring the slow march of time as they warily advanced deeper into a hungry wilderness of snarling peaks and leering defiles, with the high walls of one canyon after another frowning down on them.

At length, the marshal drew rein. He motioned for Ki to join him, which Ki did after passing the signal on to Jessie. When they were all gathered round, the marshal explained, "There's a spring and some fair graze up a bend or two, if I ain't mistaken. Y'all wait here while I see who might be camping in about there."

"I'll side you," Longarm said.

"No," Nicodemus said firmly. "You'll stick here, Deputy. I'll go have a cautious look, then come back. If it's a case o' shooting, why, then you can all help me do the job."

"I'll swap you places," Longarm suggested.

"Keep your shirt on, Custis. The day is yet a pup. I'm thinking we'll burn more'n our shares of powder before the sun goes down. And how d'you expect civilians to listen to me if my subordinates won't?"

Longarm nodded reluctantly. They watched Nicodemus ride around the next bend, where the canyon curved sharply to the right. Longarm let out a troubled sigh. "He worries me. It's like he's bound and determined to be the first to spring any trap that's set for us."

"I guess he feels it's his responsibility, maybe because we're along," Jessie said. "It takes guts to ride straight into the teeth of death like he's been doing, knowing it lies in wait."

"Takes luck, too," Ki added. "Lots of it. Old campaigners like the marshal survive on luck. That's not to say he doesn't know what he's doing. Those two ambushers were waiting to get us all within easy rifle range, and the way the marshal had us strung out sort of wrecked their plans."

"I wonder where their horses were," Longarm remarked. "I've yet to see an outlaw that'd get ten jumps from his saddle, but there weren't any along in that canyon. Or any climbing rope that I saw."

"Yeah, and as I recall, it's a long stretch to any ledge above the one they're on. Still, if they did drop down by rope, they wouldn't have left it hanging to catch our eye. It's hard to say exactly how they managed it," Ki shrugged, then added with a slight grin, "Who knows? Maybe we're chasing a bunch of mountain goats."

"I always told you we'd be hunting the cartel in high places," Jessie rejoined. "But right now, they seem to be hunting us."

Longarm cupped his ear. "Did you hear a shot a second ago?"

Jessie and Ki shook their heads.

"I would've sworn . . . You two wait here. No sense in all of us disobeying orders, and maybe I'm just dreaming things, but I've got to go check on the ol' boy before I'll rest easy."

Before they could argue, Longarm was riding swiftly on around the bend, his thoughts in ferment. Had he heard a far-distant shot? Or had that shot been an echo within his mind? His horse's hooves resounded hollow and mocking in the narrow defile. He rounded another twisting curve and saw Nicodemus's big chestnut gelding romping toward him, bridle reins lying across its neck. Longarm blocked the way. The horse came to a snorting halt, and it was then Longarm saw that a smear of crimson stained the empty saddle.

Alarmed and agitated, Longarm dismounted, ground-hitched his reins, and left both horses standing there neck to neck while he ran up the canyon, carbine in hand. He passed around another abrupt turn and saw that the canyon was widening before him. Slackening his pace, he advanced with more caution on silent feet. As his range of vision increased, he glimpsed a bearded man off ahead, and tensed, motionless.

The man wore the sun-faded, nondescript garb characteristic of old prospectors who spend their lives in futile quests for gold. He was bent over, as if even now he plied his trade, sampling the gravel deposited in this broad curve of the canyon. Then the bearded prospector straightened, and Longarm caught his breath. Marshal Nicodemus's body was stretched out limp upon the ground. As if satisfied, the man laughed gustily, while with a skill born of long practice, he spun his revolver on his trigger finger.

As he viewed that callous scene, something cracked within Longarm and turned him cold as ice. He shifted his carbine to his left hand, and drew his revolver slowly, quietly from his holster. Unobserved by the bearded man, he padded noiselessly out into the open, and was quite close before the man raised his eyes from the body. Abruptly aware that he was not alone, the man whirled, his revolver stabbing out a muzzle blast. Longarm fired two quick shots, his revolver held low, and saw his bullets pat dust from the faded vest. He watched as the man started hinging at the knees. Then he raised his revolver and threw a third shot square into the bearded face. The man toppled over and sprawled backward to the ground.

Marshal Nicodemus was not quite dead. He opened his eyes when Longarm straightened out his grizzled head and lifted it on his arm, kneeling there beside him.

"I knew you'd find me, Custis. You never could obey orders worth a damn," Nicodemus murmured faintly. "Real pretty, isn't it, up here in the mountains?" The marshal's lean fingers tightened for an instant on Longarm's arm, then grew limp.

With a smothered emotion in his chest, Longarm gazed into the marshal's face. Nicodemus seemed to smile, as if he were quite content to have died with boots and badge on, rather than uselessly in his bed. Slowly Longarm lowered the marshal's head and gently closed the sightless eyes.

A few moments later, Jessie and Ki rode up, leading the marshal's and Longarm's horses. Naturally, they were in a high state of concern. They found Longarm standing over Nicodemus in somber reverie, a faraway look in his thoughtful eyes, the rest of his features stony bleak.

"How did it happen?" Jessie demanded softly, hurrying to him.

"That's what I aim to figure out," Longarm replied calmly, and put his arm about her as if to protect and shield her from some danger he could not quite place. "Cheney died with a bullet in his back."

"That harmless gold rat killed him?" Ki asked as he stepped from the horses toward the bearded man.

Longarm nodded. "I reckon that's what Cheney judged him to be. He was a rat, all right! But not a harmless rat."

"He's not a prospector either," Ki said, bending over the man and examining his hands. "His palms are as soft as a woman's, almost. The hardest work he ever did was to toss lead. He's a gunslick."

"He *was* a gunslick," Longarm corrected. "He isn't any more."

The wide bend where they were was about ten acres in extent, they judged. An old river channel lay on their right, curving like a drawn bow with the undercut wall of the canyon hanging over it. On their left was a long, level bar of coarse gravel, with a sprinkling of large boulders here and there. The bar was of half-moon shape, and a few hardwood trees had taken root close to a spring whose flow trickled from a fault in the high cliff. It was there the canyon branched.

Near the spring, wisps of smoke curled up over a small cookfire. A blackened coffee pot nestled among the glowing embers, and a frying pan of half-cooked bacon sat on the

ground alongside. Near the fire were a cluster of pack panniers, and three large, lop-eared burros picking at what scant
forage they could find. They were still wearing their wooden
packsaddles, indicating that this was not a permanent campsite, but only a mealtime rest stop.

Satisfied after a quick look at the lay of things that the
killer had been alone, they carried Nicodemus's body in
among the trees and laid it there for the time being. By then
they had figured out how the marshal came to be backshot.
The tracks of his horse were plain upon the gravel bar,
showing where he had slowly ridden up to the cookfire and
had stopped to talk to the killer. From that bunch, more
tracks led to the spring, where the marshal had watered his
horse before he set off slowly back the way he had come.
And, as clearly as if there was sign to read, it was apparent
that the bearded man had taken his pan of frying bacon from
the fire, drawn his revolver, aimed, and fired. The horse
carried Nicodemus for a few jumps as it lunged away. Then
Nicodemus slipped limply from the saddle.

Then the killer had walked out to view the result of his
shot, and laugh as he watched Nicodemus die. Obviously
the marshal had not mentioned that others were waiting for
him, else the killer would have been warned. Nor could the
killer have made a mistake in identity, for the marshal's gold
badge was pinned prominently to his lapel. But Nicodemus's
error was easy to understand, for by every outward sign, the
man was a wandering prospector. They had all met many
such wanderers at odd places at odd times, appearing out of
nowhere on an unmarked path that seemed to have no start
or end. If given no reason to suspect otherwise, they all
could have been fooled by the man's disguise.

They went over to inspect the packs. Each pair of panniers was covered with a square of soiled canvas, upon
which lay a neatly coiled pack rope and cinch. When they
drew back the canvas, they did not find the meager grub-
stake of a luckless prospector, but fancy canned goods, hams
and bacon slabs, carefully packed eggs, bottles of bonded
whiskey, and a large supply of ammunition for various
weapons.

"Where else could all this be heading," Ki remarked with

a sly grin, "if not to the campsite of some crooks we've been after?"

"Noplace else," Jessie agreed. "And it would've gone right on to there, too, if the marshal hadn't stumbled onto it here. If it doesn't show up, in fact, they might worry and go in search of it."

Longarm voiced what they all had in mind. "Why, then let's take the stuff to them. The burros should know the way and lead us there."

They did not leave immediately. Their horses needed a break, and were picketed within reach of water and graze. A meal was prepared from the well-supplied packs. Then Longarm said, "There's no need to wash this tin plate and frying pan. We'll be using them to dig Cheney's grave. Come on. Let's do the job now."

They worked in silence among the trees, close by the wall of the cliff, scratching away the gravel and rolling larger boulders from the depression. Finally, with his revolver holstered and his badge on his breast, they gently lowered Marshal Nicodemus into his last resting place, and covered his body with squares of canvas taken from the packs. When they had finished leveling the gravel over him, they carefully marked with boulders the spot where he lay. Then they stood for a time in silence, looking down with heads uncovered, before they quietly turned away.

At the far end of the gravel bar they scooped out a shallow oblong hole, dumped in the bearded killer, and flung the gravel back over him. The panniers were lashed in place with a squaw hitch, the horses were resaddled, and the marshal's gelding was tethered on a rope to Longarm's saddle. Judging by the position of the afternoon sun, they figured that one branch of the canyon ran southwest, the other north. The tracks of the burros came in from the north, so they prodded the outlaw pack train into reluctant motion toward the southwest, and felt heartened when one of the burros automatically fell into the lead.

Presently they came to another fork. The lead burro paused uncertainly, then scrambled upward to the right, following a precarious ledge. With stolid patience, the other two animals trailed on up behind their leader. Behind them filed the three riders and four horses. Gradually the canyon bottom appeared to fall away and become filled with a soundless river of shadows. When the riders looked upward and off beyond, they seemed surrounded by looming snow-capped spires and crags banking away against the late afternoon sky.

The hazardous trail dragged endlessly on. The lead burro plodded grudgingly on, needing to be prodded every so often, seemingly following a familiar path, invisible to the riders' eyes, yet a path that seemed to lead nowhere. Flanking high peaks, cutting through boulder-strewn passes, winding among dark and narrow ravines, they nonetheless rode where the burro went, and hoped they weren't the asses.

It was getting to be sunset when they found themselves in yet another winding canyon with smooth, high walls. Abruptly the lead burro quickened its pace, the other two picking up right behind, and the trio let out brays, as if scenting water just ahead. The riders, too, quickened their pace, exchanging anxious grins. This had been a long, worrisome trail, but evidently that burro was trustworthy.

Suddenly Longarm called a halt. "If it knows where it's going and goes busting in there, I don't think we'd better bust in with it."

"You're right. We'll go up and over," Jessie said, eyeing the almost perpendicular walls. "Sure, we will. Anybody bring wings?"

"It may come to that, Jessie," Ki replied. "I doubt our saddle ropes are long enough to handle that climb. Let's backtrack some."

They returned along the canyon floor, studying the sheer sides and lofty rimrock with thoughtful care. For a good hundred yards they couldn't locate a spot that didn't require alpine equipment to scale. They kept on searching, and found that in the shoulder of the first curve back a ways, the possibilities of ascent were slightly better.

By the shoulder, they anchored their horses' reins under rocks, then from each saddle removed a saddle string. With these strong strips of leather thong, they fashioned sling straps for their carbines, while they studied and discussed the wall before them, deciding on every ledge and handhold of the route they'd have to climb. They must make no mistakes, no false starts.

Ki began, swinging his carbine across his back and gripping a handhold with steady fingers. Close behind came Jessie, then Longarm. Forty feet from the trail, they gained a thrusting projection no wider than a hand, but it served as a foothold, and each paused for a moment to flex fingers before moving on. A horizontal niche ran almost alongside them for twenty feet or more, toward their left. Like persistent, slow-creeping beetles, they worked along this crevice, clinging by their hands.

When they reached the broken apex of the shoulder, they climbed another forty feet using fingers and toes. Straddling a sliver of rock that stuck outward like a stubby horn, they pulled themselves up to a thin shelf where they were all able to perch together. There they rested, too breathless to speak, and stared at the trial below.

After a few moments, Ki continued straight upward, hand over hand, slowly, smoothly. Jessie and Longarm followed, equally careful to make no jerk or unbalanced shift that might cause them to slip. Painstakingly they ascended, sweat trickling in their eyes, clinging with the strength of one hand while exploring with the other.

Sighing wearily, Ki reached a point where the shoulder slanted inward. He rested, then climbed onward faster, but very soon the cliff face straightened again to form another wall. This was the last high step to the top. Regarding the short section up to the ragged lip of the rim, he estimated that the best hold was still the one they had figured from the trial—a plate of stone, cut away on either side and sticking out like a balcony, above him and a little to his right.

"So far, so good," he murmured, hoisting himself upward.

The toe of a boot appeared at the edge of the stone slab.

Ki stopped.

There was a scraping of boot leather. The toe vanished, and its mate showed briefly as the man turned and stepped back a pace.

Glancing down, Ki saw that Jessie and Longarm were

crouched against the wall where it angled from a slant to perpendicular again. They were craning anxiously, apparently having glimpsed the reason for Ki's suddenly stopping and flattening to the wall. But, to be sure, Ki motioned for them to be quiet and stay put. Stay? Hell, they were stuck, Ki mused bitterly; they had no way to tell when or if the man up there would go away, and odds were the man would chance to look down while he looked around, then swat three flies on the wall.

Ki mulled it over another moment. Then, wedging himself as securely as possible, he dug a *shuriken* out of his vest and called up in a hearty, cheerful voice, "Hey, mister! Do you have a match?"

"Eh?" A hatbrim appeared. Startled eyes peered down, blinking, tobacco-stained lips opening to gape, the barrel of a rifle beginning to dip low, aiming toward Ki. Ki flicked his *shuriken* underhand, sending it whirring upward in a shallow curve. It sliced through the bridge of the man's nose, burying its razored tips at an angle in his left eye. The head dropped forward, the man's big body sliding over the rim and angling directly at Ki, gathering momentum as it plunged.

Ki took one long breath, with eyes gauging the body's fall, conscious that the carbine on his back stuck upward like the point of a fishhook, ready to fasten itself under the man's belt or clothes. Weaving aside, he pressed into the slender crack to which his left hand clung. Even so, the tumbling body brushed his shoulder and all but fastened upon the point of his gun barrel. Shaken, gripping strenuously to his precarious hold, Ki heard the man strike the trail below with a sodden thud.

After a reassuring smile at Jessie and Longarm, and a moment to regain his breath, Ki began to work his way upwards as before. He reached the stone ledge, and with the remaining strength in his arms he shinnied himself up and over. A few minutes later Jessie groped for the rim. Ki pulled her up. Then, when Longarm appeared, they both helped boost him onto the top. They sat, slouching, their breaths coming in great heaving gasps while they recovered their strength.

"By God," Jessie panted, "that was a corset-burster."

Longarm rose, nodding, wheezing hoarsely. "Yeah. Smart, Ki, taking that one out quietly instead of with a noisy gunshot."

"Didn't think of that. If I'd aimed or fired, I'd have fallen."

When they had regained their feet and wind, they turned their backs to the canyon and viewed the sharp pinnacles that reared like waiting fangs beyond. A narrow stretch of flat plateau intervened. They strode on, crossing the level ground in a few minutes, and advancing cautiously among the rocks. Here there were no sheer walls to bar their way, and they climbed easily up and in between two peaks, then crawled forward through the brush to the ridge of a long, curving slope.

The slope edged an oval valley that was securely cupped among the surrounding high peaks. There was no break or mouth to the valley, though three trails led down into it from three directions. On the far side was a bold cliff facing toward where they crouched hidden, and near the cliff was a small lake, blue as turquoise in the setting sun. On the left was a field of green, where a cavvy of horses grazed and a small bunch of scattered cattle roamed at will. On the right, a grove of conifers clustered on a steep slope and ran down to the lake's edge. Some of the stand had been cut away to form a shaded clearing where the thin smoke of a campfire spiraled upward and dissipated in the dimming sky. A number of men moved or lounged lazily about the clearing, their figures made small and indistinct by distance and the intervening twilight haze.

Again they talked over how best to proceed. Unquestionably they must act fast, for at any time the man on the rim could be missed, or that maverick burro train could wander where it would be noticed and stir questions. Then the horses and the body on the trail would be found, and the hunt for them would be on. Now was the time, while they still had some small advantage and could shock with surprise. They mapped out a path which would bring them around behind and above the outlaws, agreeing on a point of vantage which would have command of their camp.

Then they dropped back the way they had come and began circling behind the intervening peaks. Forging cautiously yet rapidly, they chanced upon a trail that cut through a narrow gap. They paused to watch and listen, then dodged quickly across and into the cover of the rocks beyond. Here the narrow stretch of benchland pinched out against the peaks, and they were forced to pick their way with greater care, for the deep canyon had closed in behind them. But to climb up and down behind these peaks was nothing compared to their ascent of the canyon wall. Soon they gained the peak they had estimated as closest, and crept through its gap and down the other side.

The trees screened the camp from their view, and they reached the upper edge of the stand without being seen by any of the outlaws. Of this they felt quite sure, and though they did not know the exact number, they were certain of at least a dozen men camped down there. They advanced lower through the timber, angling more to their right. Then, gliding with all the silence possible, they crossed an open slope to an outcropping cluster of rocks midway between the cliff and the lower strip of trees. Settling themselves among these protective boulders, they took stock of their position.

They now observed something which had previously escaped their eyes. Up on the face of the cliff, built in the low, wide mouth of a flat-roofed cave, was an old and crumbling cave dwelling. Its row of unscreened windows looked out upon the valley like dark, inscrutable eyes. A crudely built pole ladder, about thirty-five to forty feet long, ran up the face of the cliff and gave access to the narrow doorway. The ladder did not appear to be many years old, which indicated it had been constructed by the outlaws camping here. Though the cliff dwelling was on a level with their own, they found it impossible to penetrate the gloom of its windows and view anything or anybody inside.

So they gave their attention to the camp. Rough voices drifted up to them, but they could make nothing of the guttural conversations. One of their number seemed to be the cook, and was now moving industriously about the fire, rattling pots and pans and Dutch-oven lids.

"Looks like we caught them at dinnertime," Jessie murmured. "Let's wait till they eat, and see if they help do our work for us."

Flashing Jessie a grin of agreement, Longarm removed his hat and pressed it flat beside his loading hand. From his pockets he took cartridges and laid them carefully on his hat, leads forward. Jessie and Ki did the same, lining up extra rounds in ways which suited them best for quickly snatching and thrusting into their carbines' magazines. They had that strip of timber covered.

The cook clanged a pan with a spoon, and the men below began converging toward the fire. Above, the three settled their elbows firmly and pressed gun stocks against their shoulders. With narrowed eyes they picked out targets, tensing ready, yet hesitating until the outlaws were all grouped around the fire, eating their last supper.

Longarm sighed a satisfied "Ahh," to himself, but it acted like a signal to Jessie and Ki. Three shots roared as one, and three men went down like the sitting ducks they were. After that it grew interesting. With startled yells and curses, the rest of the men leaped to defend themselves, some returning fire, all scrambling desperately for cover.

Ki's next bullet struck and bowled over an outlaw who was ducking behind a tree. His bullet after that struck another, whose gun was spitting lead up at the boulders. A pair of men were running for the cliff. Longarm plugged one in the kidneys, and was tracking the second when two others poured an uncomfortably close salvo at him. Jessie lost no time dropping one, then the other. She turned, levering, to find a third, while Longarm blew out the brains of that second gent.

Another man actually got as far as the ladder, and started climbing it like an ape. A silver concho glittered on his hatband, and Ki drew a moving bead and triggered. The concho vanished as if by magic, and the climbing man fell backward toward the ground. But around Ki, as well as the others, lead was whining and striking and screaming off in ricochet. Gravel and splinters of rock stung their face and eyes. As Ki reloaded, a bullet cut his hand and caromed off a rock, ripping the sleeve of Longarm's brand new jacket he had bought to replace the one ruined in Beulah. Ki did not notice his cut. His hand was snapping back the lever, bringing a fresh shell up into his rifle barrel. Longarm at once saw the tear, and smoked the air around him blue with some rather choice and inventive expletives.

Three gunmen in particular were throwing shots up at them. One whirled and headed for the trees, while another sprang for some rocks. Jessie knocked the latter man as he was diving headlong behind the rocks, and he did a strange corkscrewing twist in midair, skidded in a belly flop, and crumpled lifeless with his legs up in back of the rocks. By then Jessie had shifted and fired again, drilling the other an instant before he would have ducked behind the trunk of a pine.

The third of these gunmen stayed his ground. He sighted his rifle with care, ignoring the volley after volley that blasted down, riddling those few outlaws who were still able to flee. The man squeezed off a bullet that exploded with a vicious splat against a rock mere inches from Longarm's face. Half blinded, Longarm tightened on his trigger. His shot was a little wild, barking the tree trunk above the outlaw's head. Then Jessie's bullet, coming from her angle, sent the outlaw sprawling to his death.

Longarm blinked the rock dust from his eyes. His hammer fell with a metallic click. Muttering in disappointment, he began thumbing fresh shells into the carbine. By the time he had loaded, his vision was cleared, but the shooting had abated, and all he could view were the dead through stinging, sulfurous gunsmoke.

He stood up. "That's it?" he asked, almost disappointed.

"That's it," Jessie confirmed. "Let's go get our horses."

★

Chapter 24

Shortly on horseback they returned to the camp.

Removing their saddles, they added their horses to the cavvy grazing the field, then began the gruesome task of checking the dead outlaws strewn about the clearing and the fringe of grove. Near the still burning cookfire were the leftover biscuits and beef, and the litter of dumped or flung tin plates and cups. A little removed from the fire, blanket rolls and tarpaulin-covered beds had been spread in groups, or singly, as if the owlhoots had placed small trust in one another. Possessions were meager, mostly changes of clothing, though there were several lanterns, a couple of whiskey bottles, five denominations of poker chips, and some soiled decks of playing cards.

The gunman who had worn a concho in his hatband was crumpled against the base of the ladder to the cliff dwelling. Dragging the body aside, Ki glanced up at the ancient ruins, whose openings were dark and somehow sinister, as though haunted by what they held now and the violence they had once witnessed in the long-dead past. He turned, then, and scanned the three winding trails which disappeared from view among the tall pinnacles enclosing the secluded valley. And he surveyed the thickets and trees etching their dark pattern against the steeply rising gray slopes to the east, bordering the far edge of the valley bottom, a pleasing background against the verdant green of the meadow in between. Yet every copse and covert was a potential menace, and though his probing gaze caught no sign of danger, he could not as yet throw off a sense of hidden peril that escaped his eyes.

"No Major Pennington," Jessie declared peevishly. "No one I recognize or might even suspect as more than a bottom-rung member of the cartel, if that. Certainly no Von Blöde or Henry Gustav!"

She spoke loud enough for Ki to hear, though she was addressing Longarm as they approached him. Longarm replied, "Including the trails and climbing like we did, there must be several ways to get in and out of here. It's possible for the real clever gents to've sidestepped our ruckus. Or for them to be off somewhere, and they'll come back."

"Perhaps they're upstairs," Ki suggested, motioning toward the cliff dwelling. "Or others, maybe, who got scared and hid inside."

Longarm grinned. "I'll grab a lantern and we'll go through it. You're right, that ol' mud fort's too dim and gloomy to trust, and it'd take only one gunhand shooting from a front window to pick us all off."

After Longarm found a lantern nearby and returned, Ki started up the rickety ladder. Jessie would have followed, but Longarm barred her way, smiling. "Gal, you trail behind—same as an Injun squaw."

"Very well, Custis. This is once when you have your way," she responded with a throaty purr, and climbed upward behind him.

They stepped into a room with a high-rock ceiling and a floor that had once been leveled with puddled mud, now smooth and hard and covered with tracked-up dust. To the rear and upon either side, narrow doorways framed with rocks and timbers led to adjoining rooms through thick walls of mud and stone. This room was empty and stripped bare.

Longarm struck a match and lit the lantern. Then, with pistols in hand, he and Jessie and Ki strode into the adjoining room. It, too, was empty, and so was the next, and so on as they worked along the dwelling's outer wall. From outside, they had roughly judged the dwelling to be of no great extent, perhaps all of a dozen rooms facing out upon the valley. But they soon discovered that behind these rooms was a second row, depressingly dark; and in back of that a third row, utterly black.

It was while they were in the second row that they began to find bones. Age-whitened human bones, sometimes merely chunks of them, other times whole sections, like a rib cage or hip assembly. In one room was a complete skeleton whose skull had rolled a little to one side, a gaping hole in its top. Ki moved closer and peered down. Under the bleached bones lay a stone ax with a broken handle, mute evidence of what had been done by earlier savages who also have lived only to plunder, murder, and destroy.

Guided by the lantern, Longarm led the way through the third row. Their shadows assumed grotesque patterns on the age-old, crumbling walls as they traveled from one room to another, until finally they came to the last at the rear, a dead end with no opening leading further into the cliff—except, that is, for the little alcove in the rear wall, like a closet, which many of the chambers had. And, like many of the doorways had, the threadbare remnants of an ancient blanket hung as a rotted screen in its sagging doorway.

They took no interest in that, however, or in the room generally as they gazed about at piles of bones and rubbish. In too many other rooms they had seen the same backwash of a fierce battle, of some massacre in antiquity which had doomed this community to extinction.

"This is as far aback as we can go," Jessie said. "Satisfied?"

Ki nodded. "I guess. Let's go, there're no outlaws here."

"Well, I'm not sorry we troubled to make sure. I am kind of sorry for the Indians who once lived here. Whatever befell them must've been tragic," Longarm said, starting to lead the way out.

Abruptly the lantern flickered. The blanket in the alcove doorway billowed out at Ki, who happened to be passing by it. At the same instant there came a rustle of sound like the stirring of marshland reeds, and a gust of wind which struck everyone in the face and blew out the lantern. The wind was cold, tainted with a pungent musky odor, as if from some just-opened vault long closed. It was immediately followed by a low scraping noise, and as quickly as it arose, the air died and grew still again.

In the total dark, Longarm yelled, "What'n hell's going on?"

The answer came in a hushed pounce of suddenness. The soft tread of feet rushed in behind Ki, and the feathery touch of unseen fingertips. Ki was already ducking in a whirl, and recoiled from the fingers as if he had been caressed by a rattler. Yet somehow the attacker was able to gauge Ki's movements by that single brush, and though as blind as Ki, he was positioned better for a strike. Puma-swift, he shifted to compensate and grabbed Ki exactly as planned, tackling him from behind and locking a powerful arm beneath Ki's chin.

Head forced back, Ki felt a hot breath panting in his face as his own throat was being throttled to the point of choking him. But this hold was for stabbing, not strangling. He couldn't see a knife, any more than he could see the man, but he recognized by the moves of the body pressing against him that an upraised arm was in motion, a downward arc that would bring a knife slicing into his chest.

Simultaneously Ki countered the hold he knew he was in. He directed an elbow strike just below the attacker's breastbone, together with a smashing heel stomp on the left instep. Grunting in pain, the man relaxed his stranglehold, his knife hand wavering, his reflexive movement enough for Ki to twist around and draw his *tanto*.

Ki could sense the strength and suppleness of his opponent as he slewed away to avoid the short, single-edged blade. But not in time, and Ki felt his knife slide into the body. He sliced the blade upward. The weight stuck on his blade, then slipped off the end. The attacker never uttered a noise, the only sound being the dull slump of his collapse to the floor.

"Light the lantern," Ki called hastily.

A match flared in the dark. Jessie gasped and Longarm blurted, "Holy shit!" Hastily he fired the wick and held the glowing lantern near while they stared in wonder down at the gutted attacker.

The man was lean, wiry-muscled, light tan of skin, black of hair and eyes, and clad only in a breechclout, his face striped with warpaint. His right fist still clenched a hunting knife, and his split belly was draining quantities of blood.

"An Indian!" Jessie exclaimed.

"Yeah, and look how he's dressed. Or undressed," Longarm said, frowning. "Why, he's decked out like some red warrior of old."

Nodding, Ki moved toward the alcove. "Bring the lantern."

"Leaping to fight the white foe," Longarm continued, following Ki with the lantern held high. "Sure, that could be why he was hiding in here, or maybe he was hiding from the outlaws and mistook . . . Hell, he wasn't hiding! That wind was like a draft, opening and closing."

They heard that dry rattling sound when Ki thrust the blanket aside and went in. The rattling increased to a hollow clatter when Jessie and Longarm crowded in behind, and more rattling was triggered when the blanket fell into place in back of them. With sharp, startled exclamations, they glanced around by the lantern light.

Complete in every ghastly detail, human skeletons surrounded them upon all sides. Their entering had set the skeletons off to bowing and prancing and jiggling, leering at them through vacant eye sockets.

"Cheerful, aren't they?" Ki remarked.

"It doesn't make me want to dance," Longarm retorted. "This's just another human graveyard where the dead aren't even buried."

"Oh, these old bones are harmless," Jessie said with a shrug. Already the skeletons had fallen slack and quiet again, and hung in a dejected row around the walls with blankets at their backs—for the walls, like the doorway, were covered with tattered Indian weavings. "It's not the dead ones, but the live ones we've got to watch out for. Such as Indians coming out of nowhere. Well? What're we waiting for?"

Quickly they began searching the blanket-shrouded walls for a doorway, a passageway leading into they knew not what. One by one they elbowed the skeletons aside, starting

238

the bones jangling against one another on their tiny connecting loops of thread or wire. They moved the blankets, which hung from ropes suspended from wooden plugs set in the cave roof. They examined the walls, whose surfaces were seamed and lined with crevices like an aged, wrinkled face. Yet they found not the faintest sign of any means of entry or exit.

They stood regarding the little alcove with thorough disgust.

A new thought prompted Jessie to move along the walls again, but this time she tucked the end of each blanket up over the ropes from which they were suspended. "Now shine the lantern down by the floor, Custis," she directed, "and let's look for some spot around the base of the walls which is free of dust."

Within minutes, the lantern light revealed a fan-shaped space where the wind blowing in through the secret panel had swept the dust away cleaner than a broom. Now with all their strength and cunning they worked to find the combination to that invisible door. It turned out to be embarrassingly simple. All that was required was a powerful and continuous shove inward. A dark interior passageway was revealed, through which a strong and smelly draft of air came rushing.

The door was an irregular slab of rock artfully set on a pivot and painstakingly shaped to fit exactly the opening it had closed. Inside the time-scalloped passageway, other, smaller slabs of rock were piled close at hand. All that was required to make this exit impregnable was to pile these waiting stones against the closed door. Probably the Indian women and children did precisely that, Jessie mused thoughtfully, for this must be the path they had followed long ago, while their braves battled and died resisting the press of foes behind.

The rush of air clearly proved that this natural tunnel led to some distant vent hole under the cliff. Before their eyes lay a trail worn smooth by the passing of many feet. Very recently, perhaps, by the feet of cartel members—a tempting theory, for though there was no proof of it, there was no proof against it or for anything else, and besides, it was precisely the sort of sneaky escape hatch the cartel was fond of using. It was definitely worth checking.

So now Jessie, Longarm, and Ki moved forward without hesitation, closing the door behind them, and descending the steps down into the earth.

Chapter 25

The winding stairway had been hacked into the solid rock with primitive tools. They followed the crude steps downward for all of eight feet. Then the passage leveled and they entered one of the passageways of a great cavern where, in eons past, a subterranean river had roared through the walls of mountains. The hard-beaten trail showed that this tunnel had been dry for countless generations, for in places feet had worn its surface down a foot deep through bedrock.

Guided by the lantern, they hiked carefully along while watching for a hole to dart into at a second's notice. There were many of them. The underground trail wound its perilous course past grottos and caves whose mouths yawned at either hand, as well as skirting deep abysses where the mutter of running waters rose softly from ink-black emptiness.

Abruptly they stopped, hearing the sound of a faint patter approaching. They dove quickly into the mouth of a deep niche, Longarm hastily snuffing out the lantern, and crouched silently, weapons ready.

Moments later two braves ran by. Like Longarm had said of the first Indian, this pair was like a picture of the past flashing in front of their eyes, wearing only warpaint and breechclouts, one carrying a torch of blazing pine splinters bound together by a thin grass rope.

"And both," whispered Jessie, "are carrying bows and

arrows, just like in the old days. It isn't just a plain Indian party we seem to've bumped into. They're up to something."

Longarm nodded. "Something tied in with the outlaw camp."

"And that'd tie in the cartel," Ki added.

The runners swiftly passed from sight and sound, though Longarm waited a few moments to make certain before relighting the lantern. They continued on, the lantern glow a mere blob in the fathomless dark, until at length they could see a reflection of light on the curving walls of rock ahead. Advancing cautiously, they found they had at last come to the mouth of the long tunnel. Relieved to no longer be so riskily hemmed in, they stepped outside . . . and promptly discovered they were in as much of a squeeze as ever.

They were in a short but very deep and narrow ravine with its towering walls of glass-smooth rock shutting out all but a strip of the early night sky. The light came from the other end of the ravine, flaring out of the mouth of another great cavern. Also out of there could be heard the roll and thunder of drums, the weird incantations of screaming voices, and the screech and wail of strange instruments.

"What a hell of a noise," Longarm growled. "Makes my teeth ache."

"I think we've stumbled on a ritual, one of those strictly-by-invitation affairs," Jessie said, then turned. "They're coming back!"

Dipping into the shelter of a trailside thicket, they saw the two braves who had passed them in the tunnel burst out behind them and race toward the cavern ahead. As the braves plunged into the cavern, they began shouting and waving their arms.

Ki murmured, "Uh-oh. They must've found the first one."

"Then they better not find us here," Longarm said, and started out from the thicket, only to leap back in again when seven more braves surged from the cavern, raising an angry rumpus as they sped by and back into the tunnel. Longarm shook his head. "Well, that fairly well blocks our return. And we can't climb out or stay here."

"So let's go join the party," Jessie said.

They darted along the ravine, taking advantage of every patch of shadow on the way, knowing that these shadows which hid them could, likewise, hide their enemies as well. When they drew near the cavern's mouth, they discovered that the end wall of the ravine was jagged and sloping. Keeping to the darkest spots, they started up over the sharp rocks as rapidly as possible until they reached a high, broad shelf and saw they were skunked again. It was more than forty feet to the next ledge, and it was back to being sheer wall.

From their vantage, however, they could view inside the great opening. Here was an immense chamber in the rocks, high-ceilinged and broad—and something far more than a cave, besides. It was a temple, one which reminded Jessie of those queer, ancient places explorers were discovering, from the jungles of South America well on to the Canadian line. Beyond a blazing fire on a wide altar of stone loomed two evil shapes chiseled by ancient hands in the rock wall of the cave. Other walls had crude sign writing, painted with bright pigments which had penetrated the rock deeply, and now still retained much of their original outline and color.

Though intrigued, they were not paying the decor much attention just then. They were focusing on five captives lined up before the fiery altar, Ki drawn in particular to the young woman.

She was Chinese, about twenty-eight to thirty, wearing a work-frayed cream shirt and jodhpurs, and dainty black boots of once-fine Russian leather. She was slender and graceful and tall for her race, with a splendid mane of burnished ebon, long and silky and glowing. She probably glowed in the dark herself, Ki thought. She had that kind of incredibly beautiful skin.

She stood against a polished hardwood stake, hands tied behind her, head tilted back wearily, eyes lifted toward the ceiling. She might have been dead or unconscious, but she was not; she was indifferent, the supreme insult she could give to all that was going on around her. With a tight grin of approval, Ki then stared at the four men. They too were Chinese, and they too were larger than average, all of them

243

broad-shouldered, deep-chested, around six feet tall, in worn work garb and flat-heeled boots. And they too were tied to wooden stakes.

Down in the ravine, now, a few excited braves were ranting about, searching more for the sake of doing something than of suspecting anyone was hiding there. It was enough, though, to prompt the trio above to hustle deeper into the cavern before they were inadvertently spotted.

Following the balcony-like ledge high up near the ceiling of the giant chamber, they could look almost straight down on what was going on. Whatever hubbub was taking place elsewhere over the finding of the dead Indian was evidently not yet going to stop the solemn ceremony below. It was a death ritual. They all could see that, could all recognize it in the chanting and drumbeat marching, and the haranguing by the very obvious chief with his gourd rattles and feathered headpiece.

Then one of the two braves who had evidently discovered the body came darting in. He waited until there was a break in the tirade, and leaned forward to speak to the chief. After listening a moment, the chief threw up his hands. The noise screeched to an abrupt halt, the marching ring stopped, and the chief launched into another wildly gesturing discourse in a tongue none of the three above had ever heard before. An uproar of war screams that might have come from so many fighting eagles arose when the chief was done, dancers and bystanders scattering into the side galleries with their bows and arrows.

Then, surprisingly, the chief began speaking to the captives in English, with no trace of accent. "So somebody's finally come to try to help you. So you miss your reward for another night, and get to find ours for another day," he snarled. "But by killing the whites in the outer valley and, yes, even one of us, your friends haven't helped you or themselves. To all you intruders, this is the land of the dead. It always was so and shall be again, as you'll all know—too late!"

"That's a fancy speech from *you!*" The young woman was suddenly answering him. "The white man educated you, Mad Dog, and—"

"Red Dog, my name's Red Dog! I didn't want the poison of their school. This's our land and we are of it, a simple people. The simple way is the best way for the Quiveran." The chief yelled commands at two stalwart Indians, who rushed to the captives and released them.

The captives were bustled away into a tall, slitlike hole in the wall between the two sullen figures carved in the stone. Water was brought and the fire on the altar was soon put out. Those who dashed away came back quickly, each man carrying a modern rifle and revolver, and scurried away like swarming wolves on the scent of blood.

Jessie, Longarm, and Ki had in the meantime taken stock of the balcony-like ledge, and had seen a hole in the wall above the long slit where the Chinese people had gone. Taking advantage of the commotion below, they hurried around and located the hole. Slipping into it was slow going. They did not yet dare light a match or the lantern, and they had to feel their way with hands and feet until finally they eased out on a natural balcony in the wall of another dome-shaped room.

It was a much tinier room. Wedged in a crack in the wall below was a burning torch, while to the left was an incline, marking a place to descend. Carefully they climbed down to floor level. The room came to an end with a swing to the right, and a set of steps that led down for thirty feet to a broad ledge overlooking a black abyss. They padded on softly past an old chute of heavy planks that apparently was used as a dumping place for unwanted rock, then rounded an abrupt bend in the rocks and entered another low cavern. By now Longarm had relit the lantern, and as he lifted it a little higher, he heard Jessie gasp and his own breath come in a sharp, whistling sound.

More skeletons stood along one rough wall, a long line of them in rusty chains, some of them broken and fallen apart, others still held together by rotting strips of clothing. Some were grinning white imps in the lamplight, some had flesh-less mouths tightly closed, all of them were chalk-white.

"What is it they seem to be staring at?" Jessie asked thickly. "Shine the light over that way, Custis. What is that boxlike thing?"

"A bin!" Longarm's voice was surprised as he moved to it and ran his hand over piles of gleaming metal. "Full of gold nuggets!"

They thought they heard a door slam then, and were certain of it a moment later when a dim, wavering glow of light appeared ahead. Promptly, as if all troubles came in bunches here, footsteps sounded behind them. Glancing hastily behind them, they saw the first of a well-armed squad of Indians stalk into the room. Then there came a grunting close at hand, and they whirled frontward just in time to see a big brave enter the doorway ahead carrying a torch.

A bullet from Longarm's revolver settled it for the man who stood in the mouth of the passageway ahead. An equally quick shot from Jessie's pistol settled it for the startled man in back, and at the second roar of her Colt, the man next in line collapsed against the rest of the squad, creating further pandemonium and delay.

And now they had to run for it, if they wished to keep living. They sprinted to the doorway, pausing to disarm the dead Indian of two cartridge belts, a rifle, and a revolver. Out they went, then, and into another room where another bin of gold lined one wall and chained skeletons the other. They ran on through, hearing Indians coming—plenty of them. After that it was one room after another until they came to a pair of archways, one with a heavy door fastened by two stout wooden bars across it. They veered down the other, which had nothing in the way, only to dead-end in the mine itself, where there were picks and shovels, gold and more gold.

Hastily they backtracked to the door and threw aside the stout bars. Shots and yells were ringing at them as they barged through and snatched the heavy door closed behind them. They were in another passageway now. It was a long one with many twists and turns before it suddenly opened into a deep, well-like hole in the rocks.

"Welcome to our cozy jail, strangers," a feminine voice called in amusement from somewhere to the right. "Welcome, until you or your hostess find it best otherwise. I am Yang Shu-zhen, daughter of the late Yang Wei. Perhaps you have heard of him in the lower country."

"They must have, Shu-zhen, they come bearing gifts," one of the Chinese men responded with a bellow of laughter. "Guns! And here I was about to bounce a rock off their skulls."

By the lantern glow Ki took a close look at the woman. Her lines were lavish curves with long, tapering legs, and her face was pure Asian, with features at once delicate yet firm. Her mouth was wide and stubborn, her nose angled at a delicate tilt, but it was her eyes that caught and held him —gray eyes, flecked with gold, challenging him, appraising him, he didn't know just what, but disturbing, whatever it was.

"Shu-zhen, 'fair and precious,'" Ki murmured. "Wei, meaning 'great.'" He handed the rifle and cartridge belts to two of the men, then turned and again faced Shu-zhen, smiling as he handed her the revolver butt first. "If I'm ignorant of the name, I hear much in the name."

She laughed skeptically. "I hear much hokum that I haven't in a long time." She glanced at Longarm then. "Better snuff out your light. There's no telling what Red Dog may do or what may happen, now that you've reached us with weapons. How many have you with you?"

Longarm doused the lantern. "There's me, Custis Long; Miss Jessica Starbuck; and Ki." He explained of their coming to the camp as quickly as possible, concluding, "So you see, all we're aiming for is to get us out of here. If you want a bunch, it'll have to be made up of some of your crowd—if you've got a crowd."

"We haven't any more!" One of the Chinese men, golden-yellow-eyed and eagle-beaked of nose, stepped close to him in the darkness. "The few people who know we're here are the ones who put us here. We're in a place no one can get out of. If things go too much against Red Dog out there, all he will have to do is to withdraw his crowd and forget us, and leave us to a slow death from starvation."

"I don't plan on dying like that." Ki glanced toward the rim of the pit, which was like looking up a gun barrel. "When I go, I want it quick and over. No use stuttering death along."

"Lu Nin only mentioned a mere fact, Ki," Shu-zhen rebuked, a roguish little smile quirking her lips. "Up here, especially in the Minarets above, we do not ask many questions. We rarely answer them."

Shu-zhen was still speaking, and Ki was still studying the pit, when a boulder plummeted from high overhead. It was as large as a man, and when it struck, it broke into a thousand slivers.

"Besides, this isn't the proper place for long conversation." There was not even a hint of nervousness in her voice as she ducked under the overhang, just as another rock came hurling down.

"They know we've got guns to fight with, and they haven't got the guts to attack through the passage," Longarm growled. "Get behind anything you can and stay there. But watch that passage mouth!"

Stones were falling in a furious hailstorm as braves rolled them off the high rim, making a constant roaring and smashing. The flying bits and shards of stone whizzed around the crouching group. Ki's and Shu-zhen's eyes met for just an instant. Hers were deep gray, and in those depths Ki could almost see rattlesnakes buzzing and the dark lights of damnation burning. Then and there something told Ki that all her men might be superb fighters, but she was downright, deadly dangerous. She was an offshoot beauty of some hard-steel mountain lord, and he had an awful suspicion he was about to make a fool of himself over her.

"I mentioned a fact too, Shu-zhen," he said, easing forward and shouldering his carbine. "Here's another: I get tired of squatting around and letting the other side have all the fun." In the overhang above was a vee-shaped crack, and he stood with a lean little grin on his face as he sighted on it and watched for his chance.

It came suddenly, and his carbine tracked to meet it. There was a split-second's aim, and a crash burst up through the dust and flying rock, snatching a cry of pain and terror from up there on the rim.

"You got him, and he's coming down!" Jessie smiled widely, and Longarm gave a laugh. "Yep, his hide's good for a pair of shoes!"

The squalling Indian plunged spinning until he struck a

248

rock, his body seeming to melt right over its surface before he bounced in a spin and sprawled backward in the dust. Ki glanced at Shu-zhen, and though he couldn't be certain, he would have sworn that he saw a faint hint of a smile as she nodded. Then she spoke, her voice cold and flat.

"It's Barking Wolf. But his skin is filled with scars, and won't make good shoes. Get me Crooked Eye, and the skin will be smooth and tough. He's up there." She pointed at the rim. "Crooked Eye and Barking Dog stand in each other's shadow."

Ki brought down Crooked Eye a few minutes later. He didn't know it was Crooked Eye, but the man's head appeared right where Barking Wolf's head and shoulders had come easing out shortly before. The Indian fell silently with a bullet hole through his skull.

"Anyone else you can think of?' Ki asked.

"Red Dog!" Shu-zhen's eyes burned as if ready to shower sparks. "But give him to me alive, so he'll know when I peel his hide."

Ki's shooting, however, had stopped the bombardment of stones. A great pile of crushed rocks lay on the floor in front of them, and Longarm studied the spots where they had struck the wall. Chuckling, he pointed to one of the places where the shattering rocks had hit.

"Sometimes folks get so ornery, they overdo their own mean tricks, and they backfire on them. Look up there. D'you see what I see?"

"The walls have chunks knocked out of them!" Jessie exclaimed. "They're a puddingstone, soft enough to gouge out steps and handholds."

Longarm nodded. "Keep watch, and I'll see what I can do." Shielded by the overhang, he started inspecting the wall in many places. His big stockman's knife made a strong, sharp pick to prod about with, and at one spot he chipped out a piece of stone as broad as his hand. He saw others loosening like tile above him, but it would still take about a week's steady work, he figured, to reach the first overhang.

He had not been prodding long, though, before Shu-zhen touched him on the shoulder and pointed to an area about five feet above his head. "When you're in a well like this as long as we have been, you get to notice oddities," she said. "There's a part up there that's a slightly different color, like it's a patch, perhaps over a hole."

"Go have at it," Longarm said. He gave her the knife and a boost. She placed a foot on his knee, put another on his shoulder, and in a moment he had her standing on his shoulders while he leaned against the wall to support her as she set to work. It was slow at first. Then Shu-zhen began throwing down stones as large as a man's fist. Others came easily after that. Once a regular rain of them came spilling out.

Jessie tried her hand at it then, standing on Ki's big shoulders and working as rapidly as she could. Two of the Chinese men partnered a third team, leaving the rest to watch the rim and passageway.

"It's open!" Shu-zhen announced, smiling. She crawled into the hole, followed by Jessie, and then one by one by everybody else. Longarm was the last, drawn up inside by Ki and one of the other men.

But a new danger was making itself known by this time. Dead trunks of trees were being rolled down from the rim, crashing in thunderous booms on the rocks. Bundles of grass tumbled with them, the pile growing higher and higher. Red Dog evidently intended to force his captives to come back to him of their own accord through the passage. That was clear when fire started coming down. Flames spread swiftly, filling the big pit with a hot crackling and snapping, and boiling clouds of smoke that funneled into the hole.

Eyes smarting, lungs gagging, the escaping prisoners crawled on their hands and knees. It was not like any of the passageways they had encountered before, but was a series of small caves winding in a hopeless tangle in every direction. Eventually they reached a place where a similar ancient wall of pottery clay and stone had suffered a cave-in. They moved forward slowly, pausing to listen, then in single file they crept out between boulders onto the slope of a canyon.

They were still easing outside when voices and running feet could be heard approaching from down and along one side of the slope. A shot cracked out. Then bullets were whistling and pinging all around them, forcing them down, while Indians surged howling to overrun them. They responded with a fusillade of gunfire, the Indians attacking so close together that a blind man couldn't have missed.

The valley echoed with screaming and thrashing, but the Indians as a whole didn't panic. They even showed some discipline as they speedily fanned out and returned withering salvos of their own.

"Try to get Red Dog," Ki called. "Sometimes if you drop a chief, the braves will retreat in confusion. Or so I've heard."

They kept trying to home in on the chief, yet whatever gods he prayed to seemed to be giving him a charmed life. Other warriors fell all around him, but his gaudy feathers ducked and wove and wafted high like a standard-bearer's rallying flag. It frustrated Ki no end. Chambering a round, he took careful aim on the Indian leader, and only when he was sure he had him dead on did Ki pull the trigger.

At that precise instant the chief zigged, another brave zagged, and the slug blew a hole in the brave's chest. Ki levered and fired again. The chief leaned, making a sweeping go-get-'em gesture, and a brave next to his shoulder reeled, fell against Red Dog, then slid to the ground. Ki was starting to wonder if those damned skull fronds were a magical shield, or if the chief had somehow chanted a curse on his aim. "Damn it," Ki muttered. "Next time I'll get him."

As if this were a signal, everyone else with a firearm unleashed a volley at the chief. Bullets riddled him, and with arms vainly clenching his chest, he staggered and collapsed.

Jessie said, "Let's make a break for it."

The remaining braves were melding into a single swirling mob again, circling about their fallen leader. Up the slope, the escapees began scrambling up along the slope. A mad wail lifted from the Indians, who immediately began pursuing.

Jessie glanced at Ki. "I don't think they heard what you heard."

On they ran, plunging over the crest of the slope and into a stand of timber, with the night all around them crackling with gunfire and raging shouts, the darkness flaring with tongues of blazing powder.

★

Chapter 26

An hour passed, then two.

Weaving drunkenly, worn out with fatigue, they came out of yet another dense forest, this time at the timberline. They walked on rubbery legs, heels dragging, nine forlorn figures in the wildest, tallest, and roughest country of the Sierras, far up on the great slopes of the Devil's Minarets. Around them hovered snow-crowned summits and scruffy, bottomless crags. Yonder, as if to tantalize their burning thirst, a river tore and tossed in a frothing cataract down a mountainside, a sparkling ribbon racing down from the melting ice and snow on a great peak wrapped in a silvery halo of clouds.

Even now they could hear bullets droning in the timber behind them, bullets fired from rifles and pistols. For they were still on the run, their Indian pursuers remaining implacably determined, following their line of movement with the whine and slap of lead.

A cluster of pines, a mere thicket of green on the bald mountain dome above the timberline, lay ahead of them now. Shu-zhen motioned toward it, leading the way as she had from the start, her eyes now kindling with a gleam of hope. It was only a short distance away, but they were in the open again, and once more they heard howling shouts from below by the forest to eastward.

They turned and used precious ammunition in a rear-guard action. For the next few minutes it was like the opening guns of a hotly contested war on a raging battlefield. The death-dealing shots continued until they were into the thicket, a steady crashing and rolling of exchanged gunfire that played havoc with the chasing braves.

The shooting dwindled to scattering shots as they plunged on through the thicket. At the end of ten rods, they pushed between a low mass of limbs and entered a round clearing that overlooked a cliff. There they stopped. Jessie, Ki, and Longarm halted, startled.

The clearing was flanked with enormous stone benches surrounding a circular pavement of flat stones carefully and evenly laid together. Though they never would have expected to find such up in these remote elevations, it was not only this which startled them. It was the huge grotesque statue facing them from the absolute center of the clearing. A great-bellied, jade-eyed monstrous stone idol, it was lavishly ornamented with wrought and carved brass. Cross-legged, its right hand dropped between its knees, the other clasped flat across its stomach, it was an image of the great Oriental Buddha, a masterpiece of Chinese carving hewn from a mass of solid rock fully thirty feet high and nearly twenty feet thick.

"We're safe enough for the moment," Shu-zhen said breathlessly. "The timber will protect us up here at the foot of Buddha, as the miners who erected the shrine must have had in mind."

Even as she spoke, the crashing report of a rifle reverberated over the thicket. A bullet rocketed in from behind to smack the left shoulder of the monument, bringing a shower of fine stone sprinkling down on the young woman.

"They're still coming, Shu-zhen," Ki pointed out needlessly.

"Then, quickly, we'll be going." She addressed her four companions in a dialect of Cantonese, and with curt nods they loped away to the southwest. She turned back and said, "This way, please, to our left around the Buddha. Hurry!"

They followed her just past the image to the throne seat. There she tugged on one of the great, yard-thick slabs of stone which formed the rear wall. It swung open, revealing an archway where a short flight of steps burrowed down through the Buddha toward the cliff.

Shu-zhen paused to let them by, then pushed the door closed behind them, throwing several wrought-iron bars in place. Now everything was black, save for a patch of gray night sky about twenty yards ahead.

"May the soul of Ming Wu Li and all his followers be blessed," she murmured, moving now to head the way, "and may the great Buddha stand forever!" After a moment, she added quietly, "For as the Buddha often protected Ming Wu Li and his harassed followers in the past, he has protected me, and my father and mother long before my coming."

They were strange words, coming from a voice as gentle as a benediction. Of the three with Shu-zhen, Ki had the best understanding of it. Yet there was much here to puzzle over, he realized, though not to ask about. *We do not ask many questions; we rarely answer them,* she had said, in a lightly spoken but nonetheless thinly veiled warning not to pry. He would merely wait, and by his waiting he would learn.

Cautiously they stepped onward with nothing but their sense of touch to guide them, for Longarm had long since discarded the empty lantern. When they reached the far opening, they found they were perched on a ledge high along the side of the cliff, and after a moment of eyeing the precipitous drop, they began a torturous descent along an extremely narrow path. Notched and slashed in the steep wall, sometimes dogging segments of other natural ledges, the path led to the bottom in a series of switchbacks, with only projecting stubs of rock and occasional wire-tough roots to give steadying handholds.

At the bottom, they walked out onto a broad, flat shelf like a plateau. It was generally rectangular-shaped, its northern and southern sides bounded by creviced banks, the elongated western side facing them apparently the rim of a bottomless ravine, with mountainous slopes just yonder. By fencing or blocking the mouths of the crevices, the shelf became a natural corral for the thirty horses they could see in front of a long line of stone and mud stables.

Beyond the horses stood a round, bowl-like pool fed by

254

an icy seepage of water running through a crack. They headed straight for it to drink with deep, satisfying gulps. When their thirst was slaked, Shu-zhen took them into one of the stables, where there was a row of spare saddles and gear.

"Rope and mount whichever suits you," she said. "Be certain to catch one you can ride, or you might find yourself piled."

The horses were in splendid condition, and gave vent to their exuberant feelings by bucking and kicking. They were not wild, half-broke broncs, but were well trained, and looked fast and full of endurance. After four were selected and saddled, they were ridden at a feisty trot to a crevice in the southern slope, where Shu-zhen dismounted and lowered a rail gate so they could leave the shelf.

The trail slanted up through mounded rock. While they rode, Shu-zhen talked about this mountainous mining region, the abandoned claims and lonely ghosty towns, though she told them little that other old-timers could not have told them just as readily.

It was a world unto itself, one that had seen bitter strife from almost the beginning of the Forty-nine gold rush. Many Chinese had been among the scores lured across the Pacific to seek their fortunes, one in particular being Ming Wu Li, a scholarly devotee of the ancient Buddha, with the honorable blood of the rulers of the Ming dynasty in his veins. A hardy horde followed him to these reaches and struck it rich, so rich that it brought the curse and envy of the white ruffians less fortunate in their prospecting of the lower valleys, down where it was warmer and the trails were more passable and whiskey and rowdy night life in the dance halls easier to get.

"Bandits robbed him of much gold and killed many of his miners," Shu-zhen explained, "but Ming prospered despite the plundering. More followers flocked to him, and none stole his right to set up his temple in these hills and carve his Buddhas on the slopes."

Her three listeners had not expected Shu-zhen to talk so freely, yet they noticed that she spoke only of the dim past. Even the story of Ming Wu Li was sketchy, one that she seemed to tell them merely to occupy their thoughts and prevent them from asking questions.

Eventually they crossed a long bridge made of thick logs and covered with sand and fine gravel. Below them, far down in the black gash of a gorge, a river surged with the noise of thunder. Then they were ascending again on yet a sharper graded slope, higher and higher on a trail that widened and narrowed by turns, emerging at last onto the high, round base of a towering peak.

A chilly breeze swept against their faces as they moved on. All around were little patches of snow scattered over the green grass. They were as good as on top of the world, miles and miles of vast mountains ranges stretching beyond, bald spires lifting above timberlines with their crests white with snow. The night sky had become a startling clear sheet of dark blue dusted with stars and a crescent moon, and ribboned here and there with a feathery billow of clouds.

"And now you know, when you look at all this," Shu-zhen exclaimed, "why the honorable Ming Wu Li called this Stars of Heaven Divide."

"It takes my breath away," Jessie said, awed by the majestic beauty around them. "But you never finished telling us what happened to Ming."

"I didn't," Shu-zhen admitted. "Still, you might've guessed it. The white man is relentless when he starts to do a thing. He never lets up. Ming's broken bones lie over there in that little graveyard, where he buried the rest of his dead to keep them until he could return their bodies to China." She pointed off to the right, where half-ridden by a long hedge of snowbrush stood a strange conglomeration of up-edged rocks marking graves. "All were wiped out one summer night. Nothing was left except Ming's stone and brass gods and his temple. That is the temple up there."

She pointed upward. Until now they hadn't looked up at the peak in the center of the high flat. They even had to tilt back their heads to see the top of it. But there was the temple. Like a castle in the sky, it sat high in the air, its sloping roofs mottled with snow, its multitudes of windows and doors set with countless tiny panes of glass. A winding trail led up to it with the outer edge of the trail walled with heavy stones. Around it were frowning ramparts of log and stone.

From these, small batteries of rusty iron cannon looked down at the round plain at the base of the peak, and from hidden chimneys farther back on the curved eaves of the roofs poured banners of pale gray smoke blowing crookedly away in the crisp wind.

"The temple home of Ming Wu Ling," Shu-zhen half-whispered. "My grandfather fell heir when Ming and his men were murdered. My father, Yang Wei, ruled after my grandfather was killed facing a robber band. I took over when my father died from bullets in his back fired by assassins employed by a Prussian duke, one Von Blöde. Welcome to my abode—" She gave a sardonic laugh. "—for whatever my welcome is worth. I never ask a man's business until after—"

Something halted her. It was like the faint, faraway pop of a cork from a champagne bottle. It came from the temple, a sound floating down on the wind, and behind it there was something like a muffled cry of pain or fear that was suddenly choked short.

They reined in alongside, looking at Shu-zhen, then up at the house on the peak, then back at her. For the first time since they had met in the pit, they saw a flash of a truly contented smile.

"What is it?" Jessie asked bluntly, and in a tone that was a demand for a direct reply. "We've come this far with you, Shu-zhen. It looks like we're going all the way. Even if there's something here that you don't think we should know—"

"Soon you'd know it anyway, yes," Shu-zhen said. "There'd be no way to keep it from you. Even now, after all you've seen, you might guess a great deal."

"And I do guess as well as see," Jessie said. "You and Von Blöde's people—and believe me, we know them from bitter experience—are hard down to war, and are each having a sweet time to keep the other from gaining the winning hand."

"Von Blöde has the winning hand." Shu-zhen smiled faintly. "But come, we'll talk as we ride to that cabin yonder."

Once started, Shu-zhen was free with the story. Von

Blöde wanted Ming's temple for his headquarters, and Ming's gold fields to help finance his schemes. He was aware that Ming and, subsequently, the Yangs burned strong black powder and gave their enemies only six feet under to starve the buzzards and keep the air pure. So he waged just enough war to hold down suspicion. For ten months it was like that, a mere little spat here, another slight disagreement there. Shu-zhen's men gradually dwindled away, and in the meanwhile more and more riders straggled into the canyons below.

"Then, six months ago, Von Blöde's horde of outlaw whites and renegade Indians made their blood-spouting raid," Shu-zhen explained. "Thinned as we were, we fought. We fought them for a week before we were finally over-whelmed, and Von Blöde took over all the country west of Rampart Ridge, all the way to Thunderbird Divide. As for us, we five who survived were given along with one of my mines, as you saw, to Red Dog as payment for his warrior support."

Ki nodded. "Yes, we saw you about to be put to death."

"Oh, Red Dog threatened to put us to death most every night. It was a ritual to scare us, crush us, and to get his followers excited and give him something to rave over. If you were there, you heard him, about how his ancestors were granted the land our peoples claim now as our own."

"Quivera." Jessie sighed. "An imaginary kingdom of natives and Spanish castaways, which once was a goodly chunk of the western half of America. Red Dog wasn't the only one who was deceived into believing it."

"Believe? Red Dog?" Shu-zhen laughed cynically. "The army of yellows, he called us, had committed rape by digging, digging in his sacred earth. But that's what he had us doing all day, picking and shoveling in that old worked-out mine for gold to fill his own coffers."

By now they were nearly at the cabin. In truth it was a house, and only someone used to dwellings the size of Ming's temple could regard it in terms of a shack. It was of stone, and had the flatter, angular style of European architecture, with an earth-coated roof sprouting weeds, and a stable of sorts attached to one side.

258

"Before much of the gold gave out, when Ming had almost an army here," Shu-zhen said as they dismounted, "a caretaker couple and crew lived here to keep a closer eye on things below the temple. Since then we've kept it for shelter and stopovers, as the case may be."

They tied their horses out of sight in the stable, removed their carbines, and went into the house. It wasn't dirty, exactly, but it was dusty and had a vacant feel from long disuse. From a tight, cedar-lined cabinet Shu-zhen removed blankets, then ushered everyone to the wing of small bedrooms, told them to pick any and retire.

"It's been grueling. We need rest, and we shouldn't be disturbed way off here, so long as we don't make smoke or a light," she advised. "Still, sleep with your gun as your pillow. Good night."

Jessie said, "First, Shu-zhen, please tell me. What was that noise outside? That odd cry from the temple which made you stop?"

"Jessie, I'll say only this: Death made our wrongs. Death will right them. Now, good night. I'll be in the caretaker's bedroom." With an enigmatic smile, Shu-zhen strode to the end room and shut its door.

The beds in the little side rooms were double bunks with thin horsehair mattresses. After Ki sat hunched for a while on his bunk, he rose and left the room, padding quietly outside to relieve himself. On his return, he saw that Shu-zhen's bedroom door was ajar, and she was standing in the shadows just in back of the threshold.

He approached and murmured, "Restless?"

"There's much to do. You know what it is, don't you?"

"I've a fair idea what, not how. Vengeance."

"Punishment. For murdering people who only asked to be left alone. You don't agree? Like your friends wouldn't have approved?"

"They may or may not've, Shu-zhen, but you could've told them and they'd have understood. In fact, Jessie and you are very similar. Her father was killed by the same organization, the cartel, that Von Blöde helps run. When Alex Starbuck died, the taking of his operation had seemed a simple matter, but he'd left another fighting Starbuck behind—

259

a girl who could hold her own against any man. Sound familiar?"

"Yes, incredibly. But you haven't answered me."

"Ming Wu Li," Ki whispered after a pause, "wasn't all love and roses, by the looks of those mining rooms with the men chained against the walls, just left there to die and rot. You plead justice, but you cry vengeance, for evil cannot punish evil, it can only repay it."

"Those horrid rooms! I'd been taught Ming was a kindly, gentle master, but what a beast he must have been. A merciless, cunning old spider." She shook her head violently. "Ki ... Ki, how long must the sins of our forefathers rest like millstones on our souls?"

"I couldn't say, but at least your millstone is made out of gold. You're a rich woman because of Ming, Shu-zhen."

"As if it matters." There was a strange huskiness in her voice. It, or something, prompted Ki to step closer—something he sensed rather than reasoned, something in her presence, in her dark gray eyes as they took their bold fill of him, in her touch as they met. "As if all the gold in the world could matter, Ki. It can't buy us one single second longer together than fate has allotted."

"Shu-zhen—"

"Don't think me too silly," she muttered fiercely. "We Yangs have always gone straight to the point. We are fighting people." Suddenly she was against him, and her arms were up and around him, her breasts against his chest, a wild trembling shaking her whole body. And just as quickly his arms, swift and sure, went around her. The cartel and danger were far, far away when his lips found hers.

Almost before they were fully aware of it, they were in her room and the door was closed. Ki was undressing her. She helped by undressing him, garment by garment, until their clothing was piled around their feet. He picked her up then, her willowy-smooth body light in his arms, and laid her gently on the small bunk bed.

Her flesh had the touch of fire and came alive against him. The shiny raven hair was like dark cobwebs almost hiding her face. Ki brought her with him as they climbed toward climax, and when she erupted, it was not with a shout or a loud scream, but with a tearful, almost inaudible girlish whimper.

Afterwards, cuddling with her face nuzzling his throat, Ki could sense the delicious pain, the minor hurt of love bites and the sting of fingernail scratches on his back. He knew Shu-zhen would be one of those rare women he would never get enough of.

"So beautiful, so natural," she whispered, and lightly touched the discolored patch on his chest. "But I've hurt you. I should've been more controlled."

He kissed her breasts. "No. Don't ever hold back. Always let yourself go."

Her lips moved from his throat to his ear. In a deep whisper, she said, "Again . . . ?"

Some time later, they slept.

Some time toward dawn, Shu-zhen rolled from her bed, dressed, and silently departed. Ki didn't know when, but he sensed the loss.

Meanwhile, down the hall, Jessie and Longarm had been spending the night together in one of the bunks. They had heard the muffled conversing between Ki and Shu-zhen, though they couldn't discern the exact words being spoken, but they understood the implications of only one door snapping closed, followed by total quiet.

"It figures," Jessie murmured, smothering a chuckle. "If there's a woman within fifty miles, Ki will somehow get to her. But I'm especially glad this time. I like the girl Shu-zhen."

"Well, you should," Longarm replied. "She's a lot like you. She isn't a clinging vine that needs a trellis for support. It's the same with you, Jessie. You both expect to pay your way along the trail, and don't try to pass any bogus coin."

"What flattery," she drawled, smiling.

He grinned and hugged her, and they lay that way for quite a spell, aware of each other and stirred by the closeness. Then they were touching all over, full length, until her soft thighs spread to accept his muscular hips. With a sigh of anticipation, she felt herself part slidingly as he eased his weight down on her. Longarm kissed her as he entered. Jessie kissed back, and fire was in their lips, a fire which flamed through her flesh and goaded her to reckless abandon. Their lips still locked, he moved deep within her, and she felt him clearly with a joy that surged through her. It was this elation which made her unconsciously bend her knees and anchor her feet against the bed, causing her hips to flare upward and meet his passionate thrusts. She felt herself give in to it, to flow with the throbbing, pulsating tempo. Together they worked in frenzied ecstasy until finally they reached sweet release. Of everything else they were uncertain, but of love they were adamantly sure.

★

Chapter 27

The next morning, Yang Shu-zhen was gone.

When Jessie, Longarm, and Ki arose, they found in the kitchen two large covered platters of cold meats, cheese, and bread. No one had heard the breakfast being brought in, but no one doubted who had seen to it. Shu-zhen was a gracious, if absent, hostess.

Afterwards they saddled their horses and rode across the flat toward the spearing peak. In the cool gray of early dawn, the temple high above was opaque, wreathed in mists that would soon burn off once the sun appeared. For now, though, they fogged the view from above even more than from below, and helped the riders approach undetected through the scant cover of low boulders and wind-swept growth.

At a careful walk they circled the base of the peak, studying its weathered slopes. Other than a wagon trail, whose ruts wound up between baked rocks and weedy pockets to the temple, they could not sight any path that might scale the rim. There were ledges and breaks, but most were too steep and narrow for a horse to gain footing or follow.

On the opposite side of the peak from the trail, they reined in by a low abutment and regarded the shaggy bank before them. There was not a sound, nothing save the horses gently stirring. The dawn seemed too quiet to Jessie, almost as though it were hushed in suspense.

"Well, we can't ride any farther," Longarm declared, shaking his head. "Jessie, are you sure you want to go up and see it?"

"Shu-zhen said Von Blöde took the temple for a headquarters. So he may be there, and possibly some of his associates, or Pennington."

"Yeah, perhaps. For certain there'll be a hard-gutted gun crew." He turned to Ki, demanding, "You tell her. Tell her that's not a headquarters she wants to go walk up into, Ki, but a lion's den."

Ki chuckled. "Custis, have you ever tried stopping this lady from doing something she has her mind set on doing?"

"Afraid I have. That's why I was asking you to try."

Jessie eyed both men. "Up there isn't a den, either. It's the cartel, and I want to go and *stop* it. Now, before it worsens."

She dismounted, carbine in hand, as did Ki and Longarm. The horses acted amiably disposed to staying put, nibbling grass in a nook between boulders. Jessie headed toward the bank, the men a pace behind; yet, for all her determination, her uneasiness was sharpened by the deathly stillness. Maybe it was a trap.

Maybe she'd damn well better find out, she chastised herself, and began climbing the slope. She and the men advanced swiftly yet warily, keeping to concealment whenever possible, careful not to brush against brittle alpine scrub or set loose gravel rolling. As they wended higher, avoiding obstacles, the rising sun began producing a rainbow of gold in the east while the sky to the west grew crystal blue.

Presently they crested the rim of the peak and saw that its top was like the crater of some volcano. It had all the markings, and without a doubt it had been one that flamed and raged thousands of years before the coming of man. It was about nine hundred feet across, sunken in the center and raised on one side to a short, prowlike pinnacle. Around the rest of it were two barns, a storage silo and some small sheds, and a bunkhouse and mess hall, both built barracks style. All the outbuildings tended to face the chunky pinnacle, for atop it, buttressed by block stone walls, stood the temple.

Cautiously they eased along the outside of the rim, just below eye level, until they were at a good near angle to the temple. It appeared larger, more of a castle, than it had from below. Another stone and brass Buddha was visible on the broad veranda which ran around the entire house. Also on the veranda were eight brawny men, each a two-gun slicker if the weapons at his hips were to be believed.

Except for those eight, the peak looked to be empty, the entire ranch area seeming to have an aura of desertion. Pretty soon the gunmen ambled on around the veranda corner, and after checking that nobody else was in sight, Jessie, Ki, and Longarm dashed across the intervening open space between the rim and the bottom of the pinnacle.

A wild yell burst from up inside the house. They flattened, hugging the rock, fearing they'd been spotted and that it was a call of alarm. Instead, a gunshot cut the yelling off, followed by the noise of a short, fierce struggle or of something falling against furniture, or both. Laughter came after that, a jovial bellowing which ceased with mysterious suddenness, and then everything became quiet again.

They waited a few more minutes, baffled but satisfied they had not been discovered. Then, climbing the pinnacle to the temple's rock-ribbed foundation, they edged higher with the pinnacle's drop on one side and the temple's perpendicular wall rising on the other. The structure looming far above laid its sinister shadow across their path, as if to bar the way. A gust of wind tugged at their hatbrims and passed restlessly as if to lure them on. Beyond in the heavens, an eagle soared, wheeling and drifting along brisk currents of mountain turbulent air.

They still didn't see anybody. Other than a door slamming and some agitated talk, which sounded to be coming from a distant part of the house, they didn't hear anybody, either. They were aware only of lonesome desolation amid the rugged beauty of nature's grandeur.

Abruptly, three hemp ropes snaked down and opened nooses above their heads, looping over their shoulders, immediately pinning their arms to their sides as the slack was

265

tightened. The next instant they were swept off their feet with violent jerks, which swung them banging against the solid stone wall. As they struck, the carbines they were toting were jolted from their lasso-weakened grasps, the weapons dropping beyond their clutching hands.

Half stunned by their breathtaking wrenchings, they were dragged and lifted upward by the ropes. Peering, they glimpsed the blurred forms of three men leaning over the veranda rail, each hauling hand over hand, yanking them up along the temple's foundation. Frantically they struggled to throw off the nooses which squeezed them, but they were powerless to free themselves, helpless as hooked fish at the end of fishermen's lines. As they were reeled higher, the features of the three men above grew more distinct. The smallest was a buck-toothed, red-eyed little whelp. The tallest was a six-foot-three scarecrow with a shadow of gray beard on his cheeks and chin. The meanest-looking, who had snagged Longarm and was directing the roundup, was an average-sized gent with a heavy black beard and in all black clothes, including hat, holsters, and pistol grips.

Even while they were being ripped over the veranda rail, they fought furiously for slack in their ropes. Pulled off balance and sent staggering almost to their knees, they nonetheless managed to toss the nooses off their heads, only to be confronted by leveled revolvers.

"Stand where you stand, pards," the man in black rasped. "Ike will collect your hardware and . . . By gosh, it's a female!"

Jessie shrugged, able only to stand with Longarm and Ki, while the buck-toothed man snatched away their holstered revolvers and stuck them in his belt. He made fun of Ki for being unarmed, but nobody else laughed or cracked a smile, not even the four men who had wandered over to watch, all narrow-eyed and somber-mouthed. Like the first three, they no doubt were paid killers, ready to shoot or stab at the slightest false move.

Then, seemingly out of nowhere, another man appeared from behind the man in black. The instant she glimpsed him, Jessie knew the man was Herzog Von Blöde. He had to be; he matched the description perfectly: a squat, long-armed man in his mid-fifties, wearing a navy blue Prince Albert suit. He wore no hat, and his short cropped hair looked like dirty yellow bristles, as did the mustache on his upper lip. His ex-cavalry officer's tanned face was scarred diagonally from left eye to brutish chin by a saber slash. It was a cut which had healed poorly, so that scar tissue stood out prominently against his shallow eyes and wattled cheeks. When he spoke, his accented voice had a superior, almost arrogant tone of command.

"These people, Harter, from where did you get them?"

"Down below, sir," the man in black replied. "We saw an' caught 'em climbing up here, while we was checking on that shot. We rushed here to catch anyone runnin' out, but like last night, nobody ran out."

"You say they were coming and not going, not escaping?"

"That's how it looked. Y'mean, the shot . . . ?"

"Another man killed, *ja*, like last night." Von Blöde nodded. "Seaton's inside with his head blown apart. Come, I show you all."

Harter and the buck-toothed man gestured with their revolvers for the three prisoners to follow Von Blöde. They fell in step, and with the other gunmen dogging a few paces behind, trooped around to a scrolled oak door and entered a great room with massive furniture. It had carved beams and blackwood figurines on the walls, thick velvet drapes with a dragon motif pulled back from the windows and tucked upon heavy tasseled cords, and a brass Buddha half-smiling in the far corner to the left on a pedestal of teakwood.

Jessie merely glanced at her surroundings. She was studying the men who were already in the room, the four who were in stuffily proper attire as befitting their wealthy social class, and a fifth who was not of their station, but had on as much suit as he could muster. As she had with Von Blöde, she tried to identify them from information she could recall. She wasn't able to ignore, however, the odor of blood and gunsmoke, nor the grisly sight stretched out on a huge Oriental carpet.

The man had been a brawny six-footer, and now his big hands were thrust out on either side of him, and his legs were as straight as legs could possibly be. His mouth was gaping. Through the matted blood Jessie could see the big, bulging brown eyes, eyes that seemed to register terror even in death, eyes that had seen something before death had struck him down.

"Gawd, he's straightened out like a cross," the buck-toothed Ike muttered. "Just like th' Yakima Dude got laid out last night."

He stopped, his eyes widening. A sound had swelled over the room. It was like a moan, like a groan, and it came from everywhere, up from the old tiles covering the floor, out of the carved beams overhead, out of the very walls.

In a moment the sound was gone, but in that moment Jessie had stepped back between Longarm and Ki. Unconsciously her hands had come up, closing on their forearms, and they felt her fingers digging into their flesh while their scalps prickled, their every nerve quivered and crawled, during that ghastly moment of the death-rattling sound.

The five men Jessie had her eye on stood tense and rigid, paling, and Von Blöde seemed to be steeling himself for an ordeal. "*Ach*, it's nothing but the wind among the old tiles on the roof. Nothing ghostly. Ghosts do not shoot people." His voice was calm, with even a hint of laughter in it. "Harter, Olson, take this body out of here. Take the rug with you and wash out the blood. What are you waiting for?"

He glared about, pivoting on one boot heel. Some of the gunmen moved back from Von Blöde as if expecting him to fly at them with a whip. Others looked at the ceiling, at the floor, at the walls.

Now the strange noise came rushing back to the room. Now it was like laughter, like a spasmodic outburst of wicked chortling and smacking. It filled the entire room, this eruption of harsh mockery, inhuman, unreal, a rasping, choking noise that sounded downright unearthly.

"We're in a hell of a mess of mystery here," Harter half-whispered, an awed gleam in his eyes. The sound fell away and the room became silent again. "We oughta set fire to the place and let it burn flat!"

"I agree with you, Jim," the tall, gray man said, swallowing thickly. "It's put my pecker in a knot last night an' now this morning. We should torch the whole hellish works

268

and then get back in the clear and watch it all go up in smoke and flames."

"Olson! Harter! Take Seaton out of here now! You're just wasting time standing there looking around like sick crows. *Schnell!*"

"Yes, sir, Mist' Von Blöde," Harter said, as he and the gray man hastened to pick up the corpse. "Out we go with what's left of Al."

"But it ain't gonna be the end of it." Olson was still staring at the walls. "Whatever it is that started doin' this work is on a roll to do some more, and there ain't enough of us to stop it."

Now three of the so-called gentlemen came over to join Von Blöde. The one who wasn't quite so finely dressed was a stooped, bespectacled man who could only be Henry Gustav. By now Jessie had recognized the other two as Marcel Charvey and Stanislas Wladyslaw, both members of the cartel's inner council of five. Charvey was Parisian, with curly salt-and-pepper hair, his thick chest and heavy shoulders adding a sense of blockiness to his lined features. Wladyslaw was known as "Stash" and was something of an aesthete; he held a cheroot between his thumb and forefinger in an upturned palm, while he scanned Jessie with jaded eyes and a bored expression. But not so jaded or bored that he didn't turn to Von Blöde and ask, "Who's the crumpet?"

"A snoop."

"Oh, it's all a mistake," Jessie protested coquettishly. "We were lost and thought, since we were passing, to stop for directions."

It was then that Major Pennington walked through a side archway, and blurted, "As I live and breathe! If it ain't Jessica Starbuck!"

Silence, vast and deafening, was followed by a rumble of voices breaking out. Von Blöde lifted an eyebrow, glanced at Pennington, then looked at Jessie. "So, you're the fräulein we've heard so much about." He bowed politely. "Your derringer, *bitte.*"

"I declare, you're mystifying me."

"Mam'selle, stop acting *insensé,*" Charvey rebuked. "You, *Japonais,* you then must be Ki. Strip off your belt, knife, and vest, or be stripped. We know of them, too. And who might you be, m'sieur?"

"Deputy U. S. Marshal Custis Long. And you're under arrest."

The conversing swelled with protest, alarm, and indignation. Von Blöde quelled it swiftly, snapping loudly, *"Meine Herren,* listen! Due to Starbuck we've been weakened, we've been forced to handle this venture locally. But now our final nuisance, our last potential problem, has dropped in our laps like a plum. Now nothing can deny us! We'll have the greatest army in the West. We'll have—we'll *be*— the West!"

"Is that all you can plan, how to get something somebody else has?" Jessie asked, regarding Von Blöde with eyes as hard as glass as she handed him her derringer. "How to prey on people's fears, their griefs, their dreams, just to enrich your own selfish ends?"

Von Blöde chuckled, pocketing her weapon. "We all use one another to get ahead. That's how life operates, and for proof, simply see where it's gotten us and where it has landed you. *Ja,* here, that's how Ming and his successors got on top, by using their people as cannon fodder; and that's how we took the top away, by using much the same methods."

"And is that what Pennington and Red Dog planned, to sacrifice their ragtag believers on your behalf, so you could get to the top?"

A sputtered gasp came from Gustav. "She knows an inordinate amount about our plans, sir. Torture her and find out the truth."

"About us, Henry? What can she tell us that we don't already know?" Von Blöde eyed Jessie. "But you have been busily prying, fraülein."

"Not only me. Plenty know as much or more than I do, and are gathering forces right now to come tear the top down around your ears."

Now another of the cartel hierarchy spoke up, Enrico Dheskata, a saturnine-faced financier of Italian–Greek parentage. "Your lies are silly. Soldiers, lawmen, they have no subtlety, and if anybody knew anything outside these

270

walls, they'd be hammering the front door."

"Think again," Longarm retorted, stung. "You may think you're shrewd foxes, but you're only the devil's half-brother, and the anvil and tongs of hell to boot. You'll feel rope stretch your necks yet."

He was answered with a burst of scornful laughter. Longarm gazed about, eyes fathomless and frigid, while Ki stood alongside, his lips peeled in a thin, metallic grin. Jessie was grimly, silently alert, hearing more than their scorn. It was ever so faint, a mere whisper of the sound that had come only a few minutes before.

Pennington, still standing in the archway, had a tight smile etched on his lips. "Brave talk, from a man who's soon to die—"

He halted with a suddenly whistling breath. His head had rocked backward, his eyes bulging in their sockets, his hands clawing at his throat. Kicking and writhing, he went down, a croaking bundle of jerking nerves and rank terror in the archway.

"Meine Gott!" Von Blöde snarled, leaping toward Pennington. "What's wrong? Here, let me see. *Ach*, what's this around his neck?"

Pennington was still squirming there on the floor, still raking at his throat. Others sprang to assist Von Blöde, throwing Pennington on his stomach and holding him down, while Von Blöde found buried in his throat a mere hairline of a thread. Yet it had the strength of a wire, like a tiny ribbon of steel, breaking the skin of Pennington's neck in several places, making the blood ooze when Von Blöde ripped it free. Pennington sat up, gasping and gagging, massaging his neck.

"What is it?" Dheskata demanded. "It looks like a string."

"It is a string," Von Blöde confirmed, standing up slowly. "A silk cord. It must've been thrown from somewhere. I thought I saw some movement behind the major, something like a hand. I was looking right at him."

"Yes, it did come from behind," Pennington wheezed, wobbling to his feet. "There's something haywire as hell goin' on 'round here—"

271

A sound cut him off. It was the same laugh as the last time, and now it was coming from everywhere: the walls, the floor, the ceiling, an evil cackling that reverberated from all over the ancient house. Then all of a sudden, without any warning, all the cords holding back all the window drapes unraveled all together. The drapes swooped closed, cloaking the windows, plunging the living room into darkness.

"Strike a match!" Von Blöde thundered. "Open those drapes!"

As if responding to him, the unknown laugh chuckled again. One of the gunmen bawled, "Damn it, it's ha'nts!" The room was abruptly so filled with clamorous confusion that nobody could think. Jessie, Ki, and Longarm instantly realized that this was a chance, perhaps their only one, and dove scrambling through the ruckus for any door.

Jessie had the misfortune of being too near Von Blöde. "Not so fast, *leibling*," he snarled close by her ear, and she felt the muzzle of a revolver against her cheek. Another muzzle rammed against the ribs of her left side, and she took a shuddering breath, knowing resistance would be futile for the moment.

As soon as Ki moved to break away, the buck-toothed man sprang agile and deadly as a catamount on his back. Stumbling under the unexpected impact of his attacker's body, Ki couldn't avoid being pistol-whipped for the first moment or two. Then he swiftly threw up an arm and blocked the next blow. His free hand found the man's wrist, and with a spontaneous heave of desperation, he flung the man from his back—flung him forward and downward as hard as he could.

The buck-toothed man struck hard on his back, but somehow his flailing snatched a grip on Ki's shirt and brought Ki down with him. "He's my meat! I got him!" the man cried, flinging his legs around Ki and trying to wrench his gun hand loose for a killing shot. But he could not break Ki's iron grip. Their bodies oddly entwined, they thrashed furiously about on the floor.

The sound returned, more terrible, more awful than before. It grumbled, it grew frightfully sharp, it was as if a dozen phantoms were wailing, sighing and filling the darkened room with their mockery.

They were mocking him, Longarm thought, grunting, as a boot thudded into him. Like Ki, he had become embroiled in a whirling, panting dogfight of a melee, shrouded in sinister gloom. The noisy laughter continued longer this time, and seemed to flow right under where he and a bearded man were wrestling. It was too much for the bearded man. With a wild scream, he swung his revolver at Longarm's upturned face. Longarm twisted just in time, as the man triggered a shot at him that seared past his chin and smashed into the old ceiling, bringing down a showering cloud of white dust. Longarm countered by grabbing the man's wrist, then swiveling to crack the arm across his knee brutally enough to hear bones crack.

The gunman shrieked. His grip on the revolver slackened, and it clouted Longarm above the eye, then fell into his lap. Longarm scooped it up while punching the gunman square in the groin.

Now the entire structure of the building and its foundation seemed to shake and vibrate, as if an earthquake were trembling far beneath the ancient floors. Ki had no time to worry about that. He heard the thud of boots rushing in, and saw shadowy figures closing about him like wolves surrounding their prey. Boots stomped him, boots slugged him, and he glimpsed the swift swing of another gun barrel lashing down. Instinctively he wrenched himself to one side. The buck-toothed man's head took the blow of that down-swinging gun, and for a moment his muscles turned to rubber.

Desperately Ki grasped that moment by groping at the man's belt for his sheathed Bowie knife. Clutching its haft, he drew it out, twisted, and shoved. Its keen point slipped neatly between the buck-toothed man's ribs, and the long blade buried itself to the hilt in his heart. Immediately Ki untangled himself and rolled clear.

Before he could gain his feet, however, an unseen blow landed on Ki's skull. Pain fogged his mind, while his reflexes fought blindly for his life. Then Ki saw a giant's right hand come in from the side, and the mallet-like fist crunched against his jaw. His head snapped awry, and darkness came to Ki in a blinding flash of light.

The sound that hovered under Longarm now swept on, rocking from wall to wall, floor to ceiling. With boots and gun barrels raining blows upon him, Longarm began shooting blindly upward among his attackers. Even by his winking muzzle flares, he could not see their outlined forms kicking about him. The gunmen fell back, as some of his aimless shots drove home. Pistol empty, Ki exerted his last strength, broke free of the tight arms about his legs, and staggered up. The dark room became a blot of whirling arms and rushing figures. One struck Longarm heavily and he went down again. For him the fight was over.

The laughter tornadoed from one room to another, then washed all over the house at the same time. It came back under Jessie's and Von Blöde's feet, rising up through the very soles of their boots and appearing to climb in an icy chill through their knees and legs until it was around their hips. They both stood their ground, Von Blöde because he was determined to, Jessie because she was under his gun. In the shadowy brawl around them, there was a snarl of pain that became a sickening wail, a noise of booted and spurred feet stumbling about, and the voices of Von Blöde and other cartel men roaring orders at the top of their lungs. Finally the drapes were pulled open.

There were dead and wounded strewn on the floor, an amazing toll considering the battle had lasted scarcely any time at all. The only ones unaccounted for, however, were Longarm and Ki . . . and the strange sound. Once sunlight streamed in, the chattering laugh withered and soughed dying away.

"An' he calls it wind," Harter muttered, rubbing his jaw. "Wind in the tiles of the roof."

"I ain't scared of any cockeyed thing I can see to fight," another put in, "but there's somethin' in this damn house that no one can see. It ain't human, it ain't—"

"Catch those two men!" Von Blöde raged, glowering at his people. "They can't have gone far. They've got to be right around here close! Hurry!" He smirked at Jessie.

"Loyal of them to run out, eh?"

Boot heels thumped on the veranda, spurs crashed on the old tile floors. From down around the crater of the peak to the attic of the temple, the gunmen rushed with guns out and cocked, fingers curled on the triggers, eyes seeking two targets, Longarm and Ki. But the house and grounds were thoroughly, absolutely empty. At the end of a grueling search, the entire crew found itself mobbed together in the great living room, with every pair of eyes now studying another with fearful questions in their depths. Jim Harter was first to find voice, and the voice he found was a croak.

"Damnation, this funny business is giving me the shakes, boys!" His dark face was mottled with sickly pale blotches. "There's somethin' wrong, and I don't think the duke here knows what it is."

"I say it's the dead up and walkin'," suggested a tall, hatchet-faced man. "I say it's them chinks a-comin' back, stirrin' outa their graves and wailin' for what was done to them, for what we helped do."

"Yeah, look at that brass thang in the corner!" Olson declared, pointing a long, lean hand at the Buddha. "Look at that look on its face. He's allus kinda half-smirkin' ever' time you look at him. Damned if that smirk ain't just a teensy li'l wider now. I'll swear it is! Hell, there's a smile all over that yaller brass face!"

A mocking laugh seemed to agree with him. It came from the dining room beyond. There was not the least doubt about that, for it roared out in one ferocious shriek, and the trampling of running feet.

"There they are!" Von Blöde shouted, prodding Jessie toward the dining room in his zeal. "They're there, you heard them! Move!"

"Shoot down everything you see!" Harter bawled. "Stop at nothin' what twitches! Let's go! In a bunch now, rush 'em!"

In a flying wedge they jammed through the dining room doorway. At the end of the room they saw the door of a closet slowly swinging closed. Beyond the interior of the closet was a vault of darkness that burrowed back into the

275

thick walls. Harter fired at what looked like the flame of a bobbing candle racing away from them. Then he was at the closet, just in time to keep the door from shutting. He slammed it back open and dived into the closet with his pistols blazing at the bobbing figures of two men. The figures shuddered and abruptly collapsed in a sprawl ahead of him.

"I got 'em, boys!" Harter's voice was triumphant. "C'mon! They're down, deader 'n shit! I plugged 'em both plumb center!"

He rushed on, the others following. The figures were lying there ahead of them, the candle still burning. From the dining room outside the closet, Von Blöde and the other cartel associates hovered expectantly, watching their gunmen plunge on and come to a halt with a crash of spurred heels, just as the candle flame snuffed out.

"We . . . We . . . I'll be damned!" Harter yelped, peering by the flare of a match. "They're only straw dummies! Straw packed in men's clothes! We—"

A weird laugh answered him, one which shook the closet passage, rocketed up from underfoot, an eerie, wailing burst of sound that drove cold chills through everyone.

Then the closet door slammed shut.

Von Blöde jabbed Jessie in the side with his revolver without realizing it as he shouted, "Get that door open! Open it, fast!"

Pennington hurried to open the door. He, the cartel men, Gustav, and Jessie found themselves face to face with a wall of steel.

From the other side, the trapped gunmen were yelling and howling, sending their curses raging up and down the passage.

Listening, some of the cartel associates began to shiver a little. A thin film of sweat showed on Von Blöde's furrowed brow. *"Gott . . . Mein Gott,* I fear they're good as dead and gone to hell."

"Yes, as good as dead and gone to hell, where mongrel dogs of hate and greed belong!" The voice that responded was ghastly, and seemed to surround them in the dining room and the closet. "Our honorable dead have awaited the means to avenge their murders. Thus it is written that quick death will be for some, and a slow death will be for the others, the ones who stole possession of the temple. May your souls rest in your burning pits of fire, and may the spirit of Ming Wu Li haunt you throughout all eternity."

There was silence after that."

Chapter 28

When Ki regained consciousness, he had no idea how long he had been out since the brief, fierce brawl in the darkened living room. Nor had he any idea where he was or what had happened to him. He awoke at last, with the bleary notion that his aching head was on someone's lap, and that his face was being bathed in cool water.

Slowly he stirred, then, with the light of ancient brass lamps glowing in his face. He opened his eyes and found that he was indeed resting in a lap, a rather familiar lap. Turning, he glanced up at Shu-zhen.

"How are you?" she asked anxiously. She was smiling, and her eyes were alive and warm with affectionate interest.

"I've felt better," he allowed, smiling back.

With her hand on his arm to steady him, he sat up beside her on a bunk bed similar to the ones they had slept on the night before. She gave him a big crock of icy water, and he drank several hefty gulps from it. He was about to take another swallow when Longarm called out, "Ki, you camel, if you empty it, you get to refill it."

Ki reared a little and looked around. On another bunk Longarm was lying, with two of Shu-zhen's men attending to his cuts and bruises. Ki asked him, "What . . . what happened?"

"I'm not sure," Longarm replied, grinning at Ki from one

278

side of his puffy-lipped mouth. "I got thumped in the scuffle, I recall, by a pair of Shu-zhen's lads. They dragged me off to that Buddha in the corner up there, only it had moved, and there's a black gaping hole in the wall behind it instead. I don't think I wanted to go much, 'cause they sapped me about then, and . . ." He shrugged. "And you?"

"They must've sandbagged me right off." Ki eyed Shu-zhen, who responded with a blithely innocent expression. He stared around what was obviously an underground chamber. To his right was a stone-arched opening in the rocks. A door of wrought iron filled it. There were other arches and latticed grilles, but it was difficult to get a sense of the area. From an opening off in the shadows to his left came a hazy glow of lamplight, and the moving silhouettes of men could be seen through the archway.

Shu-zhen, noting Ki's interest, explained to him and Longarm, "Ming first struck gold here, so he built his temple above. For his heirs he mapped every secret passage and room in these long-dead workings, and his miners were thorough. They didn't leave much undone."

"And it was them, I suppose," Longarm ventured, "who made all the devilish racket we heard underfoot and roaming around the house?"

"They made a system of copper tubes that runs everywhere. Like a speaking tube system in some hotels. The upper mouths were concealed, of course. Master Ming thought of everything."

"Except why we'd be here," Ki said.

She smiled faintly. "Because our enemies are trapped up there."

"All?"

"All but the few who stole possession of the temple."

"Jessie!" Longarm sat bolt upright, groaned, and sank flat again, his head throbbing like a spinning drum. "Where's Jessie?"

"Von Blöde has her, but she's in no immediate danger."

"How can you say that? Why didn't you save her, too?"

"Von Blöde had her too well covered to risk it, Custis. I'm certain he won't just kill her; he'll use her as a hostage, which gives us time. We had no time with you two. Who knew if you'd either rashly follow the others into the passage, or be ordered to go there, where we lured them like fools madly chasing simple decoys?"

"What are you planning to do to them?"

"Do you ask as Custis Long, or as Deputy Long?"

"Shu-zhen, me and myself are sworn to uphold the law."

"Well." She rose from the bunk. "You'll know soon enough. Even now they're struggling for breath, for the passage has neither air nor light." She went to the gate and had a few low-voiced words with the beak-nosed Lu Nin. When they parted, he went to that opening on the left where Ki had seen the lamplight before. Shu-zhen came back to the bunk, saying, "No, if I left them up there much longer, they would suffocate, a slow agony. There's no thrill in death, there's no joy in torture." She sat down and stared at the leftward archway.

Over that way, where Lu Nin was, a key could be heard grating in a lock. Then there was a squeal of rusted hinges as a door was pulled closed. After that he clapped his hands, making a sound that might have come from boards suddenly popping themselves together. A resounding yell answered, coming out of the blackness of the underground room's high ceiling. Then, in a noisy, shrieking, wailing, and screaming flood, the cartel gunmen were falling through fifty feet of bitter darkness to become heaps of broken bones.

It was horrifying to witness. The old planks of a floor high above had suddenly become a long trapdoor, dropping from under the feet of the men in that dark closet passage up there. It was nightmarish for Longarm, dredging up memories he would prefer to forget, of Wolfer's glory hole pit and office trapdoor. And this was mass slaughter, as into inky black darkness with only a haze of light showing far below, plunged the entire able-bodied gun crew. Spinning cartwheels in the air, they were death-bound men hurling through space to a pile of stones in the center of the underground room.

Like smacking and splashing canvas pails of water, they started landing. The terrified, yelling men in one instant became hopelessly broken shapes. There was a moan of death here, a wail of the dying there. Death splashed blood all over the room.

"And the words of the old documents are being carried out," Lu Nin intoned gravely, leaving the iron door as if his task was done.

Longarm felt shaken to the core. "Shu-zhen, this is raw work."

"Not as raw as the work they did on us. Whatever else all those men had been, they'd been vicious, merciless killers deserving execution."

"But due process . . . the law . . ."

"Custis," Ki said quietly, "there's a doctrine that states it is better to commit a crime than to let a greater evil persist."

Longarm paused, sighing. "What's done is done. The cartel gunmen have been delivered on a bloody platter, you might say. And once done, one moves on. So let's get to moving on those seven remaining upstairs, and let's get to rescuing Jessie!"

Taking a brass lamp, Shu-zhen ushered them out of the chamber and left along the corridor. When they came to the prison where the deaths of the cartel gunmen had occurred, Lu Nin joined them to unlock the wrought-iron door. Shu-zhen looked queasy for a time, but she helped Ki and Longarm straighten out the distortedly mangled corpses.

"At least we've got fighting tools," Longarm growled as they helped themselves to revolvers and belts of cartridges from the dead men.

Finished, Shu-zhen led them leftward again on a different passage to a solid iron door. For this she had the key, which rattled in the lock, and the lock clacked harshly. Hinges wailed mournfully and, when the door cracked open, the noise of splashing trickles of water filtered up from far below.

A flash of the brass lamp showed that they were on a landing, a flight of rough stone steps leading downward, another leading up. They climbed, Shu-zhen first with the lamp, Ki following on her heels, while Longarm closed the door and came after two steps at a time. Suddenly they heard the murmur of voices. Ki stepped up beside Shu-zhen, ready to dash the light from her hands while he strained his ears to listen to the muttering voices. Longarm was poised a few steps lower, staring upward, a revolver in each hand, fully prepared to fire at anything that moved overhead.

But nothing happened, and soon they were at another set of stone stairs. The steps wound higher through natural caverns and rooms hewn out of solid rock. Voices came again, this time ahead. The end came when they reached a musty passageway and followed it until they stopped before a wall of planks. Now the voices were just on the other side.

Shu-zhen trailed her fingers along a strip of the boards to locate the hidden latch. Ki stuck the S&W .44 revolver he had chosen behind the beltless waistband of his pants, and wished to hell that he had his *tanto* and his vest full of weapons instead of the firearm. When Shu-zhen turned, smiling, and showed where she had found the latch, Ki smiled too and applied a simple neck squeeze. Her smile turned slightly sad as she slumped unconscious, Ki embracing her and laying her peacefully on the floor, where she would sleep for quite a few hours.

Longarm nodded. "Yeah, for the best. I wouldn't want her hurt."

"Her hurt? I was afraid she was going to down them all and leave none for us," Ki replied. "When she wakes up, though, it'll be me who gets hurt. I'll say I acted rashly, and you ordered me to."

"Thanks." Tensing, revolvers ready, Longarm watched Ki reach up and noiselessly move the latch. Then together they gave the planks in front of them a violent push. The planks shoved outward with a crazy rattling and smashing of dishware on shelves, and the temple's dining room was there before them.

Death roared now. There was no quarter here. Longarm and Ki triggered their licking, piercing gun flames into the leaping and snarling figures of men, whose hands were flying to weapons, their startled shouts a din rising above the sounds of the shots.

Longarm and Ki became separated almost immediately in the fury. Longarm tended toward the left, where there was the open doorway to the living room. Abruptly he was confronted by Stash Wladyslaw. If Stash was startled to see Longarm, he didn't show it. His revolver swiveled smoothly and he squeezed off a shot. He was a fast and accurate shootist with most any firearm, and especially with his usual gun.

But Stash had a problem with accuracy this time. His accuracy had been disturbed by a bullet that arrived plump in the middle of his shirt front, courtesy of Longarm. Stash's bullet fanned Longarm's cheek. Stash was determined, and managed to try again; his second shot sailed a foot over Longarm's head, his third shot into the ceiling.

Meanwhile, bullet holes were marching up Stash's shirt front. As he tipped backward, the last hole, like a neat punctuation mark, appeared just above his collar stud—a period, as it were, marking the end of this cartel bigwig. He fell with a thump that jarred the floor, blocking the doorway. Longarm went through the doorway into the living room.

Enrico Dheskata and Oscar Kinelly, the fifth member of the cartel hierarchy, were launching into action from the living room. In a far corner of the room, Von Blöde turned. Seeing Longarm in the doorway with his revolver lancing smoke, he shouted above the reverberating gunshots, "They're back! There's one now! Kill him, kill!"

His raging words were lost in a barrage of pistol fire. Everyone opened up, including Ki, who had gone around and was stalking in by way of the kitchen. Bullet barrages riddled the great room, somehow missing to hit anybody, but unnerving the cartel faction and sending them sprawling. Even Von Blöde was rattled, ducking and hopping while keeping his revolver trained on Jessie.

"Bitch! You bitch!" Von Blöde ranted at Jessie. "Thanks to you and your meddling friends, my crowning operation is jeopardized and my life imperiled. How you managed to, I've no idea, but it's left me with only one alternative—you! You're my ticket out of this!"

"Ki and Deputy Long won't—"

"They will, lest they wish to adore a corpse!" Von Blöde glanced wildly about, spotted Ki toss his emptied pistol side, and realized Ki was in so much trouble from other quarters, that he'd left himself wide open from this angle. "Maybe it won't come to that point yet, if only I . . ."

With a throb of gloating in his voice, Von Blöde held on tight to Jessie, while he shifted his pistol to shoot Ki in the back. As he began squeezing the trigger, Jessie reacted in frantic horror, lurching against him just as he shot. The blast deafened Jessie, the .45 slug skimming past her head, making her wince as she pivoted and slammed squarely into him again, grabbing the hot gun barrel and trying to wrench the revolver out of Von Blöde's grip.

A second shot discharged. It sizzled past Kinelly, making him turn and glance back. That gave Ki a chance to break out of the crossfire and Kinelly and Dheskata had trapped him in. Kinelly turned back and saw Ki bearing down on him. He didn't waste his breath on any words or swearing, but continued to bring his revolver on target in one fluid motion. "Enrico! Enrico! Here he is for us!"

Ki threw himself down, twisting his lithe body into a low-rolling somersault. Kinelly fired, just as Dheskata came around a great, deeply carved table and triggered his pistol, ignoring the risk of hitting Kinelly instead of Ki. Lead whipped inches above Ki. Kinelly's revolver was so close that it lanced flame in his eyes and singed his left cheek with powder burns.

Yet this was a trifling discomfort compared to the hellish agony Kinelly felt an instant later. For Ki, coming out of his roll virtually in front of the man, hit him with an upper-cutting *nakadata-ippon-ken* blow, the extended large dexter knuckle of his fist punching Kinelly brutally in the groin. Howling, Kinelly sagged to his knees, forgetting his revolver and letting it drop, while he cupped his groin in both hands. Ki sidestepped, and for an instant regarded the man, who was flat of face and sharp of eye, with hair an incredibly carroty hue. Then Ki hit Kinelly alongside the head with his hand in the devastating *keiko* position—the chicken-beak hand. Kinelly, his skull stove in and his brains scrambled, dropped dead.

Ki was already diving for Dheskata. Dheskata, his face gnarling with rage, aimed his pistol for a point-blank shot. Ki launched into a *tobi-geri* flying kick, sailing across the floor and striking Dheskata in the chest with his extended left foot. His ferocious spring buckled Dheskata, carrying him backward past the end of the table, the pistol firing with a deafening roar beside Ki's ear. Dheskata smashed hard against a fireplace mantel, but he remained upright, and leveled his revolver again at Ki.

Ki swiveled away from the edge of the table. Dheskata

was thumbing the hammer of his single-action Colt "Banker's Special" when Ki snatched up a floor-standing candelabrum and swung it. Dheskata had to duck, but the ornate, bent-iron branches for the candles hooked Dheskata by the neck. Again his pistol discharged, and again the bullet whispered by Ki's ear as it sped harmlessly into a wall.

The shot was still reverberating when Ki, pulling savagely on the shaft of the candelabrum, jerked Dheskata toward him. He halted Dheskata with a *yonhon-nukite*, the spearheading tips of his stiffened fingers knifing into Dheskata's throat and rupturing his trachea. With a raspy sigh, Dheskata wilted and died.

Longarm glimpsed Henry Gustav bringing his Austrian Roth-Gasser pistol to bear. He quickly triggered again. He missed in his haste, but not by much, and it caused Gustav to wheel away. In his mad turn, the rug slipped under his feet, tossing him sprawling. A fierce yell of terror came from him, as if the panicky notion had occurred to him that he could be pounced upon and shot right then and there.

Perhaps he could have been, but Longarm had a more pressing problem. He was jumping back toward another entryway when he saw the drapes moving by one window. And by the way the drapes would suddenly poke out, the person hiding in there had either a fence slat or a carbine. When Longarm lined up those suspicious ripples, he judged that Jessie appeared to be the target. Longarm eyed the drapes again. Whoever it was, his motions were precise and easy to read now that he knew what to look for.

Longarm had to shoot. His revolver bucked as he slapped lead at the drapes. There rose a howl, a shuddering from the impact. The ambusher's carbine seemed to echo Longarm's shot and drown his agonized cry. Reflexively the person grabbed, as if in dying he wished to break his lurching fall, his hand clutching at the drapes and ripping them loose. They dropped, rod and all, while he collapsed on the floor, his crouched legs still bent under him, the draperies covering him like a rumpled body shroud. Not until afterwards was the man's identity exposed. It was Major Pennington, who apparently blamed Jessie for all his problems here and in Oregon, and was determined to exact revenge, even though she was under the dubious wing of Von Blöde.

At the moment, she and Von Blöde were fighting for possession of his revolver. But she was no match for Von Blöde's greater muscle and weight, Longarm saw when he glanced her way after he shot the draperies. As he prepared to go to help her, a pistol spat at him from one of the multitude of veranda windows. He sucked in his breath, scrambling across the living room away from Jessie, having to hunt this shooter first to get any safety at all.

Jessie clung tenaciously, though she was viciously backhanded, then rocked by a sweeping uppercut. She kicked out savagely but groggily for Von Blöde's groin, her boot taking the man with a glancing blow on his thigh. He yanked the pistol barrel to one side and toward him. Jessie, muscles tensed and her weight resting on her heels, was abruptly jerked forward off balance. Before she could recover, she was toppling into Von Blöde, who tripped her and sent her sprawling on the floor behind the corner desk.

Her tenacious hold, however, refused to loosen. Von Blöde suddenly found he was being torn out of his chair. In a flash he was on her, battering her flat and trying to wrestle the pistol away. Frantically she resisted, clawing and squirming with all her strength, and in her hysteria, lashed out, kicking the legs of the desk. One leg buckled, and the desk teetered precariously, upsetting the oil lamp. Von Blöde, nor noticing or caring, crouched over Jessie and elbowed her viciously in the face, stunning her with acute pain. But just as he wrenched the pistol out of her nerveless hand, the lamp fell off the desk and landed heavily on his shoulders and neck.

More startled than hurt, Von Blöde erupted like a scalded cat. In that instant Jessie was able to break free. She scrambled away, but fingers of steel clamped her ankle and dragged her away. She could only watch petrified as Von Blöde, breathing raggedly, hovered above her and tucked her pistol safely into the waistband of his trousers.

"No more nonsense. You're coming with me." Von Blöde sucked his teeth again, looking ready to jump her.

Longarm lunged toward the veranda. The pistol blasted at him again, having the flat and solid report of Henry Gustav's

Roth-Gasser—a lethal weapon in close-quarter skirmishes, but difficult to train on a moving target. Longarm was moving along the floor as fast as he could. A bullet nipped by him and ricochetted off a copper bowl, and by then he had spotted Gustav.

Gustav was in an entry alcove for one of the side doors, and he was sighting again, his eyes glittering above the pistol. Longarm brought up his revolver and fired fast, without taking time to aim. He saw Gustav back up, flinching, then turn and vanish.

He sprinted for the alcove. A door slammed shut, then quietly, furtively opened a crack when he was almost around the corner of the alcove. He put a bullet through the door and rushed the alcove.

Behind the door, Gustav rasped furiously. "Damn you, don't try to come through! I'll kill you! I'll—" His voice broke.

The door was locked. "Henry Gustav, you're under arrest!" Longarm called, wrecking the lock with a bullet. It was his fifth, and his other revolver was empty. He had one more slug left, and no time to reload. He kicked at the ruined latch, smashing the door open as Gustav fired through it.

Gustav was backed crouching by the veranda rail, trying to keep in the shelter of the Buddha. "Put your gun down, Henry," Longarm said, waggling his pistol. "Put it down, or I put you down."

Longarm stared at Gustav coldly, his revolver steady, straight out in front of him. There was no excitement in him now. No hurry, either. It was as if there was nothing going on behind him in the house, but he had all the time he needed to place his single last shot, in that final split second when Henry Gustav fired his pistol.

The explosion of two pistol shots out there on top of the world was less than spectacular. Their black powder discharges were just swept away. No matter; Longarm's spooky coolness must have shaken Gustav to the core, for his bullet missed its mark, slamming into the temple wall in back of him. Longarm's slug hit smack on the mid-button. Gustav stiffened. The pistol in his hand wobbled, and dropped to the veranda with a hollow clunk. Gustav took a quick sidestep as though he was figuring to turn and walk away. Slowly, very slowly, he folded, holding both hands over his stomach, pitched headlong over the railing, and struck the rocks below.

Like Longarm, Ki was trying to go to help Jessie. Now with Dheskata dead, he headed toward the corner where Von Blöde hovered over her, and failed to pay as much attention as necessary when he went by a second open doorway leading into a lighted room beyond. Then, suddenly, he did. He slowed cautiously, alert senses straining for whatever might have set off his intuitive alarm, and when a sound came, he detected it—the hushed tread of boots closing in behind him.

Ki whirled. A narrow-bladed "Mexican toothpick" stabbed out at his chest. He sidestepped and countered, his left hand clutching for the knife arm, his right extending to crush the attacker's windpipe.

All he struck was air.

Marcel Charvey laughed snidely, dancing away and returning to throw a swift left-handed punch to Ki's head. Shifting his head away from the blow, Ki began to counterattack when he felt a brutal crush of his stomach muscles. The punch had been a feint, and Charvey had instantly followed through with a front kick to Ki's abdomen, only to spin and throw a back kick.

Ki swiveled, sidestepping and catching the brunt of the kick on his right hip. He continued his pivot, letting it flow into a long step that brought him in close, then heel-kicked at the man's gut. He nearly missed, for Charvey twirled smoothly to one side so Ki's foot barely grazed a hip before he landed. It was then Ki realized that Charvey had to be a *savate* fighter, a damned leaping Frenchman, possibly as fast and as deadly with his feet as Ki himself. Even as Ki came out of his drop, crouched and perfectly balanced, Charvey was on the attack again, and not merely with his feet.

Light glinted on that long, dagger-like knife as Charvey leaped, a booted foot slamming into the ridged, iron-hard muscles of Ki's abdomen, bringing a grunt from him and slamming him backward against the wall. Ki straightened to counter, barely having time to bob down and to the left, as the knife slashed upward, passing a fraction of an inch from Ki's bicep. Instantly Ki axed the blade-edge of his callused left hand down hard on Charvey's knife arm, bringing a howl of pain, but not before that slender knife was again flashing at his throat.

Ki sprang back. Charvey stepped in fast pursuit, he noticed, and again he veered and ducked backward. And again Charvey lunged, almost slitting Ki. But it also left Charvey off balance for a split second; he had been too eager, too confident, too fast, and the force and stretch of his knifing stabs caused him to lean forward. It was the sort of opening Ki had been hoping for.

Ki stamped one foot, a little trick to ensure that the foot stayed planted, flat and immovable. And with his stamp, he snapped his other foot in a *yoko-geri-keage,* executing the side-thrust kick. with savage precision, his foot sinking deep into Charvey's abdomen.

Uttering a hoarse, guttural yell, Charvey was launched off the floor and sent hurtling, doubled over, to fall jarringly, stretched out and writhing. Before he could recover, Ki had leaped on him, knees crushing his chest, snapping ribs into his lungs and rupturing his stomach and kidneys.

Rising, Ki loped on toward Von Blöde.

As hope of escape was fading within her, Jessie spied the lamp where it had dropped when Von Blöde had brushed it off him. Its flame was still fluttering weakly inside the glass flue. In a desperate last attempt, she twisted beneath Von Blöde and groped for the lamp, knocking the flue aside. Hot wick singed her fingers, and Von Blöde grappled for her arm as he realized her intentions. But her hand closed around the base of the lamp, and before he could stop her, she had hold of it in a firm grip.

"Let go! Let go of that, you silly fool!" he bellowed, rearing back and straightening to his feet. Gasping for air, Jessie prodded the lamp threateningly at him and scrambled hastily onto her knees. She thought she heard Ki, and glanced over her shoulder to make sure. Von Blöde, growling testily, dashed at her to seize the lamp away, but Jessie struck back, thrusting it burning into his face.

The lamp missed by a fraction, Von Blöde veering aside just in time. Jessie didn't hesitate to see what he would do next, but began waving the lamp frenziedly back and forth to keep him at bay. Though the flame still failed to catch him, oil spilled out of the lamp base in erratic surges, drenching his hands, spraying his shirt, and soaking into his trousers.

The fiery wick then ignited the oil.

A dazzling clap of flame exploded. Panicking, Von Blöde yelled, "Look what you've done!" He slapped at his burning shirt, held for an anguished moment in a lurching paroxysm. "Damn you!" His voice was a bleating scream. "Damn you!" Then heat and smoke caught at him, oily flames consuming his clothes and flesh.

In hellfire agony, Von Blöde fled blundering, arms flagging, through the living room. His cry of tortured pain was worse than any noise that had been pumped through the copper tubes from below. He tore outside, his clothing snapping and crackling, acrid smoke roiling from his flaming hair, and hit the rail of the veranda. He seemed to teeter tantalizingly there, then screamed as he hinged over the rail. He kept on screaming until, halfway down the pinnacle, his head smashed against a boulder. He rolled the rest of the way with his arms and legs waving grotesquely, ruby sparks swirling about them, his flesh swiftly becoming the heart of a smouldering furnace.

Standing outside, looking down at him, Jessie felt no twinge of remorse for the incinerating cartel man below. Her sympathy was all directed toward his numerous victims. She heard footsteps, and glanced back to see Ki hurrying toward her.

"Jessie! Are you—? That scream!"

"I didn't scream," she said, gazing down at Von Blöde. "I never screamed in my entire life, as you very well know."

"Yes, of course," Ki replied with a smile, leaning beside her now on the rail. "You realize what's happened, don't you?"

She nodded. "I'm afraid to believe it."

"Well, believe it." He chuckled. "Here comes a believer."

"Jessie! Jessie!" Longarm was crying, hastening over. "Jessie, that's it! That's it! It's over!" He gestured toward the house, his voice rising, his smile beaming. "They would have papers here, documents and membership lists and everything. They must. But if they don't, we got what was important. We got them. We got the cartel! Nailed it! There is no more cartel!"

With fierce exultation he swept her in an embrace. "It's over, Jessie, we've won! *You've* won!"

"There's still a lot to do, Custis," she cautioned, pressing against his chest. "Yes, and places to go. Even if we have destroyed the head of the cartel, there'll be more mopping up to do of underlings. And there may be others—oh, not as bad as the cartel, but . . . Yes, we may have won this part, and it's an important part, but the good fight may not be through for a long time yet, perhaps forever."

In the corner of the living room, the brass Buddha sat and placidly smiled as if he alone knew for certain, as if he was the god and master of the mystery. A brass idol sitting and dreaming of other days, of other people; a brass idol contemplating fights that had been waged, the blood that had been shed—and the blood that would yet be shed.

Watch for

LONGARM ON THE SIWASH TRAIL

ninety-third novel in the bold
LONGARM
series from Jove

and

LONE STAR AND THE GULF PIRATES

forty-ninth novel in the exciting
LONE STAR
series from Jove

coming in September!

JAKE LOGAN